What readers across the nation are saying about this book:

"Mac McCormick has become the Garrison Keillor of funeral service. His gift as a writer and journalist has helped to keep funeral service professionals in touch with the human side of their vocation."

-Robert Mayer, Funeral Director and Author
Embalming: History, Theory and Practice
Pittsburgh, PA

"Poignant and thought provoking – you'll enjoy this collection of essays from veteran funeral director Mac McCormick. McCormick pulls you into the story. He entertains and educates.
"It's a good read."

-John Horan
Horan & McConaty
Denver, CO

"While growing up, my family lived near two funeral homes. Any time I had met the funeral directors, they were always very kind and sincere. But I always wondered how someone could have been drawn into funeral service. 'There is nothing but sadness and never a happy story,' I thought. As an editor of a funeral service publication, I always find Mac McCormick's essays to be educational as well as inspirational. They open a window to the noblest of professional callings."

-Edward J. Defort, Editor
American Funeral Director, American Cemetery

"Mac McCormick is a storyteller of the first order, who does justice to all of his writing. His research is meticulous and his writing ensures that his subjects get the importance they deserve. Mac makes his stories come alive."

-Melissa Johnson, Funeral Director
Chicago, IL

"I have anxiously read Mac McCormick's "End Notes" in American Funeral Director for quite some time. I appreciate and enjoy the mix of his consummate knowledge of funeral service and his reminiscing and experience relating to funeral service. His book, Days of Death – Nights of Service, tends to remind me of my cherished beginnings and all the reasons I love funeral service."

-Bernard Johnson, Funeral Director

D0887046

"I have enjoyed and looked forward to reading Mac McCormick's work for the last ten years. While there are a multitude of good reasons to follow this author's writing, I will share with you mine. Mac McCormick has an uncanny gift at keeping the true meaning of funeral service grounded. His work reminds me that if I put the 'Business' of the business in the background and focus on the absolute dedication to quality of service, the business end, while not to be ignored, will thrive."

-Don Terry, Funeral Director
Florida

"Days of Death and Nights of Service concerns the positives of funeral service. We hear many negatives, but few people ever learn of the many little things that funeral directors do every day to help people heal. The history of their struggles and the long hours funeral directors give to families in their time of confusion and pain goes unnoticed by many."

-Walter A. McComb, Jr., Funeral Director
Fort Wayne, IN

"Any funeral director who becomes discouraged or doubts the validity of his effectiveness in this profession will find great encouragement in the stories and writings of Mac McCormick. In Days of Death – Nights of Service, he reinforces the positive effects of compassion, sensitivity, and sacrificial service. Excellence is the word best used to characterize the daily work and writings of the author."

-Pastor Mark Klinepeter, Chaplain
Life Support Chaplaincy

"After reading Days of Death – Nights of Service, I am reminded why I am in funeral service. Many times we only hear negative things about our profession, but this collection of stories reminds us of the many reasons we all are in funeral service, mainly the people. This book helps us remember, after the end of a long day, why we are funeral directors."

-Kevin Davis, Director of Funeral Service Education
St. Petersburg Jr. College
St. Petersburg, FL

Days of Death
Nights of Service

BY

Mac McCormick

AUTHOR:	Mac McCormick
COVER DESIGN:	Gayla Steinberg H. Donald Kroitzsh
TYPING & EDITING:	Jennifer Ullrich Patricia MacLeod
LAYOUT:	H. Donald Kroitzsh

Published by:
JARMAC Publishing
308 Spring Forest Court
Fort Wayne, IN 46804
Tel: 219-413-9210

Any unattributed quotations are by Mac McCormick

Printed and Bound in Canada

Prepared by:
Five Corners Publications, Ltd.
5052 Route 100
Plymouth, Vermont 05056 USA

Days of Death – Nights of Service
ISBN: 0-9709822-0-8 $18.⁹⁵

NOTE TO THE READER

This is a collection of short human-interest stories and thoughts I have published over the years in *American Funeral Director*. I fully realize that the average reader probably thinks it odd that funeral directors have a professional trade journal available to them, but in reality, the publishers have been issuing the magazine since 1877. My thanks go to Kates-Boylston Publications, of Iselin, New Jersey, for allowing me to republish these copyrighted stories.

I have loosely based most of the *"End Note"* stories on my experiences as a funeral director and embalmer. However, any perceived similarity to any living or dead person that I may have served, or worked with, unless otherwise noted as reality, remains coincidental, and not intentional.

By reading *"Days of Death – Nights of Service"*, I hope you will realize that the funeral directors and embalmers of today are, for the most part, caring and concerned professionals.

Mac McCormick
Fort Wayne, Indiana
December 19, 2000

About The Cover

The Florence Brokaw Martin Satterwhite Memorial remains the centerpiece of the historic and magnificent Cave Hill Cemetery, Louisville, Kentucky. Designed by the noted Philadelphia architect, Horace Trumbauer (1869-1938), with statuary sculpted by Sally James Franham (1881-1943), the Memorial occupies more than 26,000 square feet. The land alone cost more than $50,000.00 in 1928, when Dr. Preston Pope Satterwhite (1867-1948), a wealthy and prominent Louisville surgeon, purchased the site as a fitting memorial to his late wife. Trumbauer developed his design after viewing the "Temple of Love", built by the French architect, Richard Mique (1728-1794), in honor of Marie Antoinette. It is located in the Petit Trianon Gardens of Versailles. Trumbauer also based the Roman aspects of the Satterwhite Memorial on the Temple of Vesta at Tivoli.

Photo by Mac McCormick, 1999
Cover Design by Gayla Steinberg & H. Donald Kroitzsh

(Information from the author's interview of Mr. Lee Squires, Superintendent, Cave Hill Cemetery, published as Consumate Majesty, American Cemetery, March 2000.)

Acknowledgments

I am deeply grateful to the following people for their help and encouragement over the years: my father, the late Nelson A. McCormick, my mother, Glenna Jane Sultzbaugh, and the truest love of my life, the charming Jo Ann Roscoe. Without you, Jo Ann, my life would hold little meaning.

After my dad died, my loving uncle, the late Fred R. McCormick, Sr., did all that he could to be a father to me, as well as a kind benefactor. My brother, Nelson A. McCormick, II and sisters, Dr. Jane L. McCormick and Cynthia Anne Keefer, all saw me through difficult periods of my life. I am glad you did not disinherit me! Two other very special people who also deserve the deepest appreciation I can offer are Ed (WA3PUN) Bolton, and his late wife, Marilynne, and Beverly Stout.

Special thanks to the late Dr. Edward C. Johnson, who was undoubtedly the finest Funeral Service Historian in the world, for all of his encouragement. To his daughter, the eminent funeral director, and truly one of the world's finest embalmers, Melissa Johnson Williams, I can only say: Thank You for carrying on your father's legacy and for living your own brilliant life.

To the following funeral directors: Ralph Riegle, Cliff Sterner, and Jessie Minier, all of Millersburg, Pa. who have all died, you were my childhood heroes and role models. Tim Miller, Earl Hodges, Don Terry, and the late David Watt were all kind and patient during my Florida apprenticeship and internship. Kevin Davis, of St. Petersburg Junior College's Funeral Service Program and funeral director Rick Hahn, both believed in me and gave me outstanding opportunities to learn and grow. Thanks also to Bob Skaggs, for his help.

I want to offer my appreciation to Dick Sanders, a funeral director and embalmer, formerly of the Dodge Company. Also, my thanks to the learned author and also one of the world's leading embalming experts, Robert Mayer, for his kind words and even more, his support, and the textbooks he brilliantly wrote for all funeral service students.

Mr. Adrian F. Boylston and Ed Defort of Kates-Boylston Publications, publisher and editor, respectively, of *American Funeral Director* and *American Cemetery*, helped me tremendously by publishing my articles and encouraging me to continue writing more of them.

My gratitude to Jennifer Ullrich, for her untiring efforts in typing the manuscript, Patricia MacLeod for her editing skills, Gayla Steinberg for the cover design, and Don Kroitzsh for his professional assistance in producing this book.

Walter and Jean, David and Doug McComb have all been exceptionally kind and supportive of my writing and me. Please accept my gratitude. To my best friend, Mark Shrader, particularly sincere thanks for every bit of encouragement you have ever offered.

Fort Wayne, Indiana
December 19, 2000

DEDICATION

To Jo Ann Roscoe and Professor Ed Johnson:

The two finest and most decent human beings I have ever known.

x

About The Author

M ac McCormick writes a monthly column for *American Funeral Director*, the nation's leading professional trade journal for funeral directors and embalmers. He also contributes frequently to *American Cemetery* and other publications, and he began writing for Kates-Boylston Publications in 1975.

The central Pennsylvania native grew up working in one of the funeral homes in his hometown and currently works as a funeral director for D.O. McComb and Sons, Fort Wayne, Indiana. He also served as a Mortuary Affairs NCO during a portion of his United States Air Force career and worked at funeral homes in Missouri, Arizona and Florida.

Mac, who saw military service during both the Viet Nam and Panama conflicts, retired from the Armed Forces Radio and TV Service as a Broadcast Journalist. During Staff Sergeant McCormick's tour of duty in Panama, General Manuel Noriega's troops detained and injured him repeatedly. They harassed the non commissioned officer because of his high visibility as a news anchor on the Southern Command Network TV Network, which broadcast anti-Noriegia rhetoric. During his military career, the United States Air Force decorated Mac twice with the Air Force Commendation Medal. The U.S. Army rewarded SSg McCormick with the Army Achievement Medal and the Army Commendation Medal. The Army also honored him with many "Fourth Estate Awards for Excellence in Military Journalism" awards, several Keith L. Ware Awards, and in 1988, they named Mac "The John T. Anderson Military Broadcaster of the Year."

He graduated from the Defense Information School and also earned an Associate of Science Degree from the Community College of the Air Force in 1982. In 1990, Mac earned a Bachelor of Arts Degree with a major in Journalism from Thomas A. Edison State University. In 1997, he graduated with the highest honors and an Associate in Science Degree in Funeral Services from St. Petersburg Junior College.

For comments or questions, please contact Mr. Mac Cormick at Hcho4u42@home.com.

CONTENTS

ƒUNERALS OF THE ƒAMOUS

When The Bells Toll

When God in His Infinite Wisdom has seen fit to call back to His fold a human soul,

And when the earthly remains of one beloved must be laid to eternal sleep,

Then it becomes the sacred duty of our profession to assist the bereaved living in this, the last task of love for the departed.

In carrying out this sacred duty, we will do our part

With Sympathy
   With Dignity
      With Reverence

-Author Unknown

"The Undertaker"

The midnight hour, the darkest hour
That human grief may know,
Sends forth its hurried summons –
Asks me to come – I go!

I know not when the bell may toll,
I know not where the blow may fall,
I only know that I must go
In answer to the call.

Perhaps a friend – perhaps unknown –
"'Tis fate that turns the wheel –
The tangled skein of human life
Winds slowly on the reel.

And I? I am the Undertaker,
"Cold Blooded," you will hear them say
"Trained to the shock and chill of death,
With a heart that's cold and grey."

Trained – that is what they call it
How little they know the rest –
I am human, and know the sorrow
That throbs in the aching breast.

Bennett Chapple — 1903

4

END NOTES

"Good Night, Mrs. Hunter"

Clancy Romberger set his jaws firmly, fumbled with a Turkish cigarette and his favorite silver Zippo lighter, and looked out the office window at the bourgeoning traffic on Gettysburg Lane. The two shoe factories in Gurber's Mill dismissed their employees about four P.M. For about fifteen minutes, it became just about impossible to get any of our vehicles out of the livery garage, which opened onto that thoroughfare. That situation only became problematic whenever we had a death call around that time, late on weekdays.

Earlier, the telephone's jangling had sliced into the lazy stillness of that cool autumn afternoon many years ago at Romberger's Chapel of the Chimes. We had all been puttering around in the front yard of the Chapel, because it was such a truly glorious day, with moderate temperatures and tolerable humidity. The sun sent its bright rays dancing over the Red Maple trees, which wore bonnets of burnished saffron leaves, turned that shade by the recent onset of cooler weather.

Mrs. Wakley's death call came about the same time the work whistle blew at the Susquehanna Shoe Company, and I correctly surmised that we would have a delay in leaving for the removal. Mr. Romberger took the call from Markley Bushnell, the County Coroner, on the garage phone. Then he went inside to clean up and change his clothing – I followed suit, and met him in the front office. He coughed a couple of times and said that we would wait another five minutes until the traffic lessened. After issuing a few orders, he commented that we would then be off for Mrs. Wakley's house, found a few miles away at the edge of Berry Mountain.

She had been an intrepid woman, politically and socially well advanced for the day and age in which she had lived. I remember seeing Mrs. Wakley around Gurber's Mill frequently, and always in church every Sunday. Her comeliness, her handsome Scottish features and her Tam O'Shanter, replete with pheasant feathers topping it, were her trademarks.

Mr. Wakley had served as a police officer for Gurber's Mill, until his death about a dozen years before in the late 1960's. While he spent his life looking after the parking meters found in the old town square, Mrs. Wakley became heavily involved in politics and philanthropic matters.

Together, the Wakley's parented two daughters, one of whom, Barbara Wakley Caldwell, married her high school sweetheart and moved to New Hampshire. The other daughter, Ann Hunter, herself a widow, stayed at the

Wakley home remaining loyal to her mothers' every need. Mrs. Hunter's only obvious fault, which I believe was common knowledge to most of the townspeople, continued to be her dependence on alcohol.

As Clancy took the last few drags on his cigarette, I went out to the garage and checked the '56 dark grey Cadillac hearse we always exercised for removals. Everything seemed in order with the Ferno-Washington cot, and plenty of clean sheets lay in readiness. Just as I was slamming the side door shut, which consistently closed with a reassuring "thud" and "whoosh" one does not hear from the later model vehicles, Clancy came into view. After opening the garage door, I hopped in the passenger side of the coach while Mr. Romberger got behind the wheel and brought the powerful engine to life. As he gingerly backed the coach out of the garage into the remaining "factory traffic" on Gettysburg Lane and swung the huge wheel, I cast a wary glance at the riot of colorful leaves still swirling on the sprawling front yard. The boss, now busy chewing a handful of Sen-Sen Mints, headed the hearse north to Wiconisco Avenue.

The Pennsylvania Dutch that live in the Gurber's Mill area would call the Wakley home "crazy clean." Mrs. Wakley had always been a good housekeeper but when we arrived at the home, and when we finally got inside, we saw immediately that there had been some sort of problem. Drivers had parked cars everywhere on the Wakley property. Two Pennsylvania State Troopers, both of whom might have been over six feet-something in height, milled about the driveway. Several neighbors clustered about the perimeters of the home, talking quietly.

"Did Markley tell you that anything odd happened here?" I asked Clancy as he spun the massive steering wheel of the hearse hard, so he could edge it by the parked police cruiser in the driveway. "Something sure as sin is going on here," I ventured, just as a third trooper came out the side door of the Wakley home, gingerly holding a hunting rifle by its shoulder strap.

"Hulllo, chust vwhat do we have here?" Mr. Romberger said, not bothering to lessen the Pennsylvania Dutch accent he sometimes worked to conceal.

"I'm not certain, but it does not look good," I said, alighting from the hearse and following Mr. Romberger as he headed for the front of the Wakley house. It looked as if the police had spent hours unraveling yards of bright lemon colored crime scene tape, spinning it about trees, yard ornaments and various house doors.

One of the Titan sized police officers knew Clancy from Trautman's Restaurant where both often had coffee and doughnuts together. He approached the lanky undertaker, grasped Mr. Romberger's hand warmly, and huddled him off to a corner of the yard where they stood for the longest time, conferring. I began to wonder what was the topic of the "good old boys" meeting. Had a mad person killed or injured someone? A furtive glance at my watch told me that I had been standing there for only seven minutes, although it seemed much longer, when Clancy motioned for me.

"Much ado over naughtin," Clancy said, his Middle Atlantic vowel distortion at it's best. He continued, his speech starting to improve, "Ann Hunter got to drinking again when her Mom died. She got despondent, and wanted to shoot herself. Barbara called the State Troopers, who took Old Man Wakley's rifle out of the house." I thought I saw a half a smirk cross Clancy's face.

Considering all of the confusion and trouble we experienced getting to the removal, I just knew that the rest of the transfer would go smoothly. Wrong. We stepped into the dimly lit living room to find Mrs. Hunter nothing short of totally inebriated. The air smelled heavily of stale cigarette smoke, a sick room, fried foods and booze. Pastor David Lenker, of St. John's Lutheran Church, stood between the two sisters, looking very much like an unwilling referee.

It would take us another hour and a half to complete the removal. Ann, after offering us a snort, told us through heavily slurred words that she did not want us to take her mother from the house. Barbara seemed in a mood to humor her. After twenty minutes of standing and listening to Clancy, the Pastor and Barbara negotiate with the befuddled Ann Hunter, I began longingly eyeing a nearby Lazy-Boy Recliner. Eventually, wondering if they had ever heard that it makes no sense to deal with an intoxicant, I sank heavily into the chair, risking a stern talk from Clancy later. The Pastor finally steered the plastered Mrs. Hunter into a nearby side room, and we agreed with Barbara Caldwell that we would meet with the entire family the following afternoon to make funeral arrangements.

Mr. Romberger and I went upstairs to discover the late Mrs. Wakley had fallen face first into the plush carpeting of the master bedroom. Clancy and I turned heel and went outside to get our mortuary cot. We came back into the once immaculate house, completed the transfer, drove back to the funeral home, and embalmed the little Scottish lady. As I began my drive home, the clock at the First National Bank and Trust Company pronounced the time as deep into the hour of ten P.M.

Late the next morning, I sat at my desk in the back of the funeral home office and shuffled through the bulky bundle of Romberger's incoming mail. There being nothing interesting in the stack, save the current issue of *American Funeral Director*, I went to the front of the building to double check the Arrangement Room. As I passed the coffee lounge, I thought I detected the glorious aroma of Mrs. Romberger's baking. Sure enough, the German born woman had been using her culinary skills again. She always baked the delicacies whenever we had a family coming into the funeral home. After delivering the goodies, she lingered at the Chapel to brew her famous gourmet style coffee. Just as I snuck one of Mrs. Romberger's scrumptious pastries from the wide hand-painted tray, which I knew was a family heirloom, I heard a loud disturbance coming from the direction of the front door. Gulping quickly without the benefit of the much desired coffee, I moved to the funeral home's foyer.

There, supported by Mr. and Mrs. Caldwell, stood – in a matter of speaking – none other than Mrs. Ann Hunter – and I dare say, not in much better condition than the previous afternoon. After exchanging greetings and some small talk, which included a few colorful epithets from Mrs. Hunter, I guided them to the Arrangement Room. Off I went to the Embalming Room to find Clancy, and inform him that the Wakley Family had arrived more than two hours early.

Swinging open the thick door, I found Mr. Romberger dressing Mrs. Wakley.

He had been in a good mood all day, and I absentmindedly wondered what my impending message might do for him, as I knew he hated missing lunch.

"The Wakley's are here. I installed them in the Arrangement Room, and I might add that this looks like a re-run of yesterday afternoon's presentation by one Mrs. Ann Hunter," I allowed, adding "Maybe some of Mrs. R's coffee will sober her up a bit. I'm going back to finish the mail."

Clancy looked at me with exasperation and that look of disdain he normally reserved for the fluid salesman that always popped in unexpectedly. "No, Sir," he said firmly. "You are going to help me with the arrangements. Get your note pad and meet me in the Arrangement Room immediately."

The chaotic conference became one that should have been video taped for use in Mortuary Colleges across the nation. The daughters took turns squabbling with us, each other, and Mr. Caldwell, alternately. Barbara Caldwell wanted us to hold the funeral at the Lutheran Church, while Ann Hunter kept insisting loudly that she did not want us to "joy ride" her Mother around town. I took notes and have to admit that Clancy did an admirable job of keeping the clan Wakley under control and the noise level just a decibel above the proverbial low roar.

His soothing voice and obvious care for the family shone through the long afternoon, even when Ann Hunter asked us for an emesis basin in the casket selection room. "You know," she said, "You should really keep a little bag like the airlines use next to each coffin." They finally selected a handsome full couch Boyertown mahogany casket. Ann Hunter proclaimed loudly that she wouldn't sign the contract. She reasoned that we would not bury her mother in the casket, but switch it with another one before burial. Clancy very diplomatically told her that he would not allow her to sign a contract because of her condition and that she could be present at the closing of the grave. Barbara Caldwell finally acquiesced to Mrs. Hunter and agreed to hold the funeral service at Romberger's Chapel.

That night, Clancy had assigned me call duty, and answered the phones from a small apartment above the funeral home. Sometime during the small hours of the morning, the doorbell disturbed the billows of my deep slumber.

Answering the massive oak door with beveled glass panes, I found a very tipsy Mrs. Hunter. She insisted that she wanted to come inside to view her Mother. For a few seconds, I debated the wisdom of such a move. Nevertheless, I reasoned, we were there for service. So I turned on lights and ushered Ann Hunter into the front parlor where Mrs. Wakley lay in repose.

A sobering transformation came over the slight woman. She came in, walked to the casket, bent over and kissed her mother. Standing in the back of the parlor, I clearly heard her say, "Goodbye, Mother, I shall always love and miss you." With that, she turned and marched out of the Chapel. "Good Night, Mrs. Hunter," I called into the murky darkness of the central Pennsylvania night, but she had already turned the corner and was headed home.

I'd like to be able to tell you that Ann Hunter got sober, got clean, and lived a productive life. Unfortunately, just a few months after we buried her mother, Mrs. Hunter drove her car into an abandoned coal mining pit and died a slow and painful death. Markley Bushnell found her blood alcohol level to be more than twice the legal limit. We buried her in the middle of a blustery winter afternoon that year, next to her parents, on a remote hill found in Oak Lawn Cemetery. "Good Night, Mrs. Hunter, and Good Bye."

Postscript

This reminiscing demonstrates our constant role, day and night, as public servants. We must constantly be vigilant to the wants and needs of a changing society and the extended families we now serve. Despite some personal abuse and moments of sheer indignation, we must shelve any personal animosities to care for those we serve. It's not for us to pass any judgments, because we may find ourselves in a situation similar to Mrs. Hunter some day. I pray that I can be non-judgmental and have the needed strength and wisdom to serve every family well and wisely.

Of Liberty Bells
and Devoted Friends

"We must all die; we are like water spilt on to the
ground, which cannot be gathered up again."
2 Samuel 14:14

The huge Liberty Bell replica controlling the panoramic front porch of Clancy Romberger's Funeral Home easily grabs visitors' eyes and attention. It stirs their patriotism and gracefully adorns the entrance to his Atlantic style Gurber's Mill Chapel. If a person looks at the signaling device long enough, the weathering on it commands their curiosity. Despite many restorations, a slight edging of rust remains on the cast-iron bell. It causes the replica to look as though it's been guarding Clancy's portico since the installation of the original Liberty Bell in Philadelphia, found just three counties south. Local lore says that Clancy rang that bell on his veranda on only one occasion – that of the simultaneous death of a husband and wife.

In reality, though, Clancy bought the bell at an estate sale in the nearby town of Chesterville shortly after he purchased the funeral home from Jessie Trautman. Trautman & Sons, Undertakers, who served the area for almost a century, held the record for the most burials near Gurber's Mill. In the waning months of 1946 Jessie Trautman had lived almost seventy-three years. He still firmly believed in cooling boards, and he also espoused the practice of using gravity percolators for embalming.

Clancy, then just twenty-six years of age, had already experienced about as much savagery and inhumanity as a man could experience in a lifetime. Having served in the Army's 109th Infantry Division during the Second World War, with great distinction and valor, Clancy decided immediately following V-J Day to return to the East Coast. The Army discharged Staff Sergeant Romberger at Fort Dix, New Jersey, and he drove without delay to south-central Pennsylvania to talk to Mr. Trautman.

Despite the firm's name, Jessie Trautman had no heirs, just a neighborhood man, Prince Boyer, who used to help him around the funeral home. Selling to the diplomatic and quick-witted Clancy Romberger, who the community truly admired, became the best move Mr. Trautman could make.

Clancy's birthright helped him considerably, as he could easily move in the right circles of "shakers and movers." He also knew well the earthy people who toiled in the several sweat shop factories found in Old Armaugh County. The veteran could talk with the men who labored on the railroads. Mr.

Romberger made friends with those who traveled into the depths of the earth to mine the rich anthracite coal of the nearby dank and dangerous mines.

So, Clancy Romberger made his deal with Jessie Trautman to take over the neat brick funeral parlor with the Gothic stained glass windows. First, he traveled the ninety-five miles to the city of Brotherly Love to attend The Eckels College of Mortuary Science on North Sixteenth Street. Romberger knew the school had been open less than twelve years. He also knew several other graduates who had used their "G.I. Bill" to complete the new course, which lasted nine months.

Next, he became involved in every fraternal, social and economic organization in and around Gurber's Mill that he could find. Because of his war duties, he joined both the Veterans of Foreign Wars and The American Legion. Clancy quickly ascended to command positions in both patriotic organizations, and people would always see him in his uniform marching at the front of the Memorial Day parades. His pals took him through the rites of Freemasonry and Clancy soon became a Tall Cedar of Lebanon. Before long, he would wear the fez of the Ancient Arabic Order of the Nobles of the Mystic Shrine. Mr. Romberger took over the Chamber of Commerce and stayed active on the Town Council, wisely accepting a nonpartisan seat. When Gurber's Mill celebrated their one hundred and fiftieth anniversary, Clancy oversaw most of the committees.

However, what is more important over the next several post-war years is that Clancy Romberger became a very good undertaker. He went out on every death call himself, no matter the hour. Clancy embalmed all the bodies, and did his own restorative work. He got along well with the ministers in the area, most of them German Lutherans, and knew how they related to their families. Mr. Romberger had that gift of charisma that allowed him to just about always say "the right thing at the right time." Women loved him because of his startling good looks, grace, charm and debonaire appearance. Men found him to be a "man's man," who could easily talk about fishing, hunting, politics, the Second World War, or family matters. Clancy washed all of his own vehicles and religiously cleaned the funeral home daily.

Eventually, he found love when he met a blond haired, blue eyed, young and buxom German woman from a nearby mining town. Nor could Gabriella Rzepka resist the suave undertaker who conducted the services for her late aunt. Less than a year after they met, they wed in a highly emotional Catholic Mass. Years later, she would always recount how she had fallen in love with Clancy when he had so graciously held the funeral parlor door open for her at the wake. Clancy would claim Gabriella exuded the joys of "holidays and blue skies."

Over the decades, the business and Clancy's relationships flourished. Gabriella and Clancy had children, and they built a beautiful new funeral home in the Reservoir Heights section of town. They made plenty of friends, but became especially close to Norma and Paul Lewandowski.

Norma taught school for the Gurber's Mill School District, and Paul owned Ski's Habadashery Shop on Market Square downtown. Paul sometimes helped Clancy with funerals and wakes, and Norma sometimes helped Mrs. Romberger with the accounting and hairdressing, common for those days.

Together, they attended Mass, played Canasta and Golf, bowled, and raised their children. They were truly devoted friends. During the winter, the men would go off to hunters camp, and the women would stay behind at home, watching the children and the businesses. Summer vacations would find all of them at their cottages by the mile wide and scenic Susquehanna River.

Because they all played musical instruments well, the foursome made up the backbone of "Ski's Polka Band." The band included seven or eight other men and women – most of whom attempted to play the accordion. They never charged anyone for any of their performances. "Ski's Band" would play at carnivals, nursing homes, hospitals, fairs, church events, school outings, but never at any bars. The four of them had a true aversion to alcohol and never took anything stronger than the Eucharistic wine of Communion.

In life, too often, irony mixes with horror and reality. Selfish people kill innocent people through their thoughtlessness. Such became the case when twenty five year old Scott Shoff left the Chesterville Inn one Saturday evening, having consumed the better part of a bottle of Irish Whiskey. Shoff was driving southbound in the northbound lane at a high rate of speed when he crashed into Paul and Norma's car, killing them outright. As often happens with drunken drivers, Shoff escaped with minor injuries. Paul and Norma were returning from playing with the band at a nearby hospital.

It happened that I was home in Gurber's Mill on leave from the U.S. Air Force that month. I had practically grown up in the funeral business with Mr. Romberger's son. As a natural result, I always helped with any odd jobs, cleaning, removals, wakes and funerals whenever I could.

Very early the morning following the agonizing and fatal accident, the town Constable, Edgar "Cookie" Dorney, woke me out of a peaceful sleep with the news of the deaths. He told me that Mr. Romberger was waiting for me at the Funeral Home. Although I could scarcely fathom what had happened, I knew that Clancy and Gabriella would be inconsolable. I fished around in the darkness, grabbed some clothing, dressed quickly, and rushed the four miles to Romberger's' Funeral Home. As I drove the last mile to the chapel, I glanced at the dashboard clock. It read just before three A.M. Motoring the last few blocks, I thought maybe I was still asleep and dreaming – I imagined I could hear a very loud bell. The closer I got to the chapel, the louder the pealing became.

There, in the midnight shadows and silhouettes of that early Sunday morning, stood Clancy Romberger ringing the huge bell on the front porch.

Groups of his neighbors stood around, simply watching him. Mrs. Romberger rushed to me and told me that Clancy had decided to ring the bell to honor his good friends, despite the hour. I walked up onto the impenetrable dimness of the portico. After a few awkward, yet moving minutes, Clancy stopped pealing the bell and looked at me strangely. I will never forget that look of grief and horror on his face.

The next few days were a blur. I recall the removals, the embalming, the restorative work, the crowds at the double wake and the funeral, attended by more than a thousand people. Paul and Norma were deeply loved. Those services were fitting, appropriate, and a heartfelt tribute to two wonderful people.

Those were the last two funerals Clancy ever conducted. Following the Lewandowski services, he called fellow funeral director Richard Weatherbee from Harrisburg, and sold him the firm. Clancy and Gabriella retired to Florida. I went back to duty in a hell hole of an assignment in Turkey, but I will always remember that night of Liberty Bells and Devoted Friends.

Emily's Pink Shirt

"In the sweat of thy face shalt thou eat bread, til thou
return unto the ground; for out of it was thou taken; for
dust thou art, and unto dust shalt thou return."
-God, speaking to Adam in Genesis 3:19

The fragrant jaded odor of purple lilacs hung heavily in the air which impetuous summer showers had just scrubbed clean. Cars on Gettysburg Lane whizzed and skidded by Romberger's Funeral Home at an alarming speed. Those drivers were most likely unaware of the tragedy that caused the heartbreak and desolation found within the confines of our Gurber Mills Chapel. Hundreds of hushed townspeople wound around the colonial style building in several serpentine lines. Here and there, some puffed on a cigarette. A few people conversed in the rarely heard and strained tones of the Pennsylvania Dutch. Shadows of farmers and factory workers mingled with those of bankers and attorneys. That remarkable and unusual crowd maintained not only a great deal of order in the oppressive humidity, but also the truest sense of decorum and respect. In some bordering and bounteous fields, verdant regiments of summer corn stalks rustled when a slight gust of mid-June wind broke their stance of attention. A few stray dogs on the neighbor's lawn yapped at each other, the strident barks resonating off nearby Turtle Hill Reservoir.

Two of Romberger's ancient and wheezing part-timers, their polyester suits worn thin with wear, acted as sentinels and front lobby hosts. Although cantankerous and obstinate, they knew just about everyone in town by name. Besides that, they lived just down the block. I always assumed those were the reasons Mr. Romberger withstood some of their tomfooleries and territorial nagging about the chapel. The aging and crotchety duo took turns alternately gossiping about the visitors and staff and opening and closing the massive walnut doors for the hundreds of callers. Those doors, replete with small viewing devices, had long been fixtures on Mr. Romberger's father's house over on stately Union Boulevard. When Clancy Romberger built the new chapel, he took the doors from his father's home just before old Oscar Ware, the cigar chomping and baldheaded builder, demolished it to make way for a new shopping mall.

Deeper inside the funeral home, a palpable cloud of grief and devastation hovered over the chapel and adjacent viewing rooms. John Leinweber, Gurber Mill's shoemaker, sat rigidly and forlornly in the front row of armchairs that Clancy Romberger had pushed together earlier in the day. As visitors came by to murmur words of consolation to him, he would mumble a few words of thanks in return. Sometimes he would repeat the story about the deaths of his family. For all intents, however, he remained in an understandable and frozen state of shock.

Not eight feet away from Mr. Leinweber, in front of him and across the teeming sea of carmine colored floral carpeting, under soft pink and aquamarine blue cosmetic spotlights, lay the casketed remains of his wife and three children. One oversized twenty-gauge "sealer" casket held his wife, Julie, and by her side, their eleven-month-old son, Christen. To the left and right of Mrs. Leinweber's casket sat the modest ivory colored caskets of the other two children, seven-year-old Eric and twelve-year-old Emily.

In a devastating contrast, masses of cut flowers cascaded and exploded in peaks and clusters of blazing color throughout the chapel. An overflow of resplendent blooms and potted plants graced the lobby and wound its way past Mr. Romberger's arrangement office, ending somewhere inside the snug kitchen that served as a refreshment lounge. There, Gabriella Romberger, in her role as the undertaker's wife, brewed pots of steaming black coffee and served mourners some of her exquisite German pastries.

Just two days earlier, John Leinweber had returned to his home after a full day of shoe cobbling to discover a horrific and eerie scene straight out of Truman Capote's *In Cold Blood*. His daughter Emily's bloodied pink shirt hanging on the front door served as the first ghastly clue to the macabre tableau he would discover. The shoemaker found his kindhearted and loving wife of fifteen years lying dead on the kitchen floor. It became immediately apparent to Mr. Leinweber that she had struggled tremendously up to the end of her life. Close to her, he encountered the remains of their baby, obviously suffocated. Upstairs, a gunman's bullets had instantaneously ended the lives of his other two children.

Mr. Romberger and I had been washing and polishing the hearse and family car when the call from Markley Bushnell, the county coroner, came that day in the mid 1980's. We both scrambled for the phone on the garage wall to escape the mundane chore, but Old Man Romberger got there first. It was the only time in several decades that I ever saw him truly shocked.

"Oh, my Gawd," I heard him say into the plain black receiver as he stared off into space as if searching for some relief from the shard of lightning the instrument had just given him.

"Yes, we will be there; however, I must call Buff Derner and see if he can bring his hearses, too – and help me with the embalming." Mr. Romberger gently cradled the headset and sat on the nearest seat which turned out to be one of several metallic garbage cans. He gave me an odd look, shook his head and cleared his throat.

"Murders, some horrible ones, most foul." Mr. Romberger could barely pronounce the words. He spoke abruptly as he lowered his head into his hands and massaged his temples.

"It's unbelievable. Someone killed John Leinweber's entire family. All of them, even the baby. We will go to John's home, get them all, and transport them to Kroll Memorial Hospital for the autopsies. That was Markely." The undertaker tried very hard to maintain his composure. I knew he attended church, the Masonic Lodge, Tall Cedars of Lebanon, the weekly poker game, and Rotary with Mr. Leinweber.

"By God, this is a day when I wish I were in any other profession than this one. Still, this is one way that we can help John Leinweber," Mr. Romberger said, his voice laden with emotion, reflecting the burden and heartache that I knew he felt.

So we did make the removals and embalm, restore, dress, cosmetize and casket the bodies. Buff Derner, although our competitor and the only other undertaker in town, acted as our colleague. He provided us the use of his two hearses and helped us with the embalming. Clancy Romberger and I met with John Leinweber in an unforgettable and agonizing arrangement conference. I took lengthy notes on a red-lined legal pad, while Clancy tried in vain to comfort his friend, who clutched Emily's pink blood-stained shirt to his chest.

The rest of the staff handled what seemed like a million phone calls, ran the vacuum, dusted and polished every piece of furniture, knick-knack and picture in the Gurber Millers Chapel. We carried flowers, rearranged furniture, and washed and polished all the rolling stock. I fielded more phone calls and carried still more flowers. All of us tried hard not to argue with the florists, who were justifiably becoming increasingly short tempered as the viewing day drew closer.

The day and night of viewing did go by smoothly – until the phone rang in the late afternoon. I answered it, reasoning it was yet another reporter wanting details about the funerals which we would hold in the Gurber Mills High School auditorium the following day. It was Markely Bushnell again, who told me to take his call in Mr. Romberger's office. I went into the office, sat in the thickly padded swivel chair behind Mr. Romberger's massive oak desk, and gazed out the frosted glass window at the barrage of people assaulting the chapel.

"We have yet another shooting," Markley spoke, his deep voice fairly rumbling the words somewhere out of the bottom of the ocean. For a split second, for some odd reason, I recalled the image of him standing in the St. John Lutheran church choir loft singing "Jerusalem, Jerusalem," as he did each Easter without fail. He continued, "It happened up in Wilkins Glenn near the old Schaffstall Coal Mine. The State Police shot Steve Frichter in a standoff." Somehow, Markley lowered his voice yet another octave and became secretive. "It relates to the Leinweber murders. He, uh, apparently called the police, confessed to shooting Mrs. Leinweber and the children and suffocating the baby. Frichter told them to meet him up at the mines. When they got there, he started shooting at them. Mac, look, they had no choice."

"Whaaat?" My voice cracked. I had grown up with and gone to school with Steve. We attended the same Sunday School classes and learned about life together. We both were in the same Cub and Boy Scouts troops. A Viet Nam veteran, Steve suffered tremendously from what the wise guy medics over at the VA Hospital called Post Traumatic Stress. I also knew that he had been dealing with flashbacks and alcoholism. Occasionally, I'd see him sitting at the bar in the Stiff Dime when I'd go in to order the Blue Plate Lunch Special at their Grille. We'd exchange pleasantries, but he always seemed hell-bent on discussing Viet Nam. He knew that I had served a tour there in a Graves Registration Unit. Steve always wanted to talk about the old army days. Somehow or other he must have made his way to the Leinwebers' home and thought he was back in 'Nam, I reasoned.

After getting all the information from the burly coroner, I hung up the telephone, and surveyed the office in disbelief. Even looking at Mr. Romberger's Graduation Day picture where the Old Man stood replete with cap and gown at Eckle's College of Mortuary Science (Class of '46) I wasn't amused, as I always was. Opening the desk drawer, I fiddled around until I found the gold colored keys to the hearse and made my way through the crowds of people to the garage. After opening the extra-wide doors the Old Man had recently installed, I gingerly backed the late model grey Cadillac hearse out into the parking lot, still overflowing with cars, trucks and people. Switching on the headlights, I swung the magnificent vehicle around and headed out into the sunset for Kroll Memorial Hospital where I knew pathologists had just completed Steve Frichter's autopsy. Luckily, traffic to Wilkes Barre stayed light both ways because I could not concentrate on the traffic. My mind and heart were racing.

Somewhere around ten P.M., I finished embalming my old friend. I always hated it when I had to prepare my boyhood pals for burial. Frankly, it hurt, and like everyone else I hated thinking about my own mortality. Taking a quick glimpse out into the hallway, I saw people were still calling on Mr. Leinweber. The murdered in front of me, and the murderer behind me on the gleaming, porcelain embalming table, I thought.

The night held yet another shocking development for us, though. After I finished showering and dressing in the employee's lounge, Mr. Romberger came in to tell me that he had already met with Steve's mother. We would bury Steve in a direct graveside burial service the following day out in Pine Hill Cemetery sometime after we had concluded the Leinweber services, which we had scheduled for ten that morning. Mrs. Frichter wanted Steve buried the same day as his victims.

I will carry the poignant and stinging memory of that day to my own grave. My emotions rode a treacherous and painful roller coaster. My body, simply worn out from the events of the preceding five days, operated on remote control.

Somehow, Mr. Romberger, Buff Derner, the rest of the staff and I buried five of Gurber Mills own citizens that day.

Nevertheless, more than a decade and a half later, I realize that is the total sum and substance of funeral service. Deaths coming in waves. Burying your childhood friends and complete families from your hometown. Working in the embalming room until your own bones and back ache so badly one wants to simply quit. Working until this thought occurs: Why not go to Jamaica and sit on the sunny beach and drink funny drinks with umbrellas and never again think about death, embalming or caskets, or burial vaults or the FTC?

Still, that thought lasts just a few wistful moments, until you truly realize the true and fine value of American Funeral Service. It lasts just long enough until the phone rings, and a family – like the Leinweber or the Frichter clan – needs you, the undertaker, or until you see a shirt that looks like Emily's pink one.

His Finest Hour

Eileen Delaney probably would have become the next Governor of the state. Sadly, her brilliant and meteoric rise in the often seditious world of state politics came to a startling end on a treacherous and winding mountain road. A car crash killed her instantly when her late model Mercedes careened off an icy lane into an ominous chasm not far from Gurber's Mill. The former district attorney's campaign could have fared well. At least, that is what some newspaper's political pundits published in their columns. These were editorial pieces meant as a tribute to the tall, graceful woman who had accomplished so much for Old Armaugh Valley.

The Romberger Funeral Home had been unusually busy that winter. Some deaths we dealt with were due to the snow, ice and general frigidity. Winter storms had dumped inches of snow on the greater Gurber's Mills area a couple of times a week for two months. My boss and chief Undertaker Clancy ("Old Man") Romberger had hired some of his World War Two buddies to come and help us at the funeral home. They were moody, arrogant, and generally beyond their element. Whenever I had to work with these "War Buddies of the Boss," they reminded me of a song from the musical Flower Drum Song, "What are We Going to Do About the Other Generation?"

One of them took the Delaney Death Call. He garbled the message insidiously, dispatching the hearse and attendants to the wrong mountain road. This serious error understandably set the funeral home staff off on the wrong foot with the Delaney's.

Still, as I stood beside Old Man Romberger at the funeral home's front door waiting for the Delaney family that clearly austere and blue cold wintry morning, I sensed something special and unusual was about to happen. For one thing, it was a Saturday morning, and Mr. Romberger rarely left the confines of his men's club lair on the weekend. The Appalachian Room, otherwise known as the Social Room of the Gurber's Mill Hotel, served as the central meeting and greeting point for all of Old Armaugh Valley's shakers and movers.

Whenever an undertaker dispatched me to the Hotel to summon Mr. Romberger, (Remember the days before pagers and cell phones?) I would exit the meeting room with Old Man Romberger in tow, the two of us reeking of stale cigar smoke and aged liqueur.

So, when Mr. Romberger missed his weekly pinochle game with the boys, I knew something monumental was at the foundation of it. As the appointed hour neared, I pulled on a thick overcoat and hat and went outside to escort the Delaney's under the forest green canopy that fortified the entrance to Romberger's Funeral Home. A steadfast crust of dense ice had recently formed on the top of the soggy snow that blanketed the vast front lawn.

Only the hot water pipes running under the sidewalk saved the walkway from the same icy fate. I paced and stomped my feet to keep warm as the Northeasterly wind chilled the very marrow of my bones. It wasn't long before Judge Delaney and his three daughters pulled up to the funeral home in a late model pewter grey Lincoln Continental. The balance of the recently bereaved immediate family followed in a recent model Oldsmobile that decidedly had not experienced even one of our Mid-Atlantic winters. I stepped forward quickly and began opening car doors, as Mr. Romberger started maneuvering the heavy walnut door that graced the main building entrance.

The Judge remained a remarkably handsome man with a full head of wavy white hair. His Celtic features simply accentuated his affable personality as he stepped from the Lincoln with an air of authority that be-fit his West Point graduate status. He continually puffed on a Meerschaum pipe that probably cost him half my monthly pay. All three of the Delaney women were absolutely radiant, just as I remembered them from nearby Chesterville High School. The trio had participated in every school activity, sport and social event available at the school. Eventually, they all finished their education at an Ivy League University. Then they married well within their upper social class standing. Heather, Shannon, and Megan were as tall as their Dad, manifested his Irish countenance, and two of them were pregnant. Judge Delaney and his daughters were a study in composure, despite the recent tragedy that had just befallen them. Were they still in shock or denial?

"Eileen always said she wanted a happy funeral." Those were the first words of greeting from the Judge to Mr. Romberger. Mr. Romberger firmly clasped the Judge's hand and guided him by the elbow to the Arrangement Room. I knew they were close fraternity brothers as I had seen them working together at the Tall Cedars of Lebanon Summer Street Fair.

"Still, I want her to have the finest and most elegant service Romberger's offers," Judge Delaney continued as Mr. Romberger got all of the daughters and their sullen looking husbands seated around the mahogany library table used for arrangements. The Old Man nodded for me to serve the coffee, which I did, dispensing steaming carmel colored liquid into hand painted and imported bone china cups that belonged to Mrs. Romberger.

No sooner had the Judge made his pronouncement than the lot of them broke into howls and shouts. Whatever vestiges there had been of dignity dissipated into the air as the sons-in-law yammered about privacy and cost. They had read Jessica Mitford's book about unscrupulous undertakers, they claimed. All three of the sons-in-law said they knew Old Man Romberger was taking them for a ride "down the coal mine." Undertaker Romberger in turn eyed the sons-in-law with his chilling baby blues. He gave the boys a look generally reserved for me when I broke a jugular vein in the embalming room. Nevertheless, he didn't say anything. Every funeral director who is reading this account knows the type of arrangement conference this situation could have easily become. Yet, the Judge held up his hand at his churlish sons-in-law. He looked toward them much the same way I imagine he would stare down a mob in his courtroom.

"Mr. Romberger has been my friend for life. We fished together along the banks of the Susquehanna River when we were boys. We attended the same church and graduated from Chesterville High together. Everyone in this room knows that." Judge Delaney paused, for effect, I thought. I was probably enjoying his soliloquy entirely too much.

"I want to say right now that no one here, I repeat, no one, will have any bearing in the intensely personal decision about how I will bury my beloved Eileen." He stared off into the distance, a firm and resolute man, not yet broken by the cycle of grief I knew he would be enduring. The three sons-in-law looked as though their fourth grade teacher had chastised them.

Excusing myself, I went to retrieve the tray of fresh Pennsylvania Dutch pastry Mrs. Romberger had prepared for the gathering.

When I came back, the group had already decided. We would bury Mrs. Delaney from Saint John's early the following week, and we would lay her body to rest at Maple Hill Cemetery on the edge of Gurber's Mill. Area residents could honor her at two days and nights of viewing. The family did select the finest casket, vault and service Mr. Romberger proffered. We covered her forty-eight-ounce solid cast bronze casket with a lush blanket of cardinal red roses. The embalmers worked throughout the weekend to complete the necessary restorative work, and her appearance was nothing short of radiant considering all she had been through in the accident.

I felt privileged to work both days and nights of calling, and I helped Mr. Romberger at the church the day of the service. More than a thousand people attended the funeral. As we moved Eileen Delaney's casket up the aisle of Saint John's, a combined choir from several churches sang out an old Irish hymn. It was a moment of intense drama in my life I will never forget.

Judge Delaney – and the rest of the family – did maintain their stoic dignity throughout all of the services. Mr. Romberger knew that he had helped his old friend tremendously by helping him through the tedious process of burying his beloved wife. Despite having to weather a fiery storm of criticism from the sons-in-law, the funeral service of Eileen Delaney remains Mr. Romberger's finest hour and a tribute to the value of American Funeral service.

"You Never Get Used to It"

The frigid central Pennsylvania weather that winter pierced your lungs, skin, and senses simultaneously as soon as you stepped outside the door. My boss, Clancy Romberger, owned two funeral homes in Gurber's Mill that he always kept at a temperature higher than that of the orchid hothouse at nearby Henningers Florist Shoppe. The usually lovable Undertaker continuously complained about the cost of anthracite pea coal. That did not stop him from keeping me in the basement, seemingly endlessly, incessantly shoveling that damned dirty black fuel into the hopper for the twin Keystoker furnaces that also heated the hot water for the buildings. Clancy kept instructing me on the fine art of removing the ashes from the furnace and carrying them to a pile of cinders just behind the garage at the Gettysburg Lane Chapel.

What remained truly odd about the entire situation is that men and women – only a half county away – labored in dank and dark labyrinths to mine the cursed substance from mile long veins of the rich bituminous and anthracite coal. Nevertheless, that did not bring the price down, and that kept Mr. Romberger somewhat cranky throughout the entire winter.

These mines formed the fabled coal regions of Pennsylvania which a century before had helped to fuel the Industrial Revolution. The coal regions spawned football wide receiver Gary Collins, people that can talk as rapidly as a machine gun sprays bullets for five minutes without taking a breath, and the late Big Band Leader Les Brown. John O' Hara, whose ancestors lived not far from Gurber's Mill, wrote volumes about the plain Pennsylvania Dutch residents who inhabited the area. Ironically, the majority of citizens were not Dutch at all, but Germans, who denied their ancestry after the United States entered World War II. Clancy often spoke Pennsylvania Dutch, a low strain of German, to people who came to "viewings" or visitations and funerals at his funeral homes.

Gurber's Mill residents stayed busy shoveling their walks and driveways free of the record amount of snow and ice that "Noreasteners," or Northeastern storms, sent their way. By early December that year, the municipal employees were busy decorating the burgh's Christmas displays with strings of multi-colored light bulbs. This magnificent holiday exhibit included five-foot high fir trees that lined the thirty blocks throughout all of the downtown area. They strung rich green garlands high above Market Street, added old-fashioned lanterns to the middle of the garlands, and lined the Market Square Gazebo with festive wreaths.

Whenever Mr. Romberger sent me downtown for some type of errand, I would see people I knew well scurrying from store to store, hoarding the precious treasures that they had selected for Christmas gifts.

Everyone that I met on the street remained excited and talked to me feverishly about the chances for the boys' Senior High School basketball team to go forward for the State Championship. Clancy, a huge sports fan, and a graduate of Gurber's Mill High School, Class of '38, never missed a game.

The funeral homes still ran an ambulance service in those days. Since the school system required that an ambulance be present at all athletic events, and since I was the youngest staff member, I sat through most of the basketball games. The fans shouted until they were hoarse, yelled at the referees whenever they did not like a call, and stomped on the wooden floorboards until the noise level approached that of a propeller plane revving its engines. (In summary, these games were typical American sporting events.) Not much of a sports enthusiast, I usually sat sullenly in the front seat of the ambulance, munching popcorn and hot dogs, rating them on their gourmet appeal.

The basketball team had been undefeated for a number of years. Clancy somewhere got a strange notion that he wanted to coach the team. Whatever made the middle-aged funeral director think that he could do this, with his demanding schedule, remains a mystery to me to this day, decades hence. He got involved, but I think the high school administrators just let him tag along with the team to keep him happy. (Clancy donated thousands of dollars to his alma mater, and I suspect the school board wanted to appease him.)

On the Friday night before Christmas, two very popular and highly skilled team members were driving back to Gurber's Mill from Wiconisco High where they had played faultlessly in one of the biggest games of the season. Snow had begun falling during the game, and the lads were anxious to get back to Gurber's Mill.

As they drove down a particularly narrow mountain pass about eight miles out of town, they lost control of their car. It careened off the icy road crashing in the Yorkshire National Forest. The devastating crash killed both basketball stars almost instantly according to Markley Bushnell, the County Coroner.

We had received an ambulance call to come to Zerby's Mountain where the accident occurred. When we arrived, having driven as fast as the untreated roads would allow us to drive, ambulances from two other villages had also responded, but it was too late. Both boys had died.

Clancy later told me that he received the death call from both families within twenty minutes of each other, deep in the early hours of a snowy Saturday morning. He and I both took hearses and drove to Wilkes Barre to bring the boy's autopsied bodies back to Gurber's Mill. By noon, we had completed the embalming and begun the restorative work.

The families – who knew each other well – decided to hold both the "viewing" and funerals together at Saint John's Evangelical Lutheran Church in nearby Chesterville. On Monday morning we took more than two hundred floral arrangements from the funeral home to the church to surround the two boys' Boyertown full couch mahogany caskets. We transported lights, folding chairs, casket drapes, flower stands, reserved seating signs, register books, memorial donation stands, and a first aid kit.

If there was anybody in the county who did not attend the viewing and funeral, I could not prove it. The substantial crowds lined up quietly and reverently Monday afternoon and night to pay their respects. I stood in the back of the church's auditorium with Clancy. Grief was palpable throughout all of the Old Armaugh Valley, and it hung heavily in the fragrant, pollen heavy air at St. John's' Church.

I remember well the funerals and the viewing, but especially I recall when "Old Doc" Wolfe, the town's pharmacist, came to talk with Clancy about the boys' death. Clancy – like everyone else – hurt badly. Doc Wolfe asked Clancy how he got used to death and dealing with families who had suffered such a tragic loss.

"You never get used to it," Clancy said, nervously fumbling with the Zippo lighter he had carried with him during the Second World War. "You can chust never, ever can get used to it," he repeated with a heart-felt emphasis, echoing his own words, with his Pennsylvania Dutch accent clearly articulated.

Recently, I was conducting a service for a very young lady who lost her life tragically. As I stood at the front door, greeting people who came into the Chapel for visitation, one of the relatives began talking with me. She asked me how I could possibly deal with such heart-breaking situations, day after day. The older woman also wanted to know if I ever hardened my feelings.

"No," I replied, "you just never get used to it."

Shortly after I said that, I experienced a flashback to that memorable night, almost forty years ago, and I remembered Clancy and "Doc" Wolfe talking. I felt a true pang of sadness because I miss him for the kind and thoughtful person he truly was. Then, I realized how very wise Clancy Romberger was, and what good advice that is for all funeral directors.

We need always to retain compassion and care for the families that we serve daily with kindness. As professional funeral directors, we must never become so hardened – or accustomed to memorialization and ceremonies – that we are funeral robots. We just must never get used to it.

THE BROKEN NECKLACE

With one auspicious and one dropping eye,
With mirth in funeral and with dirge in marriage,
In equal scale weighing delight and dole.
-Shakespeare, Hamlet, Prince of Denmark, I, ii, 11

William Shakespeare never had in his mind the bereaved family of "Ted" North that stood in front of me in the small cemetery chapel when he wrote that prose. Nevertheless, it became inevitable that those phrases came to my mind as they quibbled among themselves about a basic decision – whether or not to open their relative's casket for public viewing.

Theodore North led Chesterville, a mid-Atlantic community, in public spiritedness. He belonged to every service organization, fraternity and social group that existed in that small Pennsylvania coal-mining town. After World War II, where he served with great distinction in the South Pacific, he returned home to prosperity, a highly decorated cavalier. Always a charmer, he opened an insurance business, which readily flourished in the next several decades. He and his wife, Betty, enjoyed and owned everything they ever wanted, except children. Eventually, they adopted two boys and two girls. Life dealt a good deck of cards to the North family, until the turbulent year of 1968.

As happened with so many American clans, that violent year tore the North family unit to hell. A grenade in a far off rice paddy blew one of the North sons to bits while he fought for supposed liberty in Viet Nam. Ted North often remarked to me that the old men in Washington cared about that damned war and not the sons and daughters of America.

Later that same year, illicit drugs took the life of one of the North daughters. Our funeral home, Romberger and Sons, buried them both out in the small German Lutheran cemetery where thirty years later, I now stood again after the death of their father.

Ted never preplanned his funeral. The deaths of his two children, adopted or not, devastated him to the point where it was all he could do to serve on the Masonic Funeral Team. He simply couldn't bring himself to address his own death. For those reasons the two remaining North children now had a dilemma deciding whether to open the casket for the upcoming visitation. Mr. North never left any instructions about his funeral service and burial wishes, and it clouded the issue of the day.

For whatever reason, the Norths now decided to use the cemetery chapel, instead of the funeral home for the visitation. They stopped by Romberger and

Sons earlier that day for a brief private viewing, but the published obituary promised the public two hours of calling at the cemetery before the funeral. This wasn't as much calling as we normally gave our families but it was what the North family wanted. Since they were both Baby Boomers, the service decidedly could have gone the way of a basic cremation with no memorialization at all.

When the funeral home staff arrived at the cramped cemetery chapel, we set up the flowers, the lights, the bier, the register stand and all of the necessary equipment. Although we had allowed quite a bit of extra time, the North family pulled in a cavalcade of cars almost an hour earlier than expected.

It's often ironic how one side of a family can be caring, giving and thoughtful while the other can be demanding, insulting and obsessive-compulsive. It's also true that we, as funeral directors, need to graciously satisfy both sides equally, despite our personal thoughts or animosities.

The greater majority of the North family told us how exceptionally pleased they were with their father's appearance in the Veteran's casket they had selected for him. A few relatives uttered the standard, "It doesn't look like Uncle Ted, his mouth isn't right." They also thought the price of the casket and professional services were clearly out of line. These family members were not shy about expressing their opinion and said they thought funeral directors were on the same level as used car salespeople. They were distant cousins of Ted North and generally used the funeral home on the other side of town.

Discussion concerning whether or not to open the casket continued for over fifteen minutes. Ted North's remaining son and daughter, now well into their late forties, leaned toward opening the casket. The balance of the family remained diametrically opposed to holding a public visitation for the World War II hero.

I had heard enough bickering and stepped out into the brisk January air. There, I hoped for a brief respite from the family's travails and possible anguish. As I stood in the churchyard beside gravestones now eerily covered with frosty white ice and snow, I had a brief longing for one of the rich Honduran cigars I gave up years ago. I sighed and contemplated the yammering inside, which by now had escalated to louder voices.

"Wonder who is in charge of this family, and why don't they get some control of this situation?" I thought to myself.

Just then, Dianne North Schaeffer stepped outside for a quick smoke. Dianne amazingly retained the ragamuffin look of the young woman I had gone through Catechism and school with, many, many years ago. She held the lighter that I knew belonged to her dad in one hand and a mentholated cigarette in the other. Taking the lighter out of her hand, I lit the cigarette and grinned at her.

"Quite a storm brewing in there," I ventured, inadvertently staring at the rich auburn curls that still decorated her winsome head.

"Yeah, and it infuriates me. These folks never had any time for Pop when he was ill, never any hours to spend with him when we had to take him over to the Deppler Nursing Home. Now, they smell money. They want to insult us by insisting we not have a public viewing for his friends. My Dad..." Dianne began, holding back the inevitable sobs and tears that I knew would come shortly.

She got a hold of herself, though, and I had to admire her. Dianne looked off toward Chesterville as the sound of distant snow plows scraping a nearby road drifted over the white-topped monuments. Somewhere nearby, a few cows offered what I thought were obscene noises. It developed into an awkward moment. Dianne started gripping her necklace and twirling it rapidly, as she puffed absent-mindedly on her cigarette. My urge for the cigar's tobacco became stronger, but it passed.

Finally, Diane literally jumped forward and simultaneously broke her necklace into what seemed like a hundred small airborne crystals of jade. I scurried to help her find the various pieces in the snow and ice. When we stood up, a different, defiant and decisive look crossed over her pleasant face. Maybe some blood had rushed to her head while she crawled around looking for the necklace components. Perhaps the proximity to the earth had galvanized her to action. Whatever, I could see the fire in her eyes.

"By God, Mac, you men did an excellent job with Dad. This is the best he has looked in years. The casket will be opened for his pals from the VFW and the Legion. That's the end of that." Dianne marched toward the crowded stone chapel.

I nodded and scurried forward to hold open the massive doors that seemed out of place for such a diminutive chapel. She called the relatives into one corner, and five minutes later, nodded at me. Mr. Romberger, who had never left the warmth of the sanctuary, and I went forward, opened the casket, and made the necessary adjustments.

Many friends of Ted North came to call on him that day. As funeral directors, we naturally wanted the family to have their wishes fulfilled about the casket being open or closed. However, since we had worked especially long hours embalming, restoring, cosmetizing and dressing Ted North, we also longed to display our skills. It's a delicate and diplomatic issue that funeral directors all deal with in their own way.

Most of the funeral directors that I interview for *The American Funeral Director* tell me that when questions arise about closing the casket, they simply hold a private family viewing before public calling. Frequently, the family is so well pleased that they leave the casket open for viewing.

If we practice our skill and art the way we know we should, then we will be like Dianne North's necklace before she began twisting it. We will maintain a perfect concentric circle of funeral science, diplomacy, good public relations, community goodwill and art. If we fail to follow accepted practices that we know work well – even if it means longer working hours, then our funeral home and staff might resemble her necklace in the snow. We can be jewels that together form something beautiful or come apart, becoming simply unrelated valuables.

"The Murder of Mrs. - Dr. Dorn"

Clancy Romberger, an excellent funeral director in our "two undertaker town," Gurber's Mill, always called the wives of local townsmen by their husband's occupation. Thus, Henrietta, wife of Butcher Edgar Hayford, became Mrs. Butcher Hayford. Clancy called Elvira Shaw, whose husband operated the Malt Shoppe, Mrs. Soda Shaw. It drove me berserk, until I learned the system, and the reason behind his fanatical malapropisms.

After a few years of serving as Clancy's "permanent apprentice" embalmer, messenger boy, car washer, chauffeur, gardener and semi-butler, I had grown accustomed to his lovable, if unconventional, mannerisms of speech and action. However, I still often wondered how "Mrs. Undertaker Romberger" tolerated Clancy's eccentricities.

One early Saturday morning in early March, decades ago, the ringing of the telephone jarred me from a solid, peaceful sleep. I had gone to bed very tired, because I had spent the previous day shoveling a great deal of unexpected snow.

The Pennsylvania Dutch who live in the area call these near-Spring precipitation events "Onion Snows."

No matter what one calls it, it was wet and heavy, and Clancy had me shovel out the entire funeral home parking lot, around his home, and also at two of his rental properties. Had I been married at that point, Clancy would have to call my wife "Mrs. Snowman Mac."

Consequently, when the loud pealing of the oversized bell of the bedside telephone interrupted my slumber, I fumbled with the receiver and spoke "Hullloo, Romberger Funeral Home" into it in a much-disoriented state.

Initially, I thought I might be dreaming, but then, many of those middle of the night death calls seem that way.

All I immediately heard was a woman literally screaming and sobbing. That woke me instantaneously, and I bolted to an upright position.

" AAAAGH.. OOOH, Murder, Murder. Mac, come quickly.. Mrs. Dorn is dead.." At first, I could not make out the voice but as the weeping and shrieks continued alternately, I suddenly realized it was Mrs. Victoria Bonawitz, mother of my best friend, "Butch" Bonawitz. Now, I was completely awake and alert.

She had worked in the stately and elegant home of Doctor and Mrs. Clarence Dorn, over in Reservoir Heights, for years. I recall that Mrs. Bonawitz cleaned and cooked for them. The proper, trim little lady even stayed with

"Mrs. Dr. Dorn" for some time, looking after her welfare after the Doctor died in a freak shooting accident during deer hunting season.

"My, God, what happened? What are you saying, Mrs. B.?" was all I could manage to get past my now inordinately stubborn lips.

"She's, she's dead, I, uh, uh, just found her, upstairs in her bedroom, when I came in for work this morning. It is so terrible. Please come over." Mrs. Bonawitz said.

"What? Have you called the High Sheriff?" I growled. " Try to calm down. I will be right over. You're at the old Dorn mansion on Bradenbaugh Court, out in The Heights?"

"Yes, I called Sheriff Fogle first thing. I just want you to come over and help me. I called Butch, but he's not at home," she managed to say, but then broke down in another spasm of tears and banshee-like wails.

I signed off, shaking my head in disbelief. Next, I dialed Clancy's private home telephone number which was getting to be all too familiar to me. My orange-colored wind-up Big Ben alarm clock with the glow in the dark face read just after five A.M. No chance the Old Man would be awake, I thought. He got it on the second ring.

"Yes?" Clancy fairly hissed into the mouthpiece. He started coughing that old hacking cough of his from too many years worth of Lucky Strikes cigarettes. He had developed a serious tobacco habit during the Second World War when he served in the South Pacific. "What is it?"

"It's me. Mrs. Bonawitz – you know, Victoria – just called. Oh, you better know this lady as Mrs. Hardware Store Bonawitz. She went in, I guess to fix breakfast for Mrs. Dorn, the doctor's wife, and found a gruesome scene. Mrs. B could hardly talk. Sounds like a homicide," I ventured, waiting for his reaction.

" Saint Jehosophat!" That was about as strong an expletive as I ever heard Mr. Romberger use. He never lost his composure. "What else do you know?"

"I know that Mrs. Bonawitz called Sheriff Fogle, who I assume is on his way out to Reservoir Heights. This is something I will wager he never dealt with before, Boss. My guess is that he will be in over his head. Gurber's Mills's finest is used to baby-sitting parking meters, and not much more. I am going over to Dorns to help Mrs. B as much as I can. Could Mrs. Romberger please catch the phones?" I asked.

"Very well. I shall leave as soon as I can." With that, I heard him hang up the telephone, and I sat there stupidly staring at the instrument for just a second. I showered, dressed quickly, and grabbed my rechargeable electric razor on my way out to the garage.

While I waited for the engine in my ancient Rambler to warm up just a bit, I scraped away at some stubborn whiskers. I knew if I tried to drive the old wreck without a bit of a warm up, it would stall and strand me. Every cell in my body desperately wanted a cup of the dark, rich European coffee that Mrs.

Romberger always brewed at our Gettysburg Lane Chapel. That would prove to be hours away. After the car engine warmed slightly, I fought with the gearshift and backed it out of the tiny building.

Gurber's Mill's roads remained a bit slushy from the residue of the "Onion Snow," and a current freezing sleet kept visibility at a minimum. As I drove by the First National Bank and Trust Company, I glanced up at the old clock, and deciphered the time as five-forty five A.M. The illuminated temperature gauge sitting smartly adjacent to the antiquated timepiece told me the air temperature was thirty-four degrees.

Reaching Reservoir Heights, I urged the little Rambler through the majestic gates, and took a sharp left to reach my destination on Bradenbaugh Lane. Despite the sleet increasing, I could make out the town's one and only police car sitting in the Dorns' driveway. The good Sheriff, of course, had left the red police lights blazing. The dilapidated jalopy responded with somewhat of a backfire as I edged it behind the police car and shut off the ignition.

Meanwhile, I saw another familiar vehicle churning through the sleet coming from the other direction, having just turned off nearby Kissinger Avenue. It was Markley Bushnell, the Coroner for Old Armaugh County.

Markley always drove a late model Black Cadillac – I suspect as much for settling the bulk of his immense girth comfortably behind the wheel as for status. He had an unnerving and unsettling method of driving in the middle of the road. Markley remained myopic through all of his life, and it never added to his driving skills. The affable Coroner pulled his Caddy up into the snow-encrusted driveway behind my old car.

After exchanging a short greeting, we headed to the imposing front door together. Markley was breathing hard, as if he had been exercising. I never knew him to take any exercise, other than lifting huge cups of coffee. He needed to do that to wash down the dozen or so freshly made doughnuts and Pennsylvania Dutch "Fasnachts" that Fritz's Bakery delivered to his office daily.

We rang the doorbell, but it was hardly necessary. Sheriff Fogle appeared, burly and breathless, and ushered us into the foyer. He had stained his uniform with blood, and a great deal of it, presumably from moving the body of the late "Mrs. Dr. Dorn." Markley gave him a quizzical look, and then the shouting began.

"You idiot! What have you done? You have tampered with the evidence," Markley bellowed at the High Sheriff, who decidedly was beginning to look more and more out of his league.

"Look, you fat slob, I just did my job, and I advise you to do the exact same and leave the police work to the professionals", retorted the Sheriff.

It went on like that for about five minutes, before Markley even saw "Mrs. Dr." Dorn's remains. I stood there, fidgeted, and wondered what had happened to Mrs. Bonawitz. Finally, Clancy arrived and knocked loudly on the massive walnut door before stepping into the lobby. He sensed the friction between the two men right away and pulled the Sheriff off to one of the Sitting Rooms. That gave me a chance to ask Markley to look for Mrs. Bonawitz when he went upstairs.

Clancy and Sheriff Fogle emerged from the Sitting Room and went upstairs. I was not sure what was proper etiquette or what was legal at a presumed murder scene so I went into the Living Room, sat down, and waited. Then, I waited, and waited some more.

After about an hour and a half, Clancy called to me from the spiral staircase. He told me to go back to the funeral home and get the hearse. (Some three decades later I still have no idea what Clancy was doing upstairs all that time.) I called back up the stairs that Markley and he would have to move their cars, so I could leave. They both came sullenly down the stairs – all we needed now was Bette Davis and some Max Steiner music, and we would have had a great Warner Brother "B" grade movie, I thought.

It took me the better part of an hour to get over to the Chapel on Gettysburg Lane and get the hearse out of the old Livery Garage. By this time, it was deep into the hour of eight o' clock. Activity in the town had increased considerably, since my earlier sojourn, and there was plenty of commerce traffic.

When I returned to Bradenbaugh Court, a circus-like atmosphere existed. Neighbors were standing out on the front lawn, cars were everywhere, and a news crew from the Wilkes Barre TV station had parked itself across the street from the Old Dorn mansion. State Police had parked at least ten of their cars up and down the street, although I did not stop to count them. I knew what many of the curiosity seekers apparently did not know – that there was a little alley that ran behind the house that would lead me to the back gate of the Estate. As everyone stared, I rotated the heavy wheel of Mr. Romberger's' slate gray 1956 Cadillac hearse and pulled away from the mob of people.

My luck held out, and I found my way down the small road to the back of the house. I went in through the kitchen door to find Sheriff Fogle talking with Dudley Decker, Editor of the Gurber's Mill *Journal-Gazette*. Brushing past them, I went to the spiral staircase one more time and called softly for Mr. Romberger.

He came down. We went to the hearse, got the removal cot, and went upstairs to transfer "Mrs. Dr." Dorn to a Wilkes Barre hospital where Markley would perform an autopsy.

A ghastly scene awaited us. Some crime scene technicians were apparently finishing an examination of what evidence the Sheriff had not destroyed. Clancy remarked that he had never seen a more horrific murder site. We made the transfer to the hospital and went back to the Funeral Home. There, finally, I got a cup of Mrs. Romberger's nectar-like coffee and some of her delicious German pastries, which she loved baking.

About one o'clock, Mrs. Dorn's daughter called from Vermont. She had notified the Wilkes Barre Hospital that we were to take charge of the viewing and the funeral, and she said she would be in the following day to make the necessary arrangements.

The Dorn Family selected a top quality Boyertown Copper casket and a day and a half of viewing, with services at St. John's Lutheran Church in nearby Centerville. Most of the people who lived in the region knew Mrs. Dorn well, and we had a full three days of work with the crowds and the flowers. The community did all that they could to remember her and to give her a fitting tribute and memorial.

One very odd thing happened during the viewing. I again saw the Sheriff, this time at the back of the funeral home parking lot, talking to several members of the media. This, no doubt, constituted the biggest case he had ever investigated. Sheriff Fogle certainly was taking advantage of every opportunity to find himself on the airwaves and in print.

We buried "Mrs. Dr. Dorn" next to her husband in Oak Lawn Cemetery with much media attention. The days returned to normal around the Gettysburg Lane Chapel, but we often remarked about "Mrs. Dr. Dorn's" unfortunate date with destiny. Clancy and I agreed that no two days in funeral service were ever alike. That, combined with the opportunity to continuously serve others, made it one of life's better career choices.

Eventually, the State Police apprehended a suspect, Larry Spatz. They believed, based on overwhelming scientific evidence and a reported confession, that he committed the murder in the course of a robbery. Spatz went to trial and was convicted, but the State had to release him a year later. What was the reason for his release? A Commonwealth Appellate Court overturned the conviction because Sheriff Fogle spoke to every media outlet he could about his discovery of Spatz as the murderer. Spatz sued the State for wrongful conviction, and in a judgment, a jury of six men and six women from another county awarded him millions of dollars.

In a fitting bit of irony, two men killed Spatz in a bar room brawl that started when he began bragging about beating the cops and the system. If he was guilty, the best summary comes from my mother who said, "Maybe God has a different opinion about Mr. Spatz."

Never Surrender

It could not have been a better or more fitting morning for the final tribute. Fluttering shards of pale sunlight punctured the dusky waters of the gently flowing Susquehanna River. Wild Canadian Geese flew overhead in strong geometric patterns of continuity. Off in the far-away edges of a nearby soupy marsh, a dog or two bayed mournfully. The Thundering Falcon, a ferry boat moored at a nearby dock and used to transport cars across the mile wide waterway, added dignity to the early hour as it majestically bobbed up and down in the murky tributary. A steady April wind punctuated the stillness of the spring morning. Still, the decades vanish from my memory as I recall Naomi Bradenbaugh's funeral service conducted on the waterfront.

Naomi loved the river and its wildlife, the boaters, the kids playfully swimming in the water, and everything about the river's rich history. She had meticulously studied how the river had helped the original Pennsylvania German and Irish settlers establish Chesterville. When old Doc Amstutz told her that she had developed terminal cancer, Miss Bradenbaugh fervently wished that Romberger and Sons, Undertakers, conduct her final rites of passage on the banks of her beloved Susquehanna River.

Naomi, the only librarian in my hometown, spent her life giving service and money to children, the needy, the community, and to anyone who needed her help. The day of her funeral ceremonies, I learned about many previously unknown charitable aspects of her life, and I suspect many other town residents did, too. Even as the insidious carcinoma enveloped her body, she used what money she had and gave it to needy students, rather than using it for medication that may have prolonged her life.

We buried her later that day in mid-afternoon at Pine Hill Cemetery as the weather changed and a fresh drizzle developed into pouring cold rain. Seas of black umbrellas sheltering mourners from a dull grey and distinctly Pennsylvania sky helped set a somber and surrealistic tone for her funeral. Any Hollywood director would have found it difficult to devise a more funereal or dignified atmosphere. While the cemetery workers gingerly lowered the massive vault into the waiting grave, I pondered the events of the previous week. A three-day visitation was then the "norm" for a traditional service. During all three days of calling, the crowds from several surrounding counties and communities never stopped appearing at the front door of the funeral home. They wanted to pay their final respects to "Miss Naomi." Callers filled several registration books with signatures and thoughts, and the firm's walls and floors fairly creaked with the weight of hundreds of floral arrangements.

Miss Bradenbaugh had no family. George Stillwell, the ancient, crusty, and cantankerous trust officer at the Chesterville Trust Company grudgingly completed the funeral arrangements. Stillwell hated dealing with any element of life that somehow did not have a dollar connected firmly to it. He originally planned to bury Miss Bradenbaugh in a cloth-covered casket with a private burial and no viewing.

Stillwell's boss and the Trust Company President, a jovial, rotund and German man called "K.O." Ottenweller, somehow heard about what was happening with plans for the popular librarian's funeral service and interceded.

I remember the day that Miss Naomi died, seeing Mr. Ottenweller fling open wide the massive Oak doors of Romberger and Sons Funeral Home. Breathless and coatless he rushed by me as I polished some brass fittings on some antiques and ran to the wide staircase that connected the funeral home to the spacious apartment above it. Ottenweller knew of the many trusts and gifts that Miss Bradenbaugh had established for others, and he wanted to make sure she had a proper burial. He began shouting for Clancy "Old Man" Romberger, the ancient proprietor of the funeral home. K.O. Ottenweller planned to meet with Mr. Romberger to undo the funeral arrangements George Stillwell had contrived for Miss Bradenbaugh.

Many decades earlier, Ottenweller had been one of the thousands of students that Naomi Bradenbaugh had urged to "Never Surrender." When a student would have a difficult time reading a word in a text or did not understand the meaning of a sentence, she would always urge them not to quit, to never surrender to the problem. On her off duty time she labored tirelessly in the town's single library. She rarely took a vacation. She preferred to sell her vacation time to the School Board, allowing her to collect the money to use philanthropically.

In the forties, Miss Naomi urged Ottenweller, an outstanding athlete and brilliant student from a dirt poor German farm family, to never surrender to the economic aspects that almost prevented him from succeeding. She tutored him, without any thought of charge, in one of his weaker subjects, Latin. When his family couldn't afford sporting gear or decent clothes for "K.O.," she arranged to secretly pay the bill. Nor was K.O. the only student for whom she ever became the mysterious benefactor. During her fifty plus years of service to tiny Chesterville Borough, she anonymously sent several students to nearby Penn State, paying all or part of their tuition. She kept only a small part of her own modest salary, enough to pay the upkeep on the ivy-covered bungalow her father had willed her. Miss Naomi's only self-indulgence was a fondness for Black Labrador Retrievers. To all of the students, and even her dogs when they were ill, she would utter her famous phrase, "Never Surrender."

Now it became Mr. Ottenweller's time to repay the woman who had helped him develop his self esteem, his moral fiber, and his very livelihood. He decided he would never surrender to mediocrity or to the sin of lack of gratitude, and he ordered the finest funeral Clancy Romberger offered.

So it came to pass that Naomi Bradenbaugh, who taught all of us never to quit, never to complain, never to surrender, took her final journey in a massive 48 Ounce cast bronze casket with a special velvet lining and inner sealer. Mr. Romberger talked to Wally Himmelberger, the finest florist in the Valley, and ordered him to find every red rose in a hundred-mile radius. A full-length blanket of crimson roses covered Miss Naomi's casket as we bore it to her waiting brass-lined vault.

Miss Naomi, Clancy Romberger, and K.O. Ottenweller all taught me some lessons of life that still apply to funeral directors today. First, we should be willing to make the necessary sacrifices to help those in need. Rothermel never sent a bill for Miss Bradenbaugh's funeral service. He decided that by not billing the bank, just that much more money would remain in the estate to help the youth of Chesterville, the main beneficiaries in her will.

Secondly, K.O. Ottenweller displayed human love, compassion and kindness. Too often in our day-to-day dealings, we often forget what an important element of funeral service these attributes are. Without these, we may as well be selling vacuum cleaners or coffee pots.

Finally, Miss Naomi, too, taught me not to surrender. When arrangements with a family are difficult, or a grieving relative verbally abuses me, or fifteen flower arrangements arrive in the middle of family viewing, I always want to remember Miss Naomi. She wasn't a funeral director, but you know, she would have made a fine one.

THE CORONER RANG TWICE

How their unwavering, quarter-century romance ended is the best place to begin. She walked briskly and simply out of the Cathedral's small prayer chapel clutching the single crimson rose that had adorned an elegant urn of hand-carved maple. When she stepped out of the dark wood-paneled narthex and through the front door with deeply beveled stained glass windows, she never looked back.

Nor did she ever contact the funeral home – or me – again, or answer the persistent messages left on her answering machine by the funeral home's after-care counselors. It was quite odd that I never heard from her after the memorial service.

During the months preceding the ceremony, I fielded more than fifty obsessive-compulsive phone calls from her. I had arranged the details of his at-need memorial service and had even ordered the solitary floral tribute that she clutched to herself as she fled the church. Also, I had to make what seemed like two hundred other calls to initially discover who he truly was and what was the true circumstance surrounding his death. I gained some valuable experience holding bank negotiations and dealt with not only the matter of a feud between his grieving sometime companion and her minister, but also some greedy out of state relatives.

Perhaps it's quite fitting that my involvement with them would end as abruptly as it began. Looking back now, the pieces all dovetailed together nicely, but initially, I never would have thought it would end with a chapel full of people paying tributes to a truly wealthy and apparently gregarious and well-liked man.

From the start, the matter was bizarre. It looked as though the funeral home would be turning to the county for payment, given the location of the remains and the lack of information surrounding this mystery man. The case stayed on the dispatch board for some days with almost no help coming from the local police department. Finally, my supervisor, aware of my penchant for handling different types of case, turned it over to me.

I considered the circumstances.

The death call came on a full moon with the coroner's special ring splintering the sepulchral stillness of that autumn night in Florida. I never really understood why the coroner did it, but he always rang twice and hung up. Perhaps it was just an odd habit that harked back to his days as a military intelligence officer during Vietnam.

We found the remains of Paul Bradley in his incredibly cluttered garret, alongside his exercise bike, personal computer, and TV. Literally, we kicked away hundreds of empty pizza boxes and fast food containers to get the removal cot through the constricted skywalk. A neighbor had not seen Bradley for weeks. He wisely became suspicious that Bradley's loft light remained on constantly, while the evening newspapers formed a huge mound on the front porch.

After the autopsy, the burly sergeant who worked for the county's chief medical officer phoned our firm and placed us in charge of the arrangements. No relatives survived Paul Bradley. None of his neighbors knew anything about him, except that he had recently retired,against his will, from a locally owned electronics factory. The sergeant said he had been in touch with the county public health officer who issued a cremation permit for Paul Bradley.

This seemed logical and legal, given the state of the remains and the lack of relatives. I took Paul Bradley to the crematory and planned to bill the township.

A few days after the cremation, I received a phone call from Paul's old boss. Good news – some Bradley's reside in either rural Minnesota or downtown Chicago. That narrowed down the number of phone calls I would have to make to about ten thousand. Then, my luck suddenly changed with the next telephone conversation with Barbara Stafford.

Barbara, as it develops, took good care of Paul Bradley for twenty-seven years. She recently quarreled with him and continued to ignore him. Barbara wanted me to know that she remained a pious woman and that nothing indiscreet had ever occurred between the two of them. Her heart belonged partially to the late Mr. Bradley, the other part to Jesus. Then she started telling me even more amazing things.

Paul Bradley had never been a pauper. Two nephews did survive him, and she gave me their addresses. He not only owned his own home but also several profitable rental properties out on the beach. The late Mr. Bradley also owned a prominent house boat, perhaps more correctly named a yacht, moored in a very exclusive harbor-marina.

Barbara suggested that I contact Bradley's attorneys. I called his office and his secretary informed me that bungling burglars had recently killed the attorney in a botched robbery attempt. Just how eccentric could this case become?

The answer arrived less than an hour later when I contacted the first nephew. His initial question to me was "How much money is there?" Neither he nor his brother could tell me anything about their recently deceased uncle, but both kept grilling me about the size of the estate.

Later in the day, I learned the name of Paul Bradley's bank. Their Trust Department assured me they would pay all of our charges, and handle all financial and legal obligations. They also named a new attorney to deal with the two nephews.

Barbara started calling me daily. She had been in touch with the Trust Officer, and they had agreed on a date two months in the future for the memorial service. Barbara called me so often that the secretaries in the office started a pool, wagering what time she would call.

The day of the memorial service arrived, and so did, much to my astonishment, dozens of flower arrangements. I filled the front of the chapel with the bouquets, easels, baskets and sprays.

The mourners arrived in such numbers that we had to use an overflow room. Despite his obvious differences with Barbara, the minister preached one of the better eulogies I've ever heard. Several people gave testimony concerning the care and love Barbara had given the eccentric and reclusive Paul Bradley over the years. Bradley's nephews arrived late for the memorial service, and left early, still badgering me with financial questions.

I stood at the back of the chapel and shook my head in amazement. It was a completely different outcome than I ever would have expected. It's decidedly true that absolutely the most unbelievable, fascinating and interesting things happen to funeral directors – even if the coroner does ring twice.

Remembering Ralph Riegle

A middle-aged funeral director recalls the sterling personal virtues and solid work ethics of his late boyhood hero and role model. One haunting question remains – how to learn more about the accomplished man and employ those traits in daily contact with families?

Funeral Director Ralph M. Riegle, 1914 – 1973

Spirited winds rustled the crackled and browning leaves of massive maple trees near the edge of my hometown's cemetery. It should have been much colder in central Pennsylvania in late October. Regardless, an ivory chill shook even my bone marrow as I stood considering the grave of the finest funeral director I had ever known. As hardened as I may have become to cemeteries over the years, I uttered a silent prayer for Ralph Riegle's soul. Then, I audibly thanked God for having known and worked for him in the late 1960s while in high school.

Scrutinizing the monument some 30 years later, I realize I need to know more about the dash on the marble that represented the short 59 years (1914-1973) that he spent on earth in the quaint Pennsylvania Dutch Valley. Many people who knew, respected, worked with, loved and had daily dealings with Ralph Riegle are still living today. Who could I talk to about him?

In a treasured scrap book of mine rests his now tattered obituary, alongside a letter from one of his aunts, Miss Kathryn Shaffer. She sent the cherished letter to me following his death while I suffered in a hell hole called Izmir, Turkey during my U.S. Air Force career. In that January 1974 message she wrote of Ralph being kind, generous and "loyal to all of the people." The elegant silver-haired schoolteacher described his dedication to our profession, and his daily thoughtfulness and warmth to her. These are great sources of biographical information, but my memory of the distinguished, caring man himself had grown "too hazy, too fast." To learn more, I knew I should talk with his only lineal survivor, a graceful woman the townspeople once called "the Undertaker's Daughter."

For many years I worked as a Broadcast Journalist for the Armed Forces Radio and Television Service, CBS Radio News and the Associated Press. I conducted literally thousands of interviews with the homeless, TV and recording stars, street people, governors and generals. The most important – and best – interview I ever conducted, though, spotlighted Christine Riegle Walter, the Undertaker's Daughter.

Christine, a Bucknell University graduate, and successful attorney J. Bruce Walter married in 1969. Tim Walter and Dana Witmer, their handsome children, are well on their way to acheive the same kind of accomplishments of their parents and grandparents.

Both Mr. and Mrs. Walter greeted me cordially at their elegant home, in a suburb of the capital city of Harrisburg. Christine shares the same broad smile her father used to give me, often when he would hand me a thick stack of American Funeral Director, which I had badgered him for endlessly.

"My Dad was a people person, and he was very good at talking with people. He made people feel important. My father was a very hard worker and very much a perfectionist at what he did. He had many contacts, was active in the community, and built up quite a business. The community had a lot of confidence in him," Mrs. Walter said.

People having confidence in Ralph Riegle surprises no one. He grew up in "Coal Country," and worked diligently to raise enough money to attend Eckles College of Embalming and Sanitary Science where he graduated in March of 1935. By 1936, the Commonwealth of Pennsylvania awarded him a funeral director and embalmer's license. In April 1938, he opened the Ralph M. Riegle Funeral Home in Millersburg. (Today, it operates as the Reinhard Funeral Home). Mr. Riegle also established and owned an appliance store in 1938, which he operated until 1960.

A heart murmur prevented him from entering World War II. Still he felt the need to make a contribution to the country he loved so dearly. Ralph Riegle went to work at an industrial plant (Brubakers) which manufactured parts for the U.S. army. He lost three fingers in an industrial accident there.

Mr. Riegle stayed active in scores of church, Masonic, civic, fraternal and professional organizations. The ever-genial funeral director served on the Board of Directors of a large Harrisburg Hospital, the Polyclinic, and worked as a director of the T.B. and Health Society of Harrisburg.

"People amaze me when they tell me, even today, of the major role my father played in their life," Mrs. Walter allowed, adding that Ralph Riegle was a loving and kind father, who with her mother, the late Helen Updegrove Riegle, always put family matters first.

The petite Mrs. Walter said that she was a young adult when she first started appreciating what her father achieved for others.

"When I was in college and my mother was terminally ill with cancer, I began thinking about the value of life and all these college kinds of things – thinking about where your own life is headed. I talked with our then Pastor, a Reverend Stokes, and commented to him that I wanted to do something with my life. I said that I wanted to work with people, not just bury them as my father did. He spoke to me and told me what an important role my dad was playing in helping people through the grieving process. The Pastor said that my father had a very important part in helping people in their lives. He truly helped me to value my father," Mrs. Walter recalled.

I will always remember Ralph Riegle teaching me the basics of embalming. Never can I forget his kindness and patience in teaching me about funeral service. Mr. Riegle took the time to instruct a poor high school kid in the basic tenets of funeral directing. Most importantly, he conducted himself as a true and devout gentleman who will always stay locked in my heart and mind as a true humanitarian.

Mac McCormick revisits the former Ralph M. Riegle Funeral Home.
(Photo by Jo Ann Roscoe)

"She Was Always There"

How long is eternity? One of the grandchildren of Alice Taussig wanted to know. We were burying Alice on a white-hot, sunny Florida afternoon in August that could not possibly have held another drop of sultry humidity.

I looked at the small, blonde imp of a girl and gazed out across the scenic cemetery, while I searched my mind for the right words to answer her question. The cemetery is on the same tract of land as the funeral home where I do my best to direct funerals and embalm mothers and fathers, grandparents and in-laws, children, uncles, nieces and nephews, and best friends. I had washed and embalmed, cosmetized, dressed, and casketed this little girl's grandmother. I had conditioned and combed Alice's hair and tried to set it, until I realized my limitations as a typical male and summoned the professional hairdresser to the preparation room.

And now…now, this miniature Alice, the only granddaughter Mrs. Taussig had surviving her, posed this meaningful question to me. Me, the man in the full personal protective gear who had dressed her only grandmother in a blue burial gown with Velcro tabs up the back. This almost-teenager probably thought that I looked like an authority figure – me, a chunky middle-aged man, standing there at the very edge of Alice Taussig's grace. I was trying to at least look cool in the oppressive and merciless Florida summer heat, despite the fact that I wore a solid black suit and rivers of sweat.

The setting for Alice's funeral could have been scripted in some cramped office in a Hollywood movie factory. Alice herself was resting in an 18-gauge rose-colored casket covered with a blanket of the deepest maroon roses and all the baby's breath the florist could find. It looked simple and dignified, with just the right feminine touch for Alice. From all accounts, she had been a kind, warm, loving and giving woman.

Stately and lush sabal palm trees stood guard at the four corners of the cemetery tent. A gleaming, porcelain-white statue of Christ looked on as I instructed the pallbearers on how to gently take Alice from the funeral coach and lead her to her final place of rest. Only the labored breathing of the old men bearing the pink casket to the grave punctuated the stillness of the sweltering hour of Alice Taussig's funeral.

The pallbearers stepped firmly onto the flourishing lawn, a carpet of green that could rival one found in Ireland. They bore Alice past monuments of sepulchre, past glistening flat bronze markers, navigated around burgeoning tropical bushes and a sylvan recess to her place of interment. Some cars and trucks on a nearby free way sounded urban farewells to the tall Nordic woman in the flower bedecked casket. The mourners coughed nervously, wiped their eyes and tried to blink away not only the blazingly hot bolts of Florida sunshine but salty tears of grief. From somewhere, perhaps nearby Tampa Bay, an amazingly cool breeze of air suddenly started blowing on the assembled crowd.

There was no doubt the little girl was related to Mrs. Taussig. They shared the same blonde Nordic features and bone structure, and perhaps the same sense of curiosity. How would I answer her question?

I thought about the words of Pastor Branson Rogers, who had officiated the service just minutes before. My eyes scanned the horizon in hopes that my favorite clergyman would still be in the cemetery and could field this question for me. But he was gone, no doubt rushing off to a wedding, or a baptism, or something to do with life, not death. And then I remembered something he had said in her eulogy.

"She was always there for everyone," the pastor had said, of the late 78-year-old native of Florida. "There was never a time when you needed her that she wasn't there."

I swallowed slightly and cast a glance at Eileen, one of the funeral service students helping with today's service. Eileen seemed as interested in my answer as the little towhead perched perilously on a wooden company chair in front of me.

"Honey, remember whenever you needed your grandma? Whenever you scraped your knee, whenever you had lost your favorite dolly, how Grandma was always there to help you?" I saw a glimpse of recognition in the 10-year-old's swollen eyes. "And remember how the minister just told everyone she was *always* there? Well, that is what eternity is – always and forever."

I saw Eileen and some other adults shake their heads in agreement, and I supposed that must have been at least an adequate and acceptable answer. No matter how much technical training and experience you have, no matter how you try to steel yourself from any real human emotions you encounter in funeral directing, no matter what kind of brave face you put on for your pals in the embalming room – a question like that from a hurting 10-year-old girl can tear your heart away from your chest and churn it to a million and one pieces.

My mind went back to the dreaded "National Boards." It had not been all that long since I had taken and, thankfully, passed them. The boards had grilled me on Restorative Art, Psychology, Sociology, Microbiology, Thanatochemistry, and all the other funeral service courses. But a good question to add to that eight-hour exam for any funeral director candidate might be, "How long is eternity?" And have a little 10-year-old girl who has been awake for days and nights crying for her dead "Gramma" ask the candidate.

If the candidate can answer her with care and compassion, if he or she can look in the deep pools of her languid eyes and give her an answer that helps her through the hurt, give the candidate the license. And if the candidate balks, or doesn't care about the little grandchildren of the world, then funeral service is not for him.

A Summer Tempest
and Apple Daddy

Torrential rains and thick squalls of raging winds from Tampa Bay had performed their duties nicely. Shreds of what once was the hunter green 60-foot awning covering the front portico of the funeral home now flapped helplessly in the ebbing stages of what was a typical Florida summer thunderstorm. Great rumblings of thunder suitable to signal the start of Armageddon continued to dominate the atmosphere as I wheeled one of the company's Lincolns into my parking spot behind the preparation room annex.

A quick glance upward solidified one of the many worries I had concerning the evening's upcoming visitation. The pervasive rain and devilish winds were going to continue and add to the already established hazards of travel in the St. Petersburg area this afternoon.

Huge pockets of rainwater filled gaps in the awning, and miniature waterfalls created by those gaps now inundated the walkway with pockets of tepid water. I ducked the newly created canvass shower heads and sloshed my way through the cascades of water from the unexpected late afternoon deluge, anxious to double-check all the details of the work I had completed earlier in the day.

Piles of limp, newly broken bushes and flowers torn from the ground by the storm littered the walkway leading to the front door of the funeral home. I was worried about the damage from the rainspouts and great gusts of winds, and not without cause.

Just inside the funeral home, in the chapel, not more than 100 yards from the spot where I now labored to move a pliant tree branch lay a man in repose who had spawned four generations of remarkable people. Besides the immediate family, there were almost 60 grandchildren, great-grandchildren, and great-great-grandchildren and all their families, expected to join with the community in viewing the human remains of a minister who left a remarkable and palpable legacy of kindness, love, and understanding.

He was a man whose grandchildren called "Apple Daddy," because he never came calling without a bag of deep red delicious apples. I had placed two fresh apples deep within the tufts of the powder blue satin lining of the Batesville 16-gauge steel casket his oldest daughter had tearfully selected just yesterday afternoon.

There was more, of course. There always is, if you allow yourself to take the time to learn a little something about the family.

He had been a minister who believed in the laying on of hands. He had worn a neatly pressed suit every day. Earlier in the week, in the selection room, I had laid one of those suits against the casket interior for the family so they could see if it would blend. He had always been a man – not vain – but proud of his professional appearance. The suit had to match, all the details of the visitations and funeral had to be just right for him.

He had been a man who played the piano, and played it well, to the Glory of God, I learned. The family had told me that with pride, during the arrangement conference, lovingly handing me a snapshot of him tickling the 88s at a church social. I stared with professional and human interest at that photo later, in the deep and waning hours of the obscure night, after I had found the block of time needed to embalm him properly. The minister needed some restorative work, and I used techniques and skills taught to me over the years by master embalmers. I rounded out his handsome face, enough to take away the jagged edges created by years of debilitating disease.

But, now, as I reached the door of the funeral home, I knew something was wrong…oh Lord, this can't be true. The storm knocked out the power. Why does this always happen when you are dealing with the nicest of families?

And…no phones. I half swam my way back to the car to get the cellular phone, that permanent attachment to any director's arm these days. Surely the electric company will tell me it will just be a matter of moments before the lights flicker and the massive air conditioning units on the roof of the funeral home click on to chill the water-logged air.

Just as I pleaded with the electric company and received absolutely no reassurance of repair performance from them, I caught a glimpse of the family starting to arrive for their private goodbyes. Great. Break out more candles, I guess. I will open the side doors to the chapel and use natural lighting for the visitation.

And now the family is here, well composed, well dressed and praying as a family unit in the well-marbled and nicely appointed foyer. Yes, they understand about the power and it's no problem.

His widow is frail, dying herself from an insidious form of cancer, a sarcoma that will soon take her to be with Apple Daddy. As she weeps, and I try to comfort her, I know any effort made for this family, or any other family, is what funeral service is all about. Hang the funeral service critics. Let them see what it feels like when a woman married to a man for 70 years turns to you and thanks you for making her husband look just like himself. There couldn't be anything better. It's families like this that help you weather all of the storms.

"We Can Get Along Without You"

From the Hospital Emergency Room's portico at noon, a muggy and translucent mid-day haze covered the nearby Great Smoky Mountains and spread out over the nearby tourist towns. The tropical conditions produced moderate rains that pelted the institution's thickly blue and green tinted windows. Rain droplets formed lazily concentric circles on the jade colored panes, creating spinning rivulets of water, which eventually dripped on waiting and luxuriant Rhododendron plants. I shifted uneasily in one of those blue hard plastic chairs that one inevitably discovers in hospital waiting areas, and looked around at the congregation of suffering souls. My back, head and legs simply hurt.

A young woman – probably still a teenager – sitting next to me eyed me suspiciously. I asked her if she was finished reading the only reading material available – a tattered copy of the July 1998 issue of *Self*. No doubt I looked like some sort of aging pervert to her. Perched on the opposite side of me, a middle-aged man with Chester Arthur style sideburns and a Woody Allen voice loudly described his union wages. For laying bricks, the union paid him well above twenty dollars an hour. I may have groaned audibly because he went off to find a coffee machine and returned shortly with a cardboard cup of foul-smelling java. His coffee container's brightly colored advertising offered Smoky Mountain Homes starting at a low one hundred and fifty thousand dollars. "Some way to spend some of my vacation time," I mused, and I realized the inevitability of time wearing down my spinal column. Age was catching up with me.

Ten days earlier, I had been moving a casketed body and failed to bend my aging knees when lifting it. Shrugging the immediate searing back pain as something muscular, I kept working. The following day, at the funeral, I served as a pallbearer for the same oversize casket. This time, I helped to carry the massive and gleaming Batesville Bronze casket up a steep hillside. Then, I had to help place the casket onto a lowering device that was unusually high because of the hill's angle.

A week after the lifting incident, I packed the van and camper and drove the six hundred or so miles to my favorite vacation spot in the world. By the time I arrived at the cool and majestic mountains of East Tennessee, the so-called muscles in my back were really "talking to me." I opted for treatment at a nearby medical center.

The staff at the hospital, to give them credit, tried to be polite. Nevertheless, some authority figure, high up in the corporate chain of medical command and administration had forgotten how the average person feels when they enter an Emergency Room. They began one of the most ludicrous greeting and triage systems imaginable. First, when I came into the Emergency Room, no one greeted me or asked me why I was there.

"A good thing it's just my back and not a Fred Sanford style heart attack," I thought. I did find a huge sign that instructed me to write my name on a hospital provided index card and place it face down in a waiting small cardboard box. Another sign ordered me to sit in one of the brightly colored "genuine synthetic material" seats.

After ten minutes or so, a licensed practical nurse summoned me to the triage area, behind a couple of closed doors. Middle aged and apparently very bored with her job, and even more indifferent to my descriptions of the searing pain, she took all my vital signs. Then, she yawned deeply, gave me a look of bewilderment and banished me to the waiting area again.

Another twenty minutes of detainment and confinement with my fellow injured and hurting patients passed. A woman from the Admissions Office approached me. She apparently was the local winner of the "Lucille Ball Look-a-Like Contest." "Lucy" asked me to amble over to the Admissions Office. There she propounded the usual questions about my health insurance and ability to pay the hospital if necessary. For once, I was glad to be childless because I really would hate to have to promise them my first-born child.

The Admissions Lady ordered me to continue to E-D-TWO just past the vending machines and to be sure to knock loudly on the door when I got there. Since I wasn't sure of the location of E-D-TWO, which turned out to be a treatment area, I asked her. She gave me one of those "men are so damned helpless" looks, and pointed the way with some fluorescent-colored and neatly sculpted fingernails.

I hobbled down the hallway and found the department in question. I gave the door a battery of knocks that would have pleased any grade school teacher and was not at all surprised when a diminutive man in teal colored scrubs stuck his head and arm out the slightly opened door.

"It'll be a great while," he said gleefully, almost with pride. "Have a seat."

Since sitting is how I had been wasting most of my precious vacation Sunday afternoon, I reasoned I had no cause to stop now and returned to the torture of the stone-like chair. An hour and twenty-five minutes later, a nurse – about my age, wearing the biggest band-aid I had ever seen on her left jaw – opened the sacred door. She ushered me into the sanctum-sanctorum, presumably, the holiest of holy places in the hospital complex, E-D-Two. There, she quizzed me about my injury and issued me a hospital gown four sizes too small for my considerable girth. I grunted and tried to fit my middle-aged body into the teenage size tunic. As she chuckled to herself and hurried off, presumably to more important cases in E-D-ONE, I absent-mindedly wondered if a patient had taken a dislike to her and had socked her on the jaw.

The six cubicles – all of which contained patients – were separated by little more than thin cotton drapes. I relished in the joy of not having to describe any problems with my digestive or reproductive systems. Next to me, a lad twenty years or so old and his mother plotted how to convince the doctor that he had broken his hand in a construction accident, rather than last night's bar room brawl. No matter, he proudly proclaimed to his mother, I will soon be a U.S. Marine, and I can take any kind of pain. My twenty-two years worth of experience in the U.S. military flashed through my mind on that statement, and I had to work to choke back a guffaw.

Following a wait of yet another forty minutes, a harried physician assistant came in, failed to introduce himself, gave me a cursory examination, and started to leave the confined cubicle without giving me a diagnosis. He appeared irritated when I asked him the nature of my malady. Eventually, I wound up with a few muscle relaxers, a misdiagnosis, and a trip to see my own physician when I returned home.

Contrived as this may seem, it's all true. How this "MASH-like" encounter can relate to all of us in Funeral Service today is abundantly clear.

Let's begin with someone entering our funeral home. Do we open the door, and greet them properly? Years ago when I worked for Undertaker Clancy Romberger, we employed a pompous retired office executive who insisted on giving everyone a bright cheery "Good Morning!" or "Hello! How are you?" Common sense and propriety dictate that a subdued greeting is in order because many families that come through our doors are decidedly **not** having a good morning, or a good day for that matter. (No matter how we tried to break the obnoxious and self-serving employee of the habit, he persisted with the cheery salutations. Clancy liked him because he had been a non-union supervisor in a factory heavily unionized, but the old man was a true troublemaker.)

Once a family member or guest enters the funeral home, do we guide them appropriately and try to help them? I've seen funeral directors open the door for someone, not utter a word to them and wait until the guest is wandering about the building before asking if they need help.

When we as funeral directors plan with families are we "sending the family down to E-D-TWO" much as the hospital staff sent me meandering at the hospital. By that I mean, are we giving the family the best treatment we can?

How is our phone etiquette? Do we transfer the calls to an answering service that knows little or nothing of proper protocol? How often does the phone ring when a family calls? Do we ever place families on "HOLD?"

When we know we have a family coming into the funeral home to make arrangements, are we standing at the door, waiting on them? Have we checked the arrangement room to be sure we have everything we need? Are there tissues available for the family? After we get the family seated, do we take a second to offer some light refreshments? Are we giving the bereaved all the information we should about merchandise and services? Do we take a few minutes to simply find out about the deceased, or do we rush into the FTC Disclosures and conclude the arrangement conference when we can because we have telephone calls to make to the minister, florist and cemetery or crematory? Are we giving our families and perhaps ourselves and Funeral Service overall a misdiagnosis?

On the day of the funeral or memorial service are we patient enough to take all the time that we need to conduct the service properly without rushing the family out of the chapel or cemetery? Have we followed up on the family a couple of days and weeks after the service to see if we can be of any further assistance?

Sometime back when I worked in Florida, I was serving a family that we might call "high maintenance." Despite my best efforts, nothing I did was right with the widower. He complained about everything, right down to my subdued tie and aftershave lotion. Try as I might, I was just not the right director for that family. "We can get along without you," was the final analysis from the bereaved man, which made me feel completely worthless. Later, I discovered that many funeral directors encounter a family such as this one from time to time.

Yet, giving the incident some space and time, I realize that he was correct. Families can get along without the individual funeral director or our funeral home. The other director's establishment down the streets is always willing to take on another family.

When we embalm, do we make the necessary "diagnosis" or case analysis, or do we simply use the same type of fluid and procedure on each case? Do we rush to finish the embalming procedure for whatever reason – lunches, other cases to work on, indifference, or the "they will be placed in the ground tomorrow" attitude?

Over the years, I have actually had embalmers – whom I know to be good men and women – look me in the face and tell me that there is never a need to aspirate any body. Once, when I worked in a southern state, I transferred a body from a large metropolitan firm to our smaller facility. Before I took possession of the case, I examined the body. The embalmer had only "bothered" to "get some fluid" into the head and hands. I called the owner of the funeral home that I worked for and explained my predicament, but not until I had confronted the other firm's embalmer and asked him about his "methods." His answer was pathetic, at best.

Funeral Directors are the very first to complain about bad publicity about embalming and prices. We fret and worry when a family we have been serving for many years turns to one of our colleagues for their services instead of us. We cringe in the coffee shop when we have to answer any hard questions. Still, have we done all that we can to make the funeral service a meaningful one? In the past few decades, the funeral directors that I have seen get some bad publicity brought it upon themselves by failing to follow simple established laws, rules, regulations and ethical practices.

Dave Hirt, the President of Batesville Casket Company, recently gave me some good advice which bears repeating. "Don't ever consider the two o' clock funeral just another two o'clock funeral, because it certainly is NOT just another funeral for the bereaved family."

Don't send your families "down the hall without directions, looking for E-D-TWO," and expect them to knock on your door and wait for substandard service. Families can and will get along without you. Let us all work together and work diligently to return Funeral Service to the higher standards we once earned.

"Shhh, He's a Funeral Director"

I had no plans to spend the better part of that sunny Florida afternoon in the sterile atmosphere of a busy Columbia Hospital emergency room. While in the employ of one of the death-care conglomerates, I was driving a removal van from one of their St. Petersburg funeral chapels to another. It was late August, the roadway was desert dry and the boulevard was choked with the ever-thickening Pinellas County traffic. My mind wanted to consider the woes of the family with whom I was about to meet to make funeral arrangements, but instead I concentrated on the constantly changing metropolitan traffic patterns.

The tourist driving behind me at 55 miles per hour (in a 35 mph zone) had other ideas, though. The police officer investigating the accident later told me the other driver had suddenly decided to take some medication. She lost control of her vehicle and failed to see the big white cargo van ahead of her moving at 25 mph. Another episode of "Florida Demolition Derby" was on the air.

My body did the required Raggedy Ann doll movements, and I felt searing pain. Simultaneously, I heard the sickening and gut wrenching sound of metal hitting metal with a sturdy impact. I remembered some sounds like that from when I was in Viet Nam, and for some seconds I was disoriented.

Surprisingly, not more than the distance of half a football field away, one of the area's many professional paramedic units was sitting at a stop light, returning from yet another motor vehicle accident. They drove past me in a surrealistic blur of sirens and lights, trying to reach the tourist, whose car looked as though she had driven it into a brick retaining wall. Through the foggy haze of my stunned mind, I reached for the cell phone and dialed 911. As I glimpsed into the rear view mirror, I saw the van's spare tire rolling through the traffic like a hula-hoop performing some bizarre mating ritual.

The other car was smoking, and some onlookers and the medics were now seemingly involved in an argument about who was going to pull the lady out of her car. Traffic continued to whiz past the accident at high speed. Welcome to Florida.

When the paramedic reached me, she opted to immobilize me and waved for the rescue unit to pull up to the removal van. Frankly, I wanted to call the funeral home to let my supervisor know what was going on out here in the street…and to get some reassurance that another funeral director would meet with the bereaved family. I knew I would be ok, but I also knew they had even more serious problems than I did.

While the medics were attempting to get me on the backboard, (such a twist of irony, as I had a couple of them in the back of the van) the conversation turned to why there was a cot and removal equipment in the van. As soon as I said I was an intern funeral director, the jokes and the inevitable comments started. (But at least I don't remember hearing the required "Where does the blood go?" comment. I suppose as medics they knew.)

Paramedic #2 was starting an I.V. on me and sounded quite serious when she said if there had been a body in the van, someone else would have had to get into it to get me on the backboard. The funeral director jokes continued the length of the eight-mile ride to the emergency room. They had me so securely attached to the gurney I could do little other than groan in pain and wince at the lines we have all heard a hundred times. In the emergency room the word went out...he's an undertaker!

Even the x-ray technician wanted to debate life after death with me. "Hold your breath, sir, and then tell me, 'What do you really think happens to people when they die?'" (I was more interested in trying to block my pain and keep the four-sizes-too-small hospital gown on my chubby body than I was in debating thanatology.)

About three hours into my emergency room visit, I saw a yellow emergency flasher light sitting atop a computer monitor, just across from my bed, go wild with action. Buzzers sounded, the light began rotating, and nurses ran to it.

"Code Blue, 32-year-old white male. Gunshot wound to the head. ETA seven minutes." Someone yelled, "Get the crash cart. Hurry!" Staff members from other parts of the hospital frantically scurried about the room.

My head and neck pain suddenly seemed very insignificant, and I said a silent prayer for the gunshot victim. From experience during my two-year embalmer's apprenticeship, though, and having embalmed many gunshot head cases, I suspected there wasn't much of a survival chance. When they wheeled him into the bay next to me, I felt ill at ease.

"I can't get an I.V. line on him."

"No pulse."

"No pupil reaction."

Confusion. Noise. And then all of a sudden, it got eerily quiet. I heard the doctor who had been attending me say firmly, "I'm going to pronounce him. Go ahead and start bagging him." I know I heard some pain in her voice though, as she issued further instructions.

Nurses and doctors left the area, but two medical attendants stayed behind to clean the body and prepare it for movement to the morgue. I couldn't help but hear the conversation, as there was only a thin cotton drape on a track separating me from the now deceased young man. While they chattered away, I suddenly heard one of them say:

"Shhh. He's a funeral director."

That leads me to the critical examination of our image. Odd, the Egyptians throwing stones at the embalmers. The scorn of two young nursing assistants trying to hide a dead body from the funeral director in the next bed.

"Hey, you two," I wanted to say, "funeral directors have a mature concept of death. We listen, we understand, we educate, support and advocate for the family of the deceased. We don't steal dead bodies out of overworked emergency rooms."

Maybe we all need to work a little bit harder to get the word out to the general public. We care. We can encourage families and even refer them to professionals, when necessary. Maybe the next time I'm in a situation like that, I'll say, "No need to shush me. I am a funeral director and proud of what I do each and every day."

A Coach to Remember

Ralph Riegle was as professional an undertaker as any whoever walked this earth. The World War II veteran had a pleasing, lyrical, Pennsylvania Dutch twang. His funeral home at the crest of Moore Street Hill was always immaculate. All of his vehicles were equally clean, shiny, and I thought, the best looking in the area, maybe even the Commonwealth.

Mr. Riegle was my childhood hero and role model – one of the two funeral directors in a small, central Pennsylvania village. The two morticians were not only located on opposite ends of town, but they held reverse credos of religions and business philosophies.

Ralph was especially fond of his hearse– a black-over-grey 1956 Cadillac, replete with a red emergency light. That light was a left over from the early 50's when the burgh had no organized ambulance service. Both of the town's funeral directors occasionally made emergency runs to the nearest hospital in Harrisburg, some 36 miles to the southeast.

As a lad of fourteen in the mid-60's, I was always busy trying to shock the townspeople, most of whom were stoic and humorless Germans. My coup that summer was letting "the crew cut" grow out into a "Beatle cut." According to most residents, that length of hair was the surest sign of a fast trip to eternal damnation.

But Ralph Riegle seemed to understand, and perhaps even like me. The ever genial "Dutchman" always let me assist him with the various errands around his spacious funeral home. In those pre-OSHA days, I would eagerly work in the prep room, sometimes even filling the percolator to the ancient gravity injector Mr. Riegle sometimes still used. I'd sweep the parking lot, dust the reposing room, take the garbage out, mow grass in the sweltering summer, and shovel snow in the bitterly cold winters.

My favorite job, though, was when he let me ride along in that '56 Cadillac hearse for a removal at one of the hospitals in Harrisburg. I thought it was a great honor to sit in the sumptuous leather seat and gaze at the pastoral scenery of central Pennsylvania. Frankly, I thought it was "pretty cool," that I was "hot stuff," and I vowed to myself that I would one day own one of these magnificent machines.

I still remember the gorgeous trappings. The appointments of that hearse were elegant and exceedingly appropriate for the era. (Would that I could own that machine now!) My heart would pound with excitement when Mr. Riegle's top notch assistance, Clarence Boyer, would push the accelerator to the floor as we merrily ascended Peters Mountain, a particularly dangerous, winding, steep, and trying summit road that led to the capital city of Pennsylvania.

One summer afternoon in 1965, heat from a high pressure weather front was blamed as a major factor in several deaths in the county. The Riegle Funeral Home was very busy with four or five families to serve – a rare occurrence for a relatively small firm – and Clarence and I were summarily dispatched to the Harrisburg Hospital morgue. We made the removal quickly.

Knowing the workload was heavy, Clarence, driving my favorite hearse on the return trip, sped along the two lane macadam road edging the sprawling Susquehanna River.

A cheerful man in his late sixties, Clarence was nevertheless a "no-nonsense" sort of fellow who wanted to get back to the funeral home in a big hurry. Clarence never missed an opportunity to embalm a body. My recollection of the events that fateful afternoon was that he kept increasing the speed of the hearse. The huge engine in that Caddy responded willingly.

I had sensations of being in a rocket sled. I also considered that it was a shame that not only was I going to die as Clarence pushed the coach to 80 mph but also that this superbly crafted, professional car was going to wind up in 30 feet of murky, coal tar-filled Susquehanna River water.

Before that happened, though, we heard the inevitable screeching of the siren of a Pennsylvania State Police cruiser. Clarence looked sheepish and edged the hearse off to the side of the hideously narrow roadway.

Pennsylvania State Police troopers in those days had to be a minimum of 6 feet 2 inches tall. At my tender age this policeman appeared to exceed that requirement by several inches. As he looked down at the elderly embalmer and me from underneath a foreboding drill instructor's hat, it now occurred to me that jail was probably preferable to my untimely demise in the river.

"Afternoon, sir...in a hurry?" the jowly trooper growled.

"Vell, now," Clarence began in his reassuring Pennsylvania Dutch manner and broke into a long-winded story about the body in the rear of the hearse leaking embalming fluid.

The "Statie," being aware that the pride of the Upper End of Dauphin County was to produce generations of talkers, just grunted.

"Ok, but slow it down. You can go." The cop just shook his head, as Clarence took off, the rear wheels of the '56 Caddy hearse generating a hell storm of gravel.

In no time flat, we were back to the rocket sled routine. Despite the encounter with the giant trooper, we arrived back at the funeral home in record time.

Years later, in late 1997, my boss assigned me to drive a coach for a fairly large funeral. Much to my delight the coach was the firm's 1993 Sayers and Scovill Masterpiece. It is the second most beautiful coach I have ever seen. Its luxuriant black/grey paint is emphasized with a minute red pin stripe that divides the frame from the roof.

A gleaming, silvery Landau bar and lantern ornamentation are just two of the reasons that it is my favorite in the coach fleet where I work.

The S&S Masterpiece Funeral Coach shows typical American pride in craftsmanship, holds the road well, and handles the way a coach should when you use it in a funeral procession.

In summary, it is stately and dependable – much like that 1956 Cadillac coach of Ralph Riegle. It reminds me of how rewarding and grand serving others in funeral service can be.

YESTERDAY, TODAY AND TOMORROW

When community members ask a funeral director to speak publicly, and especially at a high school, the invitation presents several opportunities for examination of funeral service standards and ideals.

"Why are funerals so expensive? I mean, it, uh, like costs a lot of money for a funeral, right?" the young student quizzed me in earnest, her expansive smile showing several thousand dollars of her parent's money tied up in corrective braces. No sarcasm oozed from her question. She just really wanted to know about the cost of funerals. Still, a question such as that from a 14-year-old has roots in something she had probably heard at home.

How I got into the enviable position of answering this question began with a recent telephone call from an assistant headmaster at a local private school. This school administrator, a charming and graceful lady of whom I am very fond, remained cheerful and positive as she attempted to sell me on the merits of being a guest speaker at the annual Careers Day. Not only would there be police officers with their drug-sniffing canines, but doctors, nurses, military people and restauranteurs would grace the class rooms that day. Besides, she reasoned with me, it was either me or a videotape. Which would the students prefer more of the two choices? Surely, I could be more entertaining and informative than a tape, she argued.

When the appointed day arrived, I drove to the school with some apprehension. As I pulled into the parking lot and saw the police cars with the canines, I wondered how interesting a talk about funerals could really be. That, I thought, is especially true when comparing it to a speaker with a visual aid such as a well-trained German Shepherd. No doubt they will hide some dope somewhere and command the dog to find the contraband, I thought. The kids will love that. What am I going to do? Explain the FTC general price list? Describe casket construction? Stick to my prepared comments and original "battle plan." That is exactly what I will do, I concluded. I entered the building and a gangly Ichabod Crane look-alike ushered me into the library where several men and women represented many different types of occupations. Everyone wore that ubiquitous stick-on nametag on their chest, the kind found at every city, state, and national association meeting or convention greeting table. Naturally, mine did not stick to the conservative black pin suit I thought would be appropriate for the talk. Well, I reasoned, the cops had their uniforms, as did the nurses and the chefs. Too casual attire would no doubt bring the firm under criticism. The suit remained a good choice of garb.

Well-behaved teenagers filled the school's hallways, changing their classes with more decorum than I could remember in the high schools of the 1960s.

My escort assured me that the students appreciated my attending the educational event. Very few funeral directors ever spoke at their school. I did not doubt her word.

Awkward best describes how the first class of the day progressed. Not really having a good sense of what goes on inside the brains of 15 and 16 year-olds, I began by assuring them I wasn't trying to recruit anyone to become a funeral director. I explained the educational and legal requirements, and the pros and the cons of our profession. The old adage, "It's not for everyone," surfaced during each separate class.

The questions from the students really varied. One lad who wanted to become a professional photographer showed a strong interest in rigor mortis. A couple of the young ladies asked about the cosmetic and hairdressing of the dead. Some students rolled their eyes, others looked out the window at the snow that blanketed the ground.

A shy young scholar sitting in a far corner of the room fluttered her diminutive hand in the air at me. The room and other students readily absorbed the young woman, and she was the type readily lost in any crowd. Nevertheless, her question remained absolutely the best question of the day – and perhaps all year.

"What's the most difficult part of your job?" She appeared almost hesitant to say anything, and once the words flew out of her mouth, she almost cringed.

That inquiry can give a funeral director a solid reason to pause and consider carefully what words to use for a reply. In a flash, I stopped and thought about the many years filled with thousands of removals, hour upon hour of embalming, seemingly limitless visitations, funerals and memorial services. In just a second, while I collected my thoughts, I remembered many tragic deaths, and families I have served whose grief was clearly more than any person should have to bear.

Yet the answer to her question, in my mind's eye, remained clear. When a funeral director takes a family forward to the casket for the final viewing – although he or she has a hundred other details on their mind – that, is often the most difficult moment of the day. Compared to that agony funeral directors often witness, speaking to a group of school children is easy.

Then it dawned on me. These "poor little match girls' feelings" about funeral service dated from the yesterdays of the 1960s and '70s. Any funeral director's yesterdays filled with dread or consternation in having to defend our profession in public should be long gone.

Today, the wise public speaker uses the FTC and Jessica Mitford-like criticisms to our advantage, so that funeral service can have tomorrow. Many of our national support organizations offer tips for the funeral director who speaks to groups. A director can dispel any long-standing myths about how we steal jewelry or break legs to make the deceased fit in the casket. Anytime a school or other group gives a funeral director the opportunity to talk about the merits of American funeral service, it is a time that the director should use wisely. In essence, it is a time to speak judiciously – and carefully – of yesterday, today, and tomorrow.

ᴹ Mirrors

A part timer that I work with has been slugging his way through J.K. Rawlins' well-liked book, *Harry Potter and the Sorcerer's Stone*. Rawlins wrote it as a parable for adults, in the guise of a child's book. Funeral directors and embalmers may have read it, perhaps even as I, out of mild boredom and curiosity. I also once heard a local minister give a sermon about it.

The clergyman said that in the book a mean aunt and uncle, commonplace human beings with a straight and narrow outlook on life, raise the orphan, Harry Potter. Rawlins calls these dogmatic mortals Muggles. The aunt and uncle lavish their own contemptible biological son with tremendous gifts, but treat Harry as the legendary orphan. They make him sleep under the stairs, and give him a birthday gift of a carrot or a comb. What is the reason for their mean-spiritedness?

The aunt and uncle know that Harry isn't a Muggles by birth, but a Wizard. These Wizards reclaim Harry Potter shortly after his eleventh birthday and whisk him away to Hogwarts, a type of exclusive school for Wizards.

Harry experiences plenty of terrific times at Hogwarts much as we all do at Mortuary School. However, the one event that stuck in my mind is Harry cloaking himself with invisibility to explore the dank and ominous hallways of Hogwarts. Eventually, he finds a room well removed from the main part of the school equipped with only a full length mirror dubbed "The Mirror of erised."

When Harry gazes into the mirror, he sees that which he has wanted all of his life – his family of Wizards – father, mother and grandparents. Later in the book, Harry shows the Mirror of erised to his best friend, Ron. When Ron looks into the magical mirror, he sees himself as a National Champion in the Wizards's sport of Quiddich. Ron then wants to know if the mirror tells the future.

As the reader has deciphered by now, "erised" is desire spelled backward. The purpose of Rawlins's mirror isn't to tell the future at all, but to show the person looking into the mirror what he or she most wants currently. Ron sees himself as a great athlete, but Harry Potter views his long coveted family. It's the Mirror of Desire.

In yet another notable literary allusion to mirrors, Miguel de Cervantes, writing in *Don Quixote*, shows the errant, broken-down squire, Don Quixote what he truly is, rather than the gallant and dashing Knight he wishes to be. Cervantes achieves this by forcing the feeble Quixote to gaze into a suit of mirror-lined armor worn by the Knight of Mirrors. The Knight's armor of mirrors is the best defense against folly, fantasy and foolishness. Broadway's version of Cervantes's novel, *Man of La Mancha*, expanded this continuing theme of self examination by using Aldonza's musical plea to Don Quixote, "Take the stars from your eyes, and see me as I really am."

After many years in funeral service, I often wonder if I am using Cervantes or Rawlins' mirror to evaluate my performance as a funeral director. Some almost long forgotten funeral arrangements and ceremonies brought this to mind.

During my Florida internship, a lead funeral director assigned me to drive the hearse for a funeral being held at a cemetery not far from the funeral home. A new part timer had begun work that day, and the supervisor designated him to "tail" me. When we left the funeral home for the cemetery, he drove the flower car, and I drove the hearse, as appointed. The young man rushed to the grave with the flowers as I had instructed him to do.

When the procession arrived at the grave site, however, the inexperienced employee left the flower van sitting slightly in the way of the procession parking space. Still, the drivers could park their vehicles. I went to the rear of the coach to instruct the pallbearers and move the casket to the grave. As I did so, the lead funeral director, a highly nervous and continually distraught type of man, began haranguing me about the placement of the flower van. He gave this regal performance in full view and earshot of the family. To put it mildly, I was not a happy camper that day, but owing to my interns' status kept my mouth shut – for a few days while I simmered. Eventually, I complained to the manager of the funeral home about the verbal abuse and the offending director apologized to me. It wasn't that I minded the "dressing down." What really perturbed me was the embarrassment of having it done in front of a family and co-workers.

However, examining the incident with the benefit of time and using the "Knight of Mirrors," I wonder now what responsibility I may have shirked. Did I fail to properly instruct the new employee and just expect him to automatically know where to park the van? Should I have confronted the lead director immediately after the service, spoken my mind, and possibly risked a physical confrontation? Who can say what the "correct amount of abuse" is that a funeral director should have to accept – either from a fellow staff member, a family, or a fellow employee? Shall I be a Muggle or a Wizard?

A few other examples come to mind. Also while working in Florida at a funeral home-cemetery combination owned by one of the multi-national acquisition corporations, my supervisor asked me to meet with a man who was burying an elderly aunt. This man was not pleased at all with the financial burden being placed upon him. When I presented the final "Statement of Funeral Goods and Services Selected," he literally came across the table and grabbed the lapels of my suit jacket. A few minutes later, with the approval of my boss, I showed the pugnacious funeral buyer the door and sent him to off to find, presumably, another funeral home or crematory. Did I shirk my duty? Should I have overlooked the physical abuse? Even years later, reflecting in the "Knight of Mirror armor" I think not. Being brutally honest clearly proved to this man that he should not physically grab funeral directors, even if he is unhappy with their prices.

Finally, some years ago, a young couple – obviously very much in love with each other – came to our funeral home to bury a child that had died. Many family members were present for arrangements, and it became immediately obvious to me that this was not going to be a simple viewing or funeral. The parents planned elaborate ceremonies, and each of the fourteen or fifteen relatives present had some theories about how the service should proceed. I worked hard to be very patient with everyone and took painstaking notes. It was one of those arrangement conferences where grief is so palpable a funeral director can literally feel it weighing down his or her own heart and mind. I worked many extra long hours to be certain that all aspects of the service were coordinated as the various families had requested. A day passed, and we made all of the necessary preparations for the child's visitation and funeral service.

When the parents came into the chapel to view their dead son, surrounded by banks and banks of floral tributes, the pain and agony that they had been concealing for the days since his death poured out of them, much as a river inevitably flows to the sea. Though I am childless, and perhaps sometimes too cold-hearted, my own heart ached.

The day of the service began with bright and beautiful skies. Our funeral home staff followed all of the detailed funeral service plans. We seated almost a hundred people, and the service and procession went flawlessly. When all the mourners arrived at the cemetery, the two ministers preceded the small casket and mourners to the grave. At the conclusion of the heart-wrenching service, the family released white balloons into the sky to symbolize the return of the young child's soul back to God. I watched helplessly as the young couple clung to each other, openly crying, their bodies heaving and convulsing from the pain of grief. We funeral directors deal with that kind of grief daily.

All went perfectly with the viewing and funeral service. As agonizing as I realize the visitation and funeral service was for that young couple, I recognize that it was the best beginning therapy for them to adjust to their loss, and start their grief work.

Using both the Mirror of erised *and* the Knight of Mirrors, I know that this is the type of funeral service I always want to be able to arrange for families. My very earnest hope is that I can daily remember that we must serve and work with both Muggles and Wizards.

A Matter of Licensure

Periodically, the area newspapers take a merry-go-round ride on the subjects of education, teachers, and the local school system. Headlines scream that the children aren't learning the correct material or are learning it inappropriately. Articles explain with great and lurid detail the battles between the union and non-union employees, also known as the administration. Blurbs cry out that the school boards aren't meeting diversity goals and describe with great zeal how this will harm future generations. It appears that one of the education editor's all time favorite subjects though is the standardized Indiana ISTEP testing that measures student's proficiencies in Math and English. The papers print plenty of articles dealing with how kids can read, write, count and take tests such as the ISTEP.

The furor that these articles create might help sell newspapers. Nonetheless a devoted and hardcore cadre of local school watchers love to launch tons of email to the Editorial Page. They decry how the reporters bias the articles. Letters complain about how the school system teaches – or fails to teach – students perfectly. These letters yammer about how the kids are "going to Hades in a handbasket," and so on, to the point of nausea.

Recently, a letter writer theorized that it was no wonder that Johnny couldn't read because his parents, grandparents, aunts and uncles can't read either. To support his postulation he noted that most drivers in Allen County (which reportedly has more registered cars per capita than any other county in the nation except Los Angeles County in California) apparently failed to read the simple instructions that came with the new license plate tags for the year 2000. The writer wryly noted that the one simple line instruction specifies placing the small "00" sticker over the "99" in the license plate's upper right-hand corner. Nevertheless, for whatever reason, the good residents of the county have decided to place the little sticky tags over the month, which is found in the upper *left* hand corner of the plates – perhaps because they thought that since we were starting a new generation, the stickers should have a new position on the plate.

"He's right!" I smugly observed and began counting daily the number of drivers that had failed to read the basic instructions. Every funeral procession that we lined up seemed to have plenty of drivers that simply could not get the fundamental idea of placing the sticker in the correct position. Indignance describes my attitude best, and I remained amazed at the hundreds of people who could not read. Then one day recently, I went to *my own* car to place some cleaning supplies in my trunk to take to one of our chapels. As I casually glanced down at my own license plate, I noticed that I had placed the sticker in the wrong position along with all those miscreants in our funeral cavalcades. A word much stronger and definitely more salty than the word "OOPS!" escaped my lips. It appears that I can't read or follow rudimentary instructions either. One could say that I had taken licensure with the law, and that I had been unfairly judgmental of my fellow human beings. I began to think how taking licensure and being judgmental might apply in our daily practice.

During my internship in Florida, I served a family controlled by a strong-willed man whom we might best term "a micro manager," and whom we will call Mr. Bressler. Difficulties began with the death call, which was for a pre-arranged funeral.

Mr. Bressler's father's death had decidedly not been an easy one. He suffered for months on end from a horribly debilitating and progressive disease, apparently without palliative Hospice care because Mr. Bressler refused their help. The family went through private nurse after private nurse because Mr. Bressler's Gestapo-like tactics insulted and intimidated them.

The death call came to the firm during one of those early evening Florida thunderstorms that prevent a driver from seeing three feet in front of the windshield. Consequently, it took more than an hour for us to get to the Bressler home where Mr. Bressler promptly greeted us with a barrage of epithets that would have made my Basic Training Drill Instructor proud. I noticed that most of his family cowered when he spoke and determined that we were serving a "high maintenance" family. Even the removal took almost an hour because we had to listen to a litany of instructions. During this time Mr. Bressler's wife frequently ran from the room in tears after one of his diatribes.

The following morning, the other funeral director on duty told me that Mr. Bressler had phoned during the night to give detailed instructions on exactly how he wanted his father embalmed, restored and dressed. Since I had already embalmed Mr. Bressler's father, I thought maybe this might lead to another series of problems. Later in the day, I almost literally cringed when the boss told me I would be meeting with the Bressler family to complete the funeral service arrangements. Although I knew he would be in the room with me, as required by law, I still dreaded the conference.

My concerns embodied themselves when Mr. Bressler brushed past me as he came in the front door of the funeral home, ignoring the hand I had offered to him in greeting. After I got everyone in the family seated in the arrangement room and had served them some light refreshments, Mr. Bressler began to "do his best to do his worst." (Years later I still haven't forgotten the verbal onslaught of directions, criticisms, comments and instructions he gave us.) The written list was far more extensive. He furnished us with a two-page obituary of his father, which I knew would be very costly for the newspaper to print. I thought that he would have a stroke when I gave him the cost of publishing the lengthy tribute.

The most personally insulting part of all of this was that Mr. Bressler consistently checked behind me to see if I had completed every detail exactly the way that he wanted. Had I phoned the VFW to arrange for graveside services? Well, he knew that I did. My buddy over at the Post called me to advise me that Mr. Bressler had phoned him to find out if I had made the call. What about my embalming and restorative art abilities? It became no surprise to me the second day of dealing with the Bresslers to learn that Mr. Bressler had phoned a fellow funeral director at the firm to learn if I had embalmed his father correctly. What about the newspaper? The woman who worked at the obituary desk told me a week after the funeral that she had received a couple of tongue lashings as well, and that Mr. Bressler had initially phoned her to see if I had faxed the obituary exactly as he had dictated it to me. Nor did it daze me to discover that Mr. Bressler had also contacted the soloist at the church to learn if I had ordered the right version of "Ave Maria." ("Order the Schubert, not the Bach. No Metallica, or anything like that," he had growled at me. I took that as his sense of humor.)

On the day of the visitation, a Sunday, I again waited at the front door of the funeral home, but this time I harbored more anger and frustration than any other emotion. I had been to Mass earlier in the day and one petition the priest had offered was for hospice workers, funeral directors, and those that work comforting the grieving. A sinking feeling told me I might be calling on St. Joseph of Arimathea, the Patron Saint of Undertakers and Embalmers.

When the Bressler family arrived, I masked my personal feelings and thoughts the best that I could. After all, I reasoned, I'm not a Saint. I'm a Funeral Director. Still, I remembered the petition at church earlier, and I recalled that in most states funeral service laws require funeral directors, as a condition of their license, to act compassionately. Had I acted with sufficient compassion?

As I ushered Mr. Bressler in to view his father for the first time since he had died, a complete transformation came over the man. Mr. Bressler literally fell onto his father's casket and wept deeply – a complete loss of control. When he regained his composure, he came and found me to compliment me on the appearance of his father. From that moment forward, I never heard another complaint or nasty word from the man's mouth. He was nothing but kind to the rest of the staff, and even told my boss what a good job he thought I had done for the Bressler family.

P. Aries, writing in *The Hour of Our Death* says: "There are two ways of not thinking about death – the way of our technological civilization which denies death and refuses to talk about it, and the way of traditional civilizations, which is not a denial, but a recognition of the impossibility of thinking about it directly or for very long because death is too close and too much a part of daily life."

Obviously, Mr. Bressler's manic and demanding behavior was one way in which he was coping with the death of his father. He did not want to think about the death of his father, and to display this he lashed out at everyone near him. Mr. Bressler immersed himself in finding faults with others and in over-controlling the funeral arrangements, rather than thinking about his grief or the actual death. Funeral directors are often handy targets for this type of demeanor, and we owe it to ourselves and the families we serve to conduct ourselves properly. Granted, it's very difficult sometimes to accept abusive behavior and erratic deportment. Funeral directors and embalmers need to recall not only the matter of the license but the reasons why most of us entered funeral service.

We are all humankind, and some words of the Old Testament (Ecclesiastes 3:19-22) summarize our common bonds and eventual reward for our labors:

> *"For the lot of man and beast is one lot; the one dies as well as the other. Both have the same life breath, and man has no advantage over the beasts; but all is vanity. Both go to the same place; both were made from dust, and to the dust they shall return..... And I saw that there is nothing better for a man than to rejoice in his work; for this is his lot."*

SILHOUETTES
AND THE $3 COFFEE POT

While sitting in a funeral coach at a traffic signal recently, I couldn't help myself from staring at a perfectly restored 1953 Chrysler New Yorker that pulled up to the intersection just a few lanes away from me. Absolute splendor radiated from that magnificent vehicle as well as the obvious handicraft, care, and the thousands of hours the owner used to restore it.

There was another reason why I could not end my obvious leering. During my 1960s boyhood in central Pennsylvania, a neighbor had collected five of these Chryslers and kept only one of them running. He always stored the other four in his backyard for spare parts. This conglomeration of aging cars concerned the other neighbors greatly, but I immensely enjoyed the thrill of climbing around in these washout automobiles. They had a front seat that I now suspect was of better quality than many living room sofas in the neighborhood. The steering wheel, the size of an old-fashioned washtub, provided endless hours of entertainment as I sawed away on it, pretending to drive. Some years later, these New Yorkers provided an ideal safe haven for a little youthful hanky-panky with a neighborhood young woman.

As all of these memories flashed through my mind, a 1999 Lincoln Navigator pulled up in the lane right next to me. It almost completely obscured my view of the 1953 Chrysler. Still, I could discern part of the New Yorker's silhouette through the Navigator's windows. The image of the juncture of the two superior American products, so similar, yet so diverse, froze in my mind. I saw an immediate parallel to the values and customs of funeral service, as we practiced them in the recent – and far past – and now.

Are we putting as many man hours and care into the funerals that we direct today as we did then? Do we take the time necessary to properly and thoroughly embalm and restore bodies? Shall we, as directors, take the "easy way out" and simply advise the family to close the casket? I wonder if we are asking for the price of the Navigator, yet delivering one of those jalopy Chryslers that sat rusting in that weed-infested yard? Are funeral directors today investing the hours necessary to restore some quality funeral customs of our rich American funeral service past? Do we find ourselves content with allowing the inevitable societal changes to mold and shape our profession? Where is our level of care in this mix?

Let us face it. Society no longer uses huge wreaths hung on the front door of the home of the deceased, distributes "monkey spoons," mourner's arm badges and rings, or funeral invitations. Mourners of the year 2000 do not wear black clothing for a year following the death of their loved one. Saying that directors no longer slip on formal mourning suits with tails and stove pipe hats and drive horse-drawn hearses is quite safe. (Of course, a few directors throughout the nation still own and use a horse-drawn hearse occasionally.)

We no longer measure gunfighters at the OK Corral for "toe pincher" coffins. Nor do we travel to log cabin homes with a tape measure to size up the dying for the coffin we will eventually have to build. Funeral home owners do, however, send our own "hired guns" out into the community as licensed, or sometimes unlicensed, counselors to solicit preneed funeral or cremation arrangements. A true funeral service historian can readily see the reflection of the past evident in that custom of today.

Other funerary customers have gone the way of the Edsel or Studebaker. We rarely conduct viewings or wakes of two or three-day duration anymore. Only in a few parts of the country do pallbearers wear white gloves and carnations. Perhaps in the Northeast alone are caskets carried on the shoulders of the pallbearers. Funeral directors can attribute that reflection to the highly successful arrival of the metal casket market which is a positive change in our history.

The first funeral I ever worked as an attendant honored the memory of a 16-year-old student killed in a car accident by an inebriated driver. What deserves mentioning is the care, compassion and multitudinous services rendered by that funeral home. The funeral director and his staff of two worked for three days straight, practically without any sleep. They spent hour after hour in the embalming room, restoring that 16-year-old young woman to her natural and lifelike appearance. A staff member drove 150 miles to the casket manufacturing plant to secure the specially ordered casket. The director informed the neighbors about the huge turn out of people expected at the viewing and funeral. He also planned with the state police to provide traffic control and an escort. A local florist coordinated all of the floral tributes at the funeral home viewing and the funeral which we held at the local high school. It's also truly remarkable that the director never charged the grieving family a single penny. God knows, though, he himself could not afford to give away services.

Ironically, the father of the young student, a rough and tumble coal miner of Welch descent, remained devastated by the loss, went into a type of abnormal grief for his daughter, and eventually drank himself to death. The director laid him to rest alongside his beloved daughter some three years later, almost to the day. Sadly, that superior funeral director also died in that same year from an insidious disease.

That brings us back to the values of current funeral customs and the subsequent value of the undertaker's services. Customs change from region to region, and from decade to decade. Customs that are important to people remain: the viewing, the flowers, the funeral, the grandest of all cavalcades, the funeral procession. We establish other new customs and trends, or reinvent an interest in older ones, especially with the help of the media and the Internet. Witness the interest in sea burial following the death of John F. Kennedy Jr.

We no longer want the nation to call us "undertakers." That is more the pity, since the word suggests that we will undertake to conduct the required services, and it harks back to an important time in the dateline of funeral service history. For the young woman killed by the drunken driver, the funeral director undertook all of the necessary steps – and many extra ones – to try to help the grieving family. It's a perfect word for what we do every day and a great description.

Some undertakers are so humanitarian that they will give away that which is most valuable to them – namely, their services and merchandise with the appropriate customs of the region and time. That, by itself, is a statement of value and human worth.

When I was in college, I was always short of money. One day my coffee pot stopped working, a true disaster for an apprentice working a 60-hour week while trying to fit all of his classes into a chaotic schedule. At the local hospice second hand shop, I found a little-used percolator, probably dating to the 1960s, for $3. It was a tremendous value for my money, and I established a custom of daily usage, one I still follow religiously to this day with the same coffee pot!

The values and customs of funeral service today remain very much like that coffee pot and the silhouette of the two cars. To answer a question posed earlier – we are giving families the care, courtesy, merchandise and service they need at a critical time in their lives. Funeral directors do that by drawing on the customs of the past while using new ideas from the families and our contemporaries. Undertakers continue to give their full worth for grieving families and mourners. In turn, hopefully, both mourners and directors can find in our service the unexpected and unsolicited value I found in a $3 coffee pot.

The Lord's Lightning Rod

"Do you really think there is a God?" Rusty, the retired chiropractor who worked as a part-time attendant at the funeral home, asked me. His question prompted me to make some small conversation as we took our seats in the brand new funeral coach.

"And if so, what does happen after death? You're a college boy. Why not give me all the answers?" asked the tall, distinguished-looking Irishman who held a number of degrees himself. His social tactics included often trying to debate death-related issues with me. Rusty, a widower, remained very bitter about his wife's death two years earlier. Signs of his unresolved grief consistently surfaced in our working environment.

Early one dreary summer afternoon I drove across one of the many bridges that span Tampa Bay. Wide Florida skies delivered monsoons and torrents of rain that frequently reminded me of some nasty days several decades ago that I spent in a "Garden Spot" in Southeast Asia. A thriving metropolitan mortuary sponsored this midsummer delivery trip, in a $65,000 Cadillac coach with less than 500 miles on it. Our mission amounted to transporting some casketed remains to a small chapel that sweltering afternoon.

I ignored Rusty's barbs and struggled to keep my mind and the coach on the road. The deluge reduced visibility to nearly zero, as if driving in a tropical rain forest. Thunder rumbled across the bay with The Armageddon seemingly moments away. Lightning illuminated the eerie early afternoon sky in a way unique to those Florida coastlines. After all, the St. Petersburg-Tampa area claims the dubious distinction of remaining the lightning capital of the world. Just as I began wondering how much worse the storm could get the skies opened with even stronger salvos of lightning and rain.

Finally, we reached the end of the bay bridge and made the short jaunt to the cemetery chapel. The roads leading to the memorial park were better suited for an Everglades air boat than the boss's spanking new Cadillac coach. Frankly, I had some concerns about the driving and even more worries about the weather. Rusty's nervous mannerisms combined with his continuously atheistic and cantankerous chattering did little to help the situation.

The chapel we were headed for that oppressively hot afternoon sits in the middle of a magnificent necropolis. It is well tended and perhaps the most beautiful cemetery in Florida. The theme gardens and burial areas are resplendent with lush foliage and greenery that any florist would envy. Behind the chapel sits a tropical mangrove of monstrous trees that have been growing in that area for hundreds of years.

Arriving at the tiny structure, we discovered the storm had taken its toll on the services. We couldn't move the remains into the chapel because it was swelled with mourners who were waiting for the rain to subside. Two other caskets occupied the cramped storage room in the back of the chapel. Rusty and I sat in the coach, feeling the reverberations of thunder gliding off the nearby bay. While parked at the back door of the chapel, a sudden irrepressible and inexplicable urge to move the coach sieged me. I pulled the coach down the road perhaps 50 feet from the back ramp to the chapel.

Not less than two minutes after moving the coach, as I gazed into the side rear view mirror, a great bolt of lightning struck the largest of the mangrove trees directly behind the chapel. Gargantuan tree branches – bigger than the coach in which we were sitting – crashed into the chapel and completely obliterated our previous parking spot. Had I not moved the coach, it's quite possible that Rusty and I may have been the central point of two funeral services later in the week.

"Well Rusty, do you still not believe in God?" I quipped as funeral directors and mourners alike poured out of the chapel to gaze at the tree, a good chunk of it now completely blocking the road. Heavy branches smashed the wooden walkway to the chapel into a million jagged toothpicks. It had been, literally, a close call.

Rusty did not say much to me the rest of the day but the experience caused me to think about how funeral directors are often the recipients of a different type of lightning as well.

On another afternoon in another part of the country, my supervisor advised me there was a person waiting in the foyer of the funeral home. This individual just wanted to give us some biographical information about the impending death of a relative. Seconds after introducing myself, this family member assaulted me with the following barrage:

"I know what you funeral directors do. I just moved here from another state where I dealt with your kind. I know all about you people. All I want you to do is exactly what I say and nothing more. And you had better remember that I know the law."

I knew then that nothing I did was going to assuage that person's death-related anger. Nothing I could say or do would change this family member's perception of me or the profession. Nevertheless, I stayed calm, polite, and made sure that I followed established protocol. I spent perhaps 15 minutes with the individual and could tell I was not well liked.

Some months later, the aftercare counselor reported the family member had been very critical of me – and highly pleased with the director who eventually handled the services. What had I done wrong?

Worried, I went to the funeral home owner. A kind and gentle man, he reassured me that I had been "The Lord's Lightning Rod." That person, he told me, was angry at the Lord about the upcoming family death…but could not get to Him, so I was the handiest target. Mac McCormick was accessible…why not vent on him? Further, the boss told me, whatever director had greeted that furious person at the front door would have taken "the hit."

Those wise words from the boss made me feel much better. Still, the entire bizarre episode plagues me. What was it that I did? What could I possibly have said or done to serve that family member better?

It finally dawned on me. All funeral directors take hits of lightning; yet we manage to continue our great tradition of caring for the dead to serve the living. I was spared some very dangerous lightning one time to be the recipient of a different type of lightning another time. I love funeral service enough to take more direct bolts and be the Lord's Lightning Rod.

A Sister's Lament

Written with Glenna Sultzbaugh

Few people realize it, or care for that matter, but my given Christian name is John. Mac is a nickname I simply got stuck with about a million years ago when I enlisted in the United States Air Force. My parents named me for some of my great-grandfathers and especially after an uncle of mine, John Barnhart, who died in 1938 in a tragic alcohol related car crash.

Not too long ago, I sent my mother, Glenna Sultzbaugh, who lives in central Pennsylvania, one of my *American Funeral Director* "End Note" columns that dealt with my thoughts about funeral directors needing to be uncommonly sensitive to a family's needs. She had a reaction to that story that I think is worthy of sharing with other funeral directors.

Glenna wrote me a long and poignant email about the life events surrounding the funeral of her previously mentioned brother, who died the day before his twenty-second birthday. Although the death occurred more than sixty years ago, the memory is still fresh and hurtful to her. She writes of the manner in which the undertaker traumatized her father and the family:

" Perhaps, one may wonder why I am so cold about funerals. I went to the accident scene when my beautiful brother, John Barnhart, was in the car accident with a drunken friend. My brother was with that man simply because he could keep his car repaired. As John lay dying, the doctor did not allow me to give him a drink of cold water. I know now that was proper, but when one is thirteen, it is a different story. Johnny told me, while his life was ebbing away, that he had gone with that boy so he could fix his car. Johnny also said he had his first glass of beer, would I please not tell Daddy? He died quickly.

"Our family undertaker, Howard Hetchen, came to our home immediately as a friend, not as a vulture, but truly as a friend. I held my Dad's hand when Mr. Hetchen explained every step of the funeral process. My sister, Margaret, keeps saying she does not remember any of this, but I can never forget. I am sure she has never properly dealt with his death, and she is blocking this memory of the undertaker being at our little house on Union Street.

"People in those days in central Pennsylvania, and as far as I knew all over the country, still held funerals at the home. People that I did not know began wandering in and out, even upstairs. Dad had to buy new trousers for Johnny as he had his good ones on when he died. I had to go to the insurance man to make sure Johnny had kept his life insurance paid up. It was.

"The flowers began arriving. Chairs began arriving. Uncle Al came from Philadelphia. I heard repeatedly how Aunt Alberta had been to a fortune teller and was told that a young man that she loved dearly was going to die in an automobile accident. The day that Johnny died, when my Aunt Alberta got home from the hospital from her job as a nurse, she got the grisly confirmation by telephone that the fortune teller had been correct.

"The crash disfigured Johnny's face. Howard asked me if I could convince Daddy to put Johnny in the coffin the opposite way – feet where the head should be – as the undertakers could not remove or restore the damage. Howard did try to fix up Johnny. Really, he did. Nevertheless, it was useless. For three days, it was a long procession of people in the front door and out the kitchen door. We had chairs all over our home.

"A Pastor we did not know conducted the funeral. Ours was on vacation. So very little spiritual help, especially for Dad, was available during those days. People came to the funeral who would not have given Johnny a dollar bill if he had been hungry. They shed – or at least it seemed to me – crocodile tears.

"Then at the committal service at Oak Hill Cemetery after it was over, Mr. Hetchen did the most unforgivable thing that I have ever witnessed. He asked my Daddy to step over to the grave and look down and in to see if the vault and all the burial arrangements were satisfactory.

"Now, I had four uncles standing there at the grave, and Howard knew that and knew all of them. Any one of them would have handled it gladly. My Daddy looked down into the grave. In the previous three days before the funeral, my Daddy had gained composure if not acceptance. Now, Howard Hetchen asked him to look down into the barren grave and stare at the concrete vault. He realized – in that split second – that lying there in a wooden casket inside that cold and sterile concrete burial vault was his only son, John, the joy of all the Barnharts – and he collapsed.

"I know I make remarks sometimes about my father, Homer, but I loved him and still do with all my heart. This is why I will have a memorial service – not to take anything away from the undertakers, but to try to insure no repeat of what happened to your Grandfather at the cemetery. I've made some pre-arrangements, and my church has my personal requests as to music and scripture at my funeral."

How much has changed in American Funeral service since 1938? A great deal. In the cities and communities of the Y2K millennium, it's rare that funeral directors ever go to the home anymore, except to make a removal or to deliver some paperwork. We decidedly don't embalm bodies there or haul folding chairs or any of our equipment to the family home.

Nevertheless, we still enter the home and stay there for years, if only in spirit. Witness the effect that Howard Hetchen had on my mother, decades ago. I knew Mr. Hetchen in his elder years, and he was truly a polite professional. For some inexplicable reason he apparently had a lapse in judgement at that service in 1938, and it has had long-standing effects.

I recall an error I made at a graveside service sometime back. Everything had gone perfectly with the arrangement conference, visitation, and funeral. The family was exceedingly pleased with the arrangements up to and including the graveside committal. After the Pastor gave the benediction and murmured his words of condolences to the family, I stood in front of the huge crowd of mourners to thank them for attending Elizabeth Smith's services. The problem with that was that we had just buried *Esther* Smith. After making my somber pronouncement, I couldn't figure out why so many people were looking at me oddly. I wondered if I had failed to zip an important aspect of my apparel. Later, the family called the error to my attention.

All I could do was apologize profusely and vow to myself to do better in the future.

An old saying I used to hear many times during my apprenticeship at the Hodges Funeral Home in Naples, Florida went something like this, "This family is only going to have one funeral for this person. Just remember that a director has to get it right the first time. Remember the five "p's" of a funeral: Proper planing prevents poor performance."

The older I get, the more I believe in that adage. Some of my contemporaries criticize me for my obsessive-compulsive organization of a funeral or visitation. Still, I realize that by over-planning, I am going to be assured of some peace and security in funeral directing.

A well-conducted funeral service – untroubled by anger and unforgiveness aimed at the undertaker – is one of the best gifts in life I can receive. We all know that the seeds of discontent can very easily appear at any phase of the funeral service. Small, nagging fears and doubts can easily disturb the serenity of a funeral as easily as some child skims rocks over the surface of a farm pond on a summer's afternoon.

I hope and pray in the future I am wise enough to choose the correct path of order for any funeral I conduct. Proper planning prevents poor performance. My mother never said those given words to me, but they are decidedly words of good advice to a conscientious funeral director. Why should those families we serve remember us sixty years hence for a few awkward and traumatic moments?

The Grandest Procession

When my father died, Cliff Sterner led the procession from his modest Mid-Atlantic style funeral home out to Oak Hill Cemetery. Cars pulled to the roadside showing deep and heart-felt respect for him. Twenty-five years later while I attended St. Petersburg Junior College's Funeral Service Program I learned a great deal about the history of the funeral cortege, and how it has evolved. I also discovered that drivers today have very little respect for the modern funeral caravan.

In Florida, an Orlando resident and funeral attendee recently sued the funeral home, the bereaved family, the Orlando Police Department, the funeral director – personally – and everyone else involved in managing a funeral procession. This happened as the result of a careless driver striking the side of her car after failing to see her driving in a properly organized and well-designated funeral procession. She won a huge judgment. When Florida funeral directors protested in court, one wise (or possibly wise-guy) magistrate suggested that directors plan all funeral processions with only right-hand turns. At one point, some funeral homes in Florida had completely abandoned the funeral procession because of these liability issues.

Terror is the word that could describe how many funeral directors must feel when approaching an intersection, leading a cortege without a police cruiser leading the way. A funeral director friend of mine almost required his own professional services after the driver of a semi-truck refused to stop at an intersection, coming to rest about three inches short of the lead car. I was following him in procession, driving the funeral coach, and cringed as I braced for the imminent collision.

Not long ago, I conducted services for the wife of a man whom we had buried just a few months earlier. Everything had gone perfectly with both of the services until we arrived at the cemetery, and I looked around for all the pallbearers. As I pulled the casket to the edge of the coach, a family member told me two of them were missing. They were riding in a car near the cortege's rear, and a pick up truck collided with them. The truck driver simply and adamantly refused to stop for the procession. We delayed the service until they arrived in a police cruiser, luckily unhurt.

We have all seen the impatient driver who cuts between the lead car and the coach or the pallbearers. I have personally witnessed drivers who negotiated their way between the hearse and the limo. What on earth are these thoughtless people thinking about as they pass the funeral procession at 40 miles an hour? They decidedly are not considering the sanctity of the funeral nor are they showing any respect for the dead.

A Brief History

A funeral cortege allows people the world over a final opportunity to recognize and exalt the dead. It's called a parade, procession, cavalcade, caravan, column, promenade, a movement, or even a funeral train. Historians root funeral processions in antiquity, and the word funeral itself comes form the Latin for torch "funeralis" which led the cortege. In ancient Russia, known then as Sycthia, funeral processions took up to 40 days as they wound through various villages where family members of the deceased lived.

The Romans and the Greeks often used oratory as a reason for lengthy processions. Heralds sounded out the news of the death, and orations along the way were common.

According to Dr. Kenneth Iserson, writing in *Death to Dust*, one of the lengthiest funeral caravans in history remains the funeral procession of Nero Claudius Drusus Germanicus. This Nero served as a Roman consul and fathered the Emporer Claudius. He died in Germany while leading Roman troops stationed there. Tribunes and centurions bore his body some 600 miles across the Alps allowing village officials along the route the opportunity for oration.

Scottish funeral processions could also be lengthy and uproarious. Unspoken Scottish code requires the family to bear the body back to the place of ancestry. Several Scottish funeral records report the participants consumed several hundred gallons of liquor along these arduous roadways.

Most elaborate funeral corteges have been reserved for the very rich, powerful or famous. French history reports that more than 600,000 people lined the streets to view Napoleon's second 1840 funeral procession. The Duke of Wellington, who defeated Napoleon, endures as a legend in the annals of funeral procession history. It took several months to just plan the procession which eventually had representatives from every British Army regiment. Sixteen horses could reportedly barely move the funeral car bearing the royal body.

The English weren't the first to use funeral processions as an indicator of wealth. However, aristocratic trappings were common in Britain during Victorian Days. Staples of funeral processions included elegantly appointed glass paneled hearses, mimes, and horses with elaborate plumes and rigging. Those on the criminal side of that society would not fare as well. After publicly hanging the condemned, city officials would unceremoniously dump the remains in a handcart and parade it through the streets, possibly as a deterrent to crime.

The 1865 funeral of Abraham Lincoln shines as a superior example of a fitting American funeral procession. It took two weeks for 13 locomotives to bear the slain President's body from Washington, D.C. to Springfield, Ill. Many soldiers guarded the train. Black draperies and evergreens are evident in many photographs of the cars. Newspapers of that era say that more than 6.5 million people viewed the train.

Instructors routinely show videotapes and films of John F. Kennedy's funeral procession in many history and funeral service classrooms across the nation. No one can easily dismiss announcer Arthur Godfrey's dramatic CBS Radio News coverage of the procession as he described the muffled drums and the skittish riderless horse.

I once led a funeral procession that featured a bagpiper playing as the procession wound its way through the cemetery gates. It was grand, but the poor bagpiper had to truly hustle to get to the other side of the cemetery to play the conclusion of the service.

Summary

The funeral procession enjoys an important and powerful position in our rich funeral service legacy. Whether or not the funeral cortege can ever safely regain the eminence it once commanded in the United States remains a clouded issue at best. It's my hope that funeral directors everywhere will continue to promote the funeral procession – the grandest legacy of them all.

Faith and Courage

"Faith is believing the more obstacles you have, the more opportunities there are for God to do something."
-Clarence W. Jones

If ever a maxim fit funeral service, the one written by Mr. Jones is it. The role of faith – and courage – in our honorable profession can't be under-rated. To be politically correct, I should probably omit "God" in that saying. I would have to insert the name of some 90-ish self-centered and sensitive guru of the Baby Boomers Generation in God's place. However, faith and courage do play a powerful role in all of our funeral service lives.

How often in our daily routine do we have the opportunity to overcome some difficulty to make things better for the families that we are serving? I recall a sunny, dazzling day in Florida. We were holding three visitations simultaneously at the funeral home. Grieving family members and friends filled several chapels. The smallest family (about 20 persons of mixed cultural diversity) turned out to be the loudest and downright boisterous group. An argument broke out, with yelling and cursing reverberating through the normally tranquil front foyer. Eventually, the offenders took to the sidewalk in front of the funeral home.

Other directors were busy. Stan, the retired man working the front door, looked little more than bewildered. I questioned, "What was the right decision? Should I say something to the noisy family? Why not use the Faith and Courage formula?" Have enough faith in yourself, your funeral home, and your decisions to give you the courage to carry through with the appropriate action.

Drawing on my military background, I found the most rambunctious fellow, and pulled him to the side. Staring him down, I spoke quietly – but firmly – mentioning the other families and our desire to give everyone a service with dignity. He rounded up the balance of the offenders. I suppose they took the argument over to a neighborhood bar. When they returned, they behaved. There were no complaints from any of the three families or visiting public.

In funeral service, we must have the courage necessary to accept the inevitable rejection. Families quite often vent their frustration and anger about death on the funeral director. Misunderstandings occur, and sometimes elements of the funeral service fail despite the best planning. Funeral directors and embalmers must have faith in themselves and their profession and respond positively to these challenges.

To lead funeral service into the next century, we must serve our families with courage and give them the type of service they want. The days of the "cookie cutter funeral" and the "funeral factory" are long since gone.

To follow the correct tenets of traditional American funeral service faithfully requires a single mindedness of purpose. Funeral home owners must learn to develop their faith and courage and to insist on sincerity in employees, proper embalming, cordiality, proper grooming, community involvement and good ethics. The list of areas where we all need improvement is lengthy.

Funeral service professionals must have the courage to tell the truth to families even when it is not pleasant. As an excellent example, sometimes arranging an infant's funeral can try even the faith of an atheist. Having to describe the state of human remains often requires courage and faith. We must have the courage to tell the family the true condition. After we do that, we must maintain enough faith in our embalming skills that we try to restore the remains to a life like condition.

A friend of mine is a pilot for a major airline. He related a story about receiving a frantic call from the Operations Dispatcher one Christmas Eve. The dispatcher had phoned more than 40 pilots trying to find one to fly from Miami to Cincinnati later that evening. Hundreds of people were trying to get home for the holiday. It would mean great inconvenience for my pilot friend. He would have to drive to Miami to get to the plane and then spend the better part of Christmas Eve and Day away from his own family. Nevertheless, he undertook the flight. The pilot had the courage to accept his responsibility and the faith to know the proper decision. He also showed his family that he would not lie his way out of the situation.

We, in funeral service, can find a lesson in that story, and many parallels.

How many Christmas mornings have we found ourselves in the Preparation Room instead of with our family? How many death calls have interrupted Thanksgiving Day meals?

Can you count the number of times that the buzzing of a pager has changed important life events? These circumstances show the difficult and trying nature of proper funeral service. We grumble, but we all have within us the faith and courage needed to serve our families with dignity and grace.

An Unforgettable Rural Funeral in Pennsylvania

Written with Glenna Sultzbaugh

In the "fast food society" in which we live, too often we may forget not only our own familial roots but also some origins of modern American funeral service practice. This history, written by my mother, Glenna Sultzbaugh, deftly describes how my Mid-Atlantic ancestors' funerals were more than burials of the dead – they were true social events.

Telephones will always remind me of a memorable family funeral. They definitely have been very important in my past, present and future. In the year 2000, I am sure we all take the instruments for granted, as a convenience that has always been there for us. During the nineteen-thirties, that decidedly wasn't the case. My Grandmother Barnhart, who operated a Boarding House, had one of the few telephones in Millersburg, our little town, as did my uncle, who owned a restaurant. In both cases, they needed the phones for people to call them to make reservations for lunch and dinner. At Grandma's the telephone was especially important because she conducted a boarding business featuring a lunch table open to the public. Quite the German, and one for Teutonic strictness, she always served meals promptly at noon, never even a minute or so later. While the table was large and accommodating, with a side buffet containing desserts and fruits, seating continued to be limited. Sometimes on special days, such as Pennsylvania Dutch Pot Pie Day, she offered two settings. Reservations were necessary to seat diners quickly and efficiently. Most of the prospective diners who called from their place of employment spent a nickel to use one of the few pay phones in town.

What still amazes me about telephones is that my uncle who lived in Philadelphia would call to talk to his mother, my Grandma Barnhart. Why, Philadelphia then represented a drive of more than two and a half hours. No turnpike existed in the mid-nineteen thirties. Yet his telephone call took only seconds to make. Grandma's telephone scared me. It frightened me to hear the voice, and I never did catch onto the party rings. Grandma's was two longs and three shorts. They all sounded the same to me.

It was through one of these mysterious devices that I learned of my Grandfather Brown's death. I was eight years old in February 1933. Central Pennsylvania's deadlock in a state of frigidity endured. The evergreens, other trees, and thickets of bushes created a wondrous winter wonderland with their luminescent coatings of snow and ice.

102 ♦ End Notes

That day I had come home from school to have lunch at my Grandmother's. Everyone was busy – my aunts with serving and refilling food dishes and water glasses. Even Daddy came from his job at the Johnson Baillie Shoe Company to help feed the guests. The service was family style, all one could eat, and as my Uncle Harry once said, "He who eats the fastest gets the most."

Plenty of those workers were fast eaters.

That eventful day, in the midst of all the bustle, the telephone rang. I remember that the jangling of the phone always annoyed my aunts. In those years one could not take the phone off the hook because everybody was on a party line. A phone off the switch surely would have concerned the operator who ruled the switchboard and, consequently, the town like a czarina. She would have to dispatch a messenger to the offending party's home to make the somber pronouncement that they had knocked the telephone off the hook.

The phone continued to ring, everyone continued to ignore it, and the rings seemed to get shriller. Finally, one of my aunts picked up the earpiece and called my grandmother to answer it. No one was happy about it at dinner time. People in this area of the country have always considered meal times and food as sacred. The eating at the table stopped and no one even reached for celery or carrot sticks in the interval.

My aunt whispered to Daddy, possibly in Pennsylvania Dutch. He went and stood beside Grandma trying to listen, because the phone featured a separate earpiece. Telephones today have volume control and speaker systems, but then they were boxes fastened to the wall higher than the average mouth. On the side of the box was a handle to crank to summon the operator.

We heard Grandma say, "Yes, and I will tell him. Yes, we will see. Thank you for calling to tell me." Then she hung up. Everybody in the dining room looked on expectantly, assuming she would tell my Dad about the call. She did not. Now my grandmother knew that these people had to get back to work, and that I had to go back to third grade. Politely Grandma told my aunts to resume serving. When everyone finished eating, I remember that I put on my good blue chinchilla coat. My family did not have money for real fur, and I consider myself blessed to have had that coat. Grandma tied my scarf and told me to put on my gloves and hat, which matched the coat. She said she would see me after school, and she told Daddy that she would see him after work.

I walked to school with my friend, Franny, who lived on the opposite side of the railroad tracks from where I lived. When I told her that Grandma had a phone call during lunch, Franny asked me who had called, and what was it all about? I told her that I did not know, but that I was to go to Grandma's after school instead of going home or to my uncle's restaurant. We were no sooner back in school that Franny had to tell the teacher about the phone call. I did not think that was very kind, because I wanted to be the one to tell the teacher. Even teachers were curious about telephone calls, and Miss Shuler, my teacher, asked me if anything was wrong. At that point I said that I didn't think so because Grandma was not going to tell anyone about the call until after Daddy got off from work, and I was home from school. The afternoon lingered longer than usual, and I kept returning mentally to the image of Grandma standing at the phone.

Franny walked me home and hinted that she would like to come in and play. I would have liked that. Nevertheless, I said she better not. Daddy came into the house shortly after me along with a man and a woman who greeted me cordially, as if they had known me forever. I had only ever seen these people, my Aunt Bessie and Uncle Albert Brown, a few times.

Grandma said we would all go up to her parlor. She told me to take my uncle and aunt upstairs to wait for her and Dad. She gave me the keys to the parlor which had to be kept locked because of the transient boarders. As we went up the stairs, the man and the woman talked to me. They questioned me about school and asked if I liked Grandma and my aunts. Did I ever wish that my mother had not died so I could live at home more often? They made it sound as if my own family neglected me. They did not neglect me – I was a happy third grader with good school grades even if I could not remember my mother. The Depression was beginning but I enjoyed good care. I heard talk of kids eating skimpy meals because their dads were working only part time or laid off completely. No unemployment compensation existed then. Yet, I was having my meals at a boarding house or at Uncle Earl's in the restaurant kitchen no less or having a supper at home that my sister cooked. It was grand when just our family could be together.

Unlocking the door, I allowed my aunt and uncle in first. They sat on the overstuffed sofa with its fancy doilies, and I sat on the piano bench. The inquisition began. I wish I could remember all their questions. Was I in the proper grade in school? Were my marks good? Did my Grandma, aunts, uncles, sister, brother, Daddy ever talk to me about my mother? Of course they did. Even my neighbors on Union Street talked to me about my wonderful mother. Daddy told me that my mother had a stroke while she was carrying me.

What caused the animosity between the Barnhart's and the Brown's, I cannot say. I had a slight glimmer of an idea from hearing my Barnhart aunts talking to each other. The Brown family had not come over from Liverpool for my mother's funeral.

Grandma Barnhart and my Daddy entered the room, and Grandma directly said to me, "Glenna Jane, that telephone call at dinner time was partly your business. Your grandfather, Jeremiah Brown, died during the night."

About me? Although I did not know either of my Grandparents Brown, I did know I was my Grandma Barnhart's girl, and she put her arms around me. Uncle Albert spoke to Daddy. I thought his tone of voice sharp. He asked Daddy if he were going to the funeral, and Daddy said that work was "too bad" for him to take off. With an edge to his voice, Uncle Albert told Daddy and Grandma that someone had to be there for my mother's sake. My mother's sake? My mother had left a home back in the woods behind a very small town, Liverpool, to come and work as a maid in my grandparent's boarding house. When my mother died, at age 39, they had not even come to her funeral. Yet, they expected us to travel to Grandpa Brown's funeral for her sake!

Then, Uncle Albert asked about my sister, Margaret, and brother, Johnny. Dad said that they were both working and could not take off for the funeral. Grandma offered the solution when she told Uncle Albert that I would take off from school. She would send a note to school, she said with a tone in her voice that told my Dad to back off the subject. After all, I was a grandchild. Dad fumed and fussed that he did not have a car. Albert countered that he owned one, and that it was acceptable to him that I go. My Dad and Grandmother Barnhart arranged when and where the dreaded Brown family would pick me up.

Sometime after that, my Aunt Helen and Aunt Gladyce entered the picture. To get me ready for my Grandfather Brown's funeral, they gave me a pair of black Mary Jane shoes in spite of the severe shortage of shoes. A real barber trimmed my bangs. I would wear my good green velvet Sunday School dress along with my chinchilla coat and matching hat.

In the next few days it snowed even more than it had previously. Ice formed around everything. My aunts did not want me in the car on roads like that. To cross the mile wide and picturesque Susquehanna River we had to drive south several miles out of the way to Clark's Ferry Bridge where we would pay the toll before we could drive north up the other side of the River Road to Liverpool. Uncle Albert and Aunt Bessie said that I would be fine, and they would not let anything happen to me.

Automobiles during the thirties weren't the sleek machines of today. We had to crank them to start them. Uncle Albert's car was a sedan shaped more like a box, high and long, with no seat belts. The heater hardly worked which is why my tall, middle-aged uncle wrapped me in blankets and tucked me in the back seat. Attached to the partition between the doors were glass vases filled with artificial flowers. I was not a small child but I felt lost in that huge, black leather seat.

The roads on this side of the Susquehanna River were fair but after we crossed the bridge the roads became worse. We slid and slid, and we turned around. I would sooner have been in school! Aunt Bessie chided Uncle Albert asking him if he knew how to drive. He did, and I felt some sympathy for my uncle having to endure my aunt's bickering.

Aunt Bessie told me that I was going to a very poor house, nothing like we had in Millersburg. She did tell me that she would stay near me, and she was as good as her word. My aunt was correct. I was still not prepared for the house's condition when we arrived there. It was dilapidated, needed painting and major repairs, and generally appeared very weather-worn. Plenty of cars parked around the shack, and two funeral vehicles sat in the yard as well. I had never before seen such a poor home. It was a log cabin with four rooms. A singular water pump adorned the outside porch with a washbasin hanging on the wall. A container held a comb. (My family would never have allowed me to use somebody else's comb.) Off to the side an ancient towel with plenty of grit and residue hung limply on a well-worn roller. This cabin set in the mountain will stay emblazoned in my mind no matter how long I live. Though a primitive outhouse sat in the back yard, I think electricity ran into the house. I thought, no wonder my mother wanted to leave her home.

As Uncle Albert parked the car near the hearse, I learned that Grandmother Brown would ride to the funeral with me in the back seat as Aunt Bessie was adamant that she would stay up front. The snowdrifts were icy, yet my Perry County relatives had strewn only a few ashes about the grounds.

I followed my aunt and uncle to the cabin door which opened to reveal a little woman standing there. She appeared smaller then me. My Grandmother Brown was a very simple woman with a small hairy wart on her face. This rough, backwoods woman looked at Albert and asked where Margaret and John (my brother and sister) were.

Then she hugged me and said, "Hello, Glenna Jane, come in, come in. You will want to see Grandpa." How had my grandmother raised five children in this place? If I could have asked Uncle Albert, I would have but I never had the opportunity. My cousin, Lydia, came from inside the house and guided me gently to an exceedingly small room. The room was barely big enough for the casket, a chair for Grandmother Brown to sit on, and a lectern for the preacher. In the casket reposed a small man, a little stocky, dressed neatly with his hands folded. The clothing they dressed him in was rough looking but I am sure it was his Sunday best. A spray adorned the top of the casket, and they represented the only flowers I saw that day. Since this funeral took place during the Depression, and even in the best of times this area had no money, it amazed me that there were any flowers at all.

People, relatives I never knew, and my grandparents' neighbors started telling me who they were as I went out into another room. Though the house was full to overflowing, I did get a seat. Most people stood as very little furniture filled the house. With Grandmother Brown beside the casket, the preacher at the lectern, and the undertaker just at this side of the door, the preacher began. He read about original sin, which I remember. He read several Psalms and talked about my Grandfather's Lutheran faith. The pastor called him "Jerry" not Jeremiah, as my Barnhart relatives did when they talked of Grandpa. He continued with passages from John, Corinthians and Revelations. I tried to soak that part of the scriptures in because Grandma Barnhart asked me to tell her what Bible verses the preacher used. I need not have worried, as I would hear them repeatedly before the day ended at three more funeral services for my Grandfather Jeremiah.

The preacher concluded after almost an hour. The room by then was stifling. Grandmother Brown wept, and with her children, covered Jeremiah Brown with a homemade quilt. The undertaker closed the casket. Uncle Albert and Uncle Charles helped my Grandmother, who suddenly seemed very feeble, into her coat and hat. They escorted her out into the frozen car. Truthfully they had to get everybody out of those cramped rooms, so that they could in some way maneuver the casket out to the waiting ancient hearse.

I sat in the back of the Ford with my Grandmother Brown who held my hand with her rough, work-worn hand. My uncles and some neighbors helped the undertaker, then went to their cars. I thought we were going to a cemetery.

Instead, we drove in a bizarre procession on those bumpy, icy roads to Lenninger's Lutheran church. The hearse pulled close to the steps of the church, and the pallbearers ambled out of their cars to unload the coffin to a platform with wheels. They took my Grandfather Brown into the church and wheeled him up front. The family and friends filed in and took seats while the undertaker opened the casket. Somebody went to the lectern and read even more scriptures. The preacher went to the pulpit and delivered his sermon again! One difference was the mourners could sit and not shuffle their feet throughout the hour-long sermon. When he finished, my family again adjusted the cover over my Grandpa. Everybody filed by, which was a motion that they could not have accomplished at the log cabin. Again, the undertaker closed the casket. My uncle helped Grandma Brown into his Ford. She said very little, but once she patted my hand and said she heard I was very smart. Grandma also said my mother would have been proud of me. That is the only conversation I remember having with her. Now we were surely going to the cemetery!

As we wound around on icy and dangerous country roads, it seemed to me that everybody from Perry County was in this funeral procession. (I could not believe that any other cars existed in Perry County.) After quite a lengthy ride we stopped at yet another church, this one Reformed. We repeated the procedure with the pallbearers, the undertakers and my Grandpa's casket again with the funeral director again opening it. Family, friends and neighbors all surrounded my frail Grandma in this little church.

They repeated everything. At least I think it was the funeral service – because the minister gave the entire service in Pennsylvania Dutch – but Uncle Albert said parts were spoken in pure German. By now the clock read two o'clock in the afternoon. We went to yet another place, probably a town hall. The service was shorter but almost the same. Then we went back to Lenninger's Lutheran Church Cemetery where the undertaker and pallbearers placed the casket over the open grave and opened it again, for the last time.

Aunt Bessie took me aside and told me that people in Perry County did not see each other for weeks at a time so funerals were wonderful events. They served as a time for people to get together. In that one day I know the good people of that county saw enough of Jeremiah Brown to at least remember him, and they decidedly heard his virtues extolled often enough.

Uncle Albert stood behind me. We stayed as cemetery workers lowered my Grandpa Brown's coffin into his grave. My uncle took a little gravel mixed with snow and dropped it into the vault. I could see he was crying, and for a moment I could not understand why my father disliked him. After all, he had been at my side through this entire ordeal. Hesitantly, I asked him if it were over, and if we would be going home after I talked one more time to my Grandma? He said, "Oh, my goodness, no. This will go on all afternoon, although we will not stay that long. People at the three places where we held the services have invited the mourners for food."

We went into the basement of Lenninger's Lutheran Church. Standing behind at least a dozen tables and chairs were smiling plump women wearing white aprons and neat hair nets. Everyone wanted to meet me, and many of them said how they loved Katie, my mother, who had died three years earlier. One of them told me that the family should sit and eat. Plenty of food graced the tables: sandwiches, slaw, potato chips, applesauce, and a Pennsylvania Dutch relish-salad called "chow-chow." One table held at least a dozen pies including what the ladies called "Funeral Pie," – reportedly their speciality.

Aunt Bessie whispered, "It's Raisin pie," and then said, "Taste a little of what you can manage. We have to eat a little something at each of the three churches and at your Grandma's house."

My conclusion of this day is that everybody in Perry County loved Jeremiah "Jerry" Brown, loved funerals, and loved to eat. They all lived so far back in the woods, "the sticks," that it was a joy to get out – even to attend a funeral. I believed then as I do now that they also lived to go to funerals to eat.

To finish the afternoon we went to the second church to eat. I am sure nobody at that funeral had to prepare an evening meal. The second church had pumpkin pie. My Aunt Bessie knew that I liked pumpkin pie so she brought a piece to our table for me. My Grandma Barnhart made the best pumpkin pie in the world. It was a pumpkin custard. When it was finished, a little milk stood on the top. The pie my aunt brought me was "truly pumpkin," and it tasted like squash. I was very disappointed.

During this long, difficult day, my Grandma Brown had stood up very well. She was a very little woman. She endured all the services and the excitement until the second meal. Suddenly this little woman told my uncle that she did not feel well, and that she was very warm. Before he could do anything, she fell forward in what we later learned was a stroke. A country doctor present at the funeral dinner diagnosed the stroke. With help from the neighbors, my family took Grandma home. My uncle stayed with her for a while. I never saw her again. The doctor told him it would be a matter of days. She lived about three weeks.

My Grandma Barnhart got another phone call from Perry County, extending to me an invitation to attend my Grandma Brown's funeral. Dad did not want me to miss another day of school, but I am sure that her service was very much like that of my Grandpa – a rural, unforgettable funeral.

A Captain's Tale:

Burial at Sea

Captain Aage Lindstad, a distinguished man with vibrant Nordic features and polished manners, recalls from his earliest memories that he always wanted to sail majestic ships on the open sea. That seems quite fitting for a young lad growing up in a small town just 80 miles north of Oslo, close to one of the largest inland lakes in Norway.

Drawing on his country's legendary seafaring heritage, the persistent youth worked feverishly and studied with passion. The future executive earned the required training and education he needed to become not only a sailor, but a captain who would sail stately cruise ships several times around the world.

He would eventually climb to a position as the vice president of Marine Operations of Royal Caribbean Cruise Lines, a decided world leader in the cruise line industry.

Following high school, Aage (pronounced aw-ge) went to sea for three and a half years as a cadet sailor with a Norwegian shipping line, after which he gained entrance to the world-renowned Merchant Marine Academy in Norway. The young sailor studied zealously during his three years of apprenticeship and training at the world-renowned school, graduating in 1960. He then spent two years in the Royal Norwegian Navy as a Reserve Second Lieutenant followed by a seven-year tour of duty with Norwegian American Lines.

Lindstad joined Royal Caribbean in 1969 as a Captain who supervised the building of the first ship he commanded, "The Song of Norway." He oversaw every aspect of construction of the 23,000-ton ship at the Wartsilla Shipyard in Helsinki, Finland for a year. On Nov. 7, 1970 he put the 1,000-passenger ship to sea on her maiden voyage. "The Song of Norway" was the first major passenger vessel ever to be lengthened – in 1978 shipbuilders cut it in two and added an 85 foot mid-section, bringing its weight to 38,000 tons. A cocktail lounge smartly cantilevered from the rear of the smokestack gives the ship its rakishly modern profile and worldwide recognition. That room has become the hallmark of every Royal Caribbean ship.

Captain Lindstad says burial at sea endured as a more common means of disposal during the early days of his career than in the 1990's.

"Some of the ships I commanded were on cruises that lasted up to 93 days, some for two months. The ships were much smaller, but often held up to 600 people, and we did have deaths on board those ships."

Please Bury Me at Sea

"Of course, during the late 1960's, we found much of our clientele to be in their sunset years," he continued. "Quite often when they came aboard the ship, they would hand me a sealed envelope with instruction that explained what I should do in the event of their death during the cruise. Often the instructions would say, "Please bury me at sea." In those days we had space for eight bodies."

Captain Lindstad says during burial at sea he always positioned the ship correctly. Otherwise, there be some problems. "The services would be in the early morning. Our nurses and doctors prepared the body for burial. Following washing and dressing, one of the sail makers on our vessel's staff would sew the body into a tarp. Then it would be weighted with lead or steel. Just before sunrise we would take the body to a lower deck, hold the ship steady at two to three knots ahead, place the tarp on a "slant" board, drape it with the appropriate national flag, and hold the religious services with whatever family and friends were on board the ship. We always made sure the wind remained on the opposite side of the ship from the services. After the service, or sometimes during the service, we tilted the board and buried the remains at sea."

A spokesman for Royal Caribbean's Marine Operations stressed that the services were simple, and the staff held a deep respect for everyone they buried from the vessel. "Those we buried at sea were often people who had sailed with us many, many times. They may have had close ties to the sea. Maybe the deceased even had a family who perished at sea, and they wished to join them in those deep waters," the spokesman said.

According to Captain Lindstad, clergymen of all faiths – Catholics, Protestant, Rabbis – have always been on board the ships to help travelers with their spiritual needs. Some 30 years ago, Captain Lindstad often asked them to conduct a funeral for someone who had died on board and wished to be buried at sea.

He recalled a Presbyterian minister who used to travel with Norwegian American Lines – and who often conducted funeral services on the open sea for the firm – specifically requesting that he be buried in the "middle of the Atlantic Ocean," saying simply, "This, the best place to be buried."

Times – and Regulations – Change

"Our longest cruise lasts 14 days. There's a qualified doctor on each of our majestic ships. The medical facilities are available 24-hours. In the event of anyone dying, the doctor on board will 'pronounce' the person and write a death certificate," Captain Lindstad said.

These days, owing to legalities and legal liabilities, if someone dies on one of our ships, we just place the body in our cooler. Our mortuary holding facility has space for four bodies, and that's ample because sometimes a helicopter will fly to the ship from the nearest port and pick up the remains. This all happens rather quickly. We can't just bury immediately at sea anymore."

"We return the body to its port of origin. Certain foreign countries have very strict regulations about bringing dead human remains into their territory," Captain Lindstad explained.

"Sometimes these countries require an autopsy. At any rate death on the open sea continues to be governed by laws of the nation that has its flag on the vessel. We just make sure that the death certificate reflects the death occurred in international waters at a given position," the executive told us, adding "The captain of the vessel will sign the appropriate documents. On our short cruises we experience about 10-15 deaths annually per million passengers."

"Save the Waves"

Over the past several years with the increasing trend in cremation, it's common to have Royal Caribbean passengers bring cremated remains aboard the vessel for scattering at sea.

"We honor these requests, of course," captain Lindstad said. "Our captains and staff assist these families. Just as in earlier days, we slow the ship down, make sure we are in a legally correct position, that the wind doesn't cause problems, and then commit the cremated remains to the sea; we scatter them. Usually, the family likes to toss some flowers into the water after they scatter the remains."

All ships in the Royal Caribbean fleet participate in the company's "Save the Waves" environmental program. This entails massive efforts on the part of the staff and guests to utilize proper recycling and conservation techniques, and eliminate the throwing of trash overboard. Royal Caribbean ensures that all scattering of cremated remains from their vessels are in accordance with Environmental Protection Agency Regulations.

Royal Caribbean offers more than 400 pages on the Internet's World Wide Web.

Captain May Order the Body Cast Into The Sea

Maritime law invests the captain of a ship "with the authority and responsibility for the health and safety of the crew and passengers. When a person dies aboard ship, the captain may, if he deems it necessary for the safety and health of the crew and passengers, order the body cast into the sea."

A 1941 lawsuit (Brambir v. Cunard White Star Ltd., 37 F. Sup. 906) involved a burial at sea. A man died while on a cruise from Liverpool to New York. Six days prior to the New York landing the captain ordered the deceased buried at sea. His widow sued the shipping line for failure to either embalm the body or notify her of the death.

The court dismissed the claim, noting, "A person who books passage on an ocean-going steamer implisedly acquiesces to be bound by the custom of the sea and consents to burial therein in the event of death during the voyage."

Burials are generally not permitted on or in land waterways. In some areas, there are requirements on the depth of the water, and remains must always be properly weighted in a special shroud to insure they sink to the bottom of the ocean rapidly and permanently. (Source: Mortuary Law, 9th edition, Stueve-Gillian, 1995).

Additionally, according to the Environmental Protection Agency, "Cremated remains shall be buried in or on ocean waters without regard to the depth limitations, provided that such burial shall take place no closer than 3 nautical miles from land."

All of these burials at sea, including the scattering of cremated human remains, shall be reported within 30 days to the nearest Regional Ocean Dumping Coordinator for the U.S. Environmental Protection Agency. The report needs to contain the date of and the latitude and longitude of the scattering, as well as the names of all persons scattered. The statement "I certify the cremated remains were scattered greater than three miles from land" must be included. (EPA Ocean Dumping Regulation 40, CFR 229.1.[d]) Many state and national funeral directors' organizations also offer guidance and brochures offering more information.

In the Azure Gulf Waters

Florida licensed embalmer Mary Mallie Fagan typifies one of the many funeral service professionals involved with burial at sea.

Fagan helps oversee more than two thousand death calls and funerals annually as the dispatch manager for the five Stewart Enterprise funeral homes found in St. Petersburg, Fla. She and husband, James M. Fagan, also independently operate a small business that scatters cremated human remains in the azure waters of Tampa Bay and the Gulf of Mexico.

The Fagans pilot a 28-foot Bayliner boat using a Loran device to ascertain they are at least three nautical miles from land. They have scattered as many as eleven remains on one trip, always moving the boat appropriately after each scattering. Mary and James say a few prayers and toss flowers in following the scattering. They mark the longitude and latitude and mail a handsome certificate documenting the location of the ceremony to the next of kin.

They have scattered for all faiths, honoring Jewish requests not to scatter on the Sabbath. Some families have asked them to scatter at nighttime, others at sunrise or sunset. Rough seas are the only reason the Fagans won't scatter for a family.

The Deep Six

Bob Harper, a St. Petersburg, Fla., funeral director and embalmer since 1947 recalls that "years ago, there were no regulations governing burial at sea...other than what the Navy prescribed. I'd often accompany a family taking a body out to sea for final disposition. We'd just go out to wherever the skipper considered the waters deep enough," Harper said.

"We'd get the canvas bag from an awning shop. In those days a funeral director and embalmer here in Florida had to be pretty handy with sewing with very heavy twine, because the responsibility fell to us to sew the bag shut. We'd use a 'palm,' a leather protective device that fits over the hand. The palm has a reinforced area in the center of it to protect the wearer's hand from the heavy needle we had to use. All the bodies were embalmed because in those days refrigeration of bodies here in Florida wasn't adequate. After we embalmed the body and got it into the canvas bag, we would put an engine block or window sash weights in to weight it down. Then, we'd lay it on a piece of plywood, put it in the hearse, and drive it out to the dock. A funeral director or embalmer would normally go on board. Burials from the East Coast of Florida are much easier than on the West Coast of the state. The shelves on the West Coast are so wide that the boats would have to go out about 100 miles."

Harper had some practical advice for any funeral director facing a family request for burial at sea of a body or cremated remains.

"These days, first, check with the U.S. Navy, and the Environmental Protection Agency for the correct guidance. There are also a number of funeral service guidebooks that have good information in them that will guide you through the process, which can be very complicated."

Commit These Earthly Remains To the Depths...Again

March 15, 1996: A day some Florida shrimpers will not soon forget. While trawling in 1,200 feet of water about 60 miles off the coast of the Diamond Shoal, the crew of a shrimping boat pulled up in its nets the "bagged" body of a man who had been autopsied and embalmed. The Duvall County Medical Examiner's office in Jacksonville, Fla. took possession of the man's decomposing body, thought to be in his sixties, dressed in a two-piece suite and tie and "plastics union-alls."

According to an Associated Press report and Lou Eliopulos, the chief Forensic Investigator for the Duvall County Medical Examiners Office, the shrimpers found the body – probably in the water anywhere from six to 18 months – wrapped in a "Zodiac" bag. Jacksonville area funeral directors contacted by Eliopulos said they have never heard of a "Zodiac" bag, which the shrimping crew lost.

The American Funeral Director spoke recently with Mr. Eliopulos, who theorizes very strong currents pulled the remains to the area from outside of Florida.

"Through the use of vital statistics, we've determined that this burial wasn't generated here in Florida. We had a lead out of a Miami funeral home, but that turned out to be false. It wasn't a military burial, because those are normally in uniform in a weighted casket. And the bodies generally have dog tags around the neck, or in the mouth."

The forensic investigator says that he has been given the medical examiner's permission to 'rebury' the remains at sea.

"We believe that the man's family wanted this. The funeral home in the county that handles indigent burials will handle the 'reburial'," Mr. Eliopulos said.

One conclusion drawn: The body was initially buried in some type of container that eroded away.

"Rest In Peace. . .Maybe!"

When people discover that a funeral director or embalmer is in their midst, they pummel him or her with the usual hackneyed jokes and questions. They want the director to tell a tall tale about a weird and wild event that allegedly happened in a cemetery or a funeral home.

The inevitable question about "Where does the blood go?" always surfaces. Then too, the line is heard, "A funeral director? OOH! How can anyone possibly do that job?" (The last person to ask me that was my dental hygienist as she scraped bacteria, food particles and possibly algae from my teeth.) Likewise, these new acquaintances will probably also describe a favorite story about their childhood. In this yarn, a dead body got up from the deathbed or casket and moved about mysteriously.

In truth, I have never experienced any of these supernatural encounters. The possible exception remains as some ghoulish trick my friends played during my internship at the Garden Sanctuary Funeral Home in Seminole, Florida. However, history abounds with certified and verifiable tales of the fate of various bodies, heads, hearts and other organs of the famous and near famous.

When the distinguished poet Percy Bysshe Shelley died at sea, friends and relatives decided to cremate him upon a funeral pyre. Before they could consummate the deed, someone cut his heart out and returned it to England. No records exist to tell us what happened to the great poet's heart.

In a similar story, when the Duke of Orleans died in 1723, physicians opened his body so that the crude embalmers of the day could preserve his heart and place it in a special box. However, before those embryonic embalmers could complete their task, the Duke's Great Dane ate almost a half of his heart. This upset the embalmers greatly.

At Least Davy Crockett Never Had This Problem

During his life, American frontiersman Daniel Boone did not stay in one place very long. United States historians tell us that whenever he saw smoke coming from a neighbor's cabin, he knew it was time to move to another location. By September 1820 ole' Daniel Boone died – and had made his final stop in Charette, Missouri. At least, that is what his family may have thought.

About twenty-five years after his death, some enterprising businesspeople from Frankfort, Kentucky invested large sums of money in a new project in the United States – a planned cemetery with some scenic views, walkways and neat landscaping. These men called the new resting place the Capital Cemetery.

Nevertheless, the nicety of nature and some seemingly perfect land wasn't enough enticement to induce families to bury their loved ones in the apparently perfect tract of land. Then one of the cemetery's promoters came up with an idea. Why not bury some truly famous Kentuckian in the new cemetery? The only problem was that the only well known Kentuckian was Daniel Boone – whose family and friends had buried on an obscure farm in the far off state of Missouri.

The owners of the cemetery acted quickly. They petitioned the Kentucky State Legislature to authorize burial of the famous homesteader and sharpshooter in their new capital city cemetery. Placing the request on a financial footing would have been much too obvious, so the cemetery promoters insisted that the disinterment and re-interment would be to correct the wrongful and unceremonious burial of Daniel Boone. Why, the people in Missouri had never even marked the grave with a monument!

The Kentucky state leaders next attempted to contact Nathan Boone and wrote a letter promising to spend ten thousand dollars to erect a suitable monument for Daniel Boone. However, they could not find Nathan – reportedly because of military business – and the group never obtained his authorization to move the body.

Not to be daunted, the Kentucky contingent next enlisted the services of Daniel Boone's elderly nephew, William Linville Boone, and two minor politicians and dispatched them to the Missouri farm once owned by the Boone family. Armed with letters of authorization signed by Daniel Boone's granddaughters, the unscrupulous trio attempted in July 1845 to persuade the owner of the farm, a Mr. Harvey Griswold, to allow the removal of bodies of Daniel Boone and his wife, Rebecca. Griswold insisted that he had paid extra money for the property because of the Boone burial. Further, he said he felt ill at ease allowing the removal of the body without Nathan Boone's approval. Arbitrations continued for hours, and finally, some three-dozen neighbors – some of whom were minor relatives of the late Daniel Boone – arrived.

Eventually, amid some objections, some approvals, and a great deal of confusion, the digging began. Finally, after excavating several graves (which they never bothered to recover), the Kentuckians discovered the hardwood casket of Daniel Boone, which Boone himself had reportedly crafted. Some bystanders took relics of Boone's bones, and the morbidly curious neighbors even passed his skull around for examination. The Kentucky contingent quickly left the Missouri farm with what few remains of Mr. and Mrs. Boone they could gather.

In September, with great ceremony back in Frankfort, the cemetery officials conducted a grand ceremony in front of the state capital building. They transferred the bones again, this time to new caskets. Again, the skull of Daniel Boone made its rounds, and an artist crafted a plaster cast of it. Bands played, the militia marched, politicians made speeches, and then they led a grand procession to the Capital Cemetery. Within weeks sales of lots increased significantly.

Within twenty years though, another controversy between the Kentuckians and the Missourians began. The cemetery owners failed to erect a monument on either the initial or the new grave of Daniel Boone. Indignant at having been swindled by the Kentucky delegation, the irate Missourians began a campaign to pressure the Kentucky state government to take decisive action. Quickly, the cemetery owners placed a monument on Boone's grave, but souvenir hunters soon defaced it, and workers had to restore it.

As late as 1987 forensic experts working for the State of Missouri claimed that the plaster replica made of Boone's skull proved that it wasn't Daniel Boone at all – and may have been that of a slave. Also in Missouri, a Warren County government official petitioned the governor to proclaim that Daniel Boone remains buried on the Griswold farm.

The Final Curtain

For years Hollywood has either denied or tried to support the story of Shakespearean actor John Barrymore's friends kidnappng his body from the Pierce Brothers Mortuary in Santa Monica, California. For the beloved actor, the final curtain fell on May 29, 1942. Barrymore's eminent biographer, John Kobler, writing in *Damned In Paradise – The Life of John Barrymore*, logically and calmly dispels the long held myth that some of Barrymore's pals stole his body.

The storyline – depending upon which version one reads – goes something like this: Director Raoul Walsh, Peter Lorre, Humphrey Bogart and Paul Henreid sat drinking in a bar holding a bodyless wake for Barrymore who essentially drank himself to death. Lorre, Bogart and Henreid had been busy filming *Casablanca* that day. The four versions alternately include or exclude Henreid, Lorre and Bogart in the execution of the body snatching. The stories agree that the conspirators all thought it would be appropriate to prop Barrymore up in Errol Flynn's living room where the bilious Barrymore spent the last three miserable weeks of his life. They decided to bribe the funeral home attendant and so gathered up several hundred dollars. Next, they drove to Pierce Brothers, made a deal with the night attendant promising to return Barrymore before dawn, and drove the remains to Flynn's home in Walsh's station wagon. There, with the help of Flynn's Russian butler, Alex, they propped Barrymore into a living room chair with a drink next to him. When Flynn came home and turned on the lights, he screamed in terror, horrified, and fled his house in panic.

Kobler points out that, despite the various versions of the story that one can find in books, TV, Radio and Tinseltown lore, the story remains false. He says that the so-called conspirators all claimed different funeral homes had possession of Barrymore's remains. Kobler also points out that Barrymore's long time friend, Gene Fowler, and his son sat with the body throughout the night, and that only one person came to pay their final respects to Barrymore – an aging prostitute.

Whatever the case, funeral directors from Pierce buried John Barrymore on June 2, 1945 in Calvary Cemetery on Whittier Boulevard in East Los Angeles. Appropriately enough, his epitaph reads, "Good Night Sweet Prince."

A Matter of Relativity

In April 1955, when Albert Einstein, the noted physicist died, his family followed his wishes and cremated his body. Nevertheless, twenty-three years passed before anyone realized that the autopsy team had removed most of Einstein's brain for study. A reporter from New Jersey discovered the dismal truth – one of the doctors, Thomas Harvey, took it with him when he moved to Kansas. He stored it in two glass jars underneath a beer cooler in his office. According to published reports from the mid nineteen nineties, the brain remains in Kansas – several museums refused to accept the grisly donation. Sad that a brain that donated such brilliance to humanity cannot even find a permanent resting place in one of our museums.

Abraham Lincoln – At Rest?

Novelists have written volumes about the disgraces that befell Abraham Lincoln's body, which by all written accounts one of our nations foremost embalmers, Henry P. Cattell, embalmed very well in 1865. For thirty-six years after his death, dozens of people tried to kidnap it in various fumbled attempts for either ransom or political reasons. During that period officials moved "Honest Abe" no fewer than seventeen times and opened his casket at least five times. In 1901, to end the state of flux that the great President's remains suffered, Robert Lincoln, his son, ordered government officials to encase Abraham Lincoln's casket inside steel bars. Next, they buried it ten feet deep and poured tons of concrete over the Great Emancipator at the National Lincoln Monument in Springfield, Illinois.

One loose fragment of Abraham Lincoln's skull exists at a Washington, D.C. museum, and in 1989 a college professor petitioned the government to allow him to extract genetic material from the fragment for medical research. Will we ever allow one of our greatest Presidents to rest in peace? Maybe.

ᴀɴɴᴀʟs ᴏꜰ ᴀᴍᴇʀɪᴄᴀɴ ꜰᴜɴᴇʀᴀʟ ꜱᴇʀᴠɪᴄᴇ ʜɪꜱᴛᴏʀʏ:

Colonial Autopsies, Anatomy Riots & Sordid Grave Robbers

"Good friend, for Jesus sake forbear
to dig the dust enclosed here
Blessed be ye the man that spares these stones
And cursed be he that moves my bones"
-William Shakespeare's epitaph

The Grave Robbers of Colonial America enjoyed a rich occupational heritage inherited from their European counterparts called "The Resurrectionists" or "The Sack-em Up Men". Some background knowledge of primitive autopsies conducted in the Colonial time period is necessary to completely understand the historical significance of the "New York Anatomy Riot of 1788."

An erudite medical scholar, Krumbhaar, writing in "The Early History of Anatomy in the United States" (printed in the September 1922 publication of "Annals of Medical History") noted that in "a country as young as the United States it is a comparatively easy matter to trace the growth of a science from its earliest beginning, and medicine is no exception to this rule."

Surgeons and physicians as early as the Jamestown Colony recognized the need for post mortem dissection. These doctors and teachers translated the need to examine dead human bodies into the curriculum for various brief anatomy classes.

Ample documentation exists to prove the presence of various physicians in the early United States of America. Thomas Wooton, the "Chirurgeon Gentleman of Captain John Smith" sailed to the United States on December 19, 1606 as the attending physician to the English Expedition. Samuel Fuller, also a physician, accompanied the Pilgrims on the Mayflower. Sebastian Crol and Jan Huyck, Dutch men of medicine, came with Peter Minuit during the transmigration of 1626. We know three Welsh physicians, Thomas Lloyd, Griffith Owen, and Thomas Wynne, arrived with the illustrious William Penn in1682. Various published reports confirm their assistance in founding Philadelphia and "Penn's Sylvania."

John Eliot (1604-1690) remains one of the earliest and best known authors to chronicle the activities of the various East Coast Indian tribes in the early Colonial period. On September 24, 1647, John Eliot wrote a letter from his Roxbury home to the Reverend Thomas Shephard of Cambridge, New England. In it he observed that the "young Students of Physick" were " forced to fall to practice before ever they saw an anatomy made."

Other writers – notably Firmin and Hartwell – discuss early Colonial autopsies in the January 1881 "Annals of Anatomy and Surgery." While the two physicians disagree about the literal meaning of Eliot's writing, Hartwell suggests that "this was the earliest utterance in America, in recognition of the importance of Anatomical Studies." However, both writers do maintain that John Eliot attempted to "instruct the Red Men in Anatomy and Physick."

They base this premise on his statement "Some of the wiser sort I have stirred up to this skill. I have showed them the anatomy of man's body, and some general principles of Physick."

Another suggestion of an early American autopsy comes to us from the diary of Judge Samuel Sewall of Boston, who on September 22,1676 wrote, "Spent the day from nine in the morning with Messrs. (Doctors) Brakenbury, Thompson, Butter, Hooper, Craig and Pemberton dissecting the middle most of the Indians executed the day before." Students of American funeral service history perhaps best remember Judge Sewall for his accurate and lengthy descriptions of Colonial Funeral Behavior. (See *The History of American Funeral Directing*, Habenstein and Lamers, pp. 201.)

Packard, a noted medical historian writing in *The History of Medicine in the United States* (1901) records six autopsies in New England between 1674 and 1678. A manuscripted "Order of the Council of Lord Baltimore" dated "Saint Mary's, in Maryland, July 20, 1670" directs two "Chyrurgeons" to view on Monday, August 8,1670 the head of one Benjamin Price, allegedly killed by Indians.

For a considerable period, many eminent medical writers believed Dr. Johannes Kerfbyle conducted the first autopsy held in the United States. In 1691, the doctor and five physicians acting as his assistants dissected the body of Governor Slaughter of New York who died so suddenly that civil authorities suspected poisoning.

However, Dr. Thomas Cadwalader (1708-1779) of Philadelphia began offering a course of Practical Anatomy, replete with dissections, as early as 1750. Dr. Cadwalader completed his own training in Anatomy Instruction at the University of Rheims and in London where dissection of cadavers remained a constant in medical education.

During that same year, according to Hartwell, Doctors John Bard and Dr. Peter Middleton of New York City injected and dissected the body of one Hermanus Carrol. Existing public records are vague, but it appears that the government executed Carrol for an unspecified crime. No mention of what preservative the doctors used remains on record. Officials granted Bard and Middleton the right to use Carroll's body "for the instruction of young men engaged in the study of medicine."

The scholar Krumbhaar located a rare copy of *The New York Weekly Postboy* of January 17, 1752. He found an advertisement for Dr. Thomas Wood, Surgeon, printed in that early Colonial newspaper. In his pronouncement of lectures Dr. Wood says that he will "give a Course in Osteology and Myology" in the city of New Brunswick the following month. It further reads,

"Whereas Anatomy is allowed on all lands to be the foundation of both PHYSICK and SURGERY, and consequently, without some Knowledge of it, no person can be duly qualified to practice either, this is therefore to inform the Publick.........that a Course in which all the HUMAN BONES will be separately examined, and their connections and dependence on each other demonstrated, and all the muscles of a human body dissected, the ORGANS, INFERTION, and Use of each plainly thewn. This course is proposed to be completed in the space of one month.......If proper encouragement is given in this course, he (Dr. Wood) PROPOFES foon after, to go thro' a course of ANGIOLOGY and NEUROLOGY, and conclude, with performing all the OPERATIONS of SURGERY on a DEAD BODY, the use of which will appear to every person, who considers the necessity of having at least seen them performed before he presumes to perform them himself on any of his living fellow creatures."

This announcement by Dr. Wood predates by at least two years the presumption by many medical scholars and historians that the Scotsman William Hunter offered one of the first better-known anatomical courses. Professor Hunter gave those classes at Newport, Rhode Island in 1754, 1755 and 1756. Hunter was a relative of the famous brothers – John and William Hunter.

Noted Funeral Service Education Historian Dr. Edward C. Johnson of Chicago has discussed the Hunters in several scholarly treatments. We find Johnson's most recent writing concerning the Hunters in *Embalming: History, Theory and Practice*, by Robert Mayer, Third Edition, pages 458-459.

These sporadic attempts at medical teaching pointed to the need for a medical college in the United States. The two founders of the first medical school in "British America" were Dr. William Shippen and Dr. John Morgan. They both were natives of Philadelphia who traveled to the Old World to complete their medical education, and attend lectures and demonstrations presented by the world's most eminent physicians, surgeons and anatomists. Medical educators in London, Edinburgh, Leyden and Paris offered lectures in Anatomy, complete with dissection.

In 1762, Dr. Shippen returned to the United States from European studies. Late in the summer of that year, he began teaching anatomy to a private class of about a dozen young men. Three years later, Dr. Morgan, who has been called "the Founder of American Medicine" by many medical historians also returned home to Philadelphia, having attended many European medical courses. By May 1765, Dr. Morgan had convinced the trustees of the College of Philadelphia to allow him and Dr. Shippen to begin teaching several courses in medicine including Anatomy and Surgery.

A stalwart group of some of the citizens of Philadelphia became greatly alarmed when they learned that Doctors Shippen and Morgan had opened an Anatomical Theatre. Rioters repeatedly interrupted Dr. Shippen's autopsies. Norris, writing in *The Early History of Medicine in Philadelphia*, notes that "in one of these attacks, the anatomist escaped by passing out through an alley, while his carriage, which stood before the door with its blinds raised, and which was supposed to contain him, received, along with a shower of other missiles, a musket ball through the centre of it." (sic) Norris also contends that Shippen quite often had to leave his home and conceal himself to avoid bodily harm.

A number of newspaper accounts exist today that show that Dr. Shippen addressed the public to assure them that private burial grounds had not been disturbed. His explanations state that all of his subjects were suicides (recall that most churches did not allow suicides to be buried in consecrated grounds, and that most burial ground in Philadelphia at that time belonged to the churches), or prisoners who the authorities had executed. Shippen did, rather disingenuously add, that "every now and then, one of the subjects may have come from Potter's Field." Eventually, his charisma, tact, and honorable conduct did lead at least the authorities and a small group of citizenry to respect him and support him in his attempts to educate medical students in the subject of Anatomy.

Medical educators at King's College (now Columbia College) in New York City soon began to offer courses in Anatomical Instruction. New York City ranked second in population to Philadelphia according to the first United States Census of 1760. The city of Brotherly Love had some forty two thousand people living there while thirty three thousand people called New York home. The total population of the United States was approximately four million people. At King's College, Dr. Samuel Clossy, an Irish physician and educator trained in Dublin, offered students the nation's second course in Anatomy beginning on November 25, 1763.

The then-popular prejudice against dissection fueled many acts of violence in the United States. In New York, the mass of protestors that mobbed the anatomists on Sunday, April 13, 1788, serves as one of the best examples of the serious and spectacular incidents that occurred in Colonial America. Newspapermen of the time illogically called it "The Doctor's Mob" because most of the rioting took place in and around the New York Hospital. A newspaper itself, *The New York Packet*, served as the impetus for the riot, when it reported that grave robbers stole bodies from two well-known church graveyards, Trinity and Brick Presbyterian.

The rioters had long suspected that physicians had been robbing the private graves of the city in order to obtain subjects for dissection. The newspaper report inflamed them, and moved them to action. A huge mob of people congregated at the front of the hospital, and eventually, the leaders found their way into the dissecting rooms. There, they found several human bodies in various stages of dissection. This enraged the protestors, and they seized heads, arms, legs, and fingers and began displaying the body parts at the windows for the public to view. Outside, the rioters became so angry and boisterous that administrators of the college summoned the military authorities to quell the disturbance. With the riot continuing for two more days, the militia confined the medical students in the common prison in order to protect them from the rioters.

Several different versions of the riot exist today. One newspaper account says that the military killed no one. However, Packard records that the mass of protestors knocked Baron Steuben, a government official, to the ground. In his anger, Steuben ordered the Mayor, James Duane, to have the militia fire into the mass of rioters. According to the Packard version, gunfire killed at least seven rioters, and as many were severely injured.

Hartwell, writing in *The Hindrances to Anatomical study In the United States*, quotes a newspaper report that maintains militia fire killed five persons and wounded eight persons. He further notes that the riot had some positive outcome as the New York State Legislature passed legislation prohibiting robbing graves. Legislators named that statute, (Chapter III, of the Laws of the 112th Session of New York) "An Act to prevent the odious practice of digging up and removing, for the purpose of dissection, dead Bodies interred in cemeteries or burial places." (sic)

Another case of grave robbery involves a prominent American family in 1878. Mr. John Scott Harrison, who had been a Senator and the son of the ninth President, died on May 26 of that year. His family buried him in a cemetery in north Bend, Ohio. Less than a week after the burial, Benjamin Harrison, his son whom Americans would elect President in 1888 went to Cincinnati, Ohio to search for the remains of a friend. Harrison had reason to believe that he would find the remains at the Ohio Medical College. There, instead, he found the remains of his father, John Scott Harrison. Benjamin Harrison knew that the Ohio Medical College officials were not responsible and reportedly did not pursue the matter legally. A 1989 report in the Journal of Forensic Sciences says that a professional grave robber known alternately as Dr. Henri le Caron, or Charles Morton, and his wife obtained the late Harrison's body under an agreement with the College. Family members reclaimed the elder Harrison's body and reburied it in an undisclosed location. This high profile grave robbery called attention to the medical college's need for cadavers, and many states subsequently passed laws that enabled the colleges to obtain bodies through legal means.

Habenstein and Lamers maintain that the desire to keep the dead safe from human harm influenced coffin (and so-called "vault") designers of the very early 19th century. British trade undertakers who offered families iron coffins, mortsafes, and a variety of "ghoul proof burial receptacles" also widely contributed to early American Colonial funeral behavior.

Callous American Grave Robbers

William Cunningham reportedly filled cadaver orders for the Ohio Medical College. To show the extent of his greed, he even sold them his own body, and visitors to the Cincinnati College of Medicine may view his skeleton. Dr. Thomas Sewall, a Massachusetts physician, engaged in some "double dipping" as a moonlighting grave robber. Police discovered his nighttime occupation, however, and he was eventually discredited, somewhat. Doctors Joseph Warren and John Collins Warren developed a group of "Resurrectionists" called the "Spunkers" whose biggest challenge, besides getting the body, was to not get caught, for being apprehended was the true crime. The Surgeon General's Office in Washington, D.C. served as the headquarters for George Christian's body snatching and delivery service. (For more information, read Schultz, S.M. *Body Snatching: The Robbing of Graves for the Education of Physicians*) Graves near medical schools were usually targets of grave robbers. Some reports say that graveyards near the University of Maryland School of Medicine in Baltimore are nearly empty. Former *American Funeral Director* Editor Nick Verrastro, writing in 1991, says that some of the reportedly empty graves in Baltimore such as that of Edgar Allen Poe, his wife, and her family were not robbed. (In an odd twist of fate, Poe wrote *The Premature Burial*.)

THE LIFE AND TIMES OF EDWARD C. JOHNSON

America's Embalmer Emeritus and Dean of American Funeral Service History

Edward C. Johnson is considered to be one of the leading historians of embalming and American funeral service. His illustrious career includes work as an educator and Dean at several mortuary science schools, worldwide travels to many foreign countries as a U.S. army officer and diplomat, travels to present embalming seminars with his beloved late wife Gail, the writing of more than 600 technical articles, service as an expert witness in civil court cases, the operation of a well known and highly respected Chicago funeral home and trade service, and the continuance of his scholarly Civil War writings.

(Photo by Mac McCormick)

Despite a myriad of humanitarian achievements that would swell the chests of any who had achieved much less, Edward C. Johnson prevails as one of the kindest, most thoughtful, intelligent and sensitive men one could encounter. His 50-year (1988) Illinois Funeral Directors Association citation states that he "sets an inspiring example of devotion and fidelity to the duties and obligations of the profession, with leadership and unselfish participation in the public affairs of the community."

At age 85, his hands remain as steady as those of an 18-year-old. The distinguished embalmer completes surgeons' exercises daily to keep his fingers nimble. He's still very active in his funeral business. He manages to sleep about five hours nightly. He wakes up daily at 6 A.M. and often spends the day talking with authors, students, and scholars who call on him for information on restorative art, embalming and American funeral service history.

One such author is Christine Quigley (among her works: *Modern Mummies*, *The Corpse*, and *Death Dictionary*) who has formed a unique bond with the affable professor. She values her relationship with Dr. Johnson.

"Edward Johnson is an inexhaustible source of information. As a practicing embalmer well into his 'retirement,' he keeps up-to-date with current literature. At the same time, his archives reach back half a century and more. He is generous with his time and with the resources and contacts he has built up over his long career. He is a mentor to many, myself included."

A genuinely pleasant person, Johnson continues to be a historian, journalist, loving father and grandfather, whose meaningful contributions to society need to be noted. Among them are many articles published in a number of industry magazines including *Hizone Supplements, Embalmers Monthly, Casket and Sunny Side, American Funeral Director, Canadian Funeral Service, British Embalmer,* and the *Encyclopedia Britannica.*

Timeline and Recollections

Edward C. Johnson was born on June 29, 1914 in Chicago, IL, the only child of physician Edward Wesley Johnson (1865-1952) from Jacksonville, IL and Kathryn Barbara Graef (1878-1958) of Milwaukee, WI, a monogram artist, who were married in 1911 in Chicago (another son was stillborn).

The Johnson family is of English ancestry. They first settled in either Virginia or North Carolina, moved on to Kentucky, and then on to Jacksonville, IL. Ed Johnson's grandfather, a tinsmith, operated a furniture and coffin factory.

"My father was too old for WWI," Johnson recalled, "but he had an inventive mind and in the period 1914-1918 had several inventions…among them, an aerial bomb…so in order for him to fly in military planes to test this bomb, they had to give him a brevet. My mother's father, Grandfather Graef, a German by birth, was in the Civil War, and the Union Army decorated him for his bravery." (Later, some of his grandfather's musings in the German language about the Civil War become the inspiration for Johnson's book, *All Were Not Heroes*).

From 1920-1932, Johnson attended grade school and some high school in Chicago.

In 1932, Edward's father became ill, so his aunt (his father's sister) invited the family to Spokane, Washington. His father eventually was placed in a sanitarium. Edward graduated from high school and studied pre-medicine at Spokane Junior College where Johnson competed in swimming and track and the Senate Club, a forum for public speaking.

Unfortunately, the college went bankrupt. Johnson explored other areas. Because he had a strong desire to be in the military, he enlisted in the National Guard in 1932.

The following year, he was called to active duty during the "Lumberman Riots" in Tacoma.

It was from 1934-1936 that Johnson began his funeral director/embalmer apprenticeship.

The Genesis of A Distinguished Career

"I began to look for earnest employment," Johnson said. "You know, then, jobs were very difficult to find. So, you began to think about what type of job is not very popular. Therefore, you don't have a lot of competition. You come up with grave digging. Well, that is hard work. It requires a certain degree of accuracy. They do a lot of other things, too, besides digging an empty grave. They go and disinter people, and all that sort of thing.

"You think of working in cattle processing plants, back then they were called slaughterhouses. Well, the main jobs that were there, of course, were killing cattle. You hit them on the head to stun them, then cut their throat; the next guy strings them up and disembowels them. These are not things the average person would want to do – nor was undertaking at that time. My mother thought that undertaking was a good idea. 'Oh, those gentlemen,' she said, 'they are always so well dressed, well groomed, and they carry themselves in an elegant manner', and so on. She didn't know any more than the façade she saw during a funeral," he continued.

"My mother called some undertakers in Spokane, and she found one who said he was looking for an apprentice. I worked with a gentleman by the name of Oscar G. Merager who had gone to school at the Worsham College in Chicago. He and Albert Worsham apparently hit it off very well. Merager said that Worsham treated him like a son."

Merager, who was the owner of the firm of Turnbull and Merager, was greatly interested in restorative art. The system that existed in Spokane at that time was ideal for such training. They had no city morgue. There were about five funeral homes, and about 100,000 people in the city. So the funeral directors arranged between themselves that they would rotate a coroner month and a welfare month. "Now, that did not mean that your firm automatically got the call," Johnson said. "What happened was that we would trade, either embalming or cremation. We saw a lot of serious trauma from car accidents, because the glass that was in those cars didn't shatter like it does today – there was no safety glass. We embalmed 'barefoot,' that means, without gloves. We didn't know then what we know now about bacteria and disease. I didn't know anything about anything. We used gravity injectors. We often embalmed in the funeral home. Merager had enclosed the back porch – unheated, except in the summer time."

An Illustrious Career in Embalming Almost Ends Before it Begins

An unusual situation early in Ed Johnson's career nearly resulted in the amputation of his fingers. "I remember once in January, it was very cold, and I was washing down a car. I had very chapped hands, you know, cracks in the skin. Mr. Merager came from the prep room and told me he had a removal, but that he had a funeral he had to take out…He had to go upstairs to dress. He told me to go get the permit and to go and make the removal, but be sure to be back in time for the funeral. When we got to the house, there was this little woman, with her legs painted all purple."

"When I got back, before the funeral, my instructions were to raise the arteries and inject a gallon of embalming fluid, using the gravity injector. In this case, there were areas where the purple color was black. A couple of days later, my hands started itching. Then, a red line went up my arm, and I got lumps in the axillary area. My hand became the size of a boxing glove, and I couldn't bend my fingers. Mr. Merager noticed it. I never complained, but he said, 'Come on, we are going to the doctor.' The doctor looked at it. We were upstairs in the fifth floor of the office building. I didn't know it at the time, but he had a huge rubber mallet in his hand. He told me to move toward the window, so he could have more light. Then, he told Mr. Merager and me that there was a doctor's office across the street, and to look quick, because there was a woman undressing. Next thing I knew, I felt him grab my arm, and Whack! God, I could feel that pain all the way to the base of my brain. He whacked it three or four times more. The pus flew everywhere. At one point, the doctor told me he was planning on amputating my fingers. I had to keep the hand soaked in a solution of hot Epsom salts for several days, but wouldn't let him amputate. It eventually cleared up. From this, I also developed tremendous resistance and antibodies to Strep. I have also never had a successful smallpox take. Never."

Recollections of Worsham's Class of '36

Edward Johnson served as class president of Worsham's class of 1936, and was the class valedictorian.

"After I was at the firm of Turnbull and Merager for a while, I discovered that to get a license, I either had to work as an apprentice for two years, or go to school, and then take the exam," Johnson said. "My boss suggested I go to Worsham, which he thought was the best school in the nation. I left Spokane, and went back to Chicago. Since Mr. Merager was a dear friend of Albert Worsham, he gave me a small delivery to take to him for when I got there. And the old man became very friendly to me.

"The school at that time had a unique method of teaching restorative art. You know, the way restorative art is taught today, you model on a skull and so forth. You learn a little bit about the projections and proportions, but it doesn't teach you how to actually handle a case."

Albert Worsham had anatomy dissection – four students to a body. "We embalmed those bodies ourselves first, but then we didn't dissect the head. We cut the head off the body, at the end of dissection, and put it in a crock of embalming fluid, and had the rest of the body cremated. Then, at the end of our restoration art class, for one week, all day long, all we did was restore those mutilated heads. We had little card tables that we worked at, and we then actually built a base for a nose, an ear, a jaw, then cosmetized it. This is where I got some basis of my knowledge of restorative art."

These Were Different Days...

From 1936-1940, Johnson begins work for the firm of Smith and Maginot as a funeral director and embalmer.

"In these early times, we were still embalming in the home. We were still taking casketed bodies home. We would embalm nuns in the convent with the nuns sitting there watching and praying. Those were different times. We had the rules of contagious disease. These were laws here in Chicago. We had the rule about not moving the body from the place where it died, except to the place of final disposition, such as the crematory or the cemetery. At the Contagious Disease Hospital in Chicago, there was a separate little chapel for casketed remains that had a big plate glass window, like a store front window. The entrance to it was not from the chapel side, but from an interior corridor. If you had a death in the Contagious Disease Hospital, you embalmed the body there, dressed the body there, casketed the body there, had the viewing and at the time of the funeral, an inspector from the Health Department would come around. Most of the caskets at this time were cloth-covered wood, and they would put two sealing thumbscrews into the lid and into the wood body of the casket. These tops contained lead, and they would break that off. This was supposed to prevent anyone from opening the casket at any time."

A Unique and Unusual Project Request

In 1939, Dr. Hilton Ira Jones, chemist and owner of the Hizone Chemical Company, approached Professor Johnson to work on a project at the start of World War II to collect blood from cadavers for use in the war effort. In Jones' words, the response from Americans for blood donations for the war overseas was slow. According to Johnson, the Russians developed the following system in 1939 – they elevated the body on a table, feet raised, massaged the body, and opened a jugular to collect the blood.

Jones thought that they could help the war effort after a large mid-western pharmaceutical company executive approached him with the idea. He asked Ed Johnson how they could get the funeral directors behind the idea.

The problem was – very few funeral homes had the metal-rimmed or glass-top embalming tables that could pivot to allow the elevation of the body.

"In those days, some of us still drained into a bucket that had to be emptied," Johnson said. "This presented even more challenges. We developed a new drain tube with a sterile collecting bottle. We didn't have to have permission to do this. Blood was a waste product anyway. What killed the blood collection program was racism. Members of various races vocalized their wishes that they not receive blood from an unknown source. The plan called for setting this program up in districts. We would have sent the blood to a collection station, a processing station, and onward to storage centers."

From 1940-1944, Johnson worked for the John Pedersen Funeral Home of Chicago.

During the 1940s, the National Boards were totally hand written, and the answers were subjective. Johnson helped grade mortuary service exams for four years, often grading up to 400 sets of examinations per sitting.

In 1942, Johnson wrote a major revision to *Encyclopedia Britannica* and *Universal Encyclopedia* (Embalming Sections).

World War II

Ed Johnson was taking courses in the Enlisted Reserve Corps (1939 – 1943) to become an officer. With his college, previous enlisted background and these courses, he qualified for a commission. Still, he couldn't pass the physical because of his eyesight. "At that time, they called up the National Guard, and they had the Illinois Reserve Militia, the Replacement Group," Johnson said. "I enlisted as a Corporal, in 1942, after Pearl Harbor, and I was a member of the regimental Rifle Team. I volunteered for active duty, but they kept turning me down, telling me to wait for the draft. It was all very peculiar. Finally, in early 1944, they called me up in the draft."

That year, Johnson traveled the world on tankers. Some evasive maneuvers resulted in Johnson breaking his ribs.

He received a number of service medals for his duty in

Ed Johnson on his 31st birthday "somewhere in Persia."

the Atlantic, European-Middle East, Mediterranean, as well as in the Pacific theaters of operation.

In 1945, he demonstrated embalming in Hobart, Tasmania, and Australia. In Adelaide, Australia, a local Australian Funeral Directors Association honored him at a banquet for "The History of Embalming" in *Casket and Sunny Side*, which he wrote in 1942. (See page 138.)

That same year, Johnson received his honorable discharge from the service. He returned to Chicago to work for Worsham College as assistant dean and as an instructor.

In 1947 Johnson established a funeral home and trade business in Chicago.

"It grew like topsy...at its peak, we had about 2,000 calls per year, most of them trade calls from other directors. I had former students who would call me up and say, 'Hey, Professor J., I left orders at a hospital for you to pick up a body and embalm it.' Until 1947, I didn't have a place to do the embalming. I always had to go to some friend's funeral home. Finally, I said, this is ridiculous, and I opened my own business at 813 Diversey Parkway."

In 1948 Johnson assumed duties as dean and instructor for the Post Graduate Institute of Restorative Art – a position he held for 10 years, with an average of 60 students annually.

"We developed models of rubber and plastic that you could suture, restore faces on and cosmetize," Johnson said. "We had cut out pillow tops, so that we could put that around the student's model and make it look like an actual case, viewed under various

Ed Johnson, circa 1942, when he worked for the John M. Pedersen Funeral Home in Chicago as a licensed funeral director and embalmer.

lighting situations." (He had a collection of over 1,000 life masks of his restorative art students).

Also in 1948, Johnson was commissioned in the Quartermaster Corps as a Captain, in the Graves Registration Division of the U.S. Army Reserve.

The Officer Looks Back

"We met weekly in those days, and then I had annual duty at Ft. Lee, Va., which was the Quartermaster School Headquarters and Training Point," Johnson said. "I also served in Washington, at the office of the Chief of the Memorial Branch. During my last two to three years, (1963-1966) in Washington, I served at the Office of the Chief of the U.S. Army Historical Branch."

In 1950, Johnson was a major contributor to the National Funeral Directors Association's publication of "Funeral Customs the World Over" and "The History of American Funeral Directing." He also developed a funeral service/ embalming correspondence course from Saskatchewan, Canada. (For several years, he traveled there to teach funeral service seminars. Both Professor and Mrs. Johnson presented embalming seminars in Mexico, France, Spain, England, Japan, the Philippines, and El Salvador, as well. Professor Johnson eventually received the Roblot Foundation Award, for his distinguished international work in funeral service in France and throughout all of Europe.)

Well-known author Robert G. Mayer (*Embalming: History, Theory and Practice*), a long-time friend and collaborator of Johnson, wrote that Johnson profited very little from these trips.

"During the years when he traveled doing seminar work, it is important to remember that he was not being financed by chemical companies, schools or associations – he was an independent presenter – many seminars would have been a break-even venture," Mayer said. "It was the love of sharing his knowledge of the fields of embalming and restorative art that drove him to travel and speak."

(It is fitting to note that Edward and his late wife, Gail Johnson, along with their daughter, Melissa Johnson Williams, all made contributions to Mayer's current and previous embalming texts, both in the embalming and restorative art history areas. Robert G. Mayer has also dedicated the text to Professor Johnson).

1950: Happiness

Edward Johnson fondly recalls his many memories of Gail Richardson.

"She and I hit it off perfectly. She was a licensed embalmer and funeral director. I met her in 1949 at the Post Graduate Institute of Restorative Art, while she was a student in my classes. Eventually, she and I married...and stayed so for 46 years."

Originally from the hills of eastern Kentucky, Gail Johnson served in the Navy as a pharmacist mate third class during World War II. She graduated from the Renouard School of Embalming in New York. The State Department cited her for massive assistance during the Jonestown, Guyana crisis. Mrs. Johnson also conducted studies concerning the effect of fluorescent lighting on embalmed jaundiced tissues in infants. She also enjoyed a lengthy mortuary science teaching career. Professor G. Johnson was a horseback-riding enthusiast, winning many jumping championships.

A formal portrait of Gail Johnson hangs in Professor Johnson's living room. The stately red-haired woman, 10 years younger than Edward Johnson, died at age 71 in 1995. Her remains are at rest in Arlington National Cemetery.

They have three daughters, Melissa Johnson Williams, a well-known embalmer and funeral service journalist, Paula DeSmet, and Victoria Lang. There are seven grandchildren, and one great-grandchild. One granddaughter (Melissa Johnson Williams' daughter, Bess Boffey) is planning a career in funeral service.

In 1958, Ed Johnson returned to Worsham as an adjunct professor. He taught restorative art and history of American funeral service and embalming.

The Late 1950s

The Johnsons begin composing and compiling rules and regulations for shipping human remains by air. They tested casket seals in an air pressure chamber at the University of Illinois. Together, they issued a report on "an air Pressure Test in an Altitude Pressure Chamber on Sealed Caskets" in 1958. Both Ed and Gail Johnson served as consultants to major airlines on problems relating to air shipments. Professor Johnson testified at Federal Aviation Administration hearings on the matter. He and Mrs. Johnson flew to virtually every continent testing various containers and inspecting airline procedures concerning handling human remains.

Operations in the Congo

In 1961, Ed Johnson became the first Chief of Mortuary Operations for the United Nations – a key role in the international organization. "In the period of 1960-1961, there were serous clashes in the Congo between the government and dissident groups," Johnson said. "My predecessor, a Belgian doctor who used archaic methods, would only embalm one body a day, although they might bring seven in, and he required payment in gold deposited to his account in Belgium. The Indian Army wanted U.S. embalming methods. They contacted Washington, and the job of selecting an embalmer fell to the Air Force Chief of Mortuary Operations. He called me and told me that he wanted me to go to the Congo. I said, 'What for? I'm not interested.' Well, two days later, and I won't go any further on this, I got another call from Washington."

The implication was clear. Johnson had to either go, or his reserve officer career was in jeopardy. "Finally, the personnel manager from the State Department called me and said that I could not go as an officer; that I would be going as a civilian," he said. "I went over to Leopoldville and reported to the American military attache. They attached me to the 152nd Indian Army Hospital Unit. At that time, I was a Major in the U.S. Army Reserve."

When he first arrived in the Belgian Congo in 1961, after they declared independence, U.N. troops asked Ed Johnson how many syringes he would require. He asked what they meant by syringes. The answer: "You know, like the veterinarians have."

He recalled how his predecessor embalmed: "The embalming was completed with syringes, after head and trunk evisceration. Viscera was buried in the front lawn of the hospital. He injected the body with formalin and injected the entire body, until the 'embalmer' and his assistant passed out from fumes. They crawled outside on their hands and knees and filled their lungs with air, and minutes later, after their lungs had cleared, they returned to finish the so-called embalming. You can imagine what condition the body would be in, given the hundreds of puncture marks and the extreme heat. They put the body into a coffin half full of sawdust and zinc sulfate. Then, they filled the coffin with more sawdust and zinc sulfate. The base of the inside coffin was galvanized zinc. It was soldered shut. That coffin was then placed into another coffin, this one of sheet lead. They soldered this one, too, and placed it into a hardwood coffin two inches thick, screwed down with heavy iron bands put around the heat and foot. The whole thing weighted more than 1,000 pounds."

While embalming in the Congo, Johnson used an electric injector and bribed customs officials with whiskey to get the embalming fluid into the country. Also, while there, he worked with U.N. Forces on experimental methods (alternate to dog tags) of identifying bodies.

One incident, Johnson recalled was the 1962 murder of an American Military Attache.

"I looked out in the streets of Leopoldville one morning, and I saw native troops, U.N. troops, and the Nigerian police, which were part of the U.N. Forces. I began my walk to the hospital and as I'm walking along, I see them almost every block. When I get to the hospital, everyone is going crazy. 'We've been waiting for you all morning,' they said. I asked, 'What's the matter?'"

Johnson was told that the American Military attache, Lt. Col. Stogner, had been murdered. "Somehow, the troops got the telephone to work, and they got through to the embassy," Johnson said. "Someone there said that I should get to the embassy as fast as I could, that the ambassador and some other people wanted to talk to me. I grabbed an ambulance and a Gurkha driver and went over to the embassy, and went into the ambassador's office.

"There was a group of high-ranking people there, and I was asked if I knew what had happened. I said that I heard that the American military attache had been killed, but I didn't know anything beyond that. 'Well,' they said, 'We don't know where the body is.' I asked the authorities where they were told the attache had been taken. The ambassador said: 'They told us that they took the body to the hospital, but we don't know which one.'

"I said: 'Well, that's great, because they should have brought him here.' The ambassador said, 'We know that, we know that.'"

As the discussion continued, Johnson and the ambassador were informed that the body had been found at Queen Elizabeth Hospital, but the hospital wouldn't surrender the body.

"So I asked the Colonel if I could take the ambulance and the driver to go over to Queen Elizabeth Hospital. He said, 'Of course, Major, go ahead.'

"I got over there to the hospital and the Mother Superior pretended that she didn't speak English. She was motioning all over the place. By this time, I am standing in the lobby and starting to talk a little louder, and along came a man who said, 'Pardon me, I speak French, may I translate for you?' I said, 'I would appreciate it.' I said to him, 'I want you to tell her exactly what I say to you. Don't deviate. Tell her I am an American embalmer and funeral director. My job is to prepare the American military attache's body for his return to his home in the United States. I need the body now. In the event that she equivocates, you tell her that I am also an expert with explosives, and that I suspect that they have locked the body up in an iron Quonset hut.

"Imagine this now; it's 95 degrees at seven o'clock in the morning.

"I continued: 'I'll blow the doors off that place as soon as I get back from the ordinance depot. I'll be leaving here as soon as she decides.' He told her, 'You better do this, this guy is a nut.' She handed me a key several inches long. I handed it to the driver, and we went around, and sure enough, there, in the Quonset hut, was the body of the murdered American military attache. We took him back to the hospital and into my operating room."

Attacked

"Now, I'm getting ready to go report to the Colonel when there is all this pounding on the door. I said, 'What the hell?' I opened the door, which was self-locking and quickly stepped out into the corridor of the hospital. Here's a mixed group of men, some in uniforms, some not, some rag-a-muffin looking types, some in suits. They were talking to me in French, then pointing into the room. I get the idea. They want the body. The Mother Superior had called these men right away when I took him.

"I noted that half of them were armed – some with batons, some with pistols, clubs, revolvers or rifles. I backed up against the wall, thinking that at least I won't get shot or hit in the back...maybe I will have half a chance of parrying the blow from the front. And, low and behold, they started in...they started to beat me. Fortunately, they had so many people...this was in a very narrow corridor…that they couldn't get a good swing. I don't know why they never thought of shooting me…they all thought of those rifles as clubs. One of them hit me in the jaw, and I suffered a dislocated jaw, and bruises on the top of my head and all up and down my arms.

"I should mention that every Indian Army Hospital is totally independent and self-sufficient. They don't need help from anybody. They have sweepers, they have gardeners, they have washers, painters, and they have their own armed guard to defend the place. In the meantime, the lab men were watching this. They called the armed guard, and they came in with a squad and threw this bunch that was attacking me out of the hospital compound. Literally, I saw them pick men up and throw them out of the hospital area.

"They took me upstairs and stitched me up, and gave me a quarter grain of morphine. Then they told me they wanted to take me to the operating room and put me under. I said, 'No way, I had my duty to do as an embalmer.' I went back to my operating room, embalmed the military attache under the influence of several more pain killers, and I tell you, I nearly floated home. We did eventually get a letter telling us that the funeral director back in the U.S. had received the body in excellent condition."

The blow that Edward Johnson received on his head in that struggle detached several of his lens fibers, and he woke up one morning blinded. He has experienced obscured vision over the years, and continues to have trouble to this day.

Two great funeral directors and professors visit the Great Pyramids, 1962.
(*Photo courtesy of Melissa Johnson*)

Sir Knight Edward Johnson

In 1963, the Consul General of Italy presented Ed Johnson with a ribbon and medal for great distinction: The Order of the Cavalier and the Medal of Merit of the Republic of Italy. The Republic of Italy rarely bestows these upon non-Italians, and when they are presented to anyone, it is for Distinguished Service to the Government of Italy.

The United Nations summoned Johnson, as its chief of Mortuary Operations for the Congo, U.N. forces, to deal with the aftermath of the Nov. 13, 1961, massacre of 13 Italian airmen in the Congo.

He was flown to the Congo and based at Leopoldville. U.N. intelligence forces found the bodies in February 1962 near Kindu and Major Ed Johnson and Col. Francesco Terzani of the Italian Air Force went to a secret rendezvous at Kindu after the United Nations took security measures. Protected by heavily armed Ethiopian M.P.s and three companies of Congolese infantry, the tiny cemetery was found. Johnson, civil prisoners, and U.N. personnel disinterred the bodies, flew the bodies of the 13 airmen back to Leopoldville, and treated them. Then, U.S. Globe Masters flew the bodies back to Italy. The bodies lay in state in the Italian Hangar there, and Papal Authorities celebrated Mass. The 13 Italian aviators died striving for a peaceful world. Recognizing Johnson's work in the Congo, the Italian Government singled him out in a ceremony at the Conrad Hilton.

"Their home air field was at Pisa…Their bodies are now in the wall of a chapel shaped like an airplane Hangar, which I helped design." Johnson later recalled that when they awarded the Medal of Civil Merit to him for his work in helping design that memorial.

Other Notable Points from the Edward Johnson Timeline

1973: Edward Johnson resigned from Worsham College staff.

1983: Joined staff of Malcolm X Chicago City College teaching Restorative Art, both theory and lab, Embalming Lab, Embalming Theory and Funeral Service History.

1995: The Pittsburgh Institute of Mortuary Science awarded Professor Edward Johnson a Doctorate in Professional Studies. Resigns from Malcolm X Chicago City College staff.

1995: Received the U.S. Army Outstanding Civilian Service medal for his work in the Congo.

1998: Received National Funeral Directors Association Resolution Honoring his Professionalism and Contributions to Funeral Service and Humanity.

A HISTORY

of the

ART and SCIENCE

of

EMBALMING

A condensation from a study
extending over three years

By EDWARD C. JOHNSON

Reprinted From

CASKET AND SUNNYSIDE

487 BROADWAY, NEW YORK 13, N. Y.

"Although I have embalmed at least 20,000 bodies, the achievement that I am the proudest of is the fact that I introduced a course in history to this field," Johnson said. "Before that time, we had so many legends and false ideas that it was ridiculous. When I started teaching after World War II, I taught a course in the History of Embalming as a preliminary to the course of Embalming Theory. The reason was so that you have an idea who you are, and where you fit in. You know who your professional ancestors are. I still believe that is important, although a lot of the schools today don't even mention it. Some of them have misguided ideas about some historical facts."

Melissa Johnson Williams best summed up her father's accomplishments:

"My father has lived and breathed funeral service his entire life. He has given unselfishly to the profession with his knowledge and support. He is probably exclusively responsible for the fact that we now teach 'our history' in mortuary school, something he did at Worsham before it was required. He has helped to promote us as a 'profession' instead of an industry.

"For me, personally, even as a small child I learned the importance of embalming, and that has stayed with me today. I have become a perfectionist and this, I fully blame on him. He has opened the door for me to develop my own talents within funeral service and provided me with much historical knowledge that is priceless."

Professional Affiliations

Chicago Area Funeral Director's Association, Illinois Funeral Directors Association, National Funeral Directors Association, Company of Fellows of the British Institute of Embalming, Japanese Funeral Directors Association, Mexican Funeral Directors Association, Founding member of International Federation of Thanatologists (FIAT-IFTA), Institut Francais De Thanatopraxie, American Hospital Association's Committee on the Rewriting of Manual of Autopsy Procedures, Pan American Health Group – Member of Advisory Board; Secretary General of the Inter-professional Relations Committee, composed of the Chicago Funeral Directors Association, the Chicago Medical Society, the Cook County Medical Society, etc.; International Affairs Consultant for National Funeral Director's Association for 13 years.

Commentary: Injustice for an American Officer

Edward Johnson, Lt./Col, USAR, retired, never hesitated to serve humanity, our country, the United Nations and several other countries well – unselfishly.

In the 1930's, he helped control lumbermen who were rioting in the streets of Tacoma, Washington. During the Second World War, he traveled millions of miles and represented this nation well in many different countries . . . While serving aboard a ship performing antisubmarine evasive maneuvers, a substantial and bulky barrel broke lose, and fractured several of Edward

Johnson's ribs. He sustained other painful injuries, and little medical attention was available to help him heal.

During the Congo crisis, he received a merciless beating at the hands of unidentified Congolese as he prevented them from stealing the body of a murdered American military attache. The 1962 clubbing that a mercenary rifleman gave him detached some of his eye lens support, and at one point left him blinded. (In 1999, he continues to have difficulty with his eyesight because of that beating with a rifle butt.) Despite his severe injuries, Professor Edward Johnson heard the clarion call to duty and to American Funeral Service. He embalmed Lt./Col Stogner's body while in great pain and at added danger to himself. Edward Charles Johnson never would have done this for self-glorification, or an award.

The valiant officer knew that a family was waiting, on the other side of the ocean, for those remains, so they could begin their grief work.

Also during the Belgian Congo Crisis of that decade, Edward Johnson followed his country's orders and helped recover the bodies of thirteen Italian airmen whom mercenaries had massacred. He exposed himself to the highest level of personal danger so that 13 Italian families would have their loved one's remains returned to Italy. For this, the Italian government knighted Professor Edward Johnson, and awarded him one of their highest medals.

Nevertheless, where was the gratitude of our own government? Edward Johnson, now 85, would be too modest and kind a man to ever brag about these war time achievements. His recounting of the events is an amazingly objective narrative.

Professor Johnson spikes it with personal pride in being an excellent embalmer and restorative artist, a fine officer, and a genuinely sincere and caring human being.

Despite his personal injuries, the U.S. Government denied Edward Johnson a Purple Heart. While it is true that in 1995, the U.S. Army, after protracted delay, awarded him the Outstanding Civilian Service Medal, it should have included a Purple Heart. At issue is a question of who controlled the amiable Renaissance man during the Belgian Congo crisis. Our government should have awarded this outstanding funeral director the decoration.

PASSING INTO HISTORY
EDWARD CHARLES JOHNSON
JUNE 29, 1914 – DECEMBER 5, 2000

A few years ago, when I was interviewing Edward C. Johnson for a biographical profile for *American Funeral Director*, I visited with him on several days in his cottage-like home. The affable historian had filled every possible wall, closet, room, nook and cranny with the finest and most elaborate history collection of embalming and American funeral service story texts and memorabilia anywhere in the world. Johnson fascinated me with tales of many marvelous and truly spellbinding events in his life. One of them – that he would tell with a certain faraway look in his eyes and an irony in his voice – was that his mother, Kathryn Barbara Graef Johnson, in the early 1930s, often urged him to become an undertaker.

"Oh, those gentlemen," she told him, "they are always so well dressed, so well groomed, and they carry themselves in an elegant manner."

"She didn't know anymore than the façade she saw during the funeral," Johnson remarked wryly. Eventually, Barbara Johnson found an undertaker in Spokane – Oscar G. Merager – who needed an apprentice. Merager, ironically, like Johnson, a Worsham graduate, held an early and keen interest in restorative art. Johnson developed his love of restorative art during those apprenticeship years of 1934-1936, and eventually became the most excellent of, and a national leader of, "those gentlemen."

Ed Johnson truly devoted the next 66 years of his life to humanity, working always for the good of others. His labor-filled time of 86 years decidedly eclipsed his mother's idea of mere fancy ceremonial pretense.

In the stately River Woods Funeral Chapel in suburban Chicago in late December, on a Friday night filled with the softness of a majestic snow, relatives and friends of Ed Johnson gathered to pay the esteemed author honor. Distinguished funeral service educator and writer Robert G. Mayer offered these appropriate words, in part, to a great man we will all miss – and one whom we shall never forget.

"It can be said, without hesitation, that Ed Johnson knew what he wanted to do in life – it was with desire, passion and love that he devoted himself to his work, his vocation – as an embalmer, funeral director, scholar, historical researcher, writer and teacher. Ed loved the work he did, and that is a great asset in life – to love one's work.

"He addressed the problems of his work as a challenge. Those of us in funeral service today and the families we serve are all richer because of Edward Johnson. Certainly it can be said he went far outside the lines of his profession

– Ed was not only recognized for his talents locally and statewide – but across this country. In truth, Edward Johnson was recognized internationally – and international recognition is afforded very few in any profession.

"It is because of people like Ed Johnson that funeral service and the discipline of embalming as practiced in America today can be called a profession. High standards in his preparation work and in his writing were his trademark. His opinions, techniques and writings have set definitive benchmarks for instructors and students of mortuary science as well as courts of law.

"I know Ed understood the true meaning of his work…the philosophical purpose of his work – it can be summarized in a quote by Jan Brugler – "You must express your grief at the death of a loved one. The eyes of the dead must be gently closed, and the eyes of the living must be gently opened.'

"Ed understood that – he knew that grief is the investment we make in others when we love them and lose them. Ed knew the loss good parents felt when an infant did not awaken in the morning from SIDS. Ed knew the pain that good parents felt when they gave the keys to a new car to their only child…only to have that child never return home after a traumatic accident.

"Ed knew the pain families felt when a son or daughter went into service for their country, never to return; he knew the grief when fire or trauma destroyed an entire family. Ed knew well the loss felt when a spouse suffered and died from a long debilitating disease.

"Ed, in his work, knew all about the grief of trauma and disease…Years before a long list of 'grief psychologists' existed, Edward Johnson truly knew that his work as an embalmer and restorative practitioner helped survivors of loss to take the first steps toward healing. He was indeed an artist who took pride in the work his hands produced, but even more important was the satisfactory approval of his work by the family and friends of the deceased.

"We will leave Edward Johnson in the 20th century, but not his opinions, ideas and written words – they will live on into a new century through his students and readers."

Since Ed Johnson was fiercely proud of his English-Welsh heritage, Mayer concluded his eulogy with a beautiful Anglican prayer:

"Oh, Lord, support us all the day long, through this troubled life, until the shadows lengthen and the evening comes, and the busy world is hushed, and the fever of life is over, and our work is done. Then, in thy mercy, grant Edward – and us – a safe lodging, holy rest and peace at the last."

One of Ed Johnson's final wishes was that he join his adored wife, Gail Richardson Johnson, herself a renowned funeral service expert and author, in her resting place in Arlington National Cemetery. Since both of them also served our country well in distinguished military careers, Ed has joined Gail, his beloved life partner.

May all of us find the wisdom and strength to pattern our careers and lives after the kindest, brightest and best ever of "Those Gentlemen."

The Value of the Funeral

~ Acknowledges that a life has been lived.

~ Allows people to remember and honor their loved one in a special way.

~ Serves as the central gathering place for family and friends to give emotional and physical support to one another.

~ Provides the final closure for the bereaved.

~ Initiates the grieving process.

~ Confirms the reality and finality of death.

~ Encourages mourners to face the pain of their loss and express their thoughts and feelings.

~ Helps survivors to better cope with their grief and enables them to move forward with their lives.

FUNERALS
OF THE FAMOUS

KATE SMITH:
AMERICA'S LOST TREASURE

MAY 1, 1907 – JUNE 17, 1986

Kate Smith as she appears on the album: "It's a Lovely Day." © Sony Records

The United States needed Kate Smith. She came to us at a time when we desperately required her strong, conservative and direct approach to people and entertainment. The charming and lovable singer gave us faith, true optimism and hope for the future. Her robust rendition of Irving Berlin's "God Bless America" caused hundreds of thousands of Americans in the early forties to demand that Congress name the 1938 song the National Anthem. About the same time, Kate Smith's tireless radio marathons raised more than $600 million for the World War II war bond effort. She opened doors and broke down some of society's barriers against the single working woman. Her name will remain emblazoned on U.S. History pages as one of the most popular singers of the Twentieth Century. Kate Smith remains America's Lost Treasure.

It's challenging for many of us to imagine that a time existed in the United States when people literally rushed home from work to listen to Kate Smith on AM radio. Probably, it's even more difficult for some Baby Boomers, Generation X and their children to fathom that U.S. citizens would stand reverently in public, hand over their heart, whenever they heard Smith's recording of *God Bless America*. Very few of us realize the monumental contributions the buxom and vibrant Songbird of the South made to our nation. Smith raised millions of dollars for the American Red Cross, and for decades she often fed and sheltered needy families, sending them barrels of food.

During World War II, Kathryn Elizabeth Smith traveled more than 520,000 miles entertaining troops. General John Pershing also decorated her for her work entertaining World War One troops stationed around her home of Washington, D.C., which she did when she was eight years old. She also ensured that her producers distributed her radio program at no cost to the Armed Forces Radio Network.

The 79 years between the birth and death of Kathryn Elizabeth Smith began in Washington, D.C. on May 1, 1907 rather than the 1909 figure she often quoted in interviews. Some controversy exists as to her actual birthplace. Smith erroneously began a rumor early in her career that she was born in Greenville near Staunton and the Blue Ridge Mountains of Virginia. One of her biographers suggests that she made the statement because her parents took in a boarder from the area. Her birth certificate states she was born at 211 First Street in Washington, D.C. in the northwestern shadow of the nation's Capitol Building.

To report that her parents (William H. and Charlotte Yarnell Hanby Smith) and maternal grandparents, the Hanbys, typify a turn of the century Victorian family is an understatement. For the formative years of Kate's singing career, her parents – and especially her grandparents – were quite negative, and urged her to forsake the theater.

Kate Smith reportedly never spoke until age three – when she suddenly began singing along with her mother, a Presbyterian church organist. She repeatedly embellished this story throughout her life as she did with several other personal anecdotes. We can only call that trait, however, consistent with her personality.

Pets, the usual adolescent mischief and hijinks, family, playing rough and tumble with boys, dolls, a love of fire engines that would last a lifetime, and singing filled the childhood years of Kate Smith. She entered vaudeville contests and by age 12 had won every talent competition in the Washington, D.C. area. That trend continued throughout high school.

Following graduation, Smith's parents forced her into an unwanted situation. She began nursing school and could bear it only nine months. A good friend advised her to quit because she somehow knew that Kate was destined for stardom. An appearance in another talent contest landed her a temporary billing in a show in a theater where a Broadway producer discovered her quickly. It was off to New York for the 17-year-old Kate Smith.

However, since the well-developed singer was amazingly light on her feet, the show's producer wanted her more for her buffoonery than her singing. He cast Smith into a role in *Honeymoon Lane* where she sang a song or two, but he really wanted her to be mainly the object of the show's cruel dialogue about fat people. Continually, the stinging barbs of comedian Bert Lahr reduced Smith to tears. Lahr (best known as the *Wizard of Oz*'s Cowardly Lion) remained ruthless and insensitive.

Kate Smith sheet music cover

(Interestingly, despite Lahr's attempts to continually upstage and degrade Kate Smith, she remained quite the lady throughout her life and never defamed Lahr publicly for his abusive and sadistic behavior, both on and offstage.) Smith decided to quit the show after its run.

Smith joined two more New York productions, but did not complete the third engagement, *Flying High*, before her beloved father became critically ill. The producer refused to let her miss a performance to return to Washington, and when she finally did arrive home, it was only to find the undertaker's hearse in front of the house. She refused to ever forgive producer George White for his heartlessness.

Kate Smith never read a note of music. The South's Songbird possessed perfect pitch which sometimes set her at odds with conductors and orchestras. Though she could never identify the exact type of discordant note produced by an errant musician during a recording session, she could always hear it and would stop singing until the conductor had corrected the offender.

At one notable 1938 session with the Philadelphia Orchestra, she sang a number from Puccini's opera *La Boehme* for a charity benefit. The famed and distinguished Leopold Stokowski conducted the orchestra, and Smith came to a passage she couldn't remember, or understand. She asked the distinguished conductor to whistle the notes. He asked her if she needed the lights adjusted to see the notes, to which Smith replied that she could see them fine, she just couldn't read them. He stared in awe and amazement and told her, "Never take a music lesson, Miss Smith. Your voice is a gift from God, and we should never spoil it." With that, he obligingly pursed his lips and whistled the section.

Miss Smith recorded almost 3,000 songs, 600 of which made the "Hit Parade." She sang many of these songs on the 15,000 radio broadcasts she made over a 25-year period. Her most famous – *God Bless America*. Smith and composer Irving Berlin created the God Bless America Foundation, and donated all royalties from the song to the Boy and Girl Scouts of America. Smith also sang it at both the 1940 Republican and Democratic conventions. Berlin called it "the most important thirty-two bars of music and lyrics I have ever composed." Despite Congress inserting the lyrics into the Congressional Record and a push by citizens to name it the National Anthem, both Smith and Berlin were against it. Smith argued successfully that the *Star Spangled Banner* was composed during a battle, while Berlin wrote and composed *God Bless America* – at least partially – during peacetime. To bolster this view, when Smith recorded *God Bless America*, she also recorded the National Anthem on the other side of the record.

Smith wrote the lyrics for *When the Moon Comes Over the Mountain* when she was a teenager, and the haunting melody became her signature-theme on radio for many years. She sang it on her very first radio show, *Kate Smith Sings*, on March 17, 1931.

Other showstoppers that she helped to popularize during the 1930's and 1940's include *The Last Time I Saw Paris, The White Cliffs of Dover, Did You Ever See a Dream Walking?* and *I'll Walk Alone*. She also recorded several significant anthologies of American Folk Music, now deemed classic collections.

The curvaceous singer also introduced the famed team of comedians, Abbott and Costello, and the single act of Henny Youngman to radio, thus giving them the break necessary to entertain millions of Americans for decades.

Miss Smith pioneered in early television starting in 1950 with *The Kate Smith Hour*. When the television network carrying her popular show dropped it in 1955, the public sent more than 400,000 letters of protest. She later described TV as having "bad taste, endless imitation, lack of experimentation, over production and the disrespect for the public by the many who have power in the television business but neither the talent nor the faith in the public they should have."

Everything that Kate Smith did, she did majestically. The vocalist didn't just sing a song. She belted it out for the world to hear. When Smith drove, it was fast. At mealtime, she didn't pick at her food – she enjoyed a full and flavorful meal. Kathryn Elizabeth Smith didn't drive her speedboat across Lake Placid, New York (where she maintained a summer home for many decades) at a slow speed – she opened it up full throttle. She traveled to her beloved Camp Sunshine on a semi-enclosed 24-foot Sportsman "Chris Craft" all-weather boat which she purchased at the 1938 New York City Boat Show. Reports from area residents say the boat is still in superb condition after more than 60 years of use, and the owner operates it seasonally.

It's important to note that her heart and actions toward others were as grand. Miss Smith truly led a philanthropic life, helping others. Not that Kate Smith ever looked for them, but many organizations did honor her for countless contributions and benevolence.

She never smoked or drank and often did not "fit in" with the Broadway, New York or Hollywood crowds. Miss Smith was reportedly usually very kind to everyone she encountered in her life and remained professional despite her spectacular success and immense popularity. In her lifetime the singer received more than 25 million fan letters. Only later in life, in her retirement years, did she have to hire a bodyguard, "Sal" Gelosi, a retired Marine.

Kate Smith was never exceedingly close to her sister, Helena Smith Steene, and her two daughters, Kathryn Steene Rodriguez and Suzanne Steene Andron. Toward the end of Smith's life, Steene and her daughters engaged in a series of well-publicized court battles. At one point, a magistrate evicted the Rodriguez family from Smiths home and ordered other family members not to travel with her. The conservators of Smith's estate began to claim that there wasn't enough money to pay medical bills, and they offered the singer's possessions for sale at an auction. Accountants had estimated Smith's earlier worth at $35 million.

In what Smith herself might have considered pathos and irony, she lived all of her life as a single person despite being revered by millions. After Miss Smith achieved her initial success, men did follow her and try to pursue her but they were generally trying to use her for their own selfish purposes. Despite her early writings dismissing marriage, some TV interviews later in her life reveal that she did long for a soulmate and children.

The one constant male companion in Smith's life was her manager of thirty-four years, Ted Collins. Over the years, so many people assumed Collins and Smith were married that her office issued a form letter denying it. He was not only a married man, but also, according to published reports, something of a womanizer and heavy drinker. No matter what else biographers might say about Collins, it was he who helped catapult Smith into stardom. Most writers conclude that Smith and Collins were never physical lovers despite the strong affection that Smith had for him. Her 1960 autobiography, *Upon My Lips a Song*, devotes many pages to her reaction to Collins first heart attack, and the very deep and sincere feelings she had for him.

Sometime early in the 1960's she dieted and lost 90 pounds over a four-year period. She lightened her hair and switched to fewer formal dresses. However, she later stated she was very uncomfortable that way and returned happily to "real chocolate fudge sundaes."

At varying phases in her life, Smith owned or was involved with various athletic teams. In 1969, an odd pairing of the legendary songster and the Philadelphia Flyers Hockey Team began. Management was worried that the fans weren't paying enough respect to the *Star Spangled Banner* played at the beginning of games. A team executive suggested playing Kate Smith's *God Bless America*, and the fans' attitude quickly changed.

Then, an amazing coincidence occurred. Every time the team played *God Bless America*, they won. Newspaper reports from that season say as the team improved, the record was reserved for critical games. An uncle of Kate Smith, who lived in Philadelphia, prevailed upon her to sing the song in person five times. The first three times she walked down the red carpet and sang the Berlin tune, the opponents were scoreless. Even the flyer's challengers said they realized "Kate Smith cooked their goose" and happily skated over to shake hands with the legendary contralto. At one of her first appearances, Kate Smith so surprised the 17,000 plus people in the audience that they applauded wildly for five minutes. At the conclusion of the 1975 season, the Flyers record was 41 wins, five losses and one tie on the nights that Kate Smith sang *God Bless America* either in person, or by recording.

As the years passed, Kate Smith's health declined. The colorful singer succumbed after doing battle for more than ten years with various debilitating diseases that robbed her of the ability to sing, and sometimes, even communicate. By November 1985, her diabetes progressed to the point that surgeons removed her gangrenous right leg and foot. The following May, she developed cancer in her left breast, and doctors ordered a mastectomy. Shortly after that, the great singer fell and fractured two of her cervical vertebrae.

Our nation lost one of its finest heroes Tuesday afternoon June 17 when Kathryn Elizabeth Smith died. President Reagan expressed his grief over her

death, noting that "Kate Smith was a patriot in every sense of the word. She thrilled us all with her stirring rendition of *God Bless America*, and sang with a passion that left few eyes dry." Decades before, in 1934 he had starred in a movie with her, *This is The Army*, and on Oct. 26, 1982 awarded her the Medal of Freedom.

Family members summoned funeral directors from the Raleigh, North Carolina firm of Brown-Wynne Funeral Home to care for the Songbird's remains. A funeral director from that firm told the *American Funeral Director* recently that Smith's services were "very dignified, quiet and low-key." Family members, her staff and loyal fans celebrated a Funeral Mass on June 19, a Thursday, at Our Lady of Lourdes Church in Raleigh. Following the Mass, they arranged to fly the body of Kate Smith to Washington, D.C.

According to Funeral Director Tom Hornbaker, who has

worked for the acclaimed and prestigious Joseph Gawlers Sons of Washington, D.C. for thirty-one years, Gawlers conducted Smith's second Funeral Mass Saturday, June 21 at St. Matthew's Cathedral. Almost 800 people wept as they sang *God Bless America* at the request of Father Albert G. Salmon, who had baptized Kate into the Catholic faith in 1965. (Rev. Salmon of St. Agnes Catholic Church in Lake Placid, New York also administered the Last Rites to Ted Collins when he died in a doctor's office in New York, May 27, 1964.)

The Gawler directors positioned the casketed remains of the gracious songstress, appropriately draped with the American flag, in the same area of the Cathedral that had held the late President John F. Kennedy's casket. The Requiem Mass concluded, but not the controversy that developed following Smith's death.

Family members were feuding about the placement of her remains. Some of her family wanted to bury her in Washington, D.C. near her progenitors. Smith's sister, bodyguard, and business manager, all produced handwritten letters, penned by Smith herself in 1973, describing her fear of being underground, even in death. (Reports say that Kate Smith would not even enter New York City by the Holland or Lincoln Tunnels.) She simply wished the executors of her estate to entomb her above ground in a pink mausoleum. Reportedly she had drawn up plans but had failed to clear it with the St. Agnes Catholic Church Cemetery in Lake Placid, New York where she wanted the mausoleum placed. This crucial point eventually proved pivotal in a battle of words between Kate Smith's estate and St. Agnes Church.

Once the family feuding stopped, Gawlers transferred Kate Smith's casketed body to the care of funeral director "Reg" Clark of the Lake Placid firm of The Clark Funeral Home (M. B. Clark, Inc.). He met the plane and took Kate Smith's body to a temporary receiving vault at North Elba, New York Cemetery where it remained for over a year while Kate's Smith's estate and St. Agnes Church argued over the placement of the mausoleum in the cemetery. The cemetery had never had a mausoleum and was concerned over its size, appearance and possible ostentatiousness. After the church viewed plans and set restrictions, cemetery officials and Smith's lawyers settled the matter.

Following a Memorial Mass at St. Agnes in November 1987 and a blessing of the Kathryn Elizabeth Smith mausoleum, Funeral Director "Reg" Clark entombed the famed singer. He said that the final services at the cemetery were private, and without publicity.

Still, the mausoleum now attracts plenty of attention. Editor Andy Flynn of the *Lake Placid News* says that whenever a convention is in town, the mausoleum of Kate Smith is always a stop for them.

The duty of arranging the final entombment of Kate Smith was especially sad for Mr. Clark. When contacted, he stated that he knew Miss Smith well and often spoke with her when she went out to do her shopping around the

Mausoleum of Kate Smith – St. Agnes Cemetery, Lake Placid, New York
(Photo courtesy of Andy Flynn, Editor, Lake Placid News)

Lake Placid area. "Reg" Clark called Smith "a great woman with a bubbly personality who was very down to earth and valued your friendship."

Mr. Clark remembers well a Summer Bazaar, a fund-raiser, conducted by the Saint Agnes School which is next door to the M. B. Clark Funeral Home. Kate Smith walked about the crowds, mixing and being very friendly. One reason that Mr. Clark and his wife decided to attend was the presence of a well-known local artist, Ed Schaver. The artist would paint a scene on whatever medium the customer wanted, with the payment going directly to the School. The Clarks asked Mr. Schaver to paint an old-fashioned flat iron with a mountain scene. When the artist completed his handiwork, the Clarks set off to enjoy the Bazaar, with "Reg" gingerly holding the flat iron in front of him, so that the paint would dry.

About that time, he ran into Kate Smith, and she asked, "What do you have there, Reginald?" Mr. Clark explained what he was doing with the painted flat iron. An hour or so passed and the paths of the undertaker and the singer crossed again. Ever jovial Smith belted out, "Reginald, that still can't be wet!" and Smith pressed her thumb securely against the still wet iron smudging it and leaving her print quite visible.

"Reg" Clark was visibly upset but determined not to let Smith know it. Just as he seethed inwardly, Smith, clearly embarrassed and quite apologetic, told him to go to the artist, and have Schaver paint another scene and that she would make a donation to the St. Agnes school.

"Oh, my heavens! I'm sorry," Kate Smith told "Reg" Clark. "I'm so sorry ...Well, you take it back, and have it repaired. I'll make the necessary contribution to the school." There was a momentary pause, with Smith adding coyly, "Of course, you know though, not even the FBI has Kate Smith's fingerprints!"

With that, "Reg" Clark decided to keep the iron just as it was. Ironically, the illustration on the iron depicted a winter mountainside scene. Smith's thumbprint landed just above the mountain. Mr. Clark says he is now proud to own the Smith-smudged iron adding that "with poetic license" you can simply consider Smith's thumbprint as "the Moon coming over the Mountain."

Kate Smith's thumbprint appears on this painting of a mountainscape. "Of course, you know, though, not even the FBI has Kate Smith's fingerprints!" But funeral director Reginald Clark recalled how Smith's thumbprint became part of the picture. (Photo courtesy of Reginald Clark)

The best way to eulogize Kate Smith? She will remain, always, our lost treasure, but President Franklin Delano Roosevelt eloquently honored her when he introduced her to King George VI of England, saying, "This is Kate Smith. This is America."

MARTHA RAYE:
EMPTY APPLAUSE

AUGUST 27, 1916 - OCTOBER 19, 1994

(Photo courtesy Johnny Horne, Photo Editor, The Fayetteville Observer)

Singer-comedian Martha Raye spent seventy-four of her seventy-eight years on earth entertaining people, for which the United States awarded her the Presidential Medal of Freedom shortly before her death. We perhaps best remember Miss Raye for her famous mouth and toothy grin, a curvaceous figure, a keen sense of wit, and her myriad United Servicemen Organization (USO) tours. Milton Berle once called her "one of the four funniest women on earth." Yet, Miss Raye, born Margie Yvonne Reed in a charity ward of a Montana hospital, easily qualifies as one of the nation's unhappiest female entertainers. As Berle also noted, "She lived a life of personal disaster."

Sadly, Martha Raye is still strongly and solely identified with her denture adhesive ads and her fondness for trolling up lawsuits. Even though married seven times, Martha Raye still made many financial, personal and emotional sacrifices to entertain American troops overseas during three wars. The diminutive Raye, just five-foot-three, with a voice known to resonate throughout theaters without the use of electronic amplification, sang, danced and clowned her way into the hearts of millions of Americans – especially the service men and women of Word War II, Korea, and Viet Nam. Her genealogical roots alone would supply plenty of material for a movie about the traditional unemployed and impoverished vaudevillians.

Raye's parents, Pete and Maybelle (Peggy) Hooper Reed, together formed the act of "The Girl and The Traveler." In August 1916, the Reeds appeared at the Maguire Opera House, a theater that catered to mine workers in the then mid-sized quarrying town of Butte, Montana. They often billed themselves as Irish immigrants, and it is true that Pete Reed came from County Clare, Ireland. Martha Raye's death certificate lists her mother as a Wisconsin resident. (Still, some of Raye's biographers suggest that Maybelle Hooper's mother, Theresa Sanchagrin and her father, Samuel Hooper, lived and worked in a small mining town near what is now Great Falls, Montana.)

Mrs. Reed, just nineteen and obviously very pregnant, played the piano and joined her husband in a variety of song, dance and comedy routines. In one story about her early life that Martha Raye told with some accuracy, just as her mother neared delivery of her baby, the Opera House manager left town with the box office receipts. No choice remained for Pete Reed – he took his young wife to the charity maternity ward of St. James Hospital in Butte, Montana. There, on August 27, 1916, "Peggy" Reed gave birth to a little baby girl who would eventually mug, caterwaul, jest, and earn her way from the barren and sawdust covered burlesque house boards of the Midwestern United States to the rich carpeted floors of New York's Broadway theaters. From there Martha Raye would toil her way to the sound-controlled stages of movies and television, sloshing through the combat areas of the South Pacific, Korea and Viet Nam and endangering her life to entertain troops.

For two years, the Reeds – who much like Raye – answered to a variety of Irish surnames, traveled the Midwestern theater circuit with Martha in tow. Living and working conditions remained brutal and sometimes even squalid. Soon, the Reeds expected a second child. In Grand Rapids, Michigan, stage hands and chorus women reportedly attended Mrs. Reed's second delivery – a boy, Douglas, whom the family soon nicknamed Buddy.

Family reports suggest that Martha Raye first wandered on stage before she had attained four years of age. She often played with her parent's theatrical make up and watched them practice their routines, so before she was even five years old, Miss Raye became an inherent part of the family act, singing a 1919 fox trot tune, "Jada." During a 1921 tour in Chicago, Peggy Reed gave birth to another daughter, Melodye, who would die tragically young in 1942.

Martha Raye spent her formative years in an atmosphere of grease paint, intimidation, child abuse and the stench and curse of her parent's apparent alcoholism. Many of these factors would stay rooted in Miss Raye's psyche. The Reed family eventually worked all three of their children into the act which toured throughout much of the nation on the Loew's Theater Circuit. The entire family often went hungry and slept in the car which doubled as a vehicle to transport the scenery for their act.

Martha Raye would tell reporters different stories about her education. These tales would vary – from parochial school attendance to graduation from a Chicago public school. Family members say she always nurtured a true sense of shame at her lack of education because she grew up being tutored mainly by her mother. Although Peggy Reed tried diligently, the results yielded a child only barely versed in the rudiments of reading and writing.

In 1928 twelve-year-old Martha Raye talked her way into a talent contest in Chicago during a layover in the Midwest and easily won against the dozen or so other contestants. She took home what to her amounted to a huge fortune of three silver dollars. A year or so later, following more liquor filled trips with parents who slapped and cursed their children, the Reed family landed in Cleveland, Ohio. Martha Raye auditioned for Big Band leader Paul Ash's Merry Mad Musical Gang and Orchestra. The fast talking youth successfully landed a singing job and work for her brother and father as well.

Ash, who was German born and raised in the Unites States, wrote several 1920's hits including Kay Kaiser's theme *Thinking of You*. Raye eventually was catapulted into an audition with a well known New York Producer, Charles Yates. Shortly after their arrival in New York, Peggy Reed helped her daughter Margie find a new name for herself by thumbing through the phone book. Martha Raye, Girl Singer, came into existence in 1929.

Around 1932 many theater owners stopped booking vaudeville acts because of the increasing popularity of movie theaters. Martha Raye had experienced a variety of small successes on stage with some moderately successful singers and orchestras. Generally, however, Raye sang so well that the "stars" were jealous of her ability and fired her, or failed to renew her contract. By the time she turned eighteen, Martha Raye had gained invaluable experience by auditioning for crooner Rudy Valee and singing with Dixieland Jazz impresario Louis Prima.

Miss Raye next earned an understudy position with a 1935 Broadway show, *Calling All Stars*. In the Boston production, one of the female comedic leads broke her arm, and the producer called for "Maggie" to substitute. She eagerly accepted the challenge and lurched about the stage in a mock drunken stupor. The audience loved her, and from that point Martha Raye's career of singing or dancing for her meals ended. When the show ended its run, agents began chasing her with lucrative night club offers. She returned to New York, and made some friendships that lasted throughout her life, including that of comedian Jimmy Durante.

During the next year, she traveled to Chicago and pianist-songwriter and comedian Steve Allen watched her sing and act. Allen wrote decades later that although Martha Raye possessed an extraordinarily superb talent for comedy, it only masked her ability to sing jazz perfectly. Shortly after her Chicago booking, the Century Club of Hollywood offered her a booking which eventually led to her first film role, *Rhythm on the Range*, with Bing Crosby.

During this highly acclaimed film, Raye sang "*Mr. Paginini*" which she and her fans always considered her theme song. In 1936, Paramount Film agents quickly wooed and won "Maggie" for *The Big Broadcast of 1937* with George Burns and Gracie Allen. Other films that followed include *College Holiday* (1936) and five films in 1937: *Hideaway Girl, Waikiki Wedding, Mountain Music, Artists and Models* and *Double or Nothing*. In 1938, Martha Raye starred in four more Paramount films: *The Big Broadcast of 1938, College Swing, Tropic Holiday* and *Give Me a Sailor*. She appeared in two 1939 films: *Never Say Die* and *$1,000 A Touchdown*. Critics panned most of these movies but the public loved the zany actress with the impossibly wide expanse of lips and pearly teeth.

Ironically, Martha Raye's married life began as it ended – to a hairdresser. At age twenty, she married her first husband, twenty one year old Hamilton Westmore, who worked as a makeup man and hairstylist. "Buddy" labored with his several brothers on the set of Martha Raye's first film. (Her seventh husband, forty-two year-old Mark Harris, a hairdresser from Brooklyn, married seventy five-year-old wheelchair bound Martha Raye three years before her death in 1994.)

We could readily consider Raye's first marriage a harbinger of the misfortune that would befall her many romances. Westmore and Peggy Reed, now long estranged from Pete Reed, grew to hate each other. The resulting stress between husband and mother-in-law caused considerable marital problems, and in September 1937, after just three months of marriage, the couple filed for divorce with ugly charges leveled on both sides.

Thirteen months later, in Ensenada, Mexico, Martha Raye wed Paramount's music composer David Rose (although he wrote many memorable tunes, people often remember him for his loud and brassy tune, *The Stripper*.) She did enjoy tremendous success with a recording of a David Rose tune, *Melancholy Mood* which Brunswick released on their label #8934 on September 9, 1939.

Just a few months later, in early 1940, Paramount sent Martha Raye a note – unceremoniously slipped under her dressing room door – ending their contract. The rubber mouthed comedienne suddenly found herself without employment. By spring 1940, husband David Rose, reportedly tired of Maggie's mood swings, fell in love with Judy Garland. In May, Raye and Rose divorced.

Shortly after her second divorce, Raye accepted an offer from Universal Studios for whom she made four films: *The Boys from Syracuse* (1940), *Navy Blues, Keep 'Em Flying,* and *Hellzapoppin,* all in 1941. Following a role with Al Jolson in a Broadway play, *Hold on to Your Hats,* Maggie decided to remarry before David Rose had the chance to marry Judy Garland. Consequently, later that same year, she married a thirty-eight-year-old Florida hotel executive, Neal Lang. About a month before Pearl Harbor Day (December 7, 1941), and after less than a year of marriage, citing massive living differences Maggie and Neal divorced.

With the coming of the Second World War, Martha Raye volunteered for duty in the first known USO show. Raye and a troupe of female artists including Kay Francis, Carole Landis and Mitzi Mayfair toured American and English bases throughout the Atlantic Ocean area and the United Kingdom. The grueling six-week schedules of several shows daily for six days a week caused some health and emotional stress on the artists, but they danced, sang and joked cheerfully in mess halls, auditoriums, theaters, Quonset huts, hospitals, on platforms, and, in fact, just about anywhere they could safely do the show. The tour continued in North Africa, and often while in transit in the air and on the ground, all of the performers placed themselves in great and true danger from enemy fire. Although Maggie would perhaps exaggerate some of her wartime stories, a great deal of documentation exists to prove her claims of personal perils during the tour which lasted until March 1943. For her work, the U.S. Army named Maggie an honorary U.S. Army captain.

Returning stateside, Martha Raye starred in what many fans consider her most popular film, *Four Jills in a Jeep*, loosely based on her recent USO tour in the United Kingdom and North Africa. Starring Phil Silvers, Alice Faye and Betty Grable, the film accurately portrayed some hardships endured by both entertainers and soldiers. Even if film critics disliked the film, Americans loved it.

Later that year, while filming another 20th Century Fox Betty Grable vehicle, *Pinup Girl*, Martha Raye met Nick Condos, who defended Raye against a drunk heckler in a night club. Despite their often stormy relationship, he remained the one man who purportedly provided some stability to Martha Raye. In fact, Condos accompanied Raye to Mexico in early 1944 to secure a divorce from Lang, by this time an officer in the U.S. Army. The marriage to Condos began in 1944 and lasted until another complicated divorce in 1953. Nick Condos would also father Raye's only child, Melodye, born in July 1944. They named her after Maggie's sister, who had died (reportedly of alcoholism, at age 21) while Raye worked her USO tour overseas. In October 1944, Martha Raye's brother, Buddy, died of tuberculosis. Neither Raye nor her mother attended his funeral.

By 1947, Raye's career began to sag. Her consistent arguments with her manager-husband, Nick Condos, and their public battles over finances, Maggie's dogs, Melodye, and gambling escalated. Maggie accepted a role in a Universal Studios film produced by Charlie Chaplin, *Monsieur Verdoux*. Though she decidedly had trouble reading the script, and understanding all of its nuances, Raye instinctively felt the critics and the American public would hail the film as a great classic, and that the reviews and respect for her performance would rejuvenate her ailing craft. Maggie could not foresee how the American people would turn on the anti-war and seemingly, anti-capitalist Chaplin, brand him a Communist, and blackball all of his films. Though critics handed out a smattering of good reviews, the American public has largely forgotten *Monsieur Verdoux*.

In October 1947, alcoholism claimed the life of another member of Raye's family – her mother, Peggy. Maggie experienced great difficulty with her grief work and never recovered fully from her mother's death. Two years later, in 1949, she placed her father, Pete Reed, in a Florida nursing home after selling her California home to film actress Doris Day. The Condos family moved to Miami Beach where they not only leased a home from singer Mel Torme but also purchased a nightclub where Martha could appear frequently. Raye frequently mimicked Margaret Truman, Vaughan Monroe, and the Lone Ranger. Still, she did not seem happy, her drinking increased, and in 1950 police jailed Maggie for driving under the influence of alcohol.

Her life began improving when Milton Berle contracted Maggie for some appearances on his *Texaco Star Theater*, an early televison extravaganza. It became her first live televised appearance.

In mid-1952, Martha Raye again traveled overseas to entertain troops, this time in Korea. Unfortunately, she became violently ill and had to return to the States where she and Nick commuted back and forth between her Miami nightclub and the NBC New York television studios where Martha Raye shined in *All Star Revue*. By the 1952 fall television season, NBC launched *The Martha Raye Show* which eventually featured heavyweight fighter Rocky Graziano and Caesar Romero. A year later, in 1953, the network expanded the show to an hour-long time slot.

During 1953, the tensions between Nick and Maggie had risen to a level that they simply could not negotiate. The two divorced with Maggie retaining custody of Melodye. Nick, though, continued to work as Maggie's business agent.

Never a woman to be without a husband for long, Maggie spied a new male dancer on her TV show, Edward Begley. She decided she should marry him and did so in a rushed wedding in Virginia on April 21, 1954. The marriage, of course, was a rocky one, replete with reports of excess drinking, public disputes and estrangement.

Toward the end of the Raye-Begley marriage, Maggie began to receive threats. She immediately suspected Begley and hired a bodyguard, Bob O'Shea, a Connecticut policeman with whom she became romantically involved. O'Shea later became her bodyguard, and Raye became the target of an alienation of an affection lawsuit launched by O'Shea's wife.

It would not be until late 1956 that Maggie would be able to divorce Begley – and then, only in Mexico. She and O'Shea had been living in Florida, and their legal troubles with his wife continued for some time. During this time, Raye attempted suicide by taking an overdose of sleeping pills but family members and friends alike claim it was a publicity stunt.

In November 1958, O'Shea's divorce from his wife became final, and Maggie and Bob O'Shea were married with actress Joan Crawford and her millionaire husband, Alfred Steele (Pepsi-Cola Chief Executive Officer), serving as witnesses at the ceremony. Despite their settling into a respectable Long Island home, O'Shea, the ex-cop, spent much of his time concentrating on his Detective Agency. Martha Raye stayed at home and agonized over delinquent income tax payments and the lack of employment. Steve Allen offered her several guest appearances on his TV show which she readily and gladly accepted.

Over the years, the relationship between Mother Martha and daughter Melodye had become strained owing to Raye's odd ideas about child raising – she drew heavily on the manner in which Pete and Peggy Reed had raised her. Now, as Melodye concluded her teen years, the rapport grew even more limited. In August 1959, when Maggie announced to the press – through Nick Condos – that she and O'Shea, her sixth husband, were divorcing, the strain between the mother and daughter heightened.

Martha Raye began drinking so heavily during this period that she hospitalized herself for detoxification. Shortly after her release from the treatment unit, her father, Pete Reed died in Florida. Though Maggie was never close to him, she felt a certain amount of grief and guilt following his death. To complicate matters during this trying time in her life, O'Shea made demands for huge amounts of money and property in the divorce settlement.

In 1962, 20th Century-MGM offered Martha Raye a leading role in the Billy Rose circus spectacular, *Jumbo*. Though she decidedly loved the idea, the offer and the role, she again attempted suicide. Raye did complete filming the epic which featured Jimmy Durante and Doris Day.

In early Spring 1965, Martha Raye took her first trip to South Viet Nam to entertain American troops. Later in the year, she spent three more months in remote outposts, and the GI's loved her – even if she was a grandmother near fifty years of age. She returned the following year and became an outspoken defender of the GI's serving in Viet Nam. Maggie rarely traveled with an organized USO show, often catching a hop on a military plane, or whatever she could find, to get from base to base.

During a 1966 Viet Nam USO show, the Viet Cong vociferously attacked the base where she was entertaining. For the better part of a day and night, Maggie worked alongside doctors and nurses, carrying litters, bandaging the wounded, doing anything she could to help the wounded and dying. Her efforts would not go unheralded.

By 1967, Broadway producer David Merrick offered Miss Raye the chance to play the lead in his New York production of *Hello, Dolly*. Raye, eager to return to the military men and women she often called "my family" in Viet

Nam, accepted a limited engagement. During the six-month run, she continued defending the American GI's to the press, and many prestigious organizations gave her awards for her work in the jungles of Viet Nam. For her efforts, President Lyndon Johnson named her an honorary Lieutenant Colonel in the Special Forces and authorized her to wear its distinctive beret. Additionally, the Army commissioned her as an honorary nurse; the Navy made her an Admiral; and the 101ˢᵗ Airborne Division named her a gunner's mate.

Maggie's commitment to the men and women who served in Viet Nam, her outspoken criticism of the anti-war protestors and Jane Fonda, and her work with veterans in the Veteran's Administration Hospital all undoubtedly hurt her career. During the decade of the seventies, Raye became all but forgotten. She landed feature roles in two minor films, *Pufnstuf* (1970, Universal) and *The Phynx* (Her only film for Warner Brothers, 1971). Maggie had some minor parts in several TV shows, and she became a nominee for an Emmy for her supporting performance in a 1976 made-for-TV epic *Mc Millan and Wife: NBC Mystery Movie*. That role led to a limited enagagement as a regular character on the Mc Millan and Wife TV series. Several years later, in 1978, Martha Raye accepted what would be her final motion picture assignment – a character role in *Concorde/Airport '79*, produced by Universal.

The eighties saw Maggie turn pitch woman for Polident denture adhesive. Her classic line "I've worn dentures for years, Take it from Martha Raye, the big mouth." became the target of network television parodies for decades. Maggie took some minor televison roles including one on the comedy *Alice* and accepted a few TV movie jobs.

Nick Condos died in July 1988 while Maggie attended a Special Forces reunion at Fort Bragg, North Carolina. His death, arguments over his estate, and the subsequent cremation order of Condos by Melodye, further alienated Maggie and Melodye. Martha Raye began living a bizarre life of seclusion and excluded Melodye whenever possible. The two took turns suing each other over various financial dealings.

Meanwhile, Raye's physical condition worsened, and her dependence on alcohol and medication increased. By 1991, two strokes had all but completely debilitated the once energetic singer and dancer, now seventy-five, and she remained confined to a wheelchair, adjudged legally incompetent to handle her own affairs.

Enter forty-two year-old Mark Bleefield Harris. Harris, by his own admission, a hairdresser, garment industry designer, chef, television show host, agent and producer wrangled an invitation to meet Martha Raye through an aging comic, Bernie Allen. Within two weeks, on September 25, 1991 a rabbi marries Harris and Raye. The tabloids run amok with lurid tales of the strange May-December relationship. Raye's health is so poor that the extent of her wedding night activities consists of being propped into a bar stool. That night, her abdominal pains are so bad and bleeding is so intent that Harris admits Martha Raye into a Desert Springs hospital.

Mark Harris arranged a subsequent wedding (December 28th) at the Beverly Hills Friars Club. The Army positioned a tank outside the front door for Martha Raye, and inside a color guard in Revolutionary War regalia heralded the arrival of the couple. Craftspeople constructed the Jewish wedding service canopy entirely of military camouflage material. *People* magazine reported that 100 guests openly wondered if the grande dame of the USO was finally suffering from battle fatigue because the service and groom were so strange.

No matter, Raye had already videotaped a will naming Harris the executor of her estate and leaving Melodye one dollar. Raye claimed that Harris added class and intelligence to her life.

During the year that followed, Melodye and Harris battled over who would control Maggie and her assets. Harris appeared on a variety of TV and radio talk shows, most notably on the "shock-jock" Howard Stern show, to explain how he physically took care of Raye. Around this time, Raye and Harris sued entertainer Bette Midler, claiming that her production of *"For the Boys"* was based on Raye's USO tours. The lawsuit proved fruitless, and the film, itself, failed.

In 1992, Raye suffered many strokes and subsequent hospitalizations. The squabbling between Melodye Condos and Mark Harris continued, until eventually a judge appointed a conservator who essentially placed Raye on a limited monthly budget.

During late October 1993, Maggie's doctors performed five hours of circulatory surgery on her amputating first a toe on her left foot and then, a few days later, her left leg below the knee. Harris announced plans for an Irish wake and subsequent burial at Fort Bragg, North Carolina. While Martha Raye's life ebbed away, the President ordered the award of the Presidential Medal of Freedom which two distinguished Armed Forces Representatives awarded to her. Before New Years Day, 1994, Martha Raye suffered two more strokes.

During 1994, the trio of Mark Harris, Melodye and the court-appointed conservator all fought each other on Maggie's various legal and economic issues. In February, surgeons removed part of Maggie's right leg. Martha Raye remained in a chronic vegetative state reduced to simply watching old movies, and barely able to do that because of poor eyesight. Varying stories abound about whether or not Martha Raye even knew that doctors had amputated her legs above the knee, bilaterally. Because the severe January 1994 earthquake had damaged her house, Martha Raye now had to call a Radisson Hotel room her home. Because of various legal moves by Harris, Melodye could not visit her mother without the court's permission.

On October 17, doctors admitted Martha Raye to Cedars-Sinai Hospital because of vomiting and diarrhea. Mark Harris flew east. Two days later, the

CERTIFICATE OF DEATH
STATE OF CALIFORNIA
USE BLACK INK ONLY/NO ERASURES, WHITEOUTS OR ALTERATIONS
VS-11 (REV. 7/93)

39419045636

STATE FILE NUMBER			LOCAL REGISTRATION NUMBER

DECEDENT PERSONAL DATA			
1. NAME OF DECEDENT—FIRST (GIVEN) MARTHA	2. MIDDLE	3. LAST (FAMILY) RAYE	
4. DATE OF BIRTH MM/DD/CCYY 08/27/1916	5. AGE YRS. 78 / IF UNDER 1 YEAR MONTHS DAYS / IF UNDER 24 HOURS HOURS MINUTES	6. SEX F	7. DATE OF DEATH MM/DD/CCYY 10/19/1994	8. HOUR 1345
9. STATE OF BIRTH MONTANA	10. SOCIAL SECURITY NO. 563-18-1774	11. MILITARY SERVICE 19 42 TO 19 73 NONE	12. MARITAL STATUS MARRIED	13. EDUCATION—YEARS COMPLE 12
14. RACE CAUCASIAN	15. HISPANIC—SPECIFY YES ☐ NO ☒	16. USUAL EMPLOYER SELF-EMPLOYED	
17. OCCUPATION ENTERTAINER	18. KIND OF BUSINESS THEATER/FILM/TELEVISION	19. YEARS IN OCCUPATION 74	

USUAL RESIDENCE			
20. RESIDENCE—STREET AND NUMBER OR LOCATION 1153 ROSCOMARE ROAD			
21. CITY LOS ANGELES	22. COUNTY LOS ANGELES	23. ZIP CODE 90077	24. YRS IN COUNTY 31	25. STATE OR FOREIGN COU CALIFORNIA

INFORMANT		
26. NAME, RELATIONSHIP MARK HARRIS - HUSBAND	27. MAILING ADDRESS (STREET AND NUMBER OR RURAL ROUTE NUMBER, CITY OR TOWN, STATE, 1153 ROSCOMARE ROAD, LOS ANGELES, CA 90077	

SPOUSE AND PARENT INFORMATION			
28. NAME OF SURVIVING SPOUSE—FIRST MARK	29. MIDDLE S.	30. LAST (MAIDEN NAME) HARRIS	
31. NAME OF FATHER—FIRST PETER	32. MIDDLE -	33. LAST REED	34. BIRTH S IRELAN
35. NAME OF MOTHER—FIRST MAYBELLE	36. MIDDLE -	37. LAST (MAIDEN) HOOPER	38. BIRTH SV WISCONS

FUNERAL DIRECTOR AND LOCAL REGISTRAR			
39. DATE MM/DD/CCYY 10/23/1994	40. PLACE OF FINAL DISPOSITION FORT BRAGG NATIONAL CEMETERY, FORT BRAGG, NORTH CAROLINA		
41. TYPE OF DISPOSITION(S) TR/BU	42. SIGNATURE OF EMBALMER William R. Pierce	43. LICENSE NO. 5595	
44. NAME OF FUNERAL DIRECTOR PIERCE BROS. WESTWOOD VILLAGE MORT.	45. LICENSE NO. F-951	46. SIGNATURE OF LOCAL REGISTRAR Robert C Matt	47. DATE MM/DD/CCYY 10/20/1994

PLACE OF DEATH			
101. PLACE OF DEATH CEDARS SINAI MED. CENTER	102. IF HOSPITAL, SPECIFY ONE: IP ☒ ER/OP ☐ DOA ☐	103. FACILITY OTHER THAN HOSPITAL CONV. HOSP. ☐ RES. ☐ OTHER ☐	104. COUNTY LOS ANGELES
105. STREET ADDRESS—STREET AND NUMBER OR LOCATION 8700 BEVERLY BLVD.			106. CITY LOS ANGELES

CAUSE OF DEATH				
107. DEATH WAS CAUSED BY: (ENTER ONLY ONE CAUSE PER LINE FOR A, B, C, AND D)			TIME INTERVAL BETWEEN ONSET AND DEATH	108. DEATH REPORTED TO CORON ☒ YES ☐ NO
IMMEDIATE CAUSE	(A) ASPIRATION PNEUMONIA		2 DAYS	REFERRAL NUMBER 94-56113
DUE TO	(B) MULTI CEREBRAL INFARCTION		3 YRS	109. BIOPSY PERFORMED ☒ YES ☐ NO
DUE TO	(C) ARTERIOSCLEROSIS		YRS	110. AUTOPSY PERFORMED ☐ YES ☒ NO
DUE TO	(D)			111. USED IN DETERMINING CAUSE ☐ YES ☐ NO
112. OTHER SIGNIFICANT CONDITIONS CONTRIBUTING TO DEATH BUT NOT RELATED TO CAUSE GIVEN IN 107 NO				
113. WAS OPERATION PERFORMED FOR ANY CONDITION IN ITEM 107 OR 112? IF YES, LIST TYPE OF OPERATION AND DATE. BILATERAL BELOW KNEE AMPUTATION 10/1993				

PHYSICIAN'S CERTIFICATION			
114. I CERTIFY THAT TO THE BEST OF MY KNOWLEDGE DEATH OCCURRED AT THE HOUR, DATE AND PLACE STATED FROM THE CAUSES STATED. DECEDENT ATTENDED SINCE 11/01/1993 / DECEDENT LAST SEEN ALIVE 10/19/1994	115. SIGNATURE AND TITLE OF CERTIFIER Gilbert D. Callis M.D.	116. LICENSE NO. C-24147	117. DATE MM/DD/CC 10/20/1994
	118. TYPE ATTENDING PHYSICIAN'S NAME, MAILING ADDRESS + ZIP GILBERT D. CALLIS, M.D. 444 SO. SAN VICENTE BLVD. #600, L.A., CA 90048		

CORONER'S USE ONLY			
119. I CERTIFY THAT IN MY OPINION DEATH OCCURRED AT THE HOUR, DATE AND PLACE STATED FROM THE CAUSES STATED.	120. INJURY AT WORK ☐ YES ☐ NO	121. INJURY DATE MM/DD/CCYY	122. HOUR	123. PLACE OF INJURY
119. MANNER OF DEATH NATURAL ☐ SUICIDE ☐ HOMICIDE ☐ ACCIDENT ☐ PENDING INVESTIGATION ☐ COULD NOT BE DETERMINED ☐	124. DESCRIBE HOW INJURY OCCURRED (EVENTS WHICH RESULTED IN INJURY)			
125. LOCATION (STREET AND NUMBER OR LOCATION AND CITY AND ZIP CODE)				
126. SIGNATURE OF CORONER OR DEPUTY CORONER	127. DATE MM/DD/CCYY	128. TYPED NAME, TITLE OF CORONER OR DEPUTY CORONER	

STATE	A	B	C	D	E	F	G	H	FAX AUTH. #	CENSUS TRAC

(Death Certificate courtesy of Bernard Johnson)

court notified Melodye that Martha Raye again remained hospitalized. Melodye rushed to the hospital, and attendants told Melodye that no Martha Raye existed as a patient.

Melodye returned to work, and heard on the radio that veteran comic Martha Raye had just died at age seventy-eight. Furious, Melodye returned to the hospital for answers, but all that she could discover was that funeral directors from the Pierce Brothers Westwood Village Mortuary had taken charge of her remains. This is confirmed on Raye's California Death Certificate.

(*American Funeral Director* contacted Jody White, manager of that firm, and asked for assistance in gathering details of Raye's California funeral. White refused, neither confirming nor denying that they handled the Raye services, adding that, "We handle a lot of high profile services here. I had one the other day, but I never talk about them, even if SCI pressures me to discuss it. I keep my job by keeping my mouth shut.")

Pierce Brothers conducted the initial transport, embalmed and cosmetized Raye, dressed her in her beloved Special Forces uniform, and shipped her in a Jewish-Orthodox Oak casket with the Mogen David affixed to the crest to the Rogers and Breece Funeral Home in Fayetteville, near Fort Bragg, North Carolina.

Published reports say the October 20th service held at the Santa Monica Chapel apparently was less than dignified. Melodye found out about it only by accident. Police officers drove her to the funeral home so that she could attend the service and arrive on time. At the service, Harris, escorted by one of his ever-present male companions, loudly insisted that Maggie had wanted both a Jewish wedding and funeral because she had loved him. Melodye, relegated to a seat in the very back of the chapel, rose to apologize to all of Martha Raye's true friends that Harris had not invited to the service and to all her military family and fans who also apparently had not known about it.

The following morning, Melodye discovered that the Pierce Funeral Directors had indeed shipped Martha Raye's body to the Rogers and Breece Funeral Home. There, a seasoned and affable funeral director with forty-two years experience, Osborne ("Oz") H. Owens, took control of the final arrangements for the burial of "Colonel Maggie."

Owens, who dealt with both Mark Harris and Melodye Condos recalled "that Mark Harris was very gracious, and so was she." Mr. Owens said the plane bearing the body of Martha Raye encountered delays Friday, the 21st. This presented many challenges to the Rogers and Breece directors as the airport was 80 miles away, at Raleigh-Durham. Mark Harris scheduled a viewing that evening from seven until nine P.M.

The U.S. Army and U.S. Air Force dispatched several Military Police cars to the airport. Funeral director Roy Zeitvogel, himself a retired Army NCO, drove the super stretch limousine in which Mark Harris, one of his daughters, Martha Raye's housekeeper, and a Paramount Studios executive would ride.

Marth Raye Remains – The only civilian buried at Fort Bragg's National Cemetery (Photo courtesy of Cyndi Burnham, Fayetteville Observer)

Mr. Zeitvogel asked the lead MP how fast they would be driving to the airport, since Raye's plane had arrived an hour late. "We have pulled out all stops." The policeman replied. Zeitvogel recalls the drive back from the airport exceeded seventy miles an hour. Mr. Owens said the body arrived in good condition, just minutes before the visitation was to begin. He did have to take the casket into the preparation room, and make some adjustments but said that he began the viewing for the hundred or so retired Special Forces troops that wanted to view Martha Raye by seven-fifteen.

The day of Martha Raye's military service dawned bright and sunny. Mr. Owens recalls that several hundred people attended the service with the press being kept on a flatbed truck at a respectable distance from the grave. An emissary from the Mark Harris entourage told Melodye they did not want her sitting with the family to which she aptly replied, "I am the family." Owens recalls that he drove the hearse bearing Raye's flag draped casket, and Roy Zeitvogel again drove the limo. Rogers and Breece assigned five or six extra people to help with the service.

"My main concern was dealing with, and taking care of the immediate family. Quite a bit of press attended, and they were all in place when we arrived at the Fort Bragg Cemetery where Martha Raye is still the only civilian to be buried there," Mr. Owens recalled recently.

"Her service to the military never went without heed," said Jimmy Dean, executive secretary of the Special Forces Association in Fayetteville to the Associated Press. "How many entertainers in this world would go to a country called Viet Nam where a war was going on for nine straight years, four months a year, and spend three of those months out with isolated Special Forces Detachments in camps all over the country ?"

Who, indeed, but the lovable, raspy voiced Margie Yvonne Reed, who knew so little happiness after giving so much to others, especially the U.S. military. In her declining years, she once told a reporter from *People* magazine, "I thought success in show business was everything. It isn't. I don't know what is."

Though Martha Raye's applause may have sounded empty to her, we all appreciated her more than she ever knew.

Bibliography/Sources/Suggested Readings

Interview – Oz Owens, Funeral Director, Rogers- Breece Funeral Home

Interview – Roy Zeitvogel, Funeral Director and Embalmer, D.O. McComb and Sons Funeral Home, Fort Wayne, Indiana, formerly of Rogers and Breece

Telephone Interview – Jody White, Manager and Funeral Director, Pierce Brothers, Westwood Village Chapel

The Associated Press

Newsday

Entertainment Weekly

People Magazine, various issues

Time Magazine

USA Today

Interview – Funeral Director Bernard Johnson, Culver City, California

Allen, Steve: *More Funny People*

Hope, Bob: *Don't Shoot, It's Only Me*

Pitrone, Jean: *Take It From The Big Mouth*

Agnes Moorehead:
A Passion for God, Country and Privacy
December 6, 1906 – April 30, 1974

(Photo courtesy of Dayton Daily News ©)

It is easy enough to still find Agnes Moorehead on television. Since "Bewitched" (which began its run in 1963) continues a long-standing run on a couple of the nostalgia networks, placing the feisty red-haired woman acting as a razor-tongued and sneering witch mother-in-law is simple. Separating Miss Moorehead's "Endora" persona from the deeply devout, fiercely patriotic and passionately private woman she truly was in her own life is perhaps more difficult. The character actress of stage, screen, radio and television achieved tremendous success because of the invaluable combination of talent and dedication that she possessed. Although she often portrayed drab, acrimonious and disheartened women, she was, in reality, a sparkling, kind, charming and highly intelligent woman who was reportedly equally at ease with either royalty or children.

Born December 6, 1906 to a Presbyterian minister and his wife, the Reverend and Mrs. John Henderson Moorehead, Agnes Robertson Moorehead began her life in Clinton, Massachusetts. Her mother, Mary Mildred MacCauley, a native of rural Pennsylvania, doted upon Agnes and taught her strict Protestant Irish ways. As a child, Agnes would often mimic people she would see on the street, and her father played along with her. At age three, she made what might be considered her first stage appearance when she sang "The Lord is in His Holy Temple" at her father's church. One of Miss Moorehead's biographers reports that she would often, during her childhood, come downstairs in the morning, and her mother would say, "Good Morning, Agnes," to which Moorehead would reply, "I am not Agnes, I am Princess Sybil." (Or whatever role the gifted child decided she should portray that day.) Her mother would involve herself in Agnes's fantasies. This may have been the foundation upon which Miss Moorehead would eventually build a remarkable acting career.

As a young girl, Agnes also often created plays at her parent's 320-acre Ohio farm, which was a grant to her great grandparents who came from England. (*The Journal Herald*, of Dayton, Ohio reported that President James Monroe signed the first deed to the farm, and the second deed, President John Tyler. Still other published narratives say that President John Adams signed the original deed. Later in her life, Miss Moorehead would retreat to the farm from the harsh world of the stage and Hollywood and raise alfalfa, wheat, grains and melons, and cattle, hogs and chickens.)

During Miss Moorehead's childhood, the family moved to St. Louis, Missouri. She received her early schooling there and performed in theaters by age ten. The ambitious young girl also worked with the St. Louis Municipal Opera Company for four years. In 1919, Miss Moorehead completed high school. She graduated from Muskingum College in Ohio, with a Baccalaureate degree in biology. While attending the New Concord, Ohio college, which her uncle founded, the intense young student participated in the Glee Club, the Girls Athletic Association and the Student Volunteer Group. Miss Moorehead opted to stay at the college for a year of postgraduate work in Education, Speech and English. In 1925, she transferred to the University of Wisconsin and there earned a master's degree in English and Public Speaking. (Over the years, other universities would award her many other honorary degrees, including a Doctorate of Fine Arts from Monmouth College in Illinois in April 1959 and a Doctorate in Literature from her alma mater in 1947.)

Sometime during 1926, Agnes moved to New York. There she enrolled in the American Academy of Dramatic Arts where she met her first husband, John Griffith Lee. The two were married in June 1930 but the marriage ended in divorce twenty-one years later in 1951.

While in New York, Miss Moorehead appeared in a succession of Broadway hits. These included "*Scarlet Pages,*" *All the King's Horses,*" "*Courage,*" "*Soldiers and Women,*" and "*Candlelight.*" Following these theatrical triumphs, she gave performances on a vaudeville circuit. Agnes followed the tour with another theater excursion, giving highly dramatic and successful readings, and she then began a career in radio. Miss Moorehead became a regular on Lionel Barrymore's "*Mayor of the Town.*" (She had such respect for the noted thespian that one of her most prized possessions in life was a signed photo of the distinguished Barrymore.)

Miss Moorehead appeared in Jack Benny's first radio broadcast, and she also appeared with Ed Wynn, Bob Hope, Gary Moore, Fred Allen and Milton Berle on their radio programs. She repeated the role of the bedridden woman in Lucille Fletcher's radio version of *Sorry, Wrong Number* a record twenty-six times, by popular demand. (One biographical sketch for an upcoming production read, "Toured more than any other actress, alive or dead. Once rode a circus elephant, played Little Eva on a Mississippi River boat, and scared the whey out of the nation with her performance of the doomed woman on the radio production of *Sorry, Wrong Number.*")

Agnes Moorehead also developed a recurring engagement with Orson Welles' Mercury Players. Through Orson Welles, she traveled to Hollywood to begin her distinguished career in films.

In the early 1950's, Agnes began a now famous tour of the United States and abroad with the Mercury Players reading *Don Juan in Hell*. She married actor Robert Gist in 1953. That marriage lasted six years, ending in a 1959 divorce. During the late sixties, while Miss Moorehead was filming *Bewitched*, she again cris-crossed the country with her one woman show, *An Evening with the Fabulous Red Head.*

Nineteen hundred fifty-six was Agnes Moorehead's most prolific film year, since producers released seven of her films that year. One film, *The Conqueror*, which featured John Wayne as Ghengis Khan and Agnes as his mother, remains a source of controversy to this day. The cast also included Susan Hayward, Pedro Armendariz, Ted DeCorsica, Lee Van Cleef, Thomas Gomez and Dick Powell. Moorehead, Powell, Wayne and Hayward all allegedly died of cancer. Several environmental historians claim we can directly relate these deaths to the film's Utah shooting location, which was near a U.S. nuclear testing facility. Studio heads also ordered the transport of thousands of tons of that Utah soil to the Hollywood studios for matching purposes.

Other than *Bewitched*, some of Agnes Moorehead's television credits include *Ballad of Andy Crocker* with Jimmy Dean, *Barefoot in the Park, Wagon Train, Playhouse 90, Studio One, Twilight Zone, The Rifleman, Walt Disney, The Tempest*, and *Through the Looking Glass.*

Her biographers agree that in conversation with Miss Moorehead, one of three subjects would gracefully come up as a topic – (Her love of) The United States, her religion, or her stagecraft. She read the Bible the first thing each morning and the last thing every night. Agnes Moorehead believed strongly in the efficacy of prayer.

Her deep faith and inherent Fundamentalism led her to constantly testify about her faith. Witness one of her most repeated sayings, "My life has been ruled by my beliefs." Some writers have suggested that she always alluded to her father being a minister and her religion because of the very unladylike characters she often portrayed. Reportedly, Agnes never gave an interview without mentioning her religious convictions. In August 1965, she published "*My Favorite Script*" (about the Bible) in Norman Vincent Peale's *Guideposts* magazine.

She backed her religious talk with decades of charitable work for such charities as The Cancer Society, the Arthritis Foundation, the National Cystic Fibrosis Foundation, and the Eye Dog Foundation. The devoted philanthropist also worked to benefit emotionally disturbed children and various Charity Leagues throughout California.

Agnes Moorehead maintained an ardent patriotism her entire life. She resented any criticism of the country or of any President. In 1972, both the White House and President Nixon (personally) sent her invitations to the Inauguration. Miss Moorehead was to die before the U.S. Congress impeached her friend.

Agnes was a perfectionist when it came to her stage art. According to several sources, she worked harder than most other film stars of that genre and era. Miss Moorehead would often prepare for months researching a role she was about to play. When filming, Agnes would arrive early on the filming set, and she would stay at the studio sometimes until the last technician had gone home. The various profiles of the late actress abound with tales of twenty hour shoots on location because she was such a stickler for excellence. During those long shoots, she would often engage her fellow stars with talk of philosophy rather than gossip. Agnes Moorehead was truly a well-rounded woman.

She loved animals of any kind but especially pigs. One of her associates reports that during a drive through Ohio, they stopped at a service station. A truckload of pigs pulled up next to the Moorehead vehicle, and the pigs started snorting loudly. The very distinguished Miss Moorehead began mimicking the pigs and snorted back so perfectly that the trim actress fooled the pigs. The snorting contest kept up until the truck pulled away with Agnes remarking that she loved animals so dearly, she should have become a vegetarian.

Miss Moorehead maintained a life-long passion for the colors purple, mauve and lavender. She owned a 1956 lavender Thunderbird, decorated her dressing rooms and mansions in purple, and often appeared as Endora clad in purple.

Several Moorehead experts agree that we can still learn more about her life. She was a very private person, who rarely shared anything of a truly personal nature with anyone outside her immediate family or circle of trusted confidantes. Still, Agnes Moorehead wasn't unkind – she would even keep a stack of photos by her front door to sign for any fan that came by her house.

In late 1973, the versatile Miss Moorehead began co-starring in a New York production of "Gigi." Everyone associated with her sensed that she was not well, but ever the theatrical trooper, she never complained. In January 1974, doctors from the Mayo Clinic began treating the famous actress. She checked herself into the Methodist Hospital in Rochester, Minnesota for her final hospitalization on April 9, 1974. The devout and regal realist died a few weeks later, Tuesday, April 30, 1974.

A funeral director from the Arendt-Riley Funeral Home of Rochester, Minnesota confirmed to Associated Press reporters that they had embalmed

Agnes Moorehead and transferred her remains to an out-of-town funeral home. At the behest of the Moorehead family, George C. Martin, of the George C. Martin Funeral Home in Dayton, Ohio received her remains.

Mr. Martin made the final arrangements for entombment of Agnes Moorehead's body with her aging mother, who survived the star by several years. (Agnes Moorehead's father had purchased a block of crypts at Dayton Memorial Park Cemetery and Mausoleum, 8135 North Dixie Drive, Dayton, Ohio, several decades before the actress's death.) George Martin recently told *The American Funeral Director* that he had to conduct the arrangements under a strict veil of secrecy. Although the media continually hounded him, Mr. Martin did not release the formal obituary until several days after the entombment.

Thursday, May 2, 1974, the United Press International wire service ran a news story on Miss Mooreheads' death. In this story and obituary combination, the reporter quoted Agnes Moorehead's attorney as saying that one of the actress's final wishes was that no one conduct a funeral for her. He also said another of Miss Moorehead's expressed last instructions was that doctors not reveal her cause of death although newspapers widely reported it as cancer.

Mr. Martin recalls that the Moorehead family summoned a Presbyterian minister from nearby Columbus who conducted a very brief and very private service in the Gothic looking Chapel Saturday afternoon, May 4, 1974. About fifteen family members attended the late afternoon entombment as private security officers cordoned off the entire Mausoleum and Cemetery area. Following the service, cemetery workers rolled the Crane and Breed Sixteen gauge orchid-colored casket with brushed finish into her crypt. They then secured her white marble name plate which reads simply, AGNES ROBERTSON MOOREHEAD, 1974.

George Martin was one of the last human beings to view the lavender-colored casket of the Lavender Lady. The superb actress – who was moral, confident, intellectual, philosophizing, alluring, kindly, thoughtful, and yet sometimes sharp and abrupt, rests near her beloved Father and Mother nearby in adjoining crypts. A fan, or some visitor, has placed two colorful bouquets of mainly purple artificial flowers on her nameplate along with a laminated copy of her career synopsis.

Agnes Moorehead's popularity is such that on a building wall near her star on the Hollywood Walk of Fame, visitors can see *"Agnes Moorehead is God"* spray-painted on it. Despite city workers covering the graffiti, some dedicated fan keeps returning to write the slogan.

No one has scrawled the words "*Agnes Moorehead is God*" on or near her Dayton, Ohio crypt. Yet, standing and gazing at that serene corner of the Dayton Memorial Park Mausoleum where they have entombed Agnes Moorehead, one has to get the feeling that maybe she was at least a type of God, though – of dignity, charity, Americanism and stagecraft.

Dayton Memorial Park Mausoleum, Dayton, Ohio (Photos by Jo Ann Roscoe)

The Films of Agnes Moorehead:

1941:   *Citizen Kane*, with Orson Welles. (Mercury-RKO)

1942:   *The Magnificent Ambersons*, with Joseph Cotten. She won the New York Film Critics Award for this fine film and also her first Oscar nomination.(Mercury-RKO)
Journey into Fear, with Ruth Warrick. (Mercury-RKO)
The Big Street, with Henry Fonda and Lucille Ball. (RKO Radio)

1943:   *The Youngest Profession*, with Lana Turner and Walter Pidgeon. (MGM)
Government Girl, with Olivia deHaviland. (RKO Radio)

1944:   *Jane Eyre*, with Orson Welles and Elizabeth Taylor. (20th Century Fox)
Since You Went Away, with Jennifer Jones and Claudette Colbert. (Selznick-United Artists)
Dragon Seed, with Katherine Hepburn and Walter Huston. (MGM)
The Seventh Cross, with Spencer Tracy and Hume Cronyn.(MGM)
Mrs. Parkington, with Greer Garson and Walter Huston. (MGM)
Tomorrow the World, with Frederic March. (United Artists)

1945:   *Keep Your Powder Dry*, with Lana Turner and June Lockhart. (MGM)
Our Vines Have Tender Grapes, with Edward G. Robinson and Margaret O'Brien. (MGM)
Her Highness and the Bellboy, with Hedy Lamarr and June Allyson. (MGM)

1947:   *Dark Passage*, Humphrey Bogart, and Lauren Bacall. (Warner Brothers)
The Lost Moment, Susan Hayward and Robert Cummings. (Universal-International)
Miss Moorehead played Hayward's 105-year-old aunt. The make-up reportedly took four hours to apply and over an hour to remove.

1948:   *Summer Holiday*, with Mickey Rooney and Gloria De Haven. (MGM)
The Woman in White, with Sydney Greenstreet and Eleanor Parker. (Warner Brothers)
Stations West, with Dick Powell and Burl Ives. (RKO Radio)
Johnny Belinda, with Jane Wyman and Lew Ayres. (Her second Oscar nomination-Warner Brothers)

1949:   *The Stratton Story*, with James Stewart and June Allyson. (MGM)
The Great Sinner, with Gregory Peck and Ava Gardner. (MGM)
Without Honor, with Franchot Tone and Laraine Day. (United Artists)

1950:   *Caged*, with Eleanor Parker and Lady Jane Darwell. (Warner Brothers)

1951:   *Fourteen Hours*, with Paul Douglas and Grace Kelly. (20th Century-Fox)
Showboat, with Howard Keel and Kathryn Grayson. (MGM)
The Blue Veil, with Jane Wyman and Charles Laughton. (RKO Radio)
Adventures of Captain Fabian, with Errol Flynn. (Republic)

1952:   *The Blazing Forest*, with William Demarest and John Payne. (Paramount Pictures)
Captain Black Jack, with George Sanders. (Classic Pictures)

1953:   *The Story of Three Loves*, with James Mason. (MGM: 3 part film)
Scandal at Scourie, with Greer Garson and Walter Pidgeon. (MGM)
Main Street to Broadway, with Tallulah Bankhead, Ethel and Lionel Barrymore. (MGM)
Those Redheads from Seattle, with Rhonda Fleming and Gene Barry. (Paramount Pictures)

1954:   *Magnificent Obsession*, with Jane Wyman, Rock Hudson and Otto Kreuger. This role earned Miss Moorehead her third Oscar nomination for her portrayal of a nurse. (Universal-International)

1955:   *Untamed*, with Tyrone Power and Susan Hayward. (20th Century-Fox)
The Left Hand of God, Humphrey Bogart and Lee J. Cobb. (20th Century-Fox)

1956:   *All that Heaven Allows*, with Jane Wyman and Rock Hudson. (Universal-International)
Meet Me in Las Vegas, with Dan Dailey and Cyd Charisse. (MGM)
The Conqueror, with John Wayne and Susan Hayward. (RKO Radio)
The Revolt of Mamie Stover, with Jane Russell and Richard Egan. (In two odd turns of events, Agnes Moorehead plays not only a blonde, but also the owner of a Hawaiian brothel. Called by critics "her most unlikely role."(20th Century-Fox)
The Swan, with Grace Kelly and Sir Alec Guinness. (MGM)
Pardners, with Jerry Lewis and Dean Martin. (Paramount Pictures)
The Opposite Sex, with Ann Sheridan, Leslie Nielson and Carolyn Jones. (MGM)

1957:   *Raintree County*, with Elizabeth Taylor and Montgomery Clift. (MGM)
The True Story of Jesse James, with Robert Wagner and Jeffrey Hunter. (20th Century-Fox)
Jeannne Eagles, with Kim Novak and Jeff Chandler. (Columbia)
The Story of Mankind, with her good friend, Cesar Romero. (Warner Brothers)

1959:   *Night of the Quarter Moon*, with Julie London and Nat King Cole. (MGM)
The Tempest, with Van Heflin. (Paramount Pictures)
The Bat, with Vincent Price and John Sutton. (Allied Artists)

1960:   *Pollyanna*, with Hayley Mills, Jane Wyman and Karl Malden. (Buena Vista)

1961:   *Twenty Plus Two*, with Dina Merrill and David Jansen. (Allied Artists)
Bachelor in Paradise, with Bob Hope, Paula Prentiss and Lana Turner. (MGM)

1962:   *Jessica,* with Angie Dickinson and Maurice Chevalier (United Artists)

1963:   *How the West Was Won,* with Spencer Tracy, Jimmy Stewart and Henry Fonda. (MGM)
Who's Minding the Store? with Jerry Lewis and Jill St. John. (Paramount Pictures)

1964:   *Hush, Hush Sweet Charlotte,* with Bette Davis and Olivia deHaviland. (20ᵗʰ Century-Fox)
For her role of the dowdy maid, she won her fourth Oscar nomination as best Supporting Actress.) (20ᵗʰ Century- Fox)

1966:   *The Singing Nun,* with Greer Garson and Debbie Reynolds. (MGM)

More Moorehead Mania

∾ Because of her impeccable diction, most people thought that Agnes Moorehead was British. We can correctly trace some of her speech patterns to her English grandparents. Her paternal grandfather hailed from Edinburgh, her paternal grandmother from London. Agnes Moorehead's maternal grandfather was a native of Wales and his wife originated in Dublin.

∾ She cited the great actors Orson Welles and Charles Laughton and her friend, film producer Paul Gregory, as the three most influential men in her career. Orson Welles gave Agnes Moorehead her first film role as his mother in the classic *Citizen Kane.*

∾ The only alcohol she drank was a small glass of champagne occasionally, citing a biblical reference to Christ using wine.

∾ Her concentration was so intense that toward the middle of her life, she vowed never to drive again because she would think deeply about other subjects while operating a car. One day, she was driving home from several hours worth of shooting and Agnes began thinking about one of her upcoming roles instead of the traffic. Before Miss Moorehead realized what she had done, she found herself in a crime-infested neighborhood of Los Angeles. From that day forward, she never drove again.

∾ She took time out of her hectic schedule to send thank you notes to those who served her – managers of hotels, motels, or inns, or the couple that looked after her Ohio farm while she was away from it. She hated flying, and preferred to take a bus, train, or car to distant destinations.

Sources

Funeral Director George C. Martin, Dayton, Ohio, Interview by Author

The Journal Herald, Dayton, Ohio, Wednesday, May 1, 1974 and Thursday, May 2, 1974.

United Press International, Thursday, May 2, 1974 (background information only, no quotations)

"Bewitched Forever," Herbie J. Pilato

Associated Press, Wednesday, May 1, 1974 and Thursday, May 2, 1974 (background information only, no quotations)

Guideposts, *My Favorite Script*, Agnes Moorehead, August 1965

In Rehearsal, Charles Jehlinger, AADA, 1968

Boston Herald Traveler, October 26, 1972, article by Ken Mayer

Agnes Moorehead, Dr. Warren Sherk, Dorrance & Co., 1976

Run Through, John Houseman, 1971

COLE ALBERT PORTER:
IN THE STILL OF THE NIGHT

JUNE 9, 1891 – OCTOBER 15, 1964

The cosmopolitan composer who wrote not only the music, but the words for an abundance of American standards such as I've Got You Under My Skin, Night and Day, Begin the Beguine *and* I Get A Kick Out of You, *determined new directions for other songwriters who may never match his verve. His complex and sometimes controversial personal life style almost offset the refinement of his graceful words and snappy music. How a millionaire from the Midwestern farmlands of Peru, Indiana changed the face of American songwriting forever remains a story often told. Yet, it is one that still fascinates people, more than thirty-five years after his death.*

(*Photo courtesy of Miami County Museum, Peru, Indiana*)

"I direct my Executors to arrange for my burial in Peru, Indiana. I further direct my Executors to arrange for no funeral or memorial service, but only for a private burial service to be conducted by the Pastor of the First Baptist Church of Peru in the presence of my relatives and dear friends. At such service, I request said pastor to read the following quotation from the Bible, 'I am the resurrection and the life; he that believeth in me, though he were dead, yet shall he live and whosoever liveth and believeth in me shall never die,' and to follow such quotation with the Lord's Prayer.

"I request that the foregoing be substantially the entire burial service, and that neither said Pastor nor anyone else deliver any memorial address whatsoever. I particularly direct that there be no service for me of any kind in New York City." — An excerpt from Cole Porter's will, drawn in 1962.

This matter of a public record – Cole Porter's will – issues specific stage directions for the medium sized band of mourners – a few of them distant relatives of the late song writer – that gathered at Mount Hope Cemetery in what would have been the seventy-third fall of the sophisticated composer's life. Weather reports tell us that it was a cold, rainy and windy day not unlike most autumn days in the Hoosier State's central northern tier.

Cole Porter died at 11:05 P.M. (PST) Thursday, October 15, 1964 at St. Johns Hospital in Santa Monica, California of "severe bronchopneumonia." The autopsy report cited many medical problems including "chronic nephrosclerosis, emphysema and far advanced arteriosclerosis."

Pierce Brothers Mortuary of Santa Monica, California (now closed) shipped Cole Porter's body in a standard transfer case to The Eikenberry Funeral Home (currently The Eikenberry-Eddy Funeral Home) of Peru, Indiana. Mr. Porter's two faithful valets, Burke and Eric Lindsay, accompanied the body on the trip back to Indiana.

Eikenberry funeral director Richard Murray (a graduate of the Indiana College of Mortuary Science, Class of '58) lived and worked in Peru for ten years from 1959- 1969. He recalls that he was sitting at a front office desk in the funeral home (with Mr. Eikenberry) when the Cole Porter death call came from Pierce Mortuary. Mr. Murray took it, and said he will always remember the "unusual" phone call from Pierce Brothers because a director told him, "This is Pierce Brothers Mortuary in Santa Monica. We congratulate you. We are shipping the body of Cole Porter to your firm." Richard Murray – who later became a partner with Mr. Eikenberry for a short period – told *The American Funeral Director* recently that he could never forget such an unusual way to receive a death call – with congratulations!

The Eikenberry Funeral Home provided both merchandise and services to the Cole family for Cole Porter. They received the remains, and funeral director Richard Murray helped dress Cole Porter for his burial. He states that Mr. Porter's body was very frail and slight, and that his fingers were excessively thin and long. The casket remained closed, and Mr. Murray believes that even the immediate family (which consisted of a few cousins) did not view Cole Porter's remains. Eikenberry Funeral Home directed the services Sunday, October 18, 1964 at 2:30 P.M. according to Tom Eddy, owner and manager of Eikenberry Eddy Funeral Home in Peru.

Mr. George Eikenberry worked as the lead funeral director for the Porter services. The firm conducted no formal service at the First Baptist Church (as they had for Cole's mother) and led no procession from there to the cemetery, according to Porter's specific wishes. One eyewitness said that there were "plenty of limousines and big cars" around Peru that day, even if funeral directors took no cortege to the cemetery. A huge spray of roses so completely engulfed the Belmont Bronze casket that the cardinal colored floral tribute trailed on the ground.

Richard Murray was one of the pallbearers for Cole Porter's massive casket. He says that about seventy-five people attended the private services which the Cole Family held before they made the funeral announcement to the public.

They invited all of the mourners. Mr. Murray commented that the number of people present at the funeral service surprised him. He also remembers that the Cole family wished no "big spectacle" and wanted to limit the news media and general public's intrusion into the funeral services.

Various reports concerning the Cole Porter funeral and the disposition of his remains can be found in the profusion of existing biographies. One report explains the rumor that funeral directors cremated Porter and did not bury him. (Several eyewitness accounts of the burial, including Richard Murray's, invalidate this supposition. Careful investigation reveals that people who were *not present* at the service have furnished incorrect information about the Cole Porter burial to various biographers.)

Yet another piece of simply sentimental gossip that endures about Cole Porter is that his only lineal survivors, two cousins, buried him between the two women who were most important to him in life, his wife, Linda, and his mother, Kate Cole. The truth is that the undertakers from Eikenberry Funeral Home buried him between his father (which is paradoxical since father and son were never very close in life) and his wife. Small headstones of Vermont granite scripted with only names, birth and death dates mark the family plot.

That cold and rainy afternoon in Peru, which is nearly seventy miles north of Indianapolis, the ever suave and debonair Cole Porter had now completed his full circle of life. It isn't far – only three blocks – from Mount Hope Cemetery to the huge Victorian style Porter homestead on Third and Huntington Street. At that frame house, still standing today, the legendary musician made his entrance into the world on June 9, 1891, a sweltering hot day in Miami County.

Yet, Cole Porter filled the years between those few blocks with an almost mythical musical and lyrical brilliance, a quality education, a highly successful career as a lyricist and composer, seemingly limitless travel abroad, fast living, servants, elegant cars, homes resplendent with majesty and opulence, a sham marriage (he was openly homosexual), and all the trappings of considerable wealth. Some of this affluence Porter inherited from his Midwestern family, and almost two million dollars of it from his wife, Linda Lee Thomas Cole, who was fifteen years his senior.

Cole's grandfather, J. O. Cole, also inherited wealth, and built upon it during the Gold Rush of 1849. He first worked as a miner's assistant in Maryville, California and then opened a General Store. Returning to Peru (once known as Miamisport out of admiration to the tribe of Indians found there and its location on the Wabash River banks), J. O. Cole escalated his fortune into millions by opening a brewery and ice and cold storage facility. Cole also wisely invested in an Ohio sawmill and timberland in several states including West Virginia. Because of the natural gas and coal on the West Virginia lands, J. O. Cole became even wealthier. In 1860, he married a woman from Peru, Rachel Henton. They nurtured a family with two children – Kate, born two years later, and her brother, Louis, born in 1865. Published reports say J.O. favored Kate heavily over her younger brother.

Kate Cole – born with the proverbial advantage of prosperity – experienced the finest possible upbringing that money could afford. Her parents gave her literally the very best of everything from clothing to a private East Coast finishing school education. Bullheaded and unyielding, Kate often resented her father's meddlesome ways. She eventually married on April 19,1884 an unassuming druggist of fixed assets, Samuel Fenwick Porter. Four years later, their son, Louis, died shortly after birth, and their two-year-old daughter, Rachel, died in 1890.

Sam, the druggist, remained hidden in the powerful and overbearing shadows of his father-in-law. Kate, used to wealth and position, often had difficulties with Samuel Porter's limited financial dealings. Still, in 1891, a third frail child entered this dysfunctional family environment. No one, except possibly Kate, dreamed that tiny Cole would grow up to be one of the most respected songwriters in the history of the American theater.

As Cole grew, Kate dressed him in the very best of clothing, which set him apart from his peers. One of Cole's cousins mused in a 1990 TV interview that Cole surely had a difficult life as a child, if for no reason other than the fancy clothing Kate insisted Cole wear.

The Hagenbeck and Wallace Circus used Peru as its operations base, and people came to know and love it as a "Circus Town." During the days of Cole's boyhood, there were constantly parades, and Sam Porter often played the steam calliope. Cole decided that he wanted to become a clown and cherished that idea for many years. (This love of circus lore probably helped Cole write "Be A Clown" in 1948.)

As a child, Cole composed songs about his play mates, teachers, neighbors and family. The ten-year-old Cole Porter wrote and dedicated two songs to his mother, who took them to Chicago and had them printed. Under the domineering influence of Kate, he learned to play the piano and violin and sing in the Lutheran church choir. Neither J.O. Cole nor Sam Porter approved of, or took much interest in, Cole's musical aptitude. He would later say that he remembered very little about his passive father, who died on August 18, 1927 at the age of sixty-nine. Cole often recalled stories of his grandfather predicting he would wind up at the county poorhouse.

By 1905, the fourteen-year-old Cole left Peru for a private preparatory school – Worchester Academy in Worcester, Massachusetts. The diminutive Cole fared well at both academics and various extracurricular activities. He graduated as Class Valedictorian, and his grandfather awarded him a trip to Europe.

Cole's next stop was Yale, where he eventually was a gargantuan success socially and musically, but less successful as a scholar. Initially, though, the predominantly Eastern "Yalies" snubbed Cole because of his pop-eyed and slight appearance. His clothing, again selected by Kate, also caused him a great deal of "razzing." He wrote several songs while attending the Ivy League University and enjoyed an elevated status around campus because of the football fight songs he composed. (*Bingo Eli Yale, Bulldog, Beware of Yale, Eli and Fla De Dah*, all now Yale classics.)

In 1917, Cole traveled to France. Some reports claim that he joined the French Foreign Legion during the First World War. Other accounts dispute that he ever served in any type of military unit. Yet another biographer maintains that Porter served in an ambulance unit. The 1945 (supposedly biographical) film about Cole Porter, *Night and Day*, depicts him as having served in the military. Most people who knew Porter, or anything about him, dismissed the film as "fantasy." The composer's closest friends suspect that the entire World War I military story was a tall tale, typical of the type Porter loved to invent. Regardless, during his prolonged stay in France, he associated with other eclectic people such as Ernest Hemingway, Gertrude Laurence, F. Scot Fitzgerald and Picasso.

It was in Paris that Cole met Linda Lee Thomas on January 30, 1918 at a wedding of friends. Thomas, an heir of the famous Lees' family of Virginia and a descendant of a signer of the Declaration of Independence, traveled the continent as a very wealthy American divorced woman.

It's generally agreed that Linda Lee Thomas took over where Kate had left off – as his mother. Strikingly beautiful, the professional model married Cole Porter on December 18, 1919 in a French civil ceremony. Linda and Cole related to each other on many levels – professionally, artistically, intellectually, economically – and they were good friends. Authors have written tomes about their marriage, speculating that it remained an open-ended one, but according to those closest to Porter the truth is that Linda stayed exceedingly loyal to Cole until her death.

During the years 1919-1936, Cole Porter enjoyed tremendous success as a composer and lyricist. He maintained many homes, some on the Continent, one in California, and still another in New York. He worked hard to achieve his goal of writing one Broadway musical and one film score a year. During these years, Cole and Linda traveled to Europe extensively.

In 1923, J. O. Cole died, and Cole immediately traveled to Peru to comfort his mother. Porter's grandfather, always disapproving of Cole's musical career, left him out of the will but entrusted the Cole fortune to Kate who promptly gave Cole a million dollars. Cole's father, Samuel Fenwick Porter, died on August 18, 1927 because of " complications of a nervous breakdown."

By October 1937, Cole and Linda, with their relationship tepid at best, were at least temporarily separated. On October 24th, Cole, while attending a weekend party at a wealthy socialite's home, decided to take a horse out for a ride on the Long Island estate. Although the horse's handlers had warned Cole against taking a particularly skittish horse, Porter's stubbornness surfaced, and he took the horse out riding anyway. In the woods, something scared the horse, throwing Cole onto the ground. The horse fell and rolled back and forth across both of Cole Porter's legs smashing them totally into compound fractures. Eventually, osteomyelitis developed.

Linda, who was living overseas at the time, immediately traveled to Cole's side. Although surgeons at Manhattan's Doctor's Hospital advocated amputation, Linda advised Cole against it. She knew that it would totally break his spirit to be a double amputee. Counseling against the surgery eventually proved the correct course of action. In February 1958, when Cole had to have his right leg amputated at mid-thigh, it literally stopped his creativity and productivity.

Cole, true to his mother's counseling not to tell others of one's own woe, endured the hardship stoically. He told one friend that while he was waiting for help after the horse rolled on him, he pulled out a notebook and finished composing a song on which he was working. Yet another tale involves the famed social columnist and close friend of Cole's, Elsa Maxwell. Cole reportedly told Elsa, while she was visiting him at the hospital shortly after the accident, that fifty million Frenchmen couldn't be wrong for eating horses, rather than riding them.

For the rest of his life, Cole relied on wheelchairs, canes, braces, male nurses, attendants and his valets to carry him from room to room or to help him into his car.

He constantly had a male nurse close to him. Eventually, Cole Porter willed one of them, Ray Kelly, half his interest in his copyrighted music. This is especially odd since in the later years of Porter's life, Kelly rarely even visited him.

After the second World War, Broadway critics considered Porter's works to be old fashioned. It took him more than three years to raise financial backing for a Broadway show that developed into one of his greatest hits – His adaptation of Shakespeare's *The Taming of the Shrew* which Porter deftly named *Kiss Me Kate*.

In early February 1952, Kate Cole Porter suffered a stroke, from which she never recovered, dying on August 3, 1952 at the age of ninety. Even after her death, she was true to her beloved son Cole and left the bulk of her estate to Cole except $12,000 which went to distant relatives. The Eikenberry Funeral Home buried her next to her husband, Sam, in the Mount Hope Cemetery in Peru, Indiana.

The late George Eikenberry (owner of the Eikenberry Funeral Home in Peru) often told friends and associates that Cole Porter had issued strict instructions that only white flowers be present at Kate's funeral service at The First Baptist Church of Peru. Apparently, a florist did not get the word, and neither did George until it was too late. Upon arriving for the funeral at the church, Cole Porter spied a bouquet of red carnations, and he asked that someone remove them immediately. Mr. Eikenberry, reportedly very embarrassed by this gaffe, quickly relocated the offending flowers to a back room of the church.

On May 20, 1954, the other strong woman in Cole's life, Linda Lee Thomas Porter, died in New York. Ministers conducted a short and private funeral service at St. Bartholomew's Church next to the Waldorf Astoria Towers where Linda died in her suite of rooms. Although she wished burial elsewhere, Cole arranged for transfer of her remains to Peru, and he buried her in the Cole family plot at Mount Hope. Porter, totally devastated, never left the car for her interment service.

After the 1958 amputation of his right leg, Cole Porter suffered deep depression and began to drink excessively. His favorite was Scotch, although friends and staff tried to switch him to vodka so they could dilute it without his knowledge. It simply did not work, and his use of alcohol and pain killing drugs increased steadily between the years of 1958-1964.

In those final six years, Cole Porter suffered wretched health and spent a great deal of time in hospitals. Toward the end, he reportedly told a close friend that he was very tired and simply wanted to die. The friend, shocked, asked Cole if there would be nothing that he would miss in death. Porter closed his eyes for a minute, considered the question and answered, "Yes, my two Queen Anne chairs."

So it was, that Cole Porter maintained his sharp composer's wit and ability almost to the end of his life. He died at 11:05 P.M., October 15th, 1964, " in the still of the night, when the world was in slumber" – but he left us a world greatly improved by his masterful compositions.

Cole Porter's Most Popular Songs: A Dateline

1919:   First Hit – *Old Fashioned Garden*

1928:   *Let's Do It (Let's Fall in Love)*

1929:   *You Do Something to Me*

1934:   *You're the Top, Don't Fence Me In, I Get A Kick Out of You* and *Anything Goes*

1935:   *Begin the Beguine* (Artie Shaw's recording with vocalist Tony Martin sold more than six and a half million copies in the first week the record company released it.)

1936:   *I've Got You Under My Skin, It's Delovely* and *Easy To Love*

1937:   *In the Still of the Night* (Theater lore says that Tough Studio Boss Louis B. Mayer burst into tears when he heard Cole Porter play this haunting love ballad from the MGM film *Rosalie*.)

1938:   *My Heart Belongs to Daddy*

1940:   *So Near and Yet So Far*

1942:   *You'd Be So Nice to Come Home To*

1944:   *Count Your Blessings*
1948:   *Be A Clown* and *Too Darn Hot*
1953:   *I Love Paris*
1955:   *All of You* and *Silk Stockings*
1956:   *True Love*

Bibliography/ Sources and Suggested Readings on Cole Porter

Interview – Tom Eddy, Manager, Owner & Funeral Director, Eikenberry-Eddy Funeral Home, Peru, Indiana

Interview – Richard L. Murray, formerly a Funeral Director with Eikenberry Funeral Home, Peru, Indiana. (Mr. Murray is now semi-retired having sold the majority interest of his Galveston, Indiana Funeral Home.)

Cole Porter: A Biography, Charles Schwartz, Dial Press, 1977

Cole Porter: A Biography, William Mc Brien, Alfred A. Knopf, 1998

Red, Hot and Blue: An Oral History of Cole Porter, Charles Grafton, Scarborough House, 1987

Genius and Lust, Joseph Morella and George Mazzei, Carroll & Graf, 1995

Travels with Cole Porter, Jean Howard, Harry N. Abrams, 1991

Also, for a quick overview of Porter's songs and life, you can watch *You're the Top*, with Bobby Short, Narrator, Island Art Videotapes, 1991.

Milton S. Hershey:

The Kiss of Success

September 13, 1857 – October 13, 1945

Milton Snavely Hershey, a benevolent and loving man who was the first to make the exquisite taste of milk chocolate readily available to the people of the United States, led an impeccable and highly moral life, filled with giving and caring. It was a time when other industrial titans prospered because of their workers' misery. Yet, Mr. Hershey often worked alongside his Pennsylvania factory workers for the common good.

(Photo courtesy of Hershey Community Archives)

"How does it feel to give away sixty million dollars?" The year was 1923, and a reporter grilled Milton Hershey, a man most accurately described as shy, caring, genuine, affable, and philanthropic. Mr. Hershey, in November 1918, in memory of his late wife, Catherine (Kitty) Sweeney, donated his entire estate, replete with his land holdings and 500,000 shares of the Hershey Chocolate Company to the Hershey Industrial School. (Milton and Kitty Hershey created the school initially with 486 acres of land to establish the wayward boy's orphanage in 1909.)

The school, with room and board, tuition and other school related costs endowed by the generosity of the childless Hershey couple – one of many noble gifts Milton Hershey gave to the world – would eventually graduate thousands of successful men and women (Mr. and Mrs. Hershey expected the students to "earn their keep" by doing mundane chores).

One could initially conclude that it's remarkable that the world outside the bustling – yet somehow distinctly peaceful – town of Hershey would not discover such a generous act for several years. It is a testimony to the solid and unassuming character of an industrial giant considered by millions to be the finest and most compassionate ever to grace the United States. (This is especially true when one considers how other American industrialists of the era used people ruthlessly to amass their fortunes, even to the point of death.) The humanitarian act of commissioning the school itself bespeaks volumes about the true high-minded personality of the Chocolate King. His insistence that his workers and the media not praise him probably harks back to his modest "Pennsylvania- Swiss-German plain people" upbringing.

"I didn't give away sixty million dollars. I just signed some papers."

True to his Mennonite origins, Mr. Hershey was characteristically modest about his magnanimous gift. Witness the following quotation found in the November 18, 1923 edition of *The New York Times*. "The biggest influence in a boy's life is what his dad does, and when a boy doesn't have any type of (decent) dad, he is a special mark for destiny. I am afraid that most of our orphan boys have a bad time of it, and that many will not get the right start. They tell me that youngsters who go to prison never had a chance. Well, I am going to give some of them a chance my way."

That Milton Hershey would specifically mention a fatherless child, rather than a motherless child, decidedly has some interesting psychological overtones. Mr. Hershey's own father, Henry, consistently absent from Milton's boyhood, involved himself in so many improbable and dubious money making schemes that the Hershey family was always penniless during the 1860's. With creditors constantly looking for Henry, eventually Milton's mother, Veronica (Fanny) Snavely Hershey, threw Henry out of several homes they inhabited. She also never corrected people when they incorrectly called her "the widow Hershey." Still, as a young man, Milton Hershey would not involve himself in his parent's quarrels, and did in reality enter a few business ventures with his father.

Henry Hershey, of Derry Church, Dauphin County, Pennsylvania, an area heavily populated by the Swiss-German, married Fanny Snavely, of neighboring Lancaster County on January 15, 1856. Some Hershey historians say that their relationship, fraught with many disagreements and an eventual separation, was downright odd for the times.

Henry failed to follow the tenants of the Mennonite faith which dictated simple living, drab dress, religious education and plenty of hard work. He preferred reading the classics and metropolitan newspapers and devised – at Fanny's count – seventeen different and wild conspiracies of investment and money-making. Conversely, Fanny Snavely, the daughter of a Mennonite minister, followed her religion devoutly and exactly, *after* her marriage to Henry.

According to Hershey Community Archivist Pamela Whitenack, the first few years of Henry and Fanny's marriage were happy until she realized that Henry would not live up to her expectations.

She dressed starkly in the traditional dark garb of the Amish-like religion replete with a starched white apron and prayer bonnet. Fanny prayed for guidance consistently and read her Bible daily. We could correctly call Fanny humorless and stern but she was an excellent mother to Milton Snavely Hershey. She bore him September 13, 1857 about two years into the stormy marriage in the small farming village of Hockersville, Pennsylvania. Henry and Fanny had one other child, a daughter, Serena, who lived just four years dying in 1867 of scarlet fever.

Milton Hershey's childhood was decidedly not an easy one by any standards. He had to rise early and work long, difficult hours before walking to school. The dysfunctional Hershey family battles continued, and Milton lived in several homes before he was ten years of age. Fanny and Henry quarreled constantly, and Milton's education was particularly a sticking point to Fanny who did not want her son educated in secular schools. (His mother despised and distrusted books so earnestly that upon Henry's 1904 death, she built a bonfire with his books. Published reports say neighbors could see the blaze for miles.)

Milton's formal education – which eventually amounted to a fourth grade level – was lackluster. Owing to the itinerant nature of the Hershey family, he attended several different schools. The zenith of Milton's school days was probably the presentation to one of his teachers of a large skunk that he trapped. He was very popular among his schoolmates, according to one of his biographers, and even in those days carried pockets full of sweets to present to the young women.

Henry remained eager to apprentice Milton in a trade. Being something of an errant journalist himself, in 1871 he secured an internship with a German printer, Samuel Ernst of Gap, Pennsylvania, for the fourteen-year-old Milton. The elder Hershey harbored an ulterior motive for selecting this vocation for Milton. Henry hoped that by apprenticing him, the German would continue Milton's education in the world of words.

Milton, who still had to attend to field chores while completing his apprenticeship, despised setting type and washing the rollers for *Der Waffenlose Wachter* (meaning: *The Unarmed Guard*, by one translation.) In an act of Karma comparable to Thomas Edison spilling chemicals on the train on which he worked, getting fired, and going on to greater destinies, Milton Hershey ruined the printing of a paper. He also spilled a tray of some scarce and valuable type. Editor Ernst discharged the young Hershey immediately, following a bombardment of Germanic appellations.

Joseph Royer's Confectionery store stood in the shadows of City Hall, best known as the meeting place of the Continental Congress for one day. Royer had developed a reputation for quality candies, and Milton seemed to think that he would like that line of work. Although many young men applied for the position, Royer took an immediate liking to the cherubic Milton, and hired him.

It was at Royers' Ice Cream Parlor and Garden on King Street that Mr. Hershey developed his sense of experimentation, timing and "hands on" approach to candy making. It was here at this busy shop near Franklin and Marshall College that Milton learned the basics of candy making.

By age nineteen, armed with one hundred and fifty dollars, the first of many loans from his Aunt Martha (Mattie), the journeyman Milton Hershey traveled to Philadelphia, less than a hundred miles from Lancaster. Visitors thronged to the 1876 Centennial Exposition. Initially, Mr. Hershey had a modicum of success with his small candy shop often working fourteen to sixteen hour days. Four years later, Aunt Mattie implored him to move to a larger shop and hire some help. She herself, along with Fanny, often helped Milton in his now enlarged business. Milton Hershey worked so diligently during this period that he developed a life-threatening illness. Fanny nursed him through it, and a month later he returned to work.

It was during this period that Mr. Hershey began his work with caramels. He, his mother and his aunt manufactured and wrapped them. These are not the caramels that will make his fortune though – he will not learn that successful formula until he moves to Colorado.

Between 1876-1882, his Aunt Mattie and his uncles from the Snavely family gave Milton intermittent financial assistance.

In late 1881, Henry wrote his son about the opportunities in Denver, Colorado. By the time Milton arrived in Colorado, the silver boom had gone bust. The younger Hershey found work with a confectioner and learned how to make caramels with fresh milk, resulting in a naturally chewy candy with a long shelf life. He also worked his trade in Chicago before returning to Lancaster.

There he borrowed even more money from his aunt and indulged a long held desire of his to move to New York City and open a candy shop, which he did at Number 742, Sixth Avenue. Mr. Hershey manufactured his tasty caramels again, and during the three years he stayed in New York he gained a slight modicum of success, even moving to larger quarters. His aunt and mother joined him, but fate again intervened in the youthful confectioner's life.

As Milton Hershey's business grew, he sought out larger quarters. When he made the change, the lease on his first building still had some time to run. The landlord would not release him, and he was unable to find someone to sublet the first building. He continued in New York City, but could not recover there financially. Attempting to improve his cash flow, he invested heavily into cough drops. In financial straits, he attempted to raise money for partial payment by hiring a wagon and filling it with the cough drops and selling to push cart dealers and other small merchants. Unfortunately, some kids threw firecrackers, and the horse bolted spilling his inventory onto the New York streets. The combination of the two bizarre episodes bankrupted Mr. Hershey. But this time, at least was able to pay his creditors forty cents on the dollar.

Back in Lancaster, the "Red Rose City," and twenty-eight years old, Milton wanted to borrow even more money from relatives but several of them washed their hands of him. His Aunt Mattie, however, placed her home as collateral for his loan. Also, one of his true friends, a Civil War veteran named Harry Lebkicher, came to the rescue with much needed capital. Milton started producing "Crystal A" caramels in 1886 but it was a few years later when he finally began savoring the sugary taste of success. The Lancaster Caramel Company eventually grew to a four-story building that covered an entire block, and had other plants in Mt. Joy and Reading Pennsylvania, and in Illinois. By this time, says Archivist Whitenack, Hershey employed more than two thousand workers.

One reason that Hershey's early workers were so loyal to him was his willingness to roll up his sleeves and work alongside them, on the floor of the factory. He loved tinkering and working and despised the administrative side of the business. For Milton Hershey, a superior product was indistinguishable from mastery.

"Give them quality." He often said. "That's the best advertisement in the world."

(In fact, until the late sixties, decades after Hershey's death, the company used no formal advertising campaigns.) Milton Hershey's idea of advertising was much less complicated than the Madison Avenue approach of the year 2000. His theory, upon finding a discarded candy wrapper, was to leave it in place, turning it over so that the Hershey name showed.

With his newfound wealth, Mr. Hershey began to travel the world, and one of his destinations shifted the course of American candy manufacturing history permanently. At the Chicago World Fair of 1893, Milton discovered the Columbian Exposition and became intrigued with some chocolate manufacturing machinery. Interestingly enough, he had used chocolate before to coat and flavor caramels. At the booth, he enticed the German proprietor, J. D. Lehmann, to sell him the entire display. Mr. Hershey had all of the machinery shipped back to the Lancaster Caramel Company by rail when the Exposition ended.

On April 10, 1894, Milton's beloved Aunt Mattie Snavely died at age 62 after a short illness. She was among the few people, along with Fanny and his good friend Harry, who truly believed that he would eventually become prosperous.

A business trip during 1897 to a confectionery store in Jamestown, New York jolted Milton Snavely Hershey out of his bachelorhood when he met a strikingly beautiful Irish Catholic woman of twenty-five years, Catherine Sweeney. The trips to Jamestown became so frequent that a year later, on a Wednesday morning, May 25, 1898, a priest married the unattended and handsome couple in a rectory of New York City's celebrated St. Patrick's Cathedral. Milton, age forty, found his father and brought him back to live in Derry Township after purchasing the family homestead.

For some time, Milton Hershey resisted his competitors' offers to buy the Lancaster Caramel Company from him. Still, he was truly interested in making chocolate. He sold for $500,000 in cash and 500,000 shares of the new American Caramel Company. Milton had plans, though, and kept all of the chocolate-making equipment. Mr. Hershey rented floor space from his successor and started turning out chocolate candies.

The chocolate business progressed considerably, and Milton Hershey attended to business with a newfound passion. He realized that he needed a new factory, and purchased land around his family homestead.

Milton Hershey's friends asked him how he expected to make money. The six-acre factory site – set on more than 1200 acres of undeveloped land – consisted of several limestone buildings in the middle of a cornfield, otherwise known as Derry Church in lower Dauphin County. Many critics didn't understand the Lebanon Valley offered an abundance of superior quality milk and good clean water. A work ethic remained very strong in this part of central Pennsylvania so choice labor was available. The intrepid and undisputed Lord of Chocolate broke the hilly and rocky ground for Hershey on March 2, 1903. Kitty, Henry and Fanny were all on hand. Henry would die less than a year later on February 20, 1904.

Beyond all of the physical work and bureaucratic trappings necessary to establish a factory with a town for its workers lay the quixotic vision of Milton Hershey. Very much like the film character George Bailey in the Christmas Classic, *It's a Wonderful Life*, Mr. Hershey envisioned parcels of land with parks and neatly laid out with homes for all of his workers. He wanted his workers to have the conveniences and niceties of life he never had in his early years. So he started building Hershey – Chocolatetown, USA, as we now often call it – thirteen miles from the capital of the Keystone State, Harrisburg and just twenty miles from Lancaster.

In the first ten years of the town's existence, Milton Hershey convinced the Reading Railroad to bring more lines into town, and to move the railway station from Derry Church to Hershey. He talked the federal government into establishing a Post Office. He built an inn, a bank, a department store, and began a weekly newspaper. He laid out the plans for utilities, homes, streets and parks, and provided a YWCA, YMCA, and schools. More growth followed in the next ten years, including a 10,000-acre Hershey Sugar Plantation, mill and factory that he laid out in Cuba beginning in 1916. Both the factories and chocolate business prospered.

Over the years, Milton Hershey would add a magnificent Community Center, a Junior College where residents would pay no tuition, and a huge amusement park (still operating in the year 2000).

(Photo courtesy of Hershey Community Archives)

However, misery and sadness soon overshadowed the magnificent contributions of Mr. Hershey. Around 1902, Kitty's health began diminishing when she developed an incurable nervous disorder. Though he resolutely took her to the best physicians and surgeons in the world and warmer climates, she died on March 25, 1915. On a Saturday, March 27, Milton Hershey held funeral services for his dignified and dedicated wife. Interment was at the West Laurel Receiving Vault in Philadelphia where Kitty's body remained until Milton established the Hershey Cemetery, four years later. Then Milton had her remains moved to what would become the Hershey family plot. For the remainder of his life, he would send freshly cut floral tributes to her grave twice a week.

On March 11, 1920, at aged 85 years, Fanny Snavely Hershey died. Milton Hershey buried her in the family plot in Hershey Cemetery about two miles northeast of town. In 1927, not far from his birthplace, Milton Hershey built a brick schoolhouse for the Hershey Industrial School in her memory.

During the Great Depression, Mr. Hershey did all that he could to provide for his workers. Rather than cutting back production in a panic, he maintained production standards and added building projects for the town.

In the thirties, some workers developed a dislike for Milton Hershey, despite all that he accomplished for them. On April 2, 1937, in Mr. Hershey's eightieth year, about six hundred workers seized the factory, declared a general strike and held the plant captive for five days. Reasons for this strike reportedly include dramatically reduced working hours, no grievance procedure and machine speedups.

Early April 7th, the farmers and other loyal Hershey workers told the strikers inside the factory to come out, or suffer the consequences. Late in the afternoon, the two sides fought in a bloody melee with many serious resultant injuries to the strikers.

This violence devastated Milton Hershey. Not long after that the workers voted in favor of unionization.

On September 13, 1944, Milton Hershey celebrated his eighty-seventh birthday. He liked to read his favorite newspapers, smoke his choice Coronna Cigars and listen to the radio news broadcasts. About a month later, he announced retirement from his many businesses.

Milton Hershey's doctors repeatedly told the great man "to slow down and take life easy." Nonetheless, that was an impossibility for the man Kitty Hershey called "My Little Dutchman." Sometime in late September, Milton Hershey went out with one of his civil engineers to check on a boundary line on one of his farms. It was a very warm day in the Lebanon Valley, and Mr. Hershey removed his coat.

One of Mr. Hershey's biographers states that he overtaxed his strength and developed a bad cold which his physician feared would develop into pneumonia. The doctor ordered him to the hospital Thursday, October 11th.

"We will go and see what kind of a hospital this man Hershey runs," Mr. Hershey reportedly said as the doctor and nurse helped him into an ambulance. "If he isn't running it right, I'll tell him about it." According to the biography, upon arrival at the hospital, all of the nurses lined up outside waiting for Mr. Hershey.

The Medical log notes that he was admitted to Hershey Hospital on October 11th after experiencing a coronary. His last words, spoken on the morning of October 12 were to the day nurse to the effect of, "You never thought that you would have to look at me in a cage, like a monkey in a zoo, did you?" He fell asleep almost at once and lapsed into a coma which endured until his death at 11:00 A.M., Saturday, October 13, 1945.

Milton Hershey never established a funeral home in Chocolatetown. The Bowser Funeral Home (now Tref and Bowser Funeral Home) of Hummelstown took charge of Milton Snavely Hershey's body and funeral arrangements.

Tuesday, the town that Mr. Hershey loved and founded, literally came to a standstill for his 2:00 P.M. funeral, dignified by its' simplicity. During the four hours of viewing (9 A.M. until 1:00 P.M.) before the service, Pennsylvania State Police estimated that more than ten thousand people made the pilgrimage to

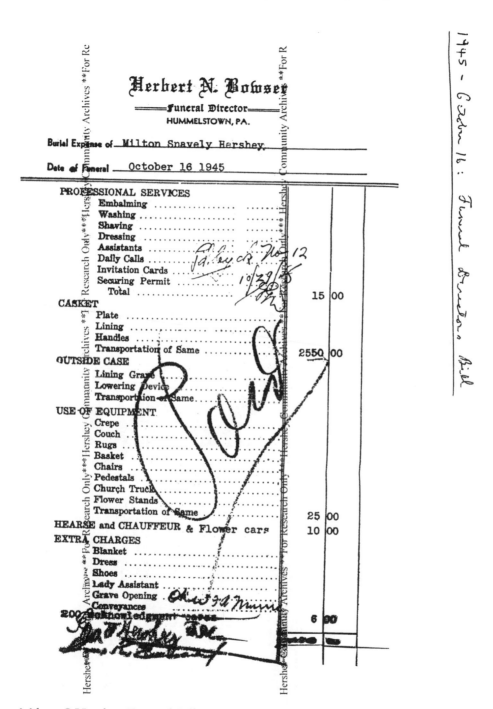

Milton S. Hershey Funeral Bill (Courtesy of Hershey Community Archives)

the Hershey Industrial School to file past his casket which the undertakers surrounded with hundreds and hundreds of baskets and sprays of all types of flowers including red roses, his favorite. Many people sent the Milton Hershey Red Rose, named after the great benefactor. The floral tributes literally created a carpet that stretched out of the school's rotunda onto the steps. Undertakers and staff from the Bowser Funeral Home transported each floral offer-

Milton Hershey's grave in the family plot, Hershey, Pennsylvania (Photo by Ed Bolton)

ing to Mr. Hershey's grave (Please see accompanying Statement of Charges for Milton Hershey's Funeral).

Six ministers – one from each church in Hershey – presided at Mr. Hershey's thirty-minute funeral. It was held in the school auditorium with 1,200 people attending including the Pennsylvania Governor Martin. The Rev. John H. Treder, vicar of All Saints Episcopal Mission said in the eulogy:

MILTON S. HERSHEY
SEPTEMBER 13, 1857
OCTOBER 13, 1945

The marker on Milton Hershey's Grave (Photo by Ed Bolton)

"Today we are gathered in this schoolroom on a Pennsylvania hillside in tribute to a man, who by God's grace was brought to this spot, somehow destined to build this community. The life of Milton Hershey will always be an inspiration in the final triumph it records of perseverance, determination, and pure hard work over failure. And men will marvel at the amazing success of this great industrial enterprise and the beauty of this model community. But when we thank God for that life, it will be for the vision it held of a better life for other men.

"When Mr. Hershey began to reap his harvest, he left not only the forgotten sheaf in the field for the fatherless, he gave not only the first fruits to God, but virtually all the sheaves, and the lives of hundreds of boys who have passed though these halls, they are the great monument that has been reared, and that will go on building as others come from broken homes into the care and guidance of this school. Indeed, the shining stone is the devotion to God and country of 915 school boys whose names are inscribed on the roll of honor, hard by the spot where today he lay in state, and surely every worthwhile action among us for the common good is a solid stone in the structure of our community."

More than 200 cars formed the mile long funeral procession to his grave at the Hershey Cemetery about two miles away on a lofty knoll overseeing Chocolatetown. The Rev. George Mack of Evangelical Lutheran Church conducted a standard Lutheran committal service at Mr. Hershey's grave.

Milton Hershey at last rejoined his beloved Kitty, Henry and Fanny in the Hershey family plot. Six students from the school served as Active Pall Bearers with top executives from the Hershey Chocolate Corporation walking behind the casket as Honorary Pall Bearers and mourners.

Milton Hershey's estate amounted to $864,724.68, after taxes and probate costs. In keeping with a lifetime of philanthropy, he gave his estate away to the Derry Township School District.

In death, even as in life, Mr. Hershey continues to set an outstanding example for all of us. A Higher Power truly blessed Milton Snavely Hershey with the Kiss of Success.

Hershey Goes To War

Since the early part of the last century, the Hershey Corporation supported the American military by working closely with them to develop food products to help the soldier in the field. As early as 1914, Hershey supplied candy to U.S. soldiers. In 1941, Milton Hershey foresaw the coming of the Second World War and organized a Council of Defense for the Hershey Community. He also established a Farm Defense program. This program began during the Depression as training for the unemployed. It shifted gears with the beginning of the Second World War. The Vocational School became a site for the National Defense Program (a federal entity), where unemployed men, both local and out of state, trained in sheet metal working and other skills useful in producing armaments. Chemists and scientists from the Army's Quartermaster Corps worked closely with Hershey chemists to perfect the "D Ration" subsistence bar, a high calorie bar laden in Vitamin B1. (The theory was to develop it so that it would taste not much better than a boiled potato, another source of the vitamin. They wanted this taste to discourage its consumption, except in emergency field conditions.) It was a government ration, packaged as such, with plain block lettering describing the contents. The wrapped bar was then placed in individual boxes dipped in wax, with the packaging to protect the candy by resisting the entrance of the elements.

A second product called the "Tropical Bar" (a heat resistant chocolate bar with an improved flavor) helped soldiers fighting in tropical climes to reportedly ward off diseases. Hershey produced more than a billion of the no-melting candy bars. During the Second World War, the U.S. Government awarded not only several military citations to the Hershey Chocolate Corporation but they also awarded the Army-Navy E flag, the nation's highest award for civilian contractor excellence. First awarded in 1942, by the end of the war Hershey Chocolate received it five times.

In the nineties, the Hershey Foods Corporation also developed a non-melting confectionery product for Operation Desert Storm, called "the Desert Bar."

Mac McCormick thanks the Legal and Corporate Relations Department of the Hershey Food Corporation for their cooperation. Thanks also to Pamela Whitenack, Hershey Community Archivist, for her kindness and valuable assistance.

Gutzon Borglum:
History Along The Skyline

March 25, 1870 - March 6, 1941

(Photo courtesy of Borglum Historical Center, Inc.)

Mount Rushmore stirs the patriotic emotions of Americans as few other sights can. Four massive presidential countenances – Washington, Lincoln, Jefferson and Roosevelt – gaze serenely across the Black Hills of barren South Dakota. Completed in 1941, the gargantuan granite sculptures not only complement the beauty of the nearby emerald pines, but also greet 2.7 million visitors annually. The granite faces loom 5,500 feet above sea level, and the sculptor scaled them to men whose height would top 465 feet. Each of the presidential heads is as tall as a six-story building. Seventeen other peaks in the area exceed seven thousand feet in height.

Sculpted with dynamite, Mount Rushmore cost $989,992.32 to create – by year 2000 standards, a mere pittance – but truly a monarch's ransom for the early 1940's. Many Americans do not know that 1) It's an unfinished work. The virtuoso sculptor behind this national treasure had intended to carve the four figures to the waist and 2) Gutzon Borglum was the phenomenal genius who crafted the majestic Mount Rushmore Memorial Park. Borglum, a colorful and yet intensely private man, remained mired in artistic and business controversies throughout his approximate 70 years of life.

Both Borglum's birth and death dates vary, according to biographer and family members.

His Cook County, Chicago, Illinois death certificate #6855 (issued March 7, 1941) lists his date of birth as March 25, 1870 and his death date as March 6, 1941. Borglum himself reportedly stated occasionally that he wasn't sure when he was born but an unfinished autobiography suggests 1867.

He was born in Idaho, formally as John Gutzon de la Mothe Borglum, son of an Idaho physician. The future artist and sculptor attended Nebraska public schools and began studying art in San Francisco at age 23, later traveling to Paris to complete his studies.

Gutzon Borglum enjoyed monumental successes before completing Rushmore. A student of the French sculptor, Rodin, his *Mares of Diomedes* was the first work by an American artist that the New York Metropolitan Museum of Art purchased. Additionally, visitors can see five Borglum statues at the U.S. Capitol Building in Washington, D.C. including the massive marble head of Lincoln found in the rotunda.

To truly understand the man, one would have to travel to the cliffs and plains of the Confederate Memorial at Stone Mountain, Georgia. It's there that Borglum learned how to skillfully carve, move and sculpt – safely – millions of tons of granite.

Stone Mountain's saga alone could fill volumes. At the turn of the century, an aging Confederate dowager, Mrs. Helen Plane, dreamed of filling the mountain with sculptures of Jefferson Davis, Robert E. Lee, and other Confederate dignitaries. She summoned and hired one of America's most prolific sculptors, Gutzon Borglum.

Borglum and Plane were almost immediately at odds during their initial 1915 meeting. Mrs. Plane – a charter member of the United Daughters of the Confederacy wanted only a 70-foot sculpture of Lee on an 800-foot cliff. Borglum told her that they could liken a project such as that to placing a postage stamp on the side of a barn. The dislike of each other began and concluded only after nine years of inadequate funding and constant confrontations between not only Mrs. Plane and Gutzon Borglum but between Borglum and the Board of Directors who had hired him. World War One also intervened and created still more confusion.

Various records report that Borglum, in February 1925, disagreed with the Board so severely that he went directly to Stone Mountain, scaled the mountain, blew up his work, and left Georgia with the State Police literally in close pursuit of him. Published reports of the day suggest that the police even fired on the noted sculptor.

No matter. For almost two years, Borglum had been in contact with the aging superintendent of the South Dakota Historical Society, Doane Robinson. During 1923, a group of South Dakota businesspeople and patriots had collected about $25,000 to create a monument to men who had made historic contributions to the West. They included General George Armstrong, Buffalo

Bill Cody, Sioux warriors, and the explorers Lewis and Clark. They would almost have filled the craggy mountainside, save for the intellect of Borglum. The Norse-American argued that the works reflect national history and be without dated references to a given period of history. He wrote, "We believe the dimensions of national heartbeats are greater than village impulses, greater than city demands, greater than state dreams or ambitions. Therefore, we believe a nation's memorials should…like Washington, Jefferson, Lincoln and Roosevelt, have a serenity, a nobility, a power that reflects the gods who inspired them and suggests the gods they have become."

Mount Rushmore's site itself presented many exciting opportunities to Borglum and his crew. Located near an isolated mining town (Keystone), Rushmore enjoyed a southern exposure, meaning it had direct sunlight most of the day. Borglum set to work testing the granite which he found free of breaks or fractures.

The project was not without its detractors. Environmentalists of the day complained how the project would ruin nature in that part of the county. Funding problems developed. Some residents complained but the site was so remote that no roads even went near Mount Rushmore.

Work began on the ponderous project.

Fortunately, on June 15, 1927, more than 10,000 South Dakotans, including a bevy of politicos, greeted President and Mrs. Calvin Coolidge for what was to be a three-week stay. The President and his wife were so delighted with the grandeur of Mount Rushmore and the area that they stayed for three months. Gutzon Borglum also rented an airplane and flew over the lodge in which the Coolidges were staying and dropped huge bouquets of Mountain flowers on Mrs. Coolidges's lawn. Borglum arranged for biologists to stock the streams in which the President fished during the day with specimens from the state fish hatchery at night.

This extended vacation of the Coolidges made it possible for Borglum to convince the President to participate in the formal dedication of Mount Rushmore's cornerstone on August 10th. After the President gave an especially stimulating speech – for which most Americans did not know him – the 60-year-old Borglum climbed the Mountain to the crest and symbolically drilled six holes to commemorate the beginning of the carving.

Workers removed 90% of the 450,000 tons of granite from the mountain with dynamite. An even more amazing notation – considering the heavy equipment and dynamite employed almost daily for a decade – is that no deaths occurred and only a handful of employees suffered minor injuries during the entire carving period.

For ten years, the project moved forward, plagued with criticisms from all levels of society, monetary problems, the elements, engineering hangups, delivery complications, and lack of roads. Nevertheless, by 1938, the bulk of the carving was completed, and Gutzon Borglum began to carve a huge Hall of Records into Mount Rushmore. He believed that this would be an appropriate place to store many of mankind's important history records.

The sculptor slowed by this point. Years of climbing around on Mount Rushmore understandably took its toll on his body. Gutzon Borglum began training his son, Lincoln, to help with the layout and blasting. The elder Borglum began spending more time at his family ranch in Hermosa, South Dakota.

In February 1941, Gutzon Borglum entered a Chicago hospital for an unsuccessful operation on his prostate. He also suffered with heart and circulatory problems. Although the death certificate reports Borglum as an inpatient for the 30 days before his death, we know that in very early March, he gave an impassioned speech in Park Ridge, Illinois for Americans to believe in their country and the values of personal liberty. His family, alarmed at his condition at the close of the speech, took him back to the hospital.

On March 6, 1941, at a reported age of 70 years, 11 months and nine days, the great sculptor died at Henrotin Hospital in Chicago with his wife, Mary Montgomery Williams, his daughter, Mary Ellis Borglum Vhay, and his son, Lincoln Borglum at his bedside. *The Chicago Tribune*, probably owing to the journalistic policies of the day, reported the following day that Borglum died of heart problems following a gall bladder ailment rather than mention the true cause of death.

The Mount Rushmore Commission immediately asked the Borglum family for Gutzon's remains. While publicly saying they appreciated the concerted effort being made to bury Borglum at Rushmore, privately they had other plans. Meanwhile, Congress passed a resolution to bury Borglum at Mount Rushmore.

Borglum's wife, Mary, writing in *Give the Man Room*, explains that Gutzon had extracted a promise from his son Lincoln to return his body to California so it could rest among the state's abundant flowers.

Two bits of pathos and irony follow Gutzon Borglum to his grave. First, he never saw Mount Rushmore totally completed. His son, Lincoln, finished the carving. The other sad circumstance is that despite being promised vast amounts of money for sculpting the mountain, Borglum died almost penniless. Family sources say that it was years before the estate was settled and much of that went to Rushmore's contractors, workmen and the doctors and hospitals.

A now totally obsolete publication gives us a fairly complete insight into Borglum's burial process. Almost six decades later, the information comes to us from the pages of *The Hizone Supplement*, the former house publication of a then prominent Wilmette, Ill. fluid manufacturer. That publication, written by the late accomplished chemist, Dr. Hilton Ira Jones, offers some unabashed support of the abilities of Chicago embalmer Larry Ward – and, of course, of Hizone chemicals, used exclusively in the embalming of the famed sculptor's remains.

The mid 1941 *Hizone Supplement* states, "The Sbarbaro Funeral Home, 708 North Wells Street, Chicago cared for the body. Mr. Larry H. Ward did the actual embalming. The body now lies in the Rosehill Mausoleum here in Chicago where it will remain until the crypt is finished which is being cut to receive it in Rushmore Mountain below the great carving that will make his name forever famous.

"The body was placed in a copper sealer casket, since the family proposes that we hold this body in such a condition that we can view it indefinitely. Mr. Ward shows the embalming procedure he used in the preparation of the body in the case report I have before me as I write. Death was due to heart failure. The body weighed about 195 pounds, the legs being somewhat dropsical. Six hours elapsed between death and embalming. He used an S & W Suprex Injector. Mr. Borglum's injection was in the carotid and the drainage from the jugular. Twelve ounces of Suprex fluid were used in the first seven quarts. The second seven quarts also contained twelves ounces of Suprex fluid. Two bottles of Hizone cavity fluid were used in the cavities. We scattered two pounds of Paulex powder between the casket and the upholstery before we sealed it and two pounds of anhydrous calcium chloride were placed in a crock between the feet. This, excepting the ordinary powder and rouge, completed the embalming. Mr. Ward reported the circulation as good and the body was 'not hard but firm.' It was four days under observation before it was finally placed in the Rosehill Mausoleum.

"Since the body is to be "under observation" for several months before the family finally moves it out to South Dakota, the probabilities are that sometime in the latter part of May or June, Mr. Ward will have the casket opened and remove the anhydrous calcium chloride since if such a large amount is left in there too long, it might cause unnecessary drying. With the removal of the calcium chloride, there probably will be put in its place a two-pound roll of absorbent cotton to help regulate the humidity in the casket.

"We are fully expecting that the body of Gutzon Borglum will remain in as perfect condition as the body of Lenin, and we are hoping to be able to control the moisture content of the body so that the body will not turn brown, as the body of Lenin has done. We know that permanent embalming is now an established fact, and we hope to be able to show in Gutzon Borglum's body the proof to the world. We fully believe that the methods and chemicals as used by Mr. Ward will bring it about. Time will tell the story."

Over a year later, in 1942, Dr. Jones published a sequel in *The Hizone Supplement* describing the current state of Borglum's body in an article entitled "Gutzon Borglum Again."

"On April 4th, with Mr. Larry Ward, the embalmer, we again examined the body of Gutzon Borglum which Mr. Ward embalmed more than a year ago and has been in the Rosehill Mausoleum in a sealer casket. Paulex Powder and anhydrous calcium chloride were used but after three months, the sealer was opened, the calcium chloride removed, and a roll of cotton placed at the feet.

"When we examined the body on April 4th, the sealer was not opened. We simply viewed the body through the glass. Of course, the body was in the same perfect condition as when embalmed – as we knew it would be. The only object was to study the effect of the cotton. We found the sealer glass on the half toward the feet where the cotton was to be entirely free from moisture condensation. There was condensation, however, on the half of the glass toward the head where there was no cotton. It is apparent now that a roll of cotton should have been placed at the head and at the feet, and then there would have been no condensation at all. We suggest that whenever cotton is used to prevent moisture condensation in a casket that two rolls be used, one at the head and one at the feet. Cotton should be unrolled all the way and the paper removed and then rolled up again and then held up by two rubber bands. You will find the cotton more effective if you dry it first by heating it in an oven before placing it in the casket."

Eventually, on October 13, 1944, the Borglum family returned the great sculptor to California and laid him to rest in Crypt A, Sarcophagus M, of Glendale's Forest Lawn Memorial Court of Honor. He slumbers on the far end of the mausoleum just underneath the Lord's Supper window. His lifelong friend Rupert Hughes wrote these words for his inscription:

His birthplace was Idaho; California first taught him Art,
Then France who gave him Fame;
England welcomed him: America called him home.
His genius for the exquisite as for the colossal
Gave permanence on canvass, in Bronze,
In marble, to moods of beauty or passion,
To figures of legend and history.
Nations, cities, colleges paid him tribute.
As patriot, he stripped corruption bare. As
Statesman, he toiled for the equality in the
Rights of man. At last he carved
A Mountain for a Monument: He made the mountain
Chant: "Remember! These Giant Souls
Set America free, and kept her free.
Hold fast your sacred heritage, Americans!
Remember! Remember!"

Gutzon Borglum's final resting place, Forest Lawn Cemetery, Glendarle, California (Photo by Anne Abe)

Quick Facts: Gutzon Borglum – Genius Sculptor

✧ Organized a bus company in Stanford, Connecticut.

✧ Became a leader of the Progressive Party in Connecticut.

✧ Investigated Airplane Manufacturing prior to American involvement in WWII.

✧ Raised Money for Czechoslovakia and Slovakia's pre-1940 war effort.

✧ Designed Coins and Medals.

✧   Wrote magazine and newspaper articles.

✧   Experimented with dynamite so long that he could remove stone by the ounce.

✧   Laid out a backwater plan for Corpus Christi, Texas.

✧   Invented an airplane.

✧   Designed roads and reconstructed historic old homes.

✧   Beautified rivers and highways and contrived waterways long before ecology was simply a political correctness.

✧   Invented hoisting equipment and long range projection devices to enable the carving of Stone Mountain and Mount Rushmore.

✧   Was knighted by the King of Denmark for his sculpture of a Royal Family Member.

Lewis Wendell Willkie:
"Deathless Loyalty"
February 18, 1892 – October 8, 1944

(Photo courtesy of Rush County Historical Society)

It may seem inconceivable today, but Wendell Willkie, a man who never held a public office one hour in his life, came relatively close to becoming the President of the United States. Add to that odd fact the reality that he was a loyal Democrat until the fall of 1939, just before he switched to the Republican Party to accept their nomination, and it seems even more incredulous.

He worked feverishly as a private citizen to alert the nation to the dangers of Nazi Germany, and essentially, united our nation to enter the Second World War as a cohesive country. Wendell Willkie was a plainspoken Hoosier – a man born in Elwood, Indiana, a town once known as the birthplace of the Ku Klux Klan. Americans took to his oratory, rugged good looks and down home appeal so well that more than twenty-two million people voted for him in the 1940 presidential election.

Born Lewis Wendell Willkie, he changed his name to Wendell L. Willkie after a clerk in the Army transposed his first and second names. With nonchalance not at all typical for the Prussian-American, he decided it would be easier to not challenge the government and let the error slide. It would be one of the very few times that Willkie, a lawyer and public utility executive by trade, would not talk back to the government.

Willkie's family was not the typical German-Prussian clan found in Indiana. All of his ancestors reportedly were involved in disputes with their governments, a trend that Wendell continued. Both of his parents were very well educated, and conversations at the Willkie household were reportedly quite intellectual.

Wendell – the third of six children – attended Culver Military Academy and the University of Indiana. He became well known on campus for fervent talks about socialism and ready criticism of student government and fraternities.

He met his wife, Edith Wilk, a librarian in Rushville, while on leave from the Army. His proposal, "I'd like to change that Wilk to Willkie." Edith agreed, and they were married in 1918 – a January wedding delayed two days because of a typical Indiana blizzard.

Wendell Willkie forged a brilliant career in the legal department of Firestone Tires but eventually tired of the office, corporate politics, and the repetitiveness of the work. After working for the Commonwealth and Southern Rail Road for a number of years, Willkie ultimately accepted a position with the Tennessee Utility System and became embroiled in a huge controversy over the Tennessee Valley Authority. He and Franklin Delanor Roosevelt feuded over rights, waterways, costs, and the concentration of power. Willkie finally brokered a deal in which the Federal Government bought the TVA properties for seventy eight million dollars.

In his private life he was considered a bright, articulate man who had some odd habits. He was constantly disheveled, never carried money, and never drove an automobile. Wendell called his own appearance poor, citing a graying mop of messy hair and his suits, "shiny with baggy seat pants."

For many years, while still married to Edith (whom he called Billie), he had an open relationship with a charming female southern historian, Irita Van Doren. They were lovers for decades, apparently with Mrs. Willkie's knowledge and consent. All three of them knew that a divorce, then, was political suicide.

Willkie's executive background and familiarity with Washington big-wigs helped ease him into the Republican presidential nomination of 1940. Almost overnight the chant was "We Want Willkie," and Willkie clubs sprang up across the nation. Citizens found his "down home on the farm in Indiana" approach to FDR's foreign and national policies refreshing, even if these same citizens did not always agree with some of Willkie's radical ideas about government. Noted columnist Walter Lippmann credited Wendell Willkie with lining up the Republican Party behind Great Britain.

Despite the fact that he lost the election to FDR, Wendell Willkie received more votes than any other Republican candidate up to that election. The record wasn't eclipsed until Dwight Eisenhower's 1952 landslide.

Following his defeat in the 1940 presidential election, Willkie stayed busy with a variety of projects. These included traveling world wide as a special envoy for the United States and upsetting a number of world leaders with his sometimes brash approach to politics. He continued to write, lecture and live at a fast pace, albeit a conservative lifestyle. Willkie argued a number of prominent civil liberty cases before the Supreme Court.

By late summer 1944, Wendell Willkie became gravely ill. While traveling to Indiana by train, Willkie struggled to open a door leading to the dining car.

By the time he arrived in Rushville, he had suffered a heart attack. Mary Sleeth, the woman who managed much of his property in central Indiana, convinced him to see a doctor. He balked, however, when the doctor suggested hospitalization. Two of Willkie's biographers, Barnes and Barnard, agree that he remonstrated to Sleeth, "I've got too many things to do and say to allow people to write me off as an old man with a bum heart."

On September 6, he returned to New York. Willkie appeared so weak at the train station that a porter and his press secretary, Lamoyne Jones, had to help him off the train. His chief's appearance shocked Jones sufficiently that he wanted to summon an ambulance. Willkie would not hear of it and promptly ordered a taxicab to take him home. Arriving at home in great pain, he asked for sedatives, and later that same day, an ambulance rushed him to Lenox Hill Hospital. Doctors admitted him for a complete physical and a rest.

Decades of careless living apparently had caught up with the illustrious son of Indiana. Once a fiercely strong man, the years of chain-smoking Camel cigarettes, a poor diet and no exercise may have caused his first of many heart attacks. Nevertheless, Rushville's leading citizen (He was the largest individual land owner in Rush County, owned four downtown business buildings, and was the largest shareholder in the Rushville National Bank) did not want the public to know the true nature of his illness. In early October, the hospital press representative said doctors were simply treating him for a stomach disorder.

For the next few weeks, Wendell appeared to recover. He wrote letters planning upcoming political dealings and disclosed plans to write yet another book. Willkie, ever the strategist, told close friends how to get into his hospital room without going past the nurses' station.

On October 4, Wendell Willkie suddenly caught a streptococcal throat infection and his temperature rose to one hundred and four degrees. His lungs filled with fluid, and Saturday, October 7, 1944, doctors alerted the public of his worsening condition. Willkie survived a total of thirteen heart attacks since entering the hospital the previous month, but not the fourteenth.

Dr. Alexander Ghiselin, ear nose and throat specialist, told a reporter from *The New York Times* that the colorful, two hundred plus pound Hoosier died of a coronary thrombosis in which a streptococcus' infection affected his heart muscle. He also said that Willkie died at 2:30 A.M. Sunday, October 8, 1944, in his sleep following two other heart attacks that night. With Willkie at his end, besides Dr. Ghiselin, were his personal physician, Dr. Benjamin Salzer, Willkie's wife, Edith, and Lamoyne Jones, Willkie's personal secretary and spokesperson since 1940.

Jones told reporters gathered at the hospital that Wendell Willkie awoke at midnight, and that the doctors decided to remove his oxygen tent, because he had improved substantially. Jones further said that when Wendell Willkie awoke, he began to joke with the nurses. As she swabbed his throat, she asked him how he felt, and he replied, "How can I talk with my mouth full of that stuff?" Mrs. Willkie arrived at the hospital about five minutes before her husband died.

"She saw him although the oxygen mask concealed his face." Dr. Ghiselin further stated, "He was still breathing. Mrs. Willkie seemed to know the exact second that death came. She wavered, and Dr. Salzer ran to her side and supported her. She would have collapsed otherwise."

Funeral directors from the Merrill Funeral Home in New York City (now closed) took charge of the great statesman's body. After embalming, dressing and cosmetizing Willkie's remains, they covered his 48-ounce seamless bronze casket with the American flag and took it to the main aisle of Fifth Avenue Presbyterian Church.

Wendell Willkie laid in state from 2:00 P.M. Monday, October 9, 1944 until his funeral services the following day at 3:00 P.M. More than sixty thousand people filed past his casket in that time. A representative from the funeral home speaking to the Associated Press said that the decision for the viewing followed many requests to the family. Thirty-five thousand people gathered outside the church for the New York services, while eight hundred people filled the pews of the flower encrusted church. Notables who attended the New York services included Eleanor Roosevelt, financier Bernard Baruch, Governor and Mrs. Thomas Dewey, President Herbert Hoover, and New York Mayor Fierello La Guardia.

The Reverend John Sutherland Bonnell, pastor and lifetime friend of Willkie's conducted the thirty-five minute service. The pastor concluded his eulogy with the words, "Wendell Willkie, thou valiant heart, hail and farewell." Following the New York service, the funeral directors sealed the casket permanently.

In Rushville, Mayor Manley Abercrombie issued a proclamation of mourning calling upon citizens of the Hoosier community to observe a ten-day period of mourning. During that period of mourning, residents were to fly their flags at half mast, and the Mayor asked businesses to close during the funeral. Most of Rushville's residents learned of the 1940 Presidential nominee's death when they attended church, and their ministers announced the death from the pulpit.

Wednesday, October 11, 1944, shortly before 9:00 A.M., the train bearing Willkie's imposing flag draped casket arrived in Rushville. (It was late because of several delays along the way.) The railroad provided a dozen men to move the massive packing crate from the train's baggage car. The twelve men carried the packing crate north down the street a short distance where the waiting hearse sat. Newsreel and other photographers were seemingly everywhere. Two local trucks, one from a mill, the other a greenhouse, moved the hundreds of floral tributes that accompanied the body from the train to the funeral home.

Funeral Directors Harry Moore and Frank Wyatt moved the casket from the street to the Wyatt Memorial Mortuary on North Main Street. Indiana

State Police Officer Lieutenant Leo Moore, serving as the head of an eight-officer honor guard, accompanied the two undertakers. (All eight officers subsequently rotated standing at attention near Willkie's casket, and all eight served at the funeral the following week.)

Around noon, reporters from the *Rushville Republican* learned that Willkie's body would remain at the Wyatt Memorial Mortuary pending the arrival of Mrs. Willkie and son, Phillip. Mrs. Willkie planned to stay in New York until Phillip, who then served as a Lieutenant in the U.S. Navy, arrived back in the United States. (The younger Willkie served on convoy duty in a foreign country during the Second World War. Mrs. Virginia Willkie, Phillip's widow, recently told *The American Funeral Director* that Phillip was traveling East on that ship when the Navy notified him of his father's early death. The Navy transferred him to a vessel heading West using a small canvas rescue vest called a Breeches Buoy.)

Funeral directors in New York distributed flowers from the New York service to hospitals throughout the city. Nevertheless, hundreds of floral tributes awaited Willkie's remains at the Wyatt Mortuary on Main Street in Rushville. By Friday, October 13, the hopelessly wilted flowers from New York that accompanied the body presented a displeasing appearance, and the Wyatt-Moore staff removed them. Still, the Willkie family instructed the Indiana funeral directors to take all the flowers from the Rushville service to nearby Camp Atterbury and Billings Hospital at Fort Benjamin Harrison in Indianapolis.

For the several days that preceded the final rites, visitors from around Indiana and the nation visited the Wyatt Memorial Mortuary to pay their final respects to the beloved Hoosier. The Secretary of War telephoned Mrs. Willkie to suggest that the Army bury Wendell Willkie in Arlington National Cemetery but Mrs. Willkie declined that honor.

Meanwhile, Indiana Governor Henry F. Schricker telegraphed Mrs. Willkie asking her for permission to lay the humanitarian's body in state at the Indiana State House or at the Indiana War memorial.

He said, in part, "The people of Indiana are bowed in grief over the untimely death of your beloved husband, and all join in an expression of sincerest sympathy in your great bereavement. In order to give this legion of sorrowing friends an opportunity to pay appropriate homage to Mr. Willkie, may I suggest that the body lie in state at the state house or war memorial prior to the final obsequies in Rushville. Mrs. Schricker joins me in a personal expression of deepest sympathy to you and Phillip in your overwhelming sorrow." The governor then ordered all state flags at the state house be flown at half mast.

Tuesday, October 17, 1944, Mrs. Willkie and Lt. Phillip Willkie arrived in Rushville by train at 9:25 A.M. Several of Wendell Willkie's closest friends, two of his former law firm partners, two brothers (Fred of Louisville, Kentucky and E.E. Willkie of Chicago, Illinois) and a sister-in-law, Mrs. Robert Willkie, of Louisville, Kentucky also attended the services.

Authorities made elaborate arrangements to handle the expected traffic for the final Willkie rites. Newspapers published the route of the cortege, which moved south on Main Street from the Wyatt Mortuary to Second Street where it turned due east to the cemetery, East Hill. Business in Rushville closed for the duration of the service.

The Willkie family asked that no one play any music, and they named no honorary pallbearers. Eight active pallbearers served, and all were Willkie farm tenants, employees or former tenants. They were Louis and Robert Berkemeier, Harold Moore, Glen Miller, Joseph Kramer, George Smiley, Frank Osterling and Ralph Brown. The funeral home provided seats for those relatives and friends attending from out of state.

Funeral Director George Todd, present owner of the Todd Funeral Home in Rushville, says that he helped the Wyatt-Moore staff with the Willkie funeral. He recalled his early relationship with Wendell Willkie:

"I knew him well. I'd go out to one of his farms, which the Berkemeir family managed and farmed, and there he would be. We used to play basketball together, and he played well."

"As to the funeral, in those days funeral homes helped each other out. I often dined with both Mr. Wyatt and Frank Moore. The Wyatt Funeral Home asked me to work at the Willkie funeral, and I considered it an honor. I told them that I would do anything I could to help."

The affable Mr. Todd revealed to *The American Funeral Director* lately, "It was a really pleasant day, weather-wise, and I helped park cars and carry flowers. About two hundred and fifty people were inside the funeral home, and another two hundred people stood out on the lawn. As I remember, we had four truck loads of flowers that went over to the cemetery. These were the big trucks, not today's mini-vans. I carried one orchid arrangement that I will never forget – it was from China's Generalissimo Chaing and Madame Meiling Kai-Shek. It took over an hour to get the procession from the cemetery to East Hill Cemetery. When the cars started pouring in, I helped park them, two abreast. That's a really big cemetery, and we got all of them parked, but it was a job."

Dr. George Arthur Frantz, pastor of the First Presbyterian Church in Indianapolis, delivered the final and solemn tribute to Wendell Willkie. He called the late politician "an ambassador of the people of the world." The Reverend Charles V. Reeder, pastor of the First Presbyterian Church of Rushville prayed and helped Dr. Frantz conduct the impressive ceremonies. Only a small portion of the huge assembly gained entrance to the funeral home while throngs of people listened to the funeral service on loudspeakers on the front lawn.

"For more than seven days the whole world has stood with uncovered and bowed head around this casket. The uncorrupted instinct for true greatness –

an instinct of all men everywhere – has given unanimous suffrage that **this** was a **man**," Dr. Frantz said.

He concluded the funeral service with, "It is hard to lose him. And we shall vehemently desire him in the day of battle. It is hard to lose such a man, citizen, friend, neighbor, brother. It is hard to lose such a husband, such a father. But it is easier because we lose him to the Immortals.

"Now, Indiana's great son has come home to stay. His family and his friends have his love forever. His fellow citizens have his deathless loyalty. His native and beloved soil have his body. His spirit is abroad and mighty in the world; his soul goes marching on.

> *"Under the wide and starry sky,*
> *Dig the grave and let me die,*
> *Glad did I live, and gladly die,*
> *And I laid me down with a will.*
> *This be the verse you gave for me:*
> *'Here he lies, where he longed to be;*
> *Home is the sailor, home from the sea;*
> *And the hunter, home from the hill.'* "

The souls of the believers are at their deaths made perfect in their holiness, and do immediately pass into glory. And so shall he be forever with the Lord."

(Photo by Jo Ann Roscoe)

Afterword

Sadly, the morning following the services for Wendell Willkie, Edith returned to the grave site with several of her friends and found that souvenir seekers had riddled the flowers. There, much to her horror, she also discovered that hundreds of visitors had mutilated the carefully designed floral displays. Someone had simply pilfered many of the massive flora, and many more of the elegant tributes were damaged. Her own spray to Mr. Willkie was badly torn, and about half of the roses and orchids were missing. Heartbroken, she returned home.

Mr. Todd adds that he again served the Willkie family, several decades later. Mrs. Virginia Willkie, Phillip's wife, called him to bury Phillip Willkie, Wendell's only child on April 10, 1974. Mr. Todd laid Phillip Willkie to rest on the same gentle slope in East Hill Cemetery where Wyatt Moore buried Wendell and Edith. Phillip Willkie's funeral cortege contained nine limousines and remains the largest funeral service that the Todd Funeral Home ever conducted.

Visitors can find Wendell Willkie's grave marked with a twelve-foot granite cross and a ledger style marker in the shape of a book with quotations from his book, *One World*. Edith and Phillip also rest in the family plot.

Just before his death, Wendell Willkie told a friend that rather than people remembering him as an unimportant President, he hoped that people would recall him as one who contributed to saving freedom at the moment of peril.

Sources

Author – Interview with Mrs. Virginia Willkie, widow of Phillip Willkie, September 2000

Author – Interview with Funeral Director George Todd, September 2000

The Rushville Republican, October 9- 20, 1944 (background information only – no quotations)

Makey, Herman, *Wendell Willkie of Elwood*, 1940, National Book Company, Elwood, Indiana

Dillion, Mary Earhart, *Wendell Willkie*, 1952, Lippincott, Philadelphia

Current Biography, 1940.p.p.s.874-876

Harland D. Sanders:
The Father of Franchising
September 9, 1890 – December 16, 1980

*His life story remains legend and legions of motivational speakers have endlessly repeated it. Still, the truth endures – A sixty-six-year-old Grandfather began what would eventually become one of the world's most successful fast food businesses with a $105 Social Security check and a determination that he would not die a failure. Harland Sanders will always be **The Father of Franchising.***

Col. Sanders cooks chicken on his 87th birthday at the dedication of the Kentucky Fried Chicken School of Restaurant Management in Salem, Indiana. (©1977, The Courier-Journal)

Kentucky's most famous son and honorary Colonel, Harland D. Sanders, actually began life on a farm near Henryville in southern Indiana on September 9, 1890. Just as he neared age six, his father died, leaving his mother with the task of raising not only Harland, but also his baby sister, Catherine, and 3-year-old brother Clarence. His mother, by all accounts, a righteous and upright Christian woman, ensured that her children learned the value of hard work. She also taught them to live by the Ten Commandments, and to avoid alcohol, tobacco, and gambling. The warnings that she gave her children early in their lives stayed with them for decades.

Col. Sanders told more than one of his biographers that his mother "wanted my brother and I to be men. She taught us how to look out for ourselves, to face responsibility, and never run from a fight or trouble. She instilled those principles in our sister as well."

The Colonel – who always believed in telling the truth, but never stepping away from the value of publicity – once told a Louisville reporter that he learned to cook at home at age five, and that he always cooked the meals at home for his brother, sister, and himself so that his mother could work. Sanders remained a consummate publicist throughout all of his life – adding every detail that he possibly could to his real life chronicle of poverty. The southern gentleman said quite often that he cooked "just like his mom did" and later when he entered the restaurant business he "kept on doing it the same way."

Around the time he reached age twelve, Harland Sanders' mother decided to remarry and to move the family to Greenwood, Indiana. Several published accounts of the future restaurant emperor's life say that he did not get along well with his stepfather. Harland announced to his mother that he would quit school, (he dropped out as a sixth grader) and leave home. With that, he packed a battered suitcase, and left.

For two years, the future Chicken King labored as a farmhand for $2 a month for a neighboring man named Sam Wilson. In 1904, a distant relative of Sanders found employment for him in New Albany, Indiana working as a conductor for the Streetcar Company. The Colonel, who manifested a deep-rooted love of railroads, often remarked that he loved that job because it had him "riding on rails."

At age 16, the future fast food magnate enlisted in the U.S. Army and soldiered for less than a year in Cuba. The Army discharged him at the rank of Private.

His next job – as a blacksmith's helper on the Southern Railroad – practically produced euphoria for the seventeen-year-old lad. Eventually, the Railroad promoted the youth to Fireman, a position that did not require him to in his own words "doodle the ashes and clean out the fire boxes."

A few years later, he married his first wife of thirty-nine years, Josie, and began working for the Pennsylvania Railroad. At some point, he worked as a service station attendant. Some variations of the next segment of the Colonel's life exist among his many biographers. A few reports suggest that he studied law by mail and worked as a Justice of the Peace, and other authors do not list this work as part of his life. Some versions say that he then managed an Ohio Riverboat steam-powered ferryboat.

Trying to better himself, Harland Sanders next alternately sold life insurance and auto tires. During one of his road trips selling tires, in the late 1920's, the Colonel crossed a cable bridge. The suspension cable broke, plummeting Sanders and his new car forty-two feet into a stream near Nicolasville, Kentucky. Relatively unhurt, he nevertheless found himself without any transportation.

The fall had virtually destroyed his new car. Sanders stayed on in Nicholasville and decided to open a service station.

The public relations-savvy salesman did so well that in 1929, a major oil company offered to build him a new gasoline station in Corbin, Kentucky on a very busy US Route #25. He advertised "Free Air" and served food to his gasoline station customers in the dining room of his living quarters. These advertising gimmicks worked effectively enough that – along with the outstanding service that he gave his customers – he made enough money to open a small restaurant and motel across the street from the filling station. He could seat over 140 people in the new restaurant.The Colonel devised his restaurant menu around his mother's manner of cooking fried chicken, served with hot biscuits and honey. Interestingly enough, the menu displayed a slogan "Not Worth It, But Mighty Good."

In 1936, Kentucky Governor Ruby Lafoon named Harlan Sanders a Kentucky Colonel because of his many contributions to Kentucky's image and cuisine. Sanders immediately began capitalizing on the honor, fully developing the role by portraying the image of a goateed and mustached Southern landowner. The gracious Colonel began constantly wearing a white plantation suit and a black string tie. He parlayed the likeness into one of the most successful and instantly recognizable celebrities in the world. Probably no one ever received more mileage from the title than Harland Sanders. The kindly grandfather often said, "The name 'Kentucky' means more to me than anyone else in the world."

1939 proved to be a banner year for Col. Sanders. First, he developed his first version of the "eleven secret herbs and spices recipe." Then, Duncan Hines, at that time a well-known national food critic, lauded Sanders food and listed the restaurant in a tour guidebook. Consequently, his motel and restaurant fared so well that he decided to open another similar business in Asheville, North Carolina.

During the Second World War, however, the U.S. Government ordered food and gasoline rationing. These problems forced the Colonel to close the Asheville restaurant. He went to work for a Seattle based national Food Corporation for almost a year. Then, the Colonel's troubles began.

First, his highly successful restaurant in Corbin, Kentucky burned. Since it remained the more important of the two, the Colonel decided to rebuild immediately. So he sold the Asheville location.

Not long after that his only son, Harland Sanders, Junior, just twenty years old, died of a streptococcal infection. Although his son's death devastated him, the Colonel once said that he consoled himself in thinking that his son had lived twenty years of a happy life, and that his son may have escaped a great deal of misery.

Shortly after Harland, Junior's death in 1948, Sanders and his wife, Josie divorced but remained good friends. Colonel Sanders remarked at the time of the divorce that he and Josie had been unhappy for most of their thirty-nine years of marriage.

In November 1949, Harland D. Sanders married Claudia Ledington Price, formerly a waitress, and one of his restaurant supervisors who had worked for him since 1930. She also helped him run various other businesses in North Carolina and Florida. Interestingly enough, Claudia met Sanders when the Depression forced her brother-in-law, George Ray, to leave his job for the Louisville and Nashville Railroad. Ray heard that Sanders needed help at his Corbin service station, and since he worked hard, the Colonel hired him.

About that time, Harland Sanders devised the idea of using the extra room at the gas station to sell food to the tourists driving from North to South and back again. He put a table and chairs in the room, and hired Nellie Ray, George's wife, and Claudia's sister to work as a waitress.

The idea became such a success that Sanders realized he needed another waitress, and asked Nellie if she knew of anyone who could help. Claudia came to work for Harland, first on a part time basis, and then, since her sister often cooked, Claudia became full time staff. She often called Sanders a human dynamo, full of energy, infecting the people who worked around him.

In 1955, Colonel Harland Sanders turned down an offer of $164,000.00 for his Corbin enterprise. A year later, the Eisenhower administration announced plans for a new Interstate (I75) that would bypass Corbin, Kentucky by seven or more miles. The announcement shattered merchants along the existing Route 25, and Sanders' business dropped radically in less than a year.

Always a man to "cut his losses," Harland Sanders auctioned the property and business for considerably less than the offer he had spurned fourteen months earlier. The Colonel paid off his debtors, and it looked as if he would live on his monthly $105 Social Security checks alone.

Harland and Claudia determined that the Colonel's chicken was their best asset. They set hard at work perfecting the Colonel's secret blend of eleven spices and herbs. Several accounts say that Sanders and his wife locked themselves in their home and fried chicken for weeks until they hit upon the right combination of ingredients. They reportedly kept meticulous records of the type of chicken used, the herbs and spices, and the cooking time.

For years, Harland believed that he could sell the recipe to restaurant owners across the nation. In fact, some five years earlier in 1952, the Colonel sold his first franchise to a long time friend, Pete Harmon of Salt Lake City. He criss-crossed the nation in his car, trying to sell the franchise to restaurant owners. Sanders asked each franchisee for a nickel for every chicken they sold. If they agreed, the Colonel simply used a handshake agreement.

Harland Sanders made more than a thousand sales calls before a restaurant owner said, "Yes." It took him two years and 1,009 sales calls before his Kentucky Fried Chicken franchise idea became successful.

By 1963, more than 600 Kentucky Fried Chicken outlets were operating in the United States and Canada. The Colonel and Mrs. Sanders initially

Everett and Mary Hall with Claudia Sanders and the Colonel at his birthday party
(*This previously unpublished photo courtesy of Mrs. Mary Taylor Hall and Stephen L. Collins*)

Registrar of Vital Statistics
Certified Copy

THE FACE OF THIS DOCUMENT HAS A COLORED BACKGROUND - NOT A WHITE BACKGROUND

FORM V.S. NO. 1-A
(Rev. 9-78)

COMMONWEALTH OF KENTUCKY
DEPARTMENT FOR HUMAN RESOURCES FILE NO. 116
REGISTRAR OF VITAL STATISTICS
CERTIFICATE OF DEATH REGISTRAR'S NO. 2275

80 32280

Registration District No. 755   Primary Registration District No.

DECEASED

1. DECEASED—NAME FIRST: Col. Harland MIDDLE: David LAST: Sanders	SEX: M—	DATE OF DEATH: Dec. 16, 1980

| 4. RACE: White/ | 5a. AGE: 90 | DATE OF BIRTH: Sept. 9, 1890 | COUNTY OF DEATH: Jefferson |

| 7b. CITY, TOWN, OR LOCATION OF DEATH: Louisville, Ky. | HOSPITAL OR OTHER INSTITUTION: Jewish Hospital |

| 8. STATE OF BIRTH: Ind. (Clark Co.) | CITIZEN OF WHAT COUNTRY: USA | MARRIED: Widowed | SURVIVING SPOUSE: Claudia Ledington |

| 12. SOCIAL SECURITY NUMBER: 237-34-7258 | USUAL OCCUPATION: Public Relations | KIND OF BUSINESS OR INDUSTRY: Ky. Fried Chicken |

| 14a. RESIDENCE—STATE: Ky. | 14b. COUNTY: Shelby | CITY, TOWN, OR LOCATION: Shelbyville | STREET AND NUMBER: Box 270 |

PARENTS

| 15. FATHER—NAME: Wilbert Sanders | 16. MOTHER—MAIDEN NAME: Margaret Dunlevy |

| 17a. INFORMANT—NAME: Mrs Claudia Sanders | 17b. MAILING ADDRESS: Box 270 Shelbyville, Ky. 40065 |

CAUSE

PART I. DEATH WAS CAUSED BY:

| 18. (a) IMMEDIATE CAUSE: Pneumonia | APPROXIMATE INTERVAL: 6 weeks |
| (b) DUE TO: Acute Leukemia | 6 months |
| (c) |

PART II. OTHER SIGNIFICANT CONDITIONS: Diabetes Mellitus

| AUTOPSY: | WAS CASE REFERRED TO MEDICAL EXAMINER OR CORONER: |

| ACC., SUICIDE, HOM., UNDET. OR PENDING INVEST. | DATE OF INJURY | HOUR | HOW INJURY OCCURRED |

| INJURY AT WORK | PLACE OF INJURY | LOCATION |

CERTIFIER

| CERTIFICATION—PHYSICIAN: I ATTENDED THE: 7 10 72 DECEASED FROM: 12 16 80 | I LAST SAW HIM/HER ALIVE ON: 12 16 80 |

| CERTIFIER—NAME: Angelo A. Ciliberti, M.D. | SIGNATURE: Ciliberti | DATE SIGNED: 12/29/80 |

| MAILING ADDRESS: 250 E. Liberty St. | Louisville, Ky. 40202 |

BURIAL

| 24a. BURIAL, CREMATION, REMOVAL: Burial | 24b. CEMETERY OR CREMATORY—NAME: Cave Hill | LOCATION: Louisville, Ky. |

| 24d. DATE: Dec. 20, 1980 | FUNERAL DIRECTOR SIGNATURE: | ADDRESS: Shelbyville, Ky. 40065 |

| 25b. NAME OF FUNERAL HOME: Hall-Taylor Funeral Home | REGISTRAR'S SIGNATURE: | DATE RECEIVED BY LOCAL REGISTRAR: JAN 6 1981 |

THE BACK OF THIS DOCUMENT CONTAINS AN ARTIFICIAL WATERMARK - HOLD AT AN ANGLE TO VIEW

I, Sandra J. Davis, State Registrar of Vital Statistics, hereby certify this to be a true and correct copy of the certificate of birth, death, marriage or divorce of the person therein named, and that the original certificate is registered under the file number shown. In testimony thereof I have hereunto subscribed my name and caused the official seal of the Office of Vital Statistics to be affixed at Frankfort, Kentucky this _____ day of _____, 20 01.

Sandra J. Davis, State Registrar

mixed the spice and herb combination in their own garage which they turned into a warehouse and workshop. The Colonel devised another advertising device – he started supplying his franchisees with paper plate mats, napkins, and glasses – all of which had the Colonel's image.

On February 14, 1964, Colonel Harland Sanders sold his far-flung food franchise business for two million dollars. He insured that his nephew and grandson became executive officers for the new firm. Among the new owners were John Brown, a Louisville attorney who would later become Governor of the Commonwealth of Kentucky and the Colonel's old friend, Pete Harmon.

Just thirteen months later, the U.S. patent Office granted Col. Sanders the exclusive rights for his method of frying chicken "finger-licking good." By this time, Kentucky Fried Chicken outlets existed in all 50 states, England, and Japan, with Col. Sanders still holding all Canadian rights.

The new Kentucky Fried Chicken owners also purchased the Colonel's likeness and hired him as their "Goodwill Ambassador" (at $40,000 per year) to travel the world and tout their product. He reportedly traveled more than 250,000 miles annually but the honeymoon between Sanders and his successors did not last long.

In 1969, Kentucky Fried Chicken listed on the New York Stock exchange, with the Colonel buying the first hundred shares. In 1971, Heublein, Inc. bought out the Brown group of investors. Three years later, the Colonel sued them for $122 million based on the premise that the company used his name and likeness with products he had not developed. That case settled out of court, and the Colonel began telling newspaper, TV, and radio reporters that the Heublein chicken amounted to "the worst he had ever tasted," and that the mashed potatoes "tasted like wallpaper paste, the gravy, sludge."

Ironically, during the years of their marriage, the Colonel and Mrs. Sanders often totally abstained from eating anything but rice and fruit, a habit they learned during periodic stays at a Durham, North Carolina Health Clinic.

Asked at age 86 if he planned to retire, Sanders quipped that he planned to work until he was 100, adding that he thought a man would "rust out" more quickly than he would wear out.

Still, death must have been on his mind, because earlier on March 31, 1972, he visited Cave Hill Cemetery and personally purchased four plots which he later re-conveyed to the Cemetery in exchange for a twelve-plot lot. Ira Mitchell, at that time Superintendent of the Cemetery, reportedly handled the transaction.

On Tuesday, December 16, 1980, Colonel Harland Sanders died at age 90 of leukemia which his doctors had diagnosed five months earlier in July. The family summoned funeral directors from Hall-Taylor Funeral Home at 1185 Main Street in Shelbyville, Kentucky.

About a week to ten days before the Colonel died, security personnel from Kentucky Fried Chicken had contacted Lee Squires who at that time worked as Grounds Manager of Cave Hill Cemetery. (Mr. Squires now serves as Superintendent/Secretary and Treasurer of Cave Hill, a position he assumed in 1996.) The security detail wanted to see the route that mourners would take from the Main Cemetery Gate to the Colonel's grave at Lot 57, Section 33, in the northeast corner of the Cemetery. Mr. Squires obliged the men who instructed him to have grounds people trim all of the lower limbs on trees that lined the route, so that buses could pass.

David V. Zimmerman, the cemetery's Secretary-Treasurer in 1980, told several Louisville media outlets that more than twelve hundred people would ride special Transit Authority of River City (TARC) buses to the grave. (KFC had chartered 27 buses to move mourners from the downtown area, hotels, and the funeral to the cemetery.) Zimmerman also told reporters that the cemetery would close the Main Gate between 11A.M. and 3 P.M.

The Colonel's body, embalmed by Bill Pruitt and dressed in his ubiquitous white linen suit with black string tie, lay in state in the Kentucky capitol rotunda on Thursday, December 18. Then, the directors moved his body to KFC Headquarters, 1441 Gardiner Lane, on December 19. His elegant walking cane lay beside him in the white Belmont Masterpiece 48-ounce solid Bronze full-couch casket. There, more than twelve hundred people filed past the Colonel's casket which funeral directors had placed in the lobby of the building. Most of the several dozen floral offerings were red and white, KFC's official colors.

Entertainer Pat Boone sang at the funeral conducted at the Southern Baptist Theological Seminary's Alumni Chapel (The Colonel had met Boone a number of years earlier at the Kentucky State Fairgrounds and had asked him if he would sing at his funeral). Officials limited attendance at both the funeral service and the burial to the Colonel's relatives and friends of the family and KFC employees. The elegant and simple front cover for the worship bulletin for Col. Harlan David Sanders' funeral depicts a communion chalice with an inlaid cross. It reads simply "Funeral Service for Colonel Harland Sanders: A Christian and Member of the First Christian Church (Disciples of Christ), Shelbyville, Kentucky." The reverse side features a distinguished portrait of perhaps the world's best known personality dressed in his white Kentucky Colonel's suit with dark pocket kerchief and his hands resting on his ever-present cane.

Services, held at the Alumni Memorial Chapel of Louisville's Southern Baptist Theological Seminary on December 20, 1980, began sharply at 11:00 A.M. Donald P. Huscad, the V.V. Cooke Professor of Organ at their Seminary, provided the prelude of organ music *O God, Our Help in Ages Past*. The Life Singers of Shelbyville's Community Youth Choir also presented entrance music. James Lee Collins, Junior, Pastor of the First Christian Church of Shelbyville, provided Words of Promise. Next, the congregation sang *Joy to the World*. (Remember that it was Christmastime.)

(Photos by Mac McCormick)

Funeral Service
for
Colonel Harland Sanders

A Christian & Member of
The First Christian Church
(Disciples of Christ)
Shelbyville, Kentucky

Worship Bulletin (Courtesy of Mr. Stephen L. Collins)

Pastor Collins gave the Invocation and then led the congregation in "A Litany of Thanksgiving for Colonel Sander's life." Eleanor Cayce sang *Beyond the Sunset*, and *It Will Be Worth it All*. J. Edward Cayce, the retired pastor from the First Christian Church of Shelbyville, read the Scriptures.

Next, as Colonel Sanders had requested him to do a number of months earlier, the well known singer-crooner, Pat Boone, sang *He Touched Me*, and *What a Friend We Have in Jesus*.

Colonel Sander's old friend from Corbin, Kentucky, John Chambers, the retired Pastor from the First Christian Church in that community gave the meditation followed by the benediction and an organ postlude.

The Colonel's grave itself features a portico fashioned after KFC Headquarters and a two-foot bust of himself, sculpted by his daughter, Margaret. A book ledger type marker, replete with three Masonic symbols, (Blue Lodge Master mason, Noble of the Ancient Arabic Order of the Mystic Shrine, and Thirty-third degree Scottish Rite Mason) reads, in part

"Col, Harland Sanders.
Born near Henryville, Ind., September 9, 1890.
Founder of Kentucky Fried Chicken Empire.
Died Louisville, Kentucky December 16, 1980."

Just beneath his inscription:

"His Beloved Wife, Claudia Ellen Sanders.
Born near London, Kentucky September 7, 1902
Truly "The Colonel's Lady"
And Co -Worker In His Enterprises
Died Shelbyville, Ky.
December 31, 1996"

Honorary Pall Bearers

✧ The Board of Directors of Kentucky Fried Chicken and Col. Sanders Kentucky Fried Chicken, Ltd. of Canada.

Active Pall Bearers

✧ Harland Morrison Adams

✧ John Foster Ruggles,III

✧ Daniel O'Deillce

✧ Aaron Lee Cummings

✧ James Trigg Adams, Junior

✧ John Foster Ruggles, Junior

✧ John Wurster, Junior

✧ James Sanders.

By The Way

A trip to the **Colonel Harland Sanders Museum**, located at KFC's World Headquarters in Louisville, Kentucky, can be well worth the time it takes to visit. The Colonel, never one to shy away from the limelight, established the Museum himself in 1978. Various displays and exhibits clearly depict the Colonel's phoenix-like rise from near destitution and hard luck to almost instantaneous success during the turbulent sixties. Visitors will discover photographs of the Colonel's first restaurant (Corbin, Kentucky), a bio-film about the Indiana native (entitled *Portrait of a Legend*), and a rare Norman Rockwell portrait of the Colonel. Also on display: old KFC commercials, the Colonel's Restaurateur of the Year Award, (aptly enough, a wire frame chicken that lays the golden egg!) and the Colonels' first cooking pot, which spews forth biographical data. Hours are Monday-Thursday 8 A.M.-4:30 P.M. and Fridays 8 A.M.-3 P.M.

Another Mecca to the Chicken King includes the **Colonel Sanders Café** in Corbin, Kentucky. The southeasterly drive from Louisville takes about two and half-hours. Travelers can find it near the site of the Colonel's very first restaurant. In 1990, owners restored it to its 1940's finery to fete the Colonel on what would have been his 100th birthday.

Yet one more shrine to the portly and courtly Sanders (and his Lady, Claudia) can be found in Shelbyville, Kentucky at **The Claudia Sanders Dinner House** easily found on U.S. 60. In the early years of the KFC dynasty, the edifice also served as Corporate Headquarters but Mrs. Sanders originally owned the property. A short stroll takes one to the former home of the Colonel, Blackwood Hall.

USA Today reports that in 1997, the most recent full year of sales figures available, KFC posted sales of $4 billion. In mid 1999, the newspaper also noted that the new animated Col. Sanders advertisements on TV were not popular with polled consumers. They noted that only 15% of those people questioned liked the campaign which features a hip-hopping bouncing Colonel "shooting hoops" (with voice supplied by actor Randy Quaid) and dancing "the funky chicken."

According to KFC, they zealously guard the original formula for the Colonel's chicken. Two separate companies blend portions of the secret mixture of the eleven herbs and spices. The company uses a computer processing system to blend the mixture, but neither company has the complete recipe. KFC, now owned by TRICON Global Restaurants, a division of PepsiCo, Inc. boasts more than 9,000 restaurants worldwide, including restaurants in China, Australia, and Moscow, Russia.

Nikola Tesla:
America's Sorcerer
July 9, 1856 – January 7, 1943

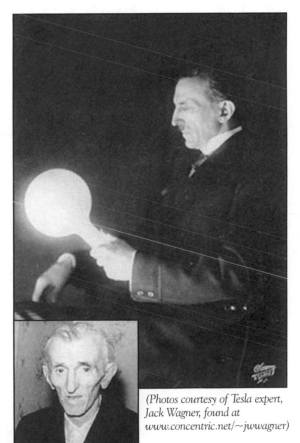

(Photos courtesy of Tesla expert, Jack Wagner, found at www.concentric.net/~jwwagner)

Almost completely forgotten by American historians, the complex genius Nikola Tesla made monumental contributions in the last century that clearly reach into the current one. The Croatian born scientist conceived unheard of ideas in his time that continue to benefit us today. Every time we turn on a radio, use the circuitry of a cell phone, or benefit from electricity, we use the master inventor's scholarly ideas that society once called preposterous.

Nikola Tesla trained in Europe in the fields of physics, mathematics and mechanics, but we can also correctly call him a dreamer. Perhaps his greatest single contribution to mankind was his promotion of alternating current, as opposed to direct current in electrical power systems.

Tesla's fellow inventor and bitter enemy, Thomas A. Edison, had to "pump up" his direct current every mile or so with "powerhouses." A simple line transformer could increase voltage in the line if Tesla's alternating current system were used. Tesla initially appealed to Edison to switch his system to alternating current, but Edison, backed by multimillionaire financier J. Pierpoint Morgan, would not budge.

Many years later, the famed George Westinghouse, head of Westinghouse Electric Corporation, agreed with Tesla and entered into a contract with the eccentric scientist to build a gigantic alternating current generator inside Niagara Falls, New York. The generator made history, sending electrical power an amazing distance of three hundred and fifty miles – all the way to New York City. Edison finally agreed that alternating current was a far superior system of power distribution than his own direct current. A bust of Nikola Tesla stands at Niagara Fills – and with good reason.

The intellectual, who actually had a Serbian heritage, also clearly laid the groundwork for the invention of radio – but he did not develop the finished product. Other men of science such as Edwin Armstrong, Reginald Fessenden and Lee De Forest would "fine-tune" and enhance radio.

Marchese Guglielmo Marconi, who most people would credit as the inventor of radio, and Tesla had an ongoing dispute over Marconi's usage of Tesla's already patented tuned radio circuitry which we can find at the heart of any radio transmitter or receiver. A lecture in 1893 by Tesla clearly proves that Tesla's disclosure was the birth of wireless communications.

In fact, Tesla sued Marconi in August 1915 over his use of Tesla's ideas and theories. A higher court eventually threw that lawsuit out of court because the lower judge could not understand the terminology. The case wound its way through many levels of courts eventually stopping at the U.S. Supreme Court which found in favor of Marconi. Finally, in 1943, the U.S. Supreme Court reversed their earlier decision in favor of Marconi ruling that Tesla had envisioned all other challengers with his rudimentary radio patents. This amounted to an unprecedented move by the Supreme Court.

However, Tesla designed the first tuned circuit for a giant oscillator and conceived of the idea of resonance through the air – between a radio transmitter and receiver – which remains at the basis of modern day radio broadcasting. Marconi tried to use Tesla's circuits in his patent applications for his radio receivers. The U.S. Patent Examiner rejected Marconi four times, but on the fifth try he cleverly hid the "Tesla tuned circuit" inside the antenna's circuitry so the Patent Examiner passed his patent on radio invention around 1904.

After World War One ended, with Marconi himself dead, the Marconi Wireless Company sued the Federal Government for failure to pay royalties due that company for the Army's use of radios during the war. The government investigated the matter and discovered that the Patent office had wrongly granted Marconi the patent on radio.

Tesla's biographers and supporters say he designed the first wireless guided model boats. Scientists now use that same principle to guide satellites on their way to other planets, and to convey drones – unmanned airplanes – to their targets saving countless lives in war.

Others in his time viewed Tesla as a very peculiar man. The scientist remained a loner who did not want the common man to bother him. His thoughts lingered constantly in the sky, dreaming up new ideas and inventions that would help his fellow man.

He primarily focused his thoughts on helping mankind; so much so, in fact that he became destitute. Clearly, we can call the genius a philanthropist, rather than a businessman. Tesla had no idea how to save money, and he died a pauper.

The Wizard's Early Life

Tesla's various biographers agree about very little. They concede that Tesla used high voltage, high frequency research to command the world's attention. Most of the biographies available agree about his friendship with Mark Twain.

Still, they don't even concur on Tesla's birth. Most list his birth as that of Serbian parents in Smiljan, province of Lika, Croatia, (then, Austria-Hungary) in the middle of a summer storm at midnight, on July 9, 1856. The dissident author, Margaret Storm, writing in *Return of the Dove* suggests that an avatar delivered him to earth as an extra-terrestrial being in the body of Nikola Tesla in 1856 to begin the New Age. (That book, self-published and printed in green ink amounts to something of an oddity by itself.)

Tesla's father, a Serbian Orthodox priest, the Reverend Milutin Tesla, married a woman from western Serbia, Duka Mandic. Duka had no formal schooling but reportedly had a photographic memory, a trait that Nikola, one of her five children, inherited.

Tesla learned to speak English, French, German, and Italian beyond his native Slavic tongues. As a lad, he devised several inventions, including one that used lightning bugs to power a small engine. Apparently, this ended when an acquaintance of his with a taste for bugs devoured the power source.

Tesla's childhood contained some tragedies, including the death of his brother, Dane, who died at the age of twelve after a horseback riding accident of some sort. Another version of the death story says he fell down a set of stairs, and in his delirium, accused Nikola of pushing him. Many writers theorize that the nightmares of Daniel's death – and the subsequent rejection of Nikola by his parents – caused some phobias and his eccentric behavior later in life.

Some obsessions that Tesla carried with him through most of his life include a severe aversion to women wearing earrings, especially pearl ones. He ordered waiters to serve his meals with eighteen napkins, so that he could polish all of his silverware before using it, and he preferred dining alone. The genius also calculated the cubic centimeters of space that each bite of food, dish or coffee cup occupied. Daily, he had hotel attendants send eighteen towels for dusting. Camphor's smell nauseated him. Tesla claimed that he could hear a fly land in a room, and that he could hear thunderclaps hundreds of miles away. Violent flashes of light plagued his mind and vision his entire life, especially when emotions were running high. Tesla often counted his steps when walking. If he dropped small squares of paper into liquid while conducting research, he developed odd tastes in his mouth. Additionally, the iconoclastic inventor would talk to himself during lightning storms, and in his autobiography, (serialized in *Electrical Experimenter*) he noted many of his "out of body experiences."

He could not bear "except at the point of a revolver" to touch another person's hair which goes a long way in explaining why he never married or had a long-lasting relationship, save a strictly platonic affair with a woman, Katherine Johnson. Mrs. Johnson was the wife of one of Tesla's friends, Robert Underwood Johnson, publisher of *Century* magazine. Over the years, according to Tesla biographer Margaret Cheney, the three of them exchanged thousands of hand delivered letters – sometimes up to three a day. Mrs. Johnson called the Serbian sage simply "Mr. Tesla," while Tesla eventually became so comfortable that he gave her a nickname, "Madame Filipov," and her husband "Luka Filipov."

From the time of his son's birth, the Reverend Tesla wanted Nikola to enter the ministry. Indeed, in remote Croatia of the late eighteen hundreds, very few career choices – save farming, the church and the army – existed. During Nikola's youth, his father insisted that he complete daily mental exercises to sharpen his reasoning and memory. Nikola's amazing photographic memory enabled him to devise and build complete inventions in his mind which later in life caused some confusion with other inventors, engineers and financiers who would want to see Tesla's ideas on paper.

Some writers suggest that Tesla may have been homosexual. However, his grand nephew, Marc J. Seifer, argues in his doctoral thesis that no evidence exists to support that claim. He does suggest that Tesla suffered from an Oedipal complex related to his brother's death. One of Tesla's other biographers, Kenneth Swezey, a journalist who remained close to Tesla in his declining years, called Tesla "an absolute celibate" and confirmed that he rarely slept.

When Nicola turned six, his family moved to Gospic. During his schooling at the Real Gymnasium, equivalent to Junior High School, Tesla did well at linguistics but truly shone in Mathematics. He calculated the answers to problems so quickly that at first his instructors thought the lad was cheating. Both his father and his uncle taught at the school.

In 1870, the family moved to Karlovac where Tesla attended an advanced school, and he discovered his aptitude for physics. During school, Nikola contracted malaria, and shortly after graduation, during an epidemic, contracted a case of cholera which lasted for nine months. Owing to his weakened condition from the earlier malady, Tesla almost died.

For a year following graduation and after his health improved, Tesla wandered the nearby mountains to regain his health and to avoid a war with the Turks. In 1875, Nikola Tesla entered the Polytechnic School in Graz with a semi-scholarship from the military. During his three years there, he developed an obsession with study, gambling, and alternating current. In 1878, failing exams because of unpreparedness, (he would often play billiards for twenty-four-hour stretches) Tesla withdrew from the school. A year later, his father died, and he returned to Budapest where he studied until he turned twenty-four years of age.

Tesla eventually found a low paying job with the Hungarian government as a telegraph engineer, which by all accounts he threw himself into with his usual vigor. Unfortunately, after a short time, he suffered a nervous breakdown claiming that he could hear the ticking of a watch three rooms away, and that the passing of a train miles away interfered with his rest. The genius recovered, and one evening while walking in the city park with a friend suddenly devised a solution to a problem with his alternating current motor that he had been thinking about for years.

By late 1882, Nikola Tesla had contributed so many improvements to the telegraph system that two friends recommended him to Edison's telephone subsidiary in Paris.

The young Serb worked diligently and solved many problems for the company, yet two of his supervisors cheated him out of money that was due him for solving a ticklish problem with the Germans. Angry, Tesla resigned and the would-be-wizard immigrated to the United States in 1884.

The New World

Problems beset Edison the day that Nikola Tesla walked into the great inventor's office. Armed with a letter of introduction, Tesla proffered it, and Edison hired him immediately, partially because of a shortage of engineers. Some months later, in a dispute over a fifty thousand-dollar stipend Edison reportedly promised him for redesigning some equipment, Tesla resigned. It was just as well as the two men differed so significantly that they disliked each other almost from the very first meeting.

Next, in early 1887, Tesla managed to meet two financiers who helped him open a laboratory in Rahway, New Jersey. There, the Tesla Electric Light and Manufacturing Company developed a system of arc lighting. Problems developed, and Tesla was forced out of his own company, essentially bankrupt. For some months, the great Tesla worked at menial positions, literally forced to dig ditches. Then good fortune shone on him because, through a friend, he obtained an introduction to George Westinghouse.

The year was 1888, and Tesla not only moved to Pittsburgh but also patented his motor and alternating method of conveying power. Westinghouse bought the patent for a million dollars, but Tesla never saw that amount because he had to pay his helpers, and other patent issues clouded the sale. Tesla finally realized around $255,000.00. Also during 1888, Tesla gave an important talk to a group of scientists about his alternating current theory.

On July 31, 1891, Tesla achieved what he later described as the most important milestone of his life – he became an American citizen. Around this time, the war between Edison and Tesla and Westinghouse began. Edison, a stubborn proponent of direct current, began electrocuting dogs and cats with alternating currents in front of audiences to show them how dangerous he thought alternating current truly was.

Tesla's mother, who impressed the young Nikola with her ability to recite long passages of Shakespeare and the Bible verbatim – although she had no formal education – died in April 1892, so Tesla was overseas at that time. He also had begun to concentrate his energies on radio.

He then suffered a period of partial amnesia. Owing to his dislike of medical doctors, Tesla decided to cure himself. He did this by sitting for hours on end trying to recall his early childhood memories. True to eccentric form, the young mastermind did manage to heal himself.

Returning to the United States in 1893, Nikola Tesla gave his now legendary lecture to the National Electric Light Association in St. Louis and the Franklin Institute in Philadelphia. The lecture described radio broadcasting in its elementary form. For the next few years, Tesla also gave some speeches and demonstrations showing how his gas filled tube lights – the forerunners of fluorescent lights – worked.

He gave one of his more unforgettable displays at the Chicago World's Fair of 1893 which he illuminated with alternating current for Westinghouse. The exposition covered more than seven hundred acres, cost more than twenty-five million dollars to produce, and offered sixty thousand exhibitors.

To show the public how the wireless lights work, he often stood on a stage and used himself as a conductor allowing hundreds of thousands of volts to pass through his own body. His clothing often would emit sparks and glimmers of halos hours after the demonstration. The Serbian maestro knew how to thrill the American people. (Later in his career, he would fake some of the more well-known photos of himself sitting among bolts of lightning surrounding his turbines and generators.)

Niagara Falls: An Extraordinary Incident

Nikola Tesla, writing in his autobiography, commented that as a child in remote Croatia, he saw a photograph of Niagara Falls and told his uncle that one day he would harness the falls' energy. Some decades later, he did just that calling it an "extraordinary incident." Both Westinghouse and General Electric used Tesla's equipment or theories, and the Niagara Falls Commission delivered an amazing amount of electricity – fifteen thousand horsepower worth of electricity – to Buffalo some twenty-six miles away to run the streetlights and street cars.

March 13, 1895 proved to be a low day in Tesla's life – his New York City laboratory and workshop (33-35 South Fifth Avenue) burned to the ground –

uninsured. Newspapers the world over reported the fire, and Tesla suffered depression. Even his good friends, the Johnsons, could not cheer him. The Serbian mastermind was unhurt, however, as he had been sleeping at his hotel at the time of the two-thirty A.M. blaze. He lived most of his life in hotels, and always had difficulty paying the bills.

Tesla soon came out of his slump and found a suitable building for a new workshop at 46 Houston Street. He wired inventors and financiers all over the globe for help and equipment. For Nikola Tesla, however, the first of many years of money problems began.

Then, shortly after getting settled in his new laboratory in 1897, he suffered some health problems caused by working on the new x-ray device that he and other inventors were checking for safety.

During that same year, the Patent Office accepted his application for a patent of his basic radio signaling equipment and theory. Just two years later, he filed for a patent for radio remote control for use in guided vehicles. The Examiners granted the patent for that application almost immediately. In 1900, they granted the patent for the radio theory and equipment he had submitted in 1897. As noted earlier, the patents were both subjects of controversies and lawsuits by other jealous inventors.

During an 1897 speech, discussing his transmission of power, a confident Tesla proclaimed that one day he could send messages to Mars. Critics, newspapers, and scientists met this statement with some degree of skepticism.

The following year, Nikola Tesla caused an earthquake of types in Manhattan when he attached an electro mechanical oscillator to an iron pillar in his laboratory. The pillar transmitted the vibrations to the core of the Manhattan soil. Just as in an earthquake, people felt the vibrations and repercussions miles away, much as in the epicenter of an earthquake. As windows broke and buildings shook, officials at the Police Department knew right away that the bizarre inventor somehow had something to do with the disturbance. They dispatched two of their finest just as Tesla realized what he had done. He took a sledgehammer to the offending equipment, explained the situation to the two amazed police officers, and then asked them to leave his lab for he had to complete his work. Tesla later told reporters that he could destroy the Brooklyn Bridge in a matter of minutes.

At the height of the Spanish-American War controversy, Tesla displayed the world's first radio controlled robotic boats at Madison Square Garden. More than fifteen thousand people attended but his display of automation almost got lost in the War news. Interestingly, what the Serbian genius did not show the public or reveal was that he had devised an unmanned and self-propelled torpedo boat replete with batteries, lights and signaling devices. It also had the ability to submerge or raise to the waters' surface upon electronic command. In a relatively few years in the United States, Tesla learned to become protective of his inventions. He received a patent for the robotic device in November of that year.

A Westinghouse attorney, Leonard Curtis, invited Tesla to move to Colorado Springs in 1899. Various financiers would help pay Tesla's expenses. He readily agreed, stating his goals as surpassing Marconi in his wireless system and learning how to send energy around the world without the use of wires. In summer of that year, he conducted dangerous experiments with lightning which we can probably compare with scenes from modern day Frankenstein movies. The maverick creator produced such a strong current that he knocked the Colorado Springs electric powerhouse out of commission by catching it on fire and plunging the entire city into darkness. Tesla sent a crew of engineers to repair the damage and returned electricity to Colorado Springs within a week.

Wardenclyffe

A short time later, critics again bombarded Tesla when he announced that he had heard rhythmic radio signals from outer space on some of his Colorado equipment. Returning to Manhattan in 1900, he further stupefied the press by announcing his plans for trans-Atlantic signaling and world radio broadcasting. Tesla planned to operate his robotic boat at a Paris exposition from his Manhattan office. Meanwhile, as always, his finances dwindled, and he went searching for financing. J. Pierpoint Morgan financed the venture for $150,000.00 but demanded that the inventor use 51% of his radio patents as collateral on the signature loan.

Tesla went searching for land and found two thousand acres on Long Island about sixty-five miles from Brooklyn. He dubbed the site Wardenclyffe. The transmitting station would rise over one hundred feet in the air, shaped much like a mushroom. Wardenclyffe's final tower rose majestically one hundred and eighty-seven feet in the air, and Tesla centered it on a shaft that contractors bore into the ground one hundred and twenty feet. The Serbian savant erroneously assumed that the U.S. Government would eventually want to use the site for coastal defense.

While his financial woes mounted with cost over runs, more bad news arrived. Marconi had signaled Newfoundland from Cornwall with equipment not nearly as elaborate as Wardenclyffe. Tesla's financial problems grew even worse, and Morgan refused him any more money. Creditors hounded Tesla, and no financier appeared willing to help the eccentric inventor. He began manufacturing small coils for medical use but it was a temporary stop gap measure. Lawsuits abounded. Tesla's stature in the world financial community declined during the years 1906-1912. In that year, Westinghouse – who had supplied equipment for Wardenclyffe – won a lawsuit against Tesla and removed some twenty-three thousand dollars worth of equipment from the site. Tesla – to continue living at the Waldorf Astoria – signed two mortgages over to the hotel to satisfy twenty thousand dollars worth of bills there. During the First

World War, wrecking crews under the guidance of the U.S. government demolished Wardenclyffe because authorities believed German spies were sending signals to the Fatherland from the mammoth structure.

Over the next few years, little monetary relief came Tesla's way as he attempted to talk J.P. Morgan, Junior (J. Pierpoint Morgan died in 1913) into financing some new projects including designs for a vertical lift airplane and an advanced turbine. Morgan, Junior advanced him fifteen thousand dollars for nine months, and started reminding Tesla that he needed to repay the original one hundred and fifty thousand that Morgan, Senior had loaned him. Tesla did earn about twenty four-thousand dollars from a German franchise on his radio equipment when a German firm built a signaling station for the U.S. Navy.

The American Institute of Electrical Engineers awarded Tesla their highest honor, the Edison Medal in 1917, but not without Tesla expressing his true opinion of the now ill Edison. Officials and friends had to coax Tesla to accept the award and attend the white tie and tails affair, which became confusing when the guest of honor left the gathering to pursue a lifetime habit – the feeding of pigeons in a nearby park.

Also in 1917, Tesla's automobile speedometer royalties amounted to seventeen thousand dollars. The funds would have continued had it not been for the World War, and the halt of production of cars.

During his sixties, illness and poverty plagued Tesla. At one point, sheriff's deputies came to seize his personal belongings. The genius was so poor at one point that to pay his two secretaries, he offered to cut the Edison Gold Medal in half and give them each a piece of it. Instead, the two declined and gave Tesla money. His lifelong obsession with pigeons continued as well, and at one point, he insisted he had a divine mystical experience with a dying pigeon, a favorite of his.

The Light Declines

On Tesla's eightieth birthday, July 9, 1936, Tesla issued a ten-page statement that debated current theories on cosmic rays. One year later, on his birthday, the Ambassador from Yugoslavia awarded him the Grand Cordon of the White Eagle, that country's highest honor.

In his diminishing years, Tesla became increasingly confused. In 1937, a taxi struck the elderly creator, and his health never improved from that time forward. He suffered heart and lung problems but generally refused medical attention. Tesla intensified his phobia of germs and did not want anyone to get within a few feet of him.

One night in very early January 1943, he summoned a messenger boy and dispatched him with an envelope containing one hundred dollars for Mark Twain, his old friend. Twain, of course, had been dead for some time, but Tesla refused to accept the messengers' explanation of Twain's death insisting that Twain had visited his room the night before.

Early Friday morning, January 8, 1943, Alice Monaghan, a hotel maid, ignored a "Do Not Disturb" sign that had been in place for two days and opened the all-powerful wizard's door to find him dead. Nikola Tesla died virtually destitute and alone at eighty- six years of age. His estate amounted to little more than two thousand dollars.

Eugene Schultz, current manager of the Frank E. Campbell Funeral Home, confirms that Tesla's staff and nephew (Sava Kosanovic) summoned funeral directors from Campbell's to make the transfer of Tesla's thin and gaunt remains to the funeral home. The staff also notified the FBI who opened Tesla's safe looking for government related files. Some biographers claim it wasn't the FBI but officials from the Office of the Custodian of Alien Property, a suggestion that seems hardly appropriate since Tesla was a U.S. citizen.

Meanwhile, at the Frank E. Campbell Funeral Home at 81ˢᵗ Street and Madison Avenue, a sculptor prepared a death mask of the great inventor. Long time friend, admirer and associate Hugo Gernsback ordered the death mask which reportedly reproduced faithfully every wrinkle and facial contour of Tesla. Gernsback had the death mask copper plated and placed it in his office.

Sunday, January 10th, Tesla laid in state at the funeral home, but according to one biographer, only twelve people, some of whom were reporters, attended the calling. That same day, Mayor Fierello La Guardia read a moving tribute/ eulogy written by Croatian author Louis Adamic over radio station WNYC.

The state funeral held Tuesday, January 12, 1943 was quite a different matter. Tesla's loyalists now elevated Tesla almost to a royalty status because of the mounting tensions between Serbs and Croats. More than two thousand people attended his funeral services, most of which the priests conducted in the Serbian tongue. Tesla's nephew decided to hold the funeral service at the Cathedral of St. John the Divine because the Serbian Cathedral wasn't completed at the time. Owing to the tension between the Serbians and the Croatians, the Bishop, a man by the name of William T. Manning, gave his permission to use St. Johns on the condition no one make any political speeches.

The funeral directors had covered Tesla's casket with the American flag in place of the usual pall but they later opened Tesla's casket for the funeral service. Four tall "halo style" candles guarded the casket corners, and priests placed the icon of the Holy Redeemer near the choir loft. King Peter II of Yugoslavia sent a huge floral offering which the Campbell funeral directors placed near the head of the casket.

Oscar Gavrilovitch of the Yugoslav Consul of New York served as Head Usher. Although Tesla had been an American Citizen for many years, the Yugoslavian government honored him by making his funeral a state function. Constantine Fotitich, Yugoslavian ambassador to the United States, represented Yugoslavia. Serbs and Croatians sat on opposite sides of the church, though.

Tesla's journalist friend, Kenneth Swezey, settled in the front row with Sava Kosanovic, Tesla's nephew.

Bishop Manning began Tesla's funeral service in English. The Very Reverend Dushan Shoukletovich, rector of the Serb Orthodox Church of St. Sava, conducted the Sermon for the Dead. He had known Tesla personally and officiated in the name of the Serbian Orthodox Church of America. Assisting him was Father Edward West, Sacrist of the Cathedral.

At the conclusion of the funeral service, Bishop Manning gave the benediction. Ambassador Fotitich led the mourners past Tesla's casket for one last viewing. The pallbearers conducted the casket in procession to a waiting hearse which took Tesla's human remains to Ferncliffe Cemetery at Ardsley-on-the-Hudson where cemetarians later cremated it.

Kenneth Swezey and Sava Kosanovic followed the hearse in a limousine provided by Frank E. Campbell to the cemetery and the waiting receiving vault.

Charlotte Muzar, transported the great sorcerer's cremated human remains to his native land in 1957. Muzar, who served Sava Kosanovic as his secretary, took the remains to the Tesla museum in Belgrade in 1957.

Many of the mysteries and controversies surrounding Tesla remain to this day. No doubt can exist, however, that Nikola Tesla's rich legacy and inventions will live on in the hearts and minds of many.

Honorary Pall Bearers For Nicola Tesla

✦ Head Honorary Pall Bearer: Newbold Morris, President, New York City Council

✦ Dr. Ernest Alexanderson of GE, inventor of a powerful high frequency transmitter and the famous Alexanderson alternator.

✦ Dr. Harvey Rentschler, Director of Research, Westinghouse Laboratories.

✦ Edwin Armstrong, Father of FM Radio.

✦ Consul General D.M. Stanoyevitch of Yugoslavia.

✦ Professor William Barton, Curator of the Hayden Planetarium of the American Museum of Natural History, New York City. (This was one of Tesla's few spots for relaxation and meditation.)

✦ Gano Dun, President of J.G. White Engineering and Tesla's early assistant.

✦ Colonel Henry Breckenridge

✦ Dr. Branko Cubrilovitch, Yugoslav Minister of Agriculture

Tesla's Major Inventions:

✧   Telephone Repeater

✧   Rotating Magnetic Field Principle

✧   Polyphase Alternating Current System

✧   Induction Motor

✧   Alternating Current Power Transmission

✧   Tesla Coil Transformer

✧   Wireless Communication

✧   Radio Theory

✧   Fluorescent Lights

✧   Experimentation with Death/Disintegrator/Beam Weapons

✧   Early Theories on the Laser Beam

✧   Tesla also held more than 700 patents.